IMMORTAL D

NINA GREEN

Pendragon Press

Publishing Details

Whilst the finding of 'St. Bees Man' was the inspiration
for this novel, the historical/factual connection ends
there. All characters and incidents in Immortal Dust are
fictional and any resemblance to persons living or dead
is purely coincidental.

Immortal Dust

Copyright © 2003 Nina Green

First published 2003 by
Pendragon Press Ltd.
Printed and bound in Wales by
Dinefwr Press Ltd.

This edition published 2022 by
Pendragon Press

Pendragon Press Ltd.

The right of Nina Green to be identified as the Author of the Work
has been asserted by her in accordance with the Copyright, Designs
and Patents Act 1988.

A CIP catalogue record for this book is
available from the British Library.

Cover created by Nina Green©

DEDICATION

IN MEMORY OF
DONALD MARTIN

Late Managing Director
GWASG DINEFWR PRESS LIMITED

With gratitude and deep affection

ACKNOWLEDGEMENTS

Grateful thanks to Deirdre O'Sullivan, Head of the Archaeological Division, University of Leicester, who led the dig that unearthed the unique preserved body in Cumbria, for her images and first hand information about the finding of 'St. Bees Man'.

Most of all, thanks to my husband Jim, for knowing and understanding – and for being my constant companion on the Quest.

ONE

The telephone shrilled, and the young woman seated at the desk lifted her head slightly and frowned before shifting her attention back to the copy she was checking. It rang again, as startling as the zip of a low-flying fighter on night manoeuvres. Sighing with annoyance, she focused her attention. It registered that this was the external line, not just one of the many in-house interruptions.

Pushing back a cluster of dark curls which immediately bounced back onto her forehead, she lifted the receiver.
"Darcy West – Manchester News."
A buzzing sound followed by a series of clicks sounded in her ear. "Darcy West," she repeated, glancing down at the copy with obvious impatience.
"Hello – are you hearing me?" The female voice at the other end was distorted, the quality of sound and the echo-effect suggestive of a mobile.
"Who is this?" Darcy demanded. The line cleared with a suddenness that was disconcerting.
"Caroline Stevens. 'That you, Darcy?"
"Caro! Great to hear you. Still lecturing at the University?"
"Sure am. Archaeology Department. Sorry – have to be brief."

In response to Caro's obvious sense of urgency, Darcy's eyes darkened slightly and her tones became   clipped and professional.
"Okay – shoot." She smiled to herself: funny how her nostrils always began to twitch whenever she sniffed a story.
"I'm up in Cumbria with the Hilldean team. A routine dig at the old priory on the cliffs at—, hey, can you still hear me?"
"Just," Darcy's 'sniff' hardened into a hunch. "Caro, your mobile is crap!" she grimaced and held the receiver an inch or so from her ear as the crackling increased in volume.

"There's a force nine blowing and it's sheeting down." Darcy winced as the line cleared. "Sorry, was I shouting?"

"For Chris'sakes Caro, just tell me."

"I am trying," Caro protested.

"Very."

"Okay, funny!! Caro said with a giggle. "It's a place called St. Gildas Bay, about eighteen miles from that weekend cottage of yours."

There arose in Darcy's mind the image of a secluded inlet ringed by sheer sandstone cliffs teeming with bird-life, and a sleepy village nestling at the foot.

"Gotcha. So give me the crack."

"A male body. Thirteen to fourteenth century at a guess. And there's a skeleton lying alongside it. Thought you would want to be first in the know. Sorry – this line is crap. It might make a news feature or something."

"I'd say so!" Darcy tapped the desk sharply with her fingernails whilst waiting for the hiss and buzz to subside.

"Still with me?" Caro inquired, then "Good," as Darcy responded in the affirmative. "Right, be at the Whitecliffe County Hospital A.S.A.P. - Dr. Piper is doing the post mortem this afternoon."

"That's a bit swift." Darcy tucked the receiver beneath chin and shoulder in order to shut down the computer. There was a slight pause before Caro spoke again.

"Deterioration sets in quickly once flesh is exposed to air."

"Flesh?" Darcy frowned and paused in replacing the cap on her fibre-tip pen. Thirteenth or fourteenth century, Caro had said, but Darcy recalled, she had also said *body* not skeleton.

There was a longer pause and a volley of clicking sounds.

"Did I not mention?" Caro's voice faded again.

"Caro?" Darcy swore beneath her breath.

"The body. It's well preserved. Absolutely unique."

"I'm leaving now". Darcy was already on her feet.

"Thanks for the lead, Caro."

"Cheers. Oh, and Darcy—,"

"Yes?"

"His eyes are green."

Darcy frowned; she must have misheard, either that or Caro
had finally flipped.

"What did you say?" she prompted,

No answer: the line was dead.

TWO

Darcy pressed a button on the intercom. "Janet – soon as you like." She was shrugging her way into her coat as her assistant entered. "Finish checking that copy through for me please – then get it down to Frank Kelly like yesterday," she instructed, slinging her bag onto her shoulder.
"Sure. Going out?"
Amused by Janet's artless probing Darcy jingled
her car keys.
"A lead. Tell Frank for me will you."

She paused for a moment, and smiled at a mental picture of her editor scowling and demanding to know what the hell she was up to now – especially as the alleged City Council corruption scandal was about to break.
"I'm driving up to Cumbria," she added, slinging her old Hilldean University scarf around her neck. "I'll ring in as soon as I've got a headline. Can you cope?"
"No probs." Janet winked.
"Good girl." Darcy nodded and headed for the door. Janet was young but a fast learner – and with the confidence to succeed in a tough business. "See you," she called over her shoulder and the door swung to as she left the office.

In the elevator she laughed aloud at feeling the familiar tingle along her nerves. The chasing up of a new lead always brought a buzz. Good old Caro, it would be great to see her again – and her sinister green-eyed friend.

****

Whipping the red coupé through the late morning traffic with an expertise born of practice, Darcy pulled out of the city and headed for the suburbs. Within fifteen minutes she was entering

7

a Georgian house with an array of brass name plates flanking its dark blue door. A letter protruded from her section of the communal rack on the wall; the cream envelope, brown ink and italic writing coupled with a Cambridge postmark all proclaimed her mother. Stuffing it into her bag to read later she crossed the hall whilst dragging a key ring from her pocket. A lucky break this ground floor flat, she reflected opening the door. It had everything: a quiet neighbourhood, nearby park and yet was convenient for the City and the Paper, and a rent within her budget – just, so that her resolve to refuse parental help was so far intact.

She paused for a moment by the large window through which the cold march sunlight streamed and excitement gripped her stomach muscles at the prospect of a new case. Hurrying to the bedroom, she stripped, put on a housecoat and headed for the bathroom. Twenty minutes later she emerged from the flat having exchanged her office gear of white shirt and black suit for cords, sweater and ankle boots. Clouds were rolling in from the west as she tossed an overnight bag onto the rear seat and slid behind the wheel.

The rain held off as far as the Lakes junction, but as the Rover swung off the M6 and sped along the dual carriageway the wipers were hard put to cope with the wind-driven wash that swept the windscreen. A brute of a ten-wheeler loomed ahead, the spray from its tyres compounding the deluge and near-zero visibility. Taking a deep breath she indicated and pulled out, gritting her teeth as the lorry driver put his foot down. Bastard, she thought pushing her foot to the floor, adding *bloody male ego* as she fought him off, but once safely past had the grace to grin at her own aggression. As the car delved deeper into Cumbria, the torrent settled to a steady drizzle and the wind sulked rather than raged. For the rest of the journey Darcy indulged in pleasant speculation about Caro's mystery man.

On reaching the hospital, she parked up, slung the

strap of her camera over her shoulder and marched
through a door marked ENQUIRIES.

"Press," she announced, flashing her card at the girl behind the
reception desk. "Dr. Piper's post mortem."

The receptionist, a serious-looking girl with gold-rimmed
glasses, and dark hair worn in a coil secured with a butterfly
clip, pulled a computer printout towards her.

"Name, please?"

"Darcy West."

"Ah yes, here we are. Theatre three. Mrs. Stevens is waiting for
you in the anteroom. Down the corridor, third door on the
left."

"Thanks. When is Dr. Piper due to start?"

"Two thirty."

"Okay," Darcy said nodding.

Passing through the doors, she glanced at the clock on the
corridor wall. Twenty past. Good. Time for a brief first from
Caro.

Her steps slowed as she reached the door of Theatre
Three. Her stomach churned, and there was a tightness in her
chest. Realisation hit as the familiar signs registered: this was
something big. The back of her neck prickled at the sudden
sense of impending danger. Then, as quickly as it arose, it was
gone. Yet the sense of being given a last chance to back out
persisted. This door was the Rubicon. A wry smile wavered
briefly on her lips; the family and friends half-jokingly accused
her of having psychic leanings: the pragmatic no-nonsense
Darcy, exposer of charlatans and debunker of myths! It was
laughable: far easier to tag these feelings 'subconscious nudges,
and put them down to the 'journalist's nose' for a story that had
brought her early promotion. Whatever the truth, she thought
pushing open the doors to the ante-room, her hunches usually
turned out to be justified - and one was bugging her now.

As she entered, the woman standing by the window
turned and her broad attractive face was illuminated by a smile.
"Darcy! So glad you could make it." Rushing forward she
enveloped Darcy in a bear hug.

9

"Hi Caro!" Darcy gasped from the depths of Caro's plump and cushiony bosom.

"Sorry, didn't mean to smother you." Caro released her and sat down again, "But – oh kiddo, it seems such an age."

"Too long." Darcy drew up a white plastic chair and dumped tote bag and camera on the rubber tiled floor. Caro seems tense, Darcy thought, then put it down to excitement. "You look great, Caro." she enthused, unconsciously lowering her voice as it echoed around the clinical room that smelled of disinfectant. "You always did know how to dress," she added admiring the earthy reds and greens of Caro's calf-length skirt, ethnic tunic and cape which showed little respect for fashion but a natural flair for colour and texture.

"Had to – with a figure like mine," Caro quipped self-deprecatingly.

"Don't put yourself down. Bet Brian has no complaints."

"Well he's not divorced me yet – despite the place being littered with ancient relics. Found a piece of bone in the bed last week but knows it's useless to complain. You seeing anyone?"

Darcy shrugged. "Nothing serious."

"Jonathan still around?"

"Just," Darcy said dryly.

"Poor Jonathan," Caro said absently, her attention diverted by the sound of footsteps as somebody approached along the corridor. She appeared to relax again as whoever it was passed by.

"He's a bastard."

"But still around – even if only just!"

Darcy ignored the playful jibe and pushed back the strand of hair that habitually flopped onto her forehead. "There's so much I want to hear," she said, smoothly changing the subject.

"We'll 'catch up' later over a drink," Caro promised. "Dr. Piper's a stickler for punctuality and he'll be here any minute."

Is that the reason you are twitchy, Darcy wondered, noting the way her friend's fingers picked at a fold of her skirt. Normally Caro was so laid back she made a sun-basked seal appear agitated by comparison.
"A bit of an ogre, is he?"
"No, a poppet really," Caro amended, glancing at the door.

Darcy leaned forward on her seat as a thought struck:
"Hey, he's not put out about me being here is he?"
"Not at all." Caro shook her head emphatically so that her thick glossy hair bounced. As though becoming aware of giving out negative signals, she beamed at Darcy and added heartily "No problem, everything's fine. Exciting, isn't it?"
"Absolutely." Darcy agreed, forcing aside her misgivings. "So," Darcy snapped open her bag and extracted a notebook and pen. "Give me a brief."

Caro leaned forward, her body tense with suppressed excitement
"As I said – a routine dig. We were hoping for evidence of a settlement predating he priory itself. We found—," she broke off as a door closed nearby, and the murmur of voices, clinking of metal on metal and the padding of boots on rubber floors issued from the adjacent room. "pottery shards, slivers of bone – the usual things," she continued, "but then, in the ruins of the chancel, we came across him." Caro jerked her head in the direction of the doors dividing ante-room and theatre.

Darcy stared. "The body is in there?" Caro nodded, and Darcy decided the reason for her disquiet lay beyond those doors, and not with her friend. "Go on," she urged.
"When we opened the vault," Caro continued, her manner detached and formal as she switched to working mode, "we found a skeleton lying beside a coffin, which when opened proved to be lined with lead. The body within was wrapped in shrouds smeared with a black pitch-like substance. "
"Why would he—," Darcy started to say, frowning. Caro ignored the interruption and carried on speaking: "We carefully pulled the wrappings aside then—," she paused and

11

glanced away as a sound like that of a metal instrument being dropped into a dish sounded from the adjacent theatre, "realising the significance of our find," she continued, her colour becoming heightened, "we replaced them until a proper examination could be made."

"But you had time to note that his eyes were green," Darcy teased.

Caro nodded. "After hundreds of years. That threw me."

"It showed," Darcy remarked, recalling the garbled telephone call, gales and atmospherics notwithstanding. "Anyway, I went down to the village and 'phoned Dr. Piper at path lab – then contacted you."

"Great stuff, but tell me," Darcy finished scribbling on her pad and looked up with a frown. "Lead lined coffins and treated shrouds – was this usual practice?"

Caro shook her head. "By no means. There are very few cases on record – Edward I being one of them." She paused and, head to one side, gave Darcy a speculative look, as though aware of the possible impact of these words, then switching into lecturer mode as Darcy opened her mouth to speak, Caro checked her with an upraised hand and continued with her story: "Edward died 1307 during the march on Scotland, making him roughly contemporary with our chappie. He had left orders with his son that his heart was to be sent to the Holy Land, but his body was to stay with the English army until Scotland was subdued."

"Bizarre." Darcy grimaced.

"Slightly eccentric," Caro agreed ironically. "It meant of course that it had to be preserved. According to Ayloffe, when the tomb was opened in 1774 the body was remarkably intact and was wrapped in a way similar to this one." Darcy's tongue moistened lips that felt dry.

"Important personages certainly," Caro modified, excitement visibly warring with professional caution.

"Great stuff. That it?" Darcy finished scribbling her idiosyncratic, but effective blend of shorthand and speedwriting on her pad.

"Actually there are a couple of things—," Caro paused and turned her head as the door opened. Mentally cursing the interruption, Darcy stuffed pen and pad into her bag and surveyed the man who had entered: tall and distinguished-looking with iron-grey hair, she noticed he walked with a slight limp.

"Good afternoon, Mrs. Stevens. And this must be Miss West," he added with a nod in Darcy's direction. "Right ladies, if you would like to join me in dressing for the occasion," he added, leading the way to the connecting door.

"What else? Spill it, Caro," Darcy demanded in a fierce whisper as they followed.

Caro paused in the doorway as though about to speak but Dr. Piper intervened.

"Now ladies, don't keep our gentleman waiting – he's not partial to twenty-first century air," he chivvied, pointedly holding the door open. There was no option but to pass through. Five minutes later, duly booted and gowned, they followed Dr. Piper into the brightly-lit theatre.

THREE

Dr. Piper peeled back the wrappings and Darcy stared at the face of the dead man. The murmurs of 'incredible'; 'beyond belief'; 'absolutely amazing' and more that rose from the assembled men and women receded from her consciousness. Whatever she had been expecting, it was not this human being, this person resembling someone who had died but a short time ago. Neither was she prepared for the potent mix of vulnerability and power: the helplessness against their lights, noise and intrusion and the violation of what should be the privacy of death, combined with a most disturbing and potent presence. The eyes – and despite fluid loss due to exposure they were still the amber-green of a trout-speckled pool – stared up at them in silent accusation.

A frisson of unease prickled Darcy's spine. She stared intently then blinked, distrusting her eyes. It was there, she had not imagined it. A glow that brought to mind the diffuse light of car headlamps reflected by mist, except that this was not yellow but rather tinged with blue. The radiance strengthened and grew until it formed a halo around his head. Her hand went to her mouth to stifle an involuntary cry. A veil of bluish vapour traced the body, swirling an inch or so above the contours in the manner of mist snaking across a forest floor. She watched mesmerised as it spread and elongated, reaching out to her in tendrils. Incapable of retreat, she watched it advance. Wisps floated around her head and she shuddered at its icy touch. The vapour was charged with energy; her scalp prickled as though something live crawled over it. Dampness and coldness seeped into her mind, permeating reality and numbing her senses.

All that is except one. A heady scent infused her being. Sweet without being cloying, the deep notes of spice and exotic oils were perfectly tempered with salt-mist, sea-wind and forest rain. Complex and ephemeral as Life itself, it bewitched her

14

with its attar of strangeness. It swirled around and within, luring her into its perfumed spiral. She felt herself being drawn upward and backward, up and away from the bright lights and sound of voices, back to the velvety dark of primordial silence. She started violently as a voice pierced the seductive cocoon. "Darcy. Are you all right?" Caro whispered, then again more urgently: "Darcy! "

Darcy opened her eyes, aware once more of her surroundings. She nodded and swallowed hard whilst struggling to regain control.
"Fine. It's just all so incredible." A feeble excuse, but it would have to do. She inhaled deeply; the scent had gone.
"Squeamish Miss West?" Dr. Piper cast a glance in her direction whilst those around him looked smug or smiled in a patronising manner.
"Certainly not." Darcy pushed back her hair and defiantly met his gaze.
"Just overwhelmed I take it, by the privilege of being allowed to witness this unique phenomenon,"
Dr. Piper taunted, glancing round at his colleagues with barely-disguised amusement.

Caro threw an anxious glance her way. Darcy shrugged dismissively, and almost afraid to look, turned her attention back to the corpse on the table. To her relief the vapour, if indeed it had ever been there, had disappeared. So, why this feeling that his eyes were watching her, and her alone? Shaking her head almost imperceptibly as though to clear it of fantasy, she concentrated on the physical features.

The high cheekbones, aquiline nose and short but vigorous dark hair suggested this had once been a handsome man. Now the lips were drawn back, the teeth partly exposed in a gruesome grin as though in appreciation of their amazement – or in triumph at cheating Death of its feast of flesh and membrane.
"Incredible – the flesh is still pink," commented a man whose faintly distracted air and untidy elegance suggested the

intellectual. "A privilege indeed. Makes one feel quite humble, wouldn't you say Piper?" he added, pushing his horn-rimmed spectacles higher onto his nose.

Dr. Piper frowned and cleared his throat. "Something like that Benson."

"A mystical moment," Darcy said softly, then flushed with embarrassment as all eyes turned her way.

"Quite." Dr. Piper continued with the task of easing away the tarred folds of the shroud where they had stuck together.

"Absolutely." the man called Benson said nodding in support. Darcy threw him a look of gratitude then turned her attention back to the body on the table. Even as they talked, the twenty-first century air had begun its inexorable work. The sheen was already beginning to fade from his eyes, the skin to assume a yellowish brown cast. Dr. Piper dropped his scalpel into a kidney dish with a decisive clunk, and hesitating for effect, peeled back the resinous shroud from the neck and shoulder area. Darcy gasped. A thong was tied tightly around the throat. So that was what Caro had been about to divulge. She frowned as her gaze moved from the cord embedded in flesh, to Caro's face Caro was staring straight ahead, deliberately avoiding eye contact.

"Very interesting, Mrs. Stevens. Mrs. Stevens?" Dr. Piper repeated, looking mildly surprised by her lack of response. Caro blinked and looked his way.

"Fascinating. One wonders at the story behind . . ."

"Absolutely. let's see if he can give us a clue," Dr. Piper interrupted with an archness that sat oddly with his pompous air. Drawing the shroud further down the body, he smiled at the involuntary chorus of exclamations. You already knew, Darcy guessed, noting the conspiratorial look he exchanged with Caro. Carefully, almost tenderly, Dr. Piper used his forceps to lift a coppery tress for them to view. A mass of hair draped the man's shoulders and chest.

Piper raised an authoritative hand, bringing the buzz of excitement under control. Darcy, focusing on work, began to jot notes on her pad.

"Obviously from some other source," Caro commented as order was restored.

Dr. Piper nodded. "I should say so, given our man's dark locks," he said dryly. "And there are no roots, so it has obviously been cut," he added, holding out the single coil and indicating the ends with the tip of his scalpel.

"From the skeleton found beside his coffin?" Caro suggested.

Dr. Piper nodded. "Probably his wife. I can confirm it is female."

"But not the identity," Darcy said swiftly, glancing up from her notes.

He paused and looked around his assembled team for support.

"Not exactly, but I think we can safely assume—,"

"We can never safely assume anything about archaic social customs," Darcy stated, shaking her head with impatience. "But Mrs. Stevens is the expert in this field," she added pointedly. Darcy ignored Dr. Piper's thunderous look and turned to her friend.

"She could have died much later, but been interred in the same grave," Caro said with a look of apology for Darcy.

"Assuming he was married," Darcy persisted, her colour rising.

"A logical assumption," Dr. Piper snapped. "Preservation of the body implies nobility – advantageous marriage would be mandatory ."

"Precisely. His wife would have to be of high birth -so why no lead coffin for her?" Darcy protested.

Momentarily diverted from the conflict, her attention was drawn once more to the body on the table. The sense of a person still being in there returned, but for sanity's sake was dismissed. Ridiculous, to suppose that this man was somehow communicating across the centuries, that he wanted them to know the truth.

"Nothing can be inferred until we determine the approximate dates of birth and death and research likely families in the area," Caro intervened, obviously sensing the descent into acrimony.

"So, shall we resume the business of the day – this post mortem examination," Dr. Piper said with icy politeness. He glanced across at a woman in a white coat who was busy adjusting settings and fitting lenses. "You'll need to be quick, there is marked deterioration already."

Out of courtesy Darcy waited until the last flash flared, then taking her camera from her bag, raised it to shoot.

"Official photographs only please," Dr. Piper rapped. The shutter clicked as he spoke.

"Miss West!" he warned, pausing in his work to glare. Darcy reluctantly lowered her camera.

"It's imperative I record each stage."

"Miss Spencer from Medical Photography is doing just that."

"Well yes, but—," Darcy started to protest, but was ruthlessly interrupted.

"Any more distractions Miss West, and I shall ask you to leave."

Darcy swallowed her frustration and fell silent.

She watched, agonised yet unable to look away as Dr. Piper made a large Y-shaped incision from shoulders to sternum and extending to the pubic area. It is a corpse, not a man, she constantly had to remind herself. The flaps of skin and muscle were carefully opened revealing the organs beneath. The heat from the overhead lights, the press of people around the table, and the clinical odour combined to make her feel faint. Closing her eyes briefly she swayed almost

18

imperceptibly on her feet.

"First post mortem?" Dr. Piper inquired with a malicious little smile.

"Certainly not." Successfully fighting off weakness, and with her concentration back in place, she ignored his patronising look.

"Body fluids still aqueous," Dr. Piper stated for the electronic recorder.

Darcy stared in disbelief at the blood that oozed from severed vessels.

Somehow, she endured the removal, weighing and analysing of organs. From somewhere far off, Dr. Piper's voice periodically intoned his findings:

"Adipocere formed within the body: fatty acid deposits found in most of the tissues and organs. This adipocere is one factor accounting for the remarkable state of preservation, the first being the resinous wrappings which excluded moisture, and inhibited the work of bacteria and insects from destroying soft tissues."

On and on it went. The pinkness of the liver, the elasticity of the heart and aorta, the freshness of mouth mucosa and so on. She took deep breaths and fought off nausea. No other post mortem examination had affected her this way. This wasn't squeamishness. She was aware of him, could sense his presence. Selective attention took over, so that a note was jotted here and there, items of information for later use. Then her attention once more spear-headed, at the words 'pathology' and 'trauma'. Now this was the stuff of journalism. How did he die? By natural causes, accident or in battle? Or was he murdered? She wondered, her excitement mounting.

Darcy's pen flew over the page as Dr. Piper's voice intoned a list of injuries: a fracture to the jaw – lower mandible broken; two broken ribs, a fracture of the hyoid bone in the neck, and here Darcy looked up sharply. There was of course, that tight cord tied around it.

"Was he strangled, Dr. Piper?" she interrupted spontaneously.

19

"Cause of death will be in my report," he said repressively. "But the nature of his injuries would not rule this out?" It was the man with horn-rimmed glasses who had spoken. Regardless of whether or not his support was intentional, Darcy threw him a look of gratitude; Piper merely grunted and got on with his work.

An uncomfortable silence settled over the assembled company, broken only by the occasional cough or clearing of the throat, or the sound of an instrument being dropped into a kidney dish. Darcy was beginning to wish herself some place else, then her attention was drawn sharply back to the pathologist who was peering closely into the thoracic cavity of the body. He resumed his work, picking and prodding and moving tissue aside with infinite care then pausing again to examine the contents. Beads of sweat trickled down his forehead and along the line of his bushy eyebrows. Darcy glanced around at the assembled faces to see if anyone else had noticed these signs of anxiety, but saw only intense concentration, boredom or, in the case of the girl monitoring the data input computer, the faint sheen of queasiness.

Dr. Piper turned and glared at his assistant who swiftly stepped forward and swabbed his brow. Darcy frowned as Piper pulled up onto his face a surgical mask that had hitherto hung neglected below his chin.
"Is anything wrong Dr. Piper?" she asked sharply, ignoring Caro's look of warning. His brows met in displeasure, but he made no reply. Darcy frowned and exchanged a look with Caro. It wasn't good enough, if this guy was exposed to risk then so were they all.
"Dr. Piper, why the mask?" she persisted.
"That's enough; I require you to leave," he grated, obviously containing his temper with great difficulty. "In fact," he said throwing the scalpel into the dish with a resounding clang, and scanning the faces before him: "I want you all to leave the room. I have completed my examination, and it only remains for me to return the organs and tidy the corpse."

At this abrupt termination, there were frowns and muttered comments from all but the female technician merely looked relieved.

"If you please." Piper stood stone-faced and resolute. As his audience filed through the door, Darcy paused on the threshold.

"You'll send me a copy of your findings?" she challenged.

"I imagine the language of my report will be above the heads of your readers."

"But not mine, Dr. Piper. I am quite capable of translating medical jargon into intelligible information."

With a backward look for the man on the operating table, Darcy allowed herself to be led from the theatre by Caro.

FOUR

"That man was a pain," Darcy commented, sipping a large gin and tonic in the bar of The Wily Weasel, a remote inn where it was possible to briefly block out the image of a long-dead knight.

"He is a bit of a stickler," Caro hedged, obviously torn between friendship and professional loyalty.

"You mean an old fart," Darcy corrected with a grin. Caro swirled the gin around in her glass, so that it caught the gleam of copper hanging from beams and the glow from a log fire burning in the grate. She appeared to be absorbed in watching a group of men who, given the frayed and weathered Barber jackets along with talk of 'tups' and 'yows', were obviously sheep farmers. Occasionally, a burst of laughter erupted as they nursed their pints and related anecdotes whilst leaning against the brass rail at the bar.

Turning back to Darcy, Caro said at last:

"He is a tad over-protective."

"Of what for God's sake?"

"The Old Priory," Caro said with a shrug. "He knows you're 'press', and that publishing this could draw sensation-seekers. I guess he envisaged the place littered with Mars wrappers and squashed Coke tins."

"Oh come on Caro!" Darcy impatiently pushed aside a battered copper ashtray. "You can't seriously think it's right to suppress news of such a find on nuisance grounds."

"Hey, I'm on your side, kiddo!" Caro held up a placatory hand. "Just tying find a reasonable explanation for his behaviour."

"Sorry!" Darcy held up her hands in surrender and grinned. "But I have to say the one you came up with is far from reasonable. Something was wrong in there; didn't you sense it?"

"Didn't you say you had to contact Janet?" Caro studied her wrist watch.

"All done!" Darcy raised her eyebrows at this abrupt change of topic. "I emailed a headline and brief for the late edition whilst you were in the loos at the car park. " She finished her drink, and twirled her glass round on the polished table so that the base squeaked and, given her friend's expression, irritated Caro. Darcy pushed it aside and gave her a penetrating look.

"Why did Piper suddenly put on a surgical mask?

Caro shrugged and folding her arms sat back on her seat. This negative body language was not lost on Darcy.

"Excitement – didn't think of it earlier?" Caro said, shrugging her shoulders.

"An old campaigner like him? And a stickler for protocol – your words. More likely he felt he didn't need one, then something changed his mind!"

Caro frowned and ran fingers irritably through her hair.

"I really don't know." Pushing aside her empty glass, she shuffled on the chair and again glanced at her watch.

"So, why don't you stay overnight at Mistletoe Cottage?" Darcy suggested, picking up the signs of imminent departure. Not for the first time, she was grateful to her parents for signing the remote cottage over to her when they swapped Lakeland breaks for holidays in France. She raised a hand to stem the flow as Caro opened her mouth to protest. "It's going dark," Darcy rushed on, "You must be hungry and we've loads to catch up on." *And there's something you are not telling me,* she silently added.

Caro rose and pushed back her seat. "I really ought to be going."

"It's a long drive to Lancaster – and at night," Darcy persisted as Caro moved towards the exit.

"Brian—"

"Will understand. Ring him from the cottage and

blame me. I'll cook supper and crack a bottle of Shiraz," Darcy cajoled, fully aware that this was Caro's favourite wine.
"Okay, you win. By the way," Caro said pausing at the door. "About Dr. Piper's report – have you really studied medicine?"
"Sixth form biology," Darcy admitted with a grin, letting the door swing to behind them.

****

A second set of headlamps rose and swept the gable of the cottage, then dipped again as Caro's car followed Darcy's to the parking area at the rear. The stand of giant pines was briefly illuminated, then retreated against an indigo sky and the dark ridge of the mountain.
"Darcy?" Caro called, her voice sharp with sudden anxiety.
"Oh, there you are – no wonder your parents let you have this place!" she added, as Darcy's torch clicked on and the beam split the darkness.
"Now you know you love it here." Darcy walked to the front door then stopped dead. Caro collided into her back.
"What is it?"
"I'm not sure." Darcy inserted the key in the lock and peered over her shoulder into the shadows.

Nothing stirred as the beam of her torch swept the parking area, and the dense undergrowth crowding the base of the pines.
"What's wrong?" Caro took hold of her arm.
Darcy caught the sharp edge of fear in her voice.
"Nothing." She shivered involuntarily, then shrugged off the feeling of being watched. "Just that dead knight spooking me out," she added lightly.
"This place is giving me the creeps," Caro complained.
"Nonsense!" Darcy pushed the door wide, "Come on, let's get that fire going."

Twenty minutes later, the flames roared satisfyingly up the chimney, with the seasoned wood crackling and glowing in the fireplace of local stone. The cottage is mellowing, Darcy thought, rising to draw the curtains. It was begrudgingly warming to human presence, shrugging off that air of cold and neglect that a place develops if unoccupied for even a short space of time. She paused, arms still above her head and her grip on the curtains instinctively tightened. It was raven-black out there, nothing visible beyond the inky square of glass. That fleeting will o' wisp must have been a reflection of flickering light from the fire.

"Any milk?" Caro called from the kitchen where she was brewing tea.
"Long Life in the pantry." The absurdity of her reply rendered the sinister mundane, and brought a smile of self-mockery to Darcy's lips. Drawing the curtains with a decisive swish, she headed for the kitchen.

An hour later, having raided the freezer, they dined on lasagne with tomatoes, olives and mushrooms, washed down with a half decent Shiraz whilst being serenaded by Pavarotti. They stretched their legs to the fire like a pair of contented cats.
"You should ring Brian."
"Uhmm." Caro, however, cheeks flushed by wine and the heat of the fire, looked disinclined to move.
"Go on. Then you can have a long soak while I 'phone Frank."
Caro frowned, and paused in levering herself out of the easy chair.
"I thought you'd contacted the office."
"I still need to talk to Frank."
"To beg a late start in the morning?" Caro hovered in the doorway.
"Or a day or so here to suss our enigmatic crusader."
"I see." Caro's face was expressionless as she dialled her home number.

The sound of water gurgling into the bath, and Caro's feet padding along the landing filtered downstairs.
Darcy opened her bag to take out the post mortem notes, but the letter from her mother – still unread – brought a pang of conscience. Scanning the sheet of cream Basildon Bond, she

learned that Jip the spaniel had gone into kennels, the garden was in bud, the antique shop thriving and they were off to France for a short break. The letter closed on the usual exhortation to take care and visit them on their return. End of guilt trip. She loved them both dearly of course, but their parochial market town existence left them in blissful ignorance of her crammed agenda and erratic lifestyle.

Obviously all was well; a 'bon voyage' telephone call on her return to the flat would suffice. She tossed letter and envelope into the fire and watched the paper scorch, curl and burst into flames. Reaching for the telephone she pressed the key that stored Frank Kelly's home number.
"Frank? Hi, Darcy here. About tomorrow . . ." Anticipating the blast of rebuke, she moved the receiver a couple of inches from her ear. "Okay, okay I know. I'm asking a couple of days here, Frank. It's a mega story." Flicking through her notes, Darcy summarised the day's events.
"I hear what you're saying," Frank's 'Morgan Freeman voice' cut in on her enthusiasm. "It's a great find," he admitted, then went on to deflate her with: "cultural history and all that crap. Great, that is, if you happen to be an archaeologist or some Oxford don. Sorry Darcy, this isn't the Telegraph Mag!"
"Give me a break, Frank! There's a story here – I can smell it."

"I want you back here like yesterday, girl. Got me? Especially with this local corruption scam set to go flash-bang into crisis." Frank's voice lost its belligerence to a wheedling note. "You wanna be in on the action, don't you?" Darcy hesitated, knowing what was on offer: a chance to be the investigating reporter on a lively local scandal which like Topsy had 'growed and growed' to national headline status. She would be in at the kill, and the reverberations would be felt in Westminster. The Nationals would be left to grind their teeth, destined to merely follow where the Manchester News had led. If she behaved herself, that is, and didn't upset Frank.
"You still there, Darcy-girl?"

The note of triumph in his voice chafed; he knew she was tempted and thought the battle already won.

"You know I'd give my left hand to be there Frank." She smiled, anticipating his reaction.

A chuckle sounded down the line.

"Spoken like a true right-handed reporter."

"But," she pressed remorselessly, "It's not there yet. Your own maxim Frank: A story on the rollers is worth two in the pub."

"Now listen to me." Frank's tone changed, as though he sensed victory drifting from his grasp. There was the chink of ice against glass and the glug, glug of whisky being poured. It was no secret that Frank had marriage trouble and was drowning it in his favourite malt. "You're top of Max Dearden's short list for this one. Your big chance; for Chris'sakes don't cock it up."

Briefly, the tightrope of indecision wobbled beneath Darcy's feet. But she had to follow her hunch – whatever the cost. With that decision came insight into the way to play it.

"Come on, you're always bemoaning the North/South divide."

"So?" Frank's voice already held a note of resignation, as though he anticipated his Waterloo.

"Here's your big chance to do something about it. If this body had been found south of Salisbury Plain the Nationals would have hyped the story to Mars and back. Features, video offers, T-shirts the full package – and you know it."

"So why gripe at me?" he growled.

"You're given the opportunity to put the North on the cultural map, show we're good for more than greyhound racing, redundancies and black pudding. And what do you do? Order me to ditch it and get my goddam' a'ss back to the frigging office!" she finished, already grinning with triumph.

"You're a devious bitch Darcy – know that?"

"Yes Frank." But she wasn't done with him yet. "There's another angle. Daniel Piper, the pathologist, tried to dissuade me from publishing my report."

"What report is that Darcy?" Frank said silkily.

"The one you're going to let me write, Frank," she said, grinning.

"Kind'a guessed it was. Hope he has more joy than me."

"No you don't. He's hiding something. I'd almost say he's running scared."

The rasp of breath sounded as he drew on a cigar, and so strong was the impression of fragrant odour that she almost expected a trail of blue smoke to coil along the line and writhe out of the mouthpiece.

"Okay Darcy, but get your roller boots on. We need to follow tonight's council news item before it goes cold. Feature length and on my desk by end of the week."

"I owe you Frank, you won't regret—,"

"You have tomorrow," he snapped, cutting her short. "Any further research, you surf the net. There's no more absconding – got me?"

"No problem." More ice clinked into the glass. "But hear me Darcy, if this council corruption thing bursts – and I can't hold it for ever – you drop this like a lump of hot shit."

"My hands won't even have time to blister."

"I ought to have fired you long ago, know that?"

"Bless you Frank."

The line went dead.

Caro, eyes closed and a rapt expression on her face, was sitting with head resting against the back of the sofa. As the last note of Pourquoi Me Reveiller died away, she opened her eyes and smiled.

"That was a super meal."

"No, you were starving."

"Don't knock freezer food," Caro raised an admonishing finger. "Take my word as a working wife!"

"I intend to," Darcy grinned, implying she had no wish to find out for herself.

"Did Brian mind you staying?" she asked, pouring coffee from the cafetière into two cups.

"No probs. He's out tonight anyway – some day course."

Darcy divided the last of the wine between their glasses, set down the coffee cups and tossed a log onto the fire. "So, must you go back tomorrow?"

Caro nodded. "I'm meeting David Watson, our Departmental Head, at eleven. He's only seen my brief message, and presumably your piece in the stop press. This is mega-news for us Darcy."

"Sure. Pity though, we could have spent some time together." Darcy, recalling Caro's negative attitude to further research, withheld her plan to visit the priory.

"We'll be returning to do a 'tidy up' job in about a week. I could stay over then."

"Great. Give me a bell and we'll fix it up." Darcy stared into the fire then sighed. "Where will he end up?"

"Try not to think in terms of 'he'. You don't rate what we did back there in theatre, do you?"

"Not much," Darcy agreed dryly. "But you haven't answered my question."

"The body may be re-interred," Caro supplied, but failed to meet Darcy's gaze.

"He'll be put on display," Darcy said, shaking her head. "Trapped in a glass case with people gawking at him."

"Does it matter – so long dead?"

Darcy's lower lip jutted, betraying her disapproval.

"I know the stuff about the body only being a receptacle for the soul, but as such we should show some bloody respect for it."

They sat for a moment in silence, drinking coffee once the wine was finished, and listening to the hiss and crackle of blazing wood as pockets of resin ignited and flared, filling the room with the fragrance of pine.

"I thought you were the one who never got involved," Caro said softly.

"So did I." Darcy sighed, and finished her coffee.

****

At first, it was like the whimpering of a child or an

animal in distress: either way, not a happy sound. Moonbeams slanted through the uncurtained window, striping the whitewash between the timbers with bars of dense black shadow to ominous effect. Ominous, sinister, bars. Bar sinister? Awaking with a start, Darcy lay on her back in bed and stared up at the ceiling beams whilst struggling to make sense of her surroundings and the tumbling stream of consciousness. This was Mistletoe Cottage, she recalled, and bar sinister was something to do with heraldic devices. Associations strung themselves together like beads on a rosary: heraldry, noble houses? The memory of a long-dead knight and his ghastly grin as they carved him up, brought her fully awake.

The whimpering filtered through to consciousness and sent a shiver of apprehension down her spine. Clinging cobwebs of sleep still shrouded reality, but the sound of fear was instantly and intuitively recognised. It took only seconds to fling back the duvet and haul herself from bed. As she reached the door a cry of pure terror ripped through the night.

FIVE

Dread clutched at Darcy's innards as she pushed open the door to the guest room. A swift glance showed the shadowed and moon-striped room to be empty apart from Caro. Her head moved erratically from side to side on the pillow, her limbs threshed as though physically fighting off an attacker. Another cry split the night and sent Darcy rushing to her side. A quick fumble, a muttered curse, and the bedside lamp clicked on, instantly neutralising the eerie effects of mottled moonlight. "Caro! Wake up!" she urged, noting Caro's pallor and the perspiration beading her face.

Caro stared blankly at Darcy.
"Leave me alone!" With a strangled cry she struggled to rise and escape the tangled bedclothes.
"Okay Caro, it's me – Darcy."
Caro's struggles lessened then ceased, and her eyes registered recognition. Darcy stuffed the spare pillow at her back and pushed her gently against it. "You were having a nightmare." Caro closed her eyes then immediately opened them again, as though terrified of returning to the abyss. She swallowed hard, and clutched the duvet to disguise the trembling of her hands. "Sorry Darcy," she apologised with a feeble smile.

Darcy went along with playing it down.
"Last time you get cheese on your supper! Shit Caro – you scared me half to death." Darcy briefly touched her hand.
"Sorry. I feel so stupid." Caro pulled a face.
"Well don't. I'll make us a drink." Darcy rose, then noting Caro's look of alarm and furtive glances at shadowed corners added: "Give me five and I'll be back."

A little more than five minutes later they were sitting with mugs of cocoa well laced with brandy.

"So what was all that about?" Darcy ventured in a matter of Caro blew on her cocoa then took another sip. Darcy's eyes narrowed with suspicion: classical playing-for-time behaviour, often encountered in the interview situation. She changed to a bantering technique.

"Talk to me please?"

"As you said – just a nightmare."

"About?"

"Stupid really." Caro looked at the moon-washed window "That knight – I thought he was here, and you know, alive."

"Not stupid just natural." Darcy let out a sigh of relief. "The excitement of the find – and my mozzarella – getting to you, that's all."

"But the discovery was marvellous, buzzy stuff, whereas this was well, horrible," Caro's fingers plucked at the duvet. She hesitated, then added quietly: "and menacing." She pushed back her dishevelled hair and gnawed her bottom lip.

"You know," Darcy began, "for all your advice about not personalising it, I guess you subconsciously felt a little uncomfortable about what was done in that theatre."

Caro put her head to one side and gave Darcy a quizzical look. "I would expect you to be the one having nightmares; I didn't think he had got to me."

Darcy gave Caro a thoughtful look, but refrained from commenting on her dropping of the objective 'it' in favour of the personal 'he'.

"Try to sleep now."

Gathering up the mugs, Darcy left them on the landing and returned to her bedroom.

SIX

The following morning brought a crispness and buttermilk sun rich with the promise of spring. Darcy stepped outside, stretched luxuriously and filled her lungs with mountain air that carried the scent of pine.

"Now I have an inkling of why you trail to this god-forsaken spot." Caro, apparently none the worse for her nocturnal experience, paused on her way to the car to admire the backdrop of rugged fells.

"It is beautiful," Darcy agreed, taking in trees pregnant with greenery, each embryonic bud bursting its sticky brown womb. The blackthorn too was beginning to blossom, virginal white stark against barbed and stunted black.

"Look – they're like lambs' tails," Caro said with delight, touching the hazel catkins that trembled in the light wind.

"God's own country as they say up here." Darcy touched a web that spanned two sprigs of a glossy-leaved camellia. The movement sent a female blackbird foraging amongst the dead leaves at the base of the shrub, cluck cluck clucking for cover.

Caro placed her bag on the rear seat of her ancient Volvo. "And to think I had you tagged as a townie!" "Oh I love my job," Darcy said with a grin, "and that means being where the action is." She leaned against the open door as Caro eased herself into the driving seat. "But when it all gets too much, you know, the late nights and the booze, the talk and the whole crazy raz – this is where I come to recharge."

"Countryside retreat - can't be bad!" Caro opened the window after Darcy slammed the door. "Oh, almost forgot: our St. Gildas Man, there was an inscription on the vault. Don't get too excited," she warned as Darcy's face lit up, "it's incomplete."

"But it's a start," Darcy enthused. "Photograph?"

"I'll email you a copy today," Caro promised starting up the engine.

Darcy watched Caro's car bump down the track until it was out of sight. Minutes later she was still standing there, a thoughtful frown creasing her forehead. Shrugging off a sense of unease, she went back inside to prepare for her visit to the priory.

****

St. Gildas Bay drowsed beneath sheer sandstone cliffs of vibrant red. Darcy parked up on a strip of common land, a scrubby limbo of sand and rocks between where the village petered out and the beach began. The area supported the odd hawthorn or hazel shrub: gaunt wind-sculpted bonsai stretching spindly arms inland, and bracing their stunted backs against the encroaching sea. It has been too long, Darcy told herself. There were cobwebs on her boots, a disgusting state of affairs, she thought with a grin whilst striding out with pleasure. She could smell freedom on the breeze that tugged at her hair and jacket, and taste it on the salt-tang it carried. After stopping off at the village post office for a local map and guidebook, Darcy made for the track that would take her to the abandoned priory.

The path cut a pale scar across the flank of the sheer cliff face. Up and up she climbed, removing her sweater and tying it around her waist as she became too warm. To either side, pale primroses and coltsfoot peered from amongst the blue-green foliage spikes of sea pinks not yet in bloom. Along the cliff edge golden gorse released its honey-scent, seduced by an unseasonable warmth that was destined not to last. Shielding her eyes, Darcy peered out to sea: a bank of grey cloud was inexorably rolling inland. For the moment however, the sun warmed her back and filled her nostrils with the perfume of bluebells and violets.

At the crest of the cliff, she stopped to rest awhile and consult her map. The priory was situated on the next headland. She sat as close to the edge as she dared with her back against a rock. The empty sea stretched out to a wide horizon, and creamed the rocks immediately below. With hypnotic rhythm the waves broke, swirled and pounded, surging and sucking, devouring the rocks then receding, gathering strength for the next assault. Here, the cliffs reached a height of some three hundred feet and the drop to the water was sheer. The rosy sandstone was striated, eroded into long ridges that housed colonies of bemused-looking puffins, quarrelsome terns and guillemots, fulmars and razor bills and sombre cormorants. They perched and jostled in rows, constantly settling and rising above the lime-spattered cliff in ever-changing patterns of flight. The air was filled with their keening and quarrelling as they vied for precious nest sites along the over-populated ledges.

Her mind wandered over the events of the previous day, tentatively touching the memory of St. Gildas Man as Caro had dubbed him, and lingering over the subtle change in her friend. At first there was a temptation to put it down to her marriage, to having simply outgrown their friendship. But last night the closeness had returned, along with glimpses of the old Caro. The nightmare, or whatever it was, had temporarily destroyed her defences. But why erect them at all against an old friend? After all, it was Caro who sought her out and not the other way round, Darcy thought in distress. She watched the gulls for several minutes then decided it was time to go. The priory was a fair stride away yet. She zipped up her jacket, suppressing a shiver. The sun had disappeared behind the marauding cloud and a chill wind pinched her face.

The path now dipped steeply to a deserted cove before climbing to the next headland. Her breath was laboured, and her thigh muscles ached, but as the goal drew nearer her heart beat quicker with something other than exertion. The wheeling of birds overhead, the whirring of wings and wild cries intensified her excitement.

The ancient priory of St. Gildas stood starkly against a brooding nimbus sky. Unzipping a pocket in her jacket, she took out a camera and reeled off several shots of the crumbling walls and vertiginous foreground. This was the sort of moody atmosphere she needed to write convincingly about the place, with the sea pounding the rocks below, and a westerly salt-laden wind flattening the weather-bleached grasses of the cliff top. What a desolate spot to build a monastic retreat; no fear of distractions here. One thing stood out as sharply as the jagged ruins of the bell tower set against a livid sky: the incongruity of the knight's body being first painstakingly preserved, then buried here, miles from civilisation.

Why at a priory? she wondered. A benefactor? A member of the local gentry who had ceded some land or other gift to the order? The memory of that string cutting into the flesh of his neck immediately mocked the theory. Were they to believe he had been strangled, then given a costly burial in a prominent place of the church? It didn't make sense – any of it. And then there were the provocative tresses of female hair draped around his neck and chest. What of that – and the woman buried at his side?

Still preoccupied with the enigma, she entered what, according to the guidebook, was the ruined chapter house. It was not difficult to picture the cowled brethren gathering here after matins whilst the abbot presided over the reading of the lesson, a chapter of the Rule and the confession and punishment of errant brothers. After jotting down notes and taking more photographs she wandered on to what had been the dormitory. It was easy to imagine the monks rising in obedience to the bell to sing the night office of nocturnes. It took some devotion to leave the warmth of bed and blanket in the small hours of a winter's night to brave wind, rain and snow to reach the church.

Through the ruined archway lay the chancel where the vault and body were found. The atmosphere in here was oppressive, as though the earth and stones were aware of the recent desecration and resented it. The vault was sheeted over with blue, heavy-duty plastic and surrounded by soil piles and rocks, the evidence of excavation. Temporary barriers had been erected, bearing ludicrous warning notices that made Darcy smile. The danger of trespass in this desolate place must be remote to say the least.

She frowned and stooped to examine a set of footprints in the soft earth on the far side of the barrier, then smiled: of course, one of the men from Caro's team. It had to be a male, unless Caro had taken to wearing size eleven boots, she thought grinning at the image this conjured up. He must have forgotten something, and stepped over the barrier before leaving. She half turned to go, but a flash of gilt against the dark earth caught her eye. Stepping over the barrier she picked up a cigarette butt and frowned over the distinctive black paper and elegant gold tip which had caught her attention. Sobranie Black Russian. She hadn't seen one of those since her Hilldean days: one of her tutors – an aging and eccentric professor – had smoked them, not the sort of cigarette one would normally associate with someone from Caro's team. An inquisitive villager perhaps, someone with a predilection for local history – and Russian cigarettes? Possible but unlikely she decided.

She put it to her nose and sniffed. The end had not yet hardened, and it lacked that stale smell of one that was long-dead. Someone must have been here a short while ago. The realisation made her spin round. A figure glimpsed from the corner of her eye brought her stomach lurching towards her throat. The shadow flickered across her consciousness then was gone, but the sense of somebody watching persisted. An involuntary shiver made her untie her sweater and pull it over her head. It was cold in here, colder than outside.

She breathed in deeply, aware of a half-familiar scent. She sniffed the cigarette butt experimentally, but shook her head; it was not the source of the odour. Another deep breath filled her lungs and jogged her memory with a sweetness that was not cloying, the heady notes of spice tempered with salt mist, sea wind and forest rain, a perfume charged with emotion and impossible to forget. Her heart put in an extra beat, bringing that sickening jolt that made it feel as though it had skipped one instead. The scent took her back to the pathology theatre – and St. Gildas Man.

Unbidden, there arose images of him, not in death but alive with vitality, dark hair springing back from wide brow, skin fresh and supple over his bones, astride his horse, armour gleaming and sword in hand, or whispering secrets into the ear of some lady of the court. The more Darcy thought of him, the greater her need to know. About the lady of the mysterious locks too, whether she had been mistress or wife; his hopes, fears and aspirations – and the manner of his death. And most of all his identity. Discover that and the rest would surely follow.

"I'll find out," she vowed aloud on impulse, standing at the head of the vault. It could have been her imagination, but it seemed that the atmosphere in the chancel marginally lightened. The smell of earth and dampness filled her nostrils, replacing the perfume which haunted her memory. If there was a sinister story behind it all, maybe he would rest more easily if it were told. Whimsical but appealing, a thought which made her smile. Setting the flash mechanism on her camera, she took some shots, and psyching herself up for the long trek back to the village, left the chancel.

Once outside, she looked around her in dismay. The mizzle that had softened the distant headland had closed in, obscuring the horizon. Looking back, she saw that the ruins were reduced to dark smudges drifting in and out of wispy cloud. The path was visible for some twelve metres ahead then faded into the mist. She recalled with anxiety how, in places, it ran dangerously close to the edge of the cliff. The air touched her face and clothes with damp fingers, and she instinctively turned up her collar against the chill.

The silence was unnerving. Even the birds were quiet. Gulls wheeled overhead, grey ghosts lacking sound or substance. The feeling that something or someone tracked her with invisible threat, grew with every step. The greater her determination not to slacken pace and look back, the greater the urge to do so. She paused and listened, heart thumping, then walked on. For a moment it seemed the chanting of those ancient monks reached her through the mist.

Did any other living being, she wondered peering through the murk, inhabit this unreal world? The suck and rattle of waves on shingle warned of breakers and white crests of foam three hundred feet below. The path began to rise over the second headland, and once crested, should lead her down to the village of St. Gildas and the car. The chatter of running water told her the bridge, remembered from the outward journey, was at hand. Relief evaporated; here the path divided. Left or right? Upper or lower track? The memory eluded her. Preferring to steer away from the cliff edge, she decided on the higher route.

Her feet stumbled over unfamiliar ground. It had been foolish to trust Cumbrian weather, especially so early in the year, she admitted pushing blindly on whilst trying to quell a rising panic. To be lost was bad enough, but worse still was of the sense of being followed. A furtive glance over her shoulder brought a buzz of shock to her stomach as a figure loomed in the half-light. The breath left her body in a rush of relief – a bush distorted by half-light and distance. Nonetheless, unpleasant thoughts arose like a swarm of flies at a dunghill. Maybe the person who left that cigarette stub was still around, was stalking this isolated cliff. But then her imagination shifted, bringing fresh terrors.

What if that shadow glimpsed in the chancel was not real? In her present situation, it was not hard to imagine St. Gildas Man haunting the spot where his body had lain prior to being violated. Another glance behind brought a stifled cry to her lips. Get yourself together girl, she exhorted herself, as the ghostly white shape turned out to be nothing more alarming than a cruising gull. Ten minutes later the cool breath of a breeze on her face promised a change in the weather which was fortunate, because Lakeland mist could linger for days at a time. Within ten minutes or so, it had noticeably thinned and a soft persistent drizzle was taking its place. She had no memory of the hawthorn hedge looming ahead, nor the shadowy mass beyond that suggested a farmhouse.

"Stop right there!"

Darcy cried out as a man stepped out of the mist and blocked her path.

SEVEN

Once the shock of the man's appearance had passed, Darcy realised he had spoken with authority rather than menace. Her nerve restored she coolly returned his appraisal: a six-footer with slim build but broad shoulders, he had an 'intelligent face' and given the cultivated voice, probably belonged to some profession. Yet there was about him too something of the wildness of these windswept cliffs and heather-clad crags, the sort of man, she guessed, who would not care too much what people thought of him. Judging by his boots, cords and waxed jacket he was also a local landowner.

"You gave me a fright," she accused. The man's eyes, which mirrored the smoke blue of the distant hills, widened slightly as though in surprise at her tone. Obviously he was unaccustomed to being challenged, but if he expected her to tug the proverbial forelock he was in for a disappointment.

"You are trespassing." He blocked her path, hands thrust into his pockets and an unforgiving look on his face. Arrogant bastard! A pity, because he's rather tasty, Darcy found herself thinking,

"I don't see any notices," she snapped.

"I don't believe this." He sighed and ran fingers through his hair. "I suggest you refrain from wandering the fells until you have learnt to read a map and fathom the rights of way." He then fuelled her anger further by adding: "And how to use a compass."

"And I suggest you chill out and keep a civil tongue in your head," she fired back. "I haven't exactly run rampage through crops, dropped litter or left open gates – if there were any to leave open," she added, indicating the expanse of moorland with a sweeping gesture of her arm. "As for getting lost, the mizzle came down without warning."

"Precisely my point about the compass," he said smoothly. "And there's more to the country code than shutting gates, but forgive me, a townie couldn't be expected to know."

"Excuse me, my property is a short drive from here."

The satisfaction Darcy felt at making this statement evaporated beneath his studied appraisal. She knew he was correctly assessing her salon-cut hair, expensive jacket and too-new hiking boots.

"And you come up every month or so – am I right?" he taunted. That she could not deny her cottage was that despised thing a 'second home' was galling beyond measure.

"And you," she was stung into replying, "are presumably one of those land owners who gobble up acres and take pleasure in denying others access."

Her reward was to see the anger leap to his eyes and stain his cheeks with colour.

"I am never fickle about land. I respect it, and the rights of others. It's a pity you don't appear to do the same."

"If you will direct me to the path for the village, I shall be only too pleased to get off your land." Now that she had succeeded in ruffling his composure, she could make her exit without losing face. He poked forcefully at a clod of earth with the tip of his boot.

"Back to Sheep Howe – that hill over there – skirt it on the right, then follow the beck until—," he broke off as a cacophony of excited barking and yelping erupted from behind. Flattening his lip he emitted a shrill whistle. Two Springer spaniels appeared, ears flying and each falling over the other in their haste to reach his side.

"Down Mab, sit Brock."

Tongues lolling, the dogs subsided at his feet and glanced inquisitively from Darcy to their master.

"Oh, come on, I'd better show you," he said turning his

attention back to Darcy. "Otherwise," he added ungraciously as she tried to protest, "you're sure to get lost again."
Calling the dogs to heel he set off, leaving Darcy no option but to follow.

They walked in silence, her unwelcome guide walking ahead, at what was for him obviously an easy pace. The two spaniels periodically vanished and reappeared as they chased through sea-grass and dead bracken. Darcy almost had to run to keep up with their master, and tried not to breathe too loudly lest he guess she was winded. The brisk walk seemed to improve his temper; he stopped at the bridge and said affably:
"What brought you up here alone then?"
"A wilful urge to trespass."
At this a gleam of amusement showed in his eyes.

Sensing that he was about to smile, and being unsure how to deal with it, she looked away. He dug his hands deeper into his pockets.
"Sorry if I was over the top back there. I get fed up with townies yomping over my land all summer. Okay, okay," he held up a placating hand as Darcy looked thunder. "I wasn't referring to you. I accept you were genuinely lost."
"So why the fuss?" she demanded.
"You jumped down my throat."
"You challenged me and gave me a fright."
"I guess we have to share the blame!" he said, smiling suddenly. "By the way, I'm Brant Kennedy, and as you'll have guessed," he added provocatively, "that's my place back there." He waited, eyebrows raised inquiringly but Darcy refrained from offering her name in return. "Look," he said breaking the awkward silence, "I'll be going down to the village in an hour or so; let me buy you a drink at the Old Priory."
"I don't think so." Darcy moved to pass, and he instantly stepped aside.
"No problem. Just a friendly gesture."

The transient look of hurt and embarrassment that

43

he didn't quite manage to conceal caught her by surprise.
"Maybe I'll drop in," she conceded.
"Fair enough. I'll be there around six." He turned and began to walk away, then paused. "Will you manage from here?"
"No problem." The rain had washed away the mist and the path was clearly visible. Darcy walked on, smiling to herself as the two spaniels tore past.

Three quarters of an hour later, she reached the village. For most of the return journey the encounter with Brant Kennedy had occupied her thoughts. During the first stretch he was an arrogant bastard whose smile had come too late; during the latter stage of the walk however, her antagonism had modified. He had tried to make amends, and experience had taught her that information came from the most unlikely sources. Brant Kennedy could have left that cigarette stub at the priory. If so, what was he doing there, and what did he know about St. Gildas man? As a reporter it was her duty to find out, she told herself, unlocking the car. Glancing at her watch, she changed walking boots for shoes and parked up at the Old Priory Inn.

Once inside, she sought and found the ladies toilets. Old fashioned but clean with a refreshing lack of coordinated curtains and dried flower arrangements, was her verdict. Nature had called back there on the cliff, but to squat behind a bush with that man loose on the fell had been out of the question. Who knows, he might have had binoculars. The image thus conjured made her grin at her reflection in the mirror above the wash basin. A quick brush of the hair and a spray of *Ghost* completed her preparations. Staring critically into the mirror, she shrugged and made her way to the bar.

A quick scan confirmed that Brant Kennedy was not amongst the occupants, who judging by appearances were either farmers or walkers. Her column and the intended feature in mind, she surveyed her surroundings: the whitewashed walls were hung with old prints depicting medieval monastic life, whilst quills, ink stands, goblets and censors were mounted on the exposed beams of the ceiling. However, a patina of dust and an interesting shade of verdigris on the copper absolved the place from the charge of being twee. Recalling the stub up at the priory, she bought a packet of cigarettes from a machine in the corner and slipped them into her bag.

Perching on a stool at the bar, she returned the landlord's greeting. Publicans, she had learned early in her career, provided excellent sources of local material. Meals, he informed her, were not normally served until later but he could rustle up egg and chips, an offer which Darcy gratefully accepted.
"Reet then. I'll just go and get that organised," he said, after drawing a half pint of Guinness at her request.

He reappeared a few minutes later. "Been walking then?"
"Up to the old priory." Darcy wiped froth from the end of her nose and nodded.
"Turned reet claggy up there around three'ish," he commented while serving an elderly man with a foaming tankard of ale.
"Thanks, George," he said, drawing himself a half at the invitation of his customer and returning to Darcy to drink it.
"Tell me! I got lost," she said with a rueful grin. "Met a man up there," she added casually, "name of Brant Kennedy."
"Oh, aye." The landlord picked up a snowy cloth and polished the already gleaming surface with a circular motion. "Put you reet, did he?"
"You could say that."
The landlord smirked. "Ticked you off for trespassing did he?"
"Good and proper."
Her host stuck out his lower lip and nodded in sympathy.
"Aye he would. A tad abrupt like, but that's just his way."
He turned and disappeared at a cry of 'one egg and chips' from the nether regions of the bar.

"That was great," Darcy enthused, finishing off a

45

meal that had come garnished with mushrooms, tomatoes and an extra egg. "Tell me," she said pushing aside her plate and wiping her hands on a serviette, "what does this Kennedy guy do up there – sheep farming?"

"Not him." The landlord paused in polishing a glass. "Something to do with the Ministry – and that weird building back of Sheep Howe."

"What sort of thing?" Darcy sipped her Guinness.

"As I heard, summat to do with the weather. Mebbe we should blame him for all the blessed rain we've been having, eh?" He chuckled and resumed his polishing. "He's a bit cagey like, but then," he added, replacing the glass on the shelf and leaning across the bar to speak in conspiratorial tones, "it could be classified stuff."

"Surely not out here," Darcy said frowning.

He shrugged. "Folks worry about the nuclear plant down the coast there. Questions get asked – you know, about this global warming stuff. Anyway, the Government have to pretend they're doing summat about it; that's where I reckon Kennedy comes in. Mind you, nobody living down there shouts too loud like. Jobs isn't it? Practically every family in the area has someone working there."

"I see." As she watched him take down another glass and begin to polish it, Darcy's mind raced. This could explain Kennedy's over-reaction to her being on his land: perhaps he had something to hide, something connected with nuclear emissions. Whatever the reason, it was imperative now that she speak with him, but first there was a personal matter to clarify.

"It's a remote spot, does he live up there alone?" she asked casually.

"Aye. The landlord continued rubbing the glass then glanced furtively at the door before speaking: "He was married." He leaned forward and continued in the hoarse undervoice of the seasoned gossip, "but she left him." He placed the second glass next to the first on the shelf, shook out his cloth and pursed his lips in a gesture that amply conveyed a sense of scandal before adding: "Another fella."

"How long ago was that?" Darcy asked, looking suitably sympathetic.

"Three or four year back." He stuck out a full lower lip and wagged his head. "It's left him a bit sour like, not over-trusting of women."

"I would never have noticed." Darcy said sarcastically. She was about to say more, but stopped as the landlord looked past her shoulder saying loudly, and obviously for her benefit:

"Evenin' Mr. Kennedy, a pint of the usual?"

Darcy forced herself not to turn round, and ordered another drink instead.

"A coke with ice and a slice of lemon please, when you're ready,"

"That's all right Tom, put it on mine," a voice that she recognised said from behind as she took out her purse to pay.

"Mr. Kennedy." She turned as though in surprise. "Thank you."

Brant Kennedy, dressed now in navy cords and a Jersey sweater that deepened the blue of his eyes, stood at her shoulder and took a long pull from the pint of Jennings Bitter set before him by Tom.

"Would you prefer something stronger?" he inquired.

"Coke's fine; I'm driving."

"You decided to come then." He wiped a line of creamy froth from his upper lip with the back of his hand. The chrome of a Rolex watch looked extraordinarily attractive against the tanned skin, Darcy noted.

"I had to eat," she said coolly.

"You're still sore at me."

She swivelled round on the stool to confront him. "Why should I be?" she said calmly, implying that he and the incident were of no significance. A faint flush of embarrassment rose in his cheeks which gave her a sense of satisfaction and went some way to evening the score. "Sit down," she ordered, patting the adjacent stool. "I don't like talking to men who loom over me."

He failed to smile in response and seemed about to refuse, but then shrugged and sat down. Exhibiting even greater reluctance, the landlord moved away in response to calls for service. The place was filling up, a couple of dozen men were milling about pint in hand, chatting or propping up the bar and several couples were hovering at the tables.

"Well you know who I am," Brant Kennedy said pointedly, wiping the base of his glass on a beer mat, and added when she failed to respond: "And as we seem to have a truce here – what's your name?"

Darcy hesitated then shrugged and smiled.

"Darcy West."

His expression took her by surprise. Surely he hadn't recognised the name, not up here in the wilds of Cumbria.

"The reporter?"

"Correct." Obviously he had.

"I do business in Manchester from time to time," he explained on seeing her look of surprise. "I've seen your column in the News."

"Seen but not read?"

"Read but not approved."

"Why not?"

"Stylish but hard-nosed."

"I'm paid to be uncompromising."

"And bloody minded?"

To her annoyance, Darcy felt her cheeks burn. It was not a pleasant feeling having the tables turned. Criticism and condemnation went with the job, she told herself; in a way they told her she was doing it right. Damn this man, his opinion shouldn't matter any more than the next punter's – but it did. "You can't please all the people . . ." she quipped, then hated herself for being flippant. "Not if you speak out instead of courting approval," she added, seeking to redeem herself.

"Or seek to be merely sensational."

"I believe in what I write," she said stiffly.

"I'm not challenging your integrity Darcy."

"So what are you questioning?"

He shrugged and gave her a long hard look.
"Your apparent lack of humility. Are you never afraid you might be wrong?"
"Humility doesn't sell papers."

"I don't envy you your job." He looked at her hard and long, in a way that made her feel oddly vulnerable. She shuffled on her seat and fidgeted with a beer mat. In order to regain her composure she turned and watched as a man entered with a dog slinking at his heels in the manner of all sheepdogs. She smiled faintly as it licked its lips, perhaps in anticipation of a saucer of ale in return for a day's work on the fell.
"Share them?"
"I was thinking the terms of this truce are pretty one-sided." It was time to shift the focus away from herself. "You know all about me, but how do you earn your living?"

"I'm an astronomer." He swabbed drips from the base of his glass with a beer mat. Darcy swivelled round to face him again.
"That's different."
He shrugged. "Not the glamorous job people think it is."
"Hardly mundane though. What are you working on?"
"Nothing too exciting."
He seemed outwardly unperturbed by her questions, but the body language said it all: arms folded across his chest and one leg crossed over the other away from herself. Training as a reporter had taught her to watch for such signs, now it was second only to breathing.
"You can tell me; I won't quote you, honest!" she prompted with a provocative change of tack.

Amusement sparked in his eyes, but the slightest nod of his head told her he accepted her word.
"I'm in charge of the small observatory behind Sheep Howe, the hill—"
"You showed me," she interrupted dryly.
"So I did. He gave her one of his rare smiles.

49

"Anyway, I'm attached to the Ministry so—" he paused
as though wondering how to continue without giving offence.
"So you have to keep stum," she finished for him.
"Something like that." He looked apologetic. "I can say I'm
reporting on cosmic conditions and their possible effect on
national and global climate."
The well-rehearsed official P.R. version, she thought with a sigh
of impatience.
"Cosmic rather than nuclear emissions?" she provoked.
He gave her a look which said 'you should know better' and
raised his glass to drink.

        "I used to look up at the stars for ages as a kid," she said
trying a different approach. "They still fascinate me; I would
love you to show me around your observatory."
Pint glass halfway to his mouth, he gave her a sceptical look
that was far from promising.
"Hey, this isn't the reporter speaking. All strictly off the record,
I promise." She licked her forefinger and crossed her heart so
that he had to laugh.
"Okay," he said, watching her face. "I don't see why not."
She rummaged in her bag, took out a pad and scribbled two
numbers on it.
"The first is the cottage, I'll be there until tomorrow; the other
my direct line at the Paper. Give me a bell and we'll fix it up."
He nodded and pocketed the numbers.

        "So, what took you up on the cliffs?"
"The body found at the priory."
"Ah, the Hilldean University dig." He ran a finger around
therim of his glass until it emitted a high-pitched note.
"Correct." He had obviously read her piece in the
local rag. "Not far from your place, have you been to
check it out?"
"No." An unequivocal answer, then he smiled as though to
temper his abruptness. Recalling the cigarette stub found in the
chancel, she took the packet of cigarettes from her bag and
offered it.
"No thanks."

"Not one of your vices?"

To her frustration, a woman's voice cut in before he could answer.

"Brant! It's been ages. Still living in splendid isolation?"

Brant excused himself and turned to speak to the cool blonde who had appeared at his shoulder.

"Hi, Helen," he greeted her, but made no move to introduce Darcy. She castigated herself for not asking him earlier: now she had no way of knowing if he simply was not in the mood, or did not use cigarettes period and therefore could not be the unknown smoker at the crypt.

"Look, I'm sorry—," he apologised, looking uncomfortable.

"No problem. Time I was on my way." Darcy slipped off her stool and walked to the door.

Looking back, she saw that Brant and the unknown woman were deep in conversation. She was evidently not his 'ex'; they were too at ease together. A new girlfriend? Intent on her emotions, Darcy failed to notice the shadow slip from behind the door, but did feel a vague trespass on her privacy. As she looked over her shoulder, the man flitted across her field of vision then disappeared in the crush of people. As she slipped the cigarettes into a bin by the door, she was left with an image of black brows: livid slashes on a white face. More disturbing though than any visual memory, was a residual aura of something indefinable, but decidedly unpleasant.

EIGHT

During the return drive, Darcy shrugged off the unpleasant memory of the stranger and occupied herself with thoughts of Brant Kennedy. On arriving at Mistletoe Cottage, she decided he disturbed her far more than he should and was best forgotten. With this resolution in mind, she strode purposefully to the front door and once within, set about making first a fire, then a pot of tea.

Despite a cheerful blaze in the hearth, loneliness and a sense of anti-climax brought on an all time low. Time to open that bottle of Bollinger that somehow had never got drunk. There was something sad though about drinking champagne alone; bubbly definitely was not a solitary tipple. So why tonight? Despair at the sterility of her relationship with Jonathon? Or something to do with meeting a bolshi stranger on a cliff top?

The popping of the cork was a poignant sound with no-one to laugh and exclaim as froth surged, ballooned and slid down the neck of the bottle. She had never caught the knack of opening one without spills; Jonathon could, but then Jonathon would, damn him. On her birthday he had replaced the milk on the step with a magnum, then just when she thought he was not coming, had whisked her off to Paris for a midnight supper and bed. Oh yes, Jonathon was great in bed, but when the love-stains were cold on the sheets it was a different story. There was something frightening about the way he could retreat like a snail into its shell. Granted, that had been her personal agenda: romance and sex without strings, but Jonathon was too good at it.

She poured champagne into a glass and carried it over to the settee by the fire. Bathed, and wearing a towelling wrap she was in reflective mood. Was Caro right? Was it time to think less about her career and, as she hinted, more about committing to a relationship? But then one couldn't go out and buy one like a bottle of red in a supermarket. Lifting her glass she grimaced and put it down again; the champagne had gone flat. Time to call Jonathon, before reflection slid down the slippery slope to self-pity.

The ringing-out tone sounded in her ear with monotonous regularity. She was about to replace the receiver when he spoke, giving his name.
"Hi Jonathon, it's Darcy."
"Darcy! Great to hear from you."
The pause was slight.
"I thought maybe you were out."
"No just taking a bath."
Liar, she thought dispassionately, you have a woman there, you bastard. Hating herself, she went along with the game. "So, you're all wet and dripping and naked. Jonathon, how on earth shall I sleep tonight with that image in my mind?"
"Well you won't darling, will you? I can quite understand that."
"Conceited bastard."
His throaty laugh sounded in her ear. "Love you too, darling! Where are you calling from?"
"The cottage."
"Right. Hang on a sec will you."
She heard a door close and knew it was to prevent his woman companion from overhearing.

"And I can just picture you, Darcy, all pink and warm by the fire – and naked beneath your negligee. Am I right?" he breathed a minute or so later.
She couldn't help smiling. "Close enough."
"Not by half. Wish I was there with you. You know one day I'll have to visit your cosy cottage."
One day, she thought with bitterness but heard herself say "That would be fun."
There was a waffling on the line then the chink of bottle on glass. "What are you doing at that benighted spot? I thought it was only for weekends?"

53

"Following up a lead."

"An outbreak of foot and mouth – or sheep shagging?"

"Very funny Jonathon. I'll tell you tomorrow when
I get back."

"I'll book a table at Zeffirelli's – you know that little Italian job
you liked."

"Great."

"Look must dash now ."

"Yes, you must be getting cold," she said maliciously.

"What? – oh er, yes, that's right," he blustered, and she
laughed, knowing it had slipped his mind that he was supposed
to be wet from the bath.

"What's funny Darcy?"

"Nothing, Jonathon. See you."

She stared into the fire then rose, picked up the bottle and
poured the rest of the champagne down the sink.

She lay sleepless in her bedroom beneath the eaves.
Jonathon was always selective, ever discreet – but never
faithful. Unaccountably, Brant Kennedy came to mind. He
would never replace milk with champagne, but neither could
she imagine him screwing other women when involved in a
relationship. But such a man would expect, as well as give,
commitment. Whatever, he probably would not call which was
a pity, because she really would have liked to see his
observatory. It was her last thought before drifting
into sleep.

A strident sound woke her up. Disoriented, she stared at
the moonlit ceiling. For a second she thought herself back at
her Manchester flat, but the beams and window did not fit. The
constant shrilling of the telephone brought her consciousness
back to Mistletoe Cottage. The hands of the luminous clock
showed ten past midnight. Who would be ringing her here at
this hour? She struggled into a sitting position and groped
for the telephone on the bedside cabinet.

"Yes?" she inquired in a tone to discourage untimely chat.

"Where the hell have you been Darcy? I rang at least six times this evening." Frank Kelly's voice was thickened by drink and anxiety. "Well?" he barked.
"Chasing my lead," she muttered, stuffing the pillow against the headboard. "Hey, what is this Frank?"
"I want you in my office at nine sharp."

Darcy ran a hand through her tangled hair.
"Okay, no problem. Except you interrupted a beautiful sexy dream."
For once her editor failed to respond with humour.
"Just be there."
"Why the urgency?" she pressed.
"Just get your a'ss back here – and no cock ups."
"Okay chief, but—"
There was a click and the line went dead.

****

"But you gave me the go-ahead."
The following morning at nine sharp, she stared at him in disbelief.
"I've changed my mind."
"But why? You owe me that much." Darcy watched as he popped a Remgel into his mouth. That nervous dyspepsia of his would one day become an ulcer.
"I owe you nothing." He picked up the cigar that was smouldering in the ash tray to avoid looking her in the eye.
"I don't believe this." Darcy ran fingers through her hair in agitation.
"You'd better," he growled, and rammed the butt between his teeth.
"If the Town Hall Scandal hasn't broke yet, then what's in the way?"
"Forget it – and go get some work done."
Pulling a sheaf of papers towards him he flicked ash dismissively from the front of his waistcoat.

Darcy shifted her weight nervously from one foot

55

to the other, looked longingly at the door then at his thatch of hair as he pored over the documents.

"Just one good reason Frank," she implored, risking a last try. He looked up and considered her for a moment.

"The Chief," he said at last, clamping his teeth on the end of his cigar. Darcy's eyes widened.

"Max Dearden took me off a local story? Come on Frank, he doesn't even know I exist."

"Seems he does now," Frank Kelly muttered with a shrug.

"But what interest can this story hold for him?" Darcy protested

Frank passed a hand wearily over his eyes.

"Who knows. Maybe he has inside info. on the Town Hall scam. Perhaps he wants you on immediate standby; I said you were on his short list for it. "

"So clue me up. Has the Treasurer's secretary agreed to an interview?"

"No change." He picked up his pen and unscrewed the cap, a clear signal for her to leave.

"On my own time and expenses?" she pushed warily.

"For the last time – there will be no Medieval Man story carried in the News. Not if you were to offer to buy your own bloody space! Got it?"

"Oh sure. I've got it."

"And don't slam the—"

The crash of the door behind her brought some small measure of satisfaction.

Coffee was a must. Her token was rejected, so she reinserted it and thumped the side of the hot drinks machine with unnecessary force, then cursed beneath her breath. A jet of steaming liquorice-coloured liquid overshot the cup and splashed her shoes and ankles. She scowled, took a tissue from her pocket and dabbed at her legs.

"Okay Darcy?" The frown faded as she turned. Geoff worked on copy for Frank and was a treasure. He was watching her with an anxious expression.

"Sure, just authority run wild in there." With a jerk of her head she indicated Frank's office.

"He'll get over it," Geoff said with a grin, shoving his perpetually slipping glasses higher up on his nose.
"Sure." Darcy extracted the plastic cup and made her way to her office.

But would he? It was doubtful. Seldom had she seen Frank in such an implacable mood. You cocked-up and got a bollocking that was soon forgotten – that's how it ran with Frank. But this was something different; what could have happened inside the space of twenty four hours? Somebody must have got to Max Dearden, otherwise he would never interest himself in so parochial a matter. And that somebody, she thought sipping coffee whilst staring at the ant-inhabited Lego metropolis below her window, had to be Daniel Piper.

There's one way to find out, she thought, heading for the lift. She punched the button for the top floor, but as the lift began to rise, so did the doubts. It took power to influence Max Dearden, and it was doubtful that a provincial pathologist had that much muscle to flex. And why should anyone with that kind of clout be interested in St. Gildas Man? The gliding open of the lift doors put an end to speculation.

Rosemary Strickland's office was next to Max Dearden's suite. She had been his P.A. for over ten years, and her protection of his privacy, person and reputation was legendary. Darcy entered in response to the peremptory call from within. As she greeted the occupant, she was struck as always by the disparity between temperament and outward appearance. The woman seated at the desk pushed back the blond curls which framed a peaches and cream complexion.
"Sit down Darcy, be with you in a second."
The voice, Darcy reflected cynically, would have softened considerably and taken on a musical note had Rosemary Strickland's visitor been male. As always, the marshmallow bosom and curvy hips were accentuated by a frilly blouse and

softly draped skirt which, regardless of fashion, ended just above her dimpled knee. Three inch heels and seamed stockings were *de rigeur*, as was Chanel No. 5. Altogether, she presented to the unsuspecting male a fantasy come true: that elusive blend of femme fatale and comforting mother-figure. What they initially failed to discern was an underlying ruthlessness and ambition that made Maxwell look like a small-town hustler.

"What can I do for you?" The baby blue eyes travelled critically over Darcy's face and figure. And was there a touch of wariness in there? Darcy couldn't be sure.
"The Save the Children Project – has a date been fixed for the Fun Run?" Darcy improvised.
"Not yet. I'll send a memo down."
"Good!" Darcy effected an exaggerated sigh of relief. "Not started training yet."
"I'm sure you'll manage, dear." The eyes glazed with boredom, and Rosemary Strickland pointedly looked away and double-clicked the computer mouse.
"So, how are things, Rosemary."
"Snowed under as usual, but this place would grind to a halt if I shirked like some I could name." The clipped tones of impatience gradually faded as she warmed to her favourite topic, that of her indispensability, though whether this was real or imagined Darcy could never decide. "That Joyce Underwood is still on the sick," the other woman continued in spiteful tones, "and Karen swears she spotted her at that Raves disco or whatever they call it the other night. But then what do you expect, when heads of department go screwing their typists instead of setting a proper example." And so the stream of bile spewed on.

Apart from the occasional nod or comment, Darcy allowed Rosemary Strickland's martyred tones to flow without interruption.
"It's lovely now though isn't it?" she broke in at last, interrupting a lengthy diatribe about last week's weather.

"Looks like Spring has finally sprung!" She gestured at the sun streaming in through the plate glass window. "Mind, it doesn't seem to have Frank's sap rising yet," she added with an innocent smile.

"Been giving you a hard time, has he?" Rosemary clicked out of the menu and looked pleased: it was always satisfying when others fell from favour; it served to emphasise one's own privileged position.

"Bit my head off. Has the Chief been giving him a roasting or something?" Darcy's cheeks were aching from holding the smile, but Rosemary seemed unaware of being pumped.

"Not that I know of," she said chattily, shaking her head and making the blond curls bounce. "Oh, but wait a minute, yes there was a call," she said almost to herself, "Max did speak to someone, and seemed mighty tetchy afterwards. Now then, was it Special Branch – no the Home Office, that was it, so he may have had a go at Frank then."

She paused, and her Barbie-doll cheeks flushed pink as though she was suddenly aware of being indiscreet. Her eyes lost their previous limpid softness and became stone-like with suspicion.

"I have a report to finish," she said abruptly, obviously deciding she had said too much. Darcy recognised this as a dismissal that could not be ignored. Special Branch? The Home Office? Why had Rosemary Strickland thought of both when trying to remember who had called? Confusion over two separate calls – or over the exact identity of a single one? Given that the police counterpart of MI5 came under Home Office rule, the latter option seemed the most likely. As she made her way back to the lift, Darcy's mind was in turmoil.

NINE

That evening, Jonathon picked her up at the flat in the vintage Bentley that was the envy of friends and enemies alike. He was looking good in a dark blue suit that set off his Saxon colouring, and Zeffirelli's fulfilled all expectations: the antipasto were appetising, the salad crisp, the tagliatelle and sauce delicious and the regional wines and cheeses were both superb. So why, she thought as they drove to his apartment, this flatness and lack of a buzz? No problem, she assured herself: the fact that Frank had pulled her off the story still rankled, then there was her preoccupation with the call from the Home Office.

So far, she had kept quiet about both issues. During the meal, Jonathon had kept her entertained with the latest gossip about town and it had seemed inappropriate to launch into gloom and doom. He had got everything right until that habitual and irritating last minute trip to the men's toilets, which was probably unfair of her, because safe sex was more important than spontaneity. But did he have to buy condoms on the night, thus underlining the reason for taking her back to his flat? She recalled her loneliness at the cottage, and suddenly his company seemed more desirable than the promise of passionate sex. As she instinctively snuggled closer, he looked down at her and smiled.
"Happy?"
"Uhmm. I rather think I am."
She was surprised to find that it might be true. Maybe they did have something worthwhile going.

The Bentley purred round the corner into the exclusive mews court where Jonathon lived. Right now, with her head resting on his shoulder, and his familiar scent in her nostrils, there didn't seem a whole lot wrong with commitment. The minimalist décor of Jonathon's flat mirrored his personal appearance: clean lines, expensive taste and stylish cool. One of his old flames, Darcy recalled tossing her handbag onto a chair, was an interior designer and had probably given the place a make-over. Jonathon switched on two art deco lamps, clicked on the C.D. remote control bringing forth late-night music and poured her a generous measure of Cointreau.

"Drink darling?" he asked belatedly as he was already holding out the glass. Slick or just fondly familiar? she found herself wondering, then ashamed of her cynicism, settled for the latter.

"Thanks." Accepting the glass she sat on a white leather settee.

Jonathon joined her, and soon she was in his arms and his lips were insistent on hers, his hand slipping inside her blouse to cup her breast and causing her breathing to sharpen and quicken.

"You know, I really have missed you." He sounded faintly surprised, and winding one of her curls around his finger, playfully tugged as though to pay her back for causing him discomfort. She pulled away a little in order to see his expression.

"You mean you've missed this?"

"Silly question. Of course I have."

His hands were slipping her silk jacket from her shoulders, his lips pressed against the exposed white skin. The familiar flame of desire kindled and leapt deep inside and her kisses were now every bit as hungry and demanding as his.

"And so have you," he whispered, his tongue teasing first the lobe of her ear, then probing the sensitive shell-curled rim whilst his fingers found and exulted at the telling thrust of her nipples. This, she thought self-mockingly as he led her into the bedroom, is where common sense and resolve get discarded along with her clothes.

Jonathon was as cool, hard and slim as the chrome rail beneath her hands as she arched and rose to meet him in climax. As the bubble of tension exploded leaving her drained and empty, she let out a long drawn-out sigh and released the rail, allowing one arm to lie limply along the damp sheen of his shoulders. She remained still for a time, eyes closed, allowing the shock waves to ebb and diminish. As he groaned, rolled over and collapsed on the bed beside her, she looked down at him and for the first time was vaguely disturbed by the way he rarely spoke during lovemaking. Something to do with silence and depersonalisation.

"So what was wrong, Darcy?" he said now as they leaned against a bank of pillows and sipped a nightcap.
"Why do you ask?" She shrugged, and sipped her drink.
"I had to work harder."
"So did I."
He moved round, resting his weight on one elbow in order to see her face.
"Do I have a rival?" he asked lightly, slipping his forefinger beneath one of her curls to flip it back from her forehead. She stared at him, momentarily disconcerted by the image of a Heathcliff-surly stranger striding the cliffs and accusing her of trespass.
"I'm sure you would know," she bantered, recovering her composure.

He looked amused, but the smile didn't reach his eyes.
"Like I said – a rival?"
Darcy picked up the lighter resting on his gold cigarette case on the bedside table, and absent-mindedly flicked it on and off, then with a sigh, dropped it back again.
"I'll have one of those."
Wordlessly she handed him the case and lighter.
"I've had a shit of a day, that's all," she said in response to his quizzical look. Jonathon dropped back against his pillows, lit a cigarette, pulled on it deeply and slowly exhaled.
"Never mind. You're here with me now, so forget about it."
"Could you forget it – if the Clifford Anderson deal fell through?" To land the computer magnate's account, she knew, had become an obsession.
"That's different."

"Is it? Why?" she demanded, half turning to face him.
"Okay, tell me what's eating you."

Briefly, she related the finding of St. Gildas Man and her stormy interview with Frank Kelly.
"Have you been listening?" she demanded as he stubbed out his half-smoked cigarette.
"Of course, darling." He slipped his hand between her thighs. Darcy contracted her muscles to discourage him.
"So what do you think I should do?" she demanded.
"Relax for starters sweetheart; you're strangling my thumb."
"I'm serious, Jonathon."
"So am I – and so is our mutual friend."

Half turning, he nuzzled his hardness against her whilst the fingers of his free hand caressed her breast.
"Later, I promise." She removed his hand from her groin. "But right now I need to talk. I want your advice."
He looked at her with a puzzled expression, as though seeing a stranger in his bed.
"I think ," he said deliberately whilst stroking her hair, "you should finish your Cointreau, lie back, and let me make slow luxurious love to you for the rest of the night."
She sat upright, dislodging his other hand from her breast.
"Do you care at all about me Jonathon – or only about my anatomy?" She felt and saw his immediate withdrawal. His eyes glazed over with wariness; the alarm was set in the empty house from which he had already fled. Swinging her legs over the side of the bed, Darcy reached for her clothes.
"What are you doing?" he demanded.
"Isn't it obvious?"
"I thought you were staying the night."
She pulled her silk top over her head and fastened her skirt.
"I don't think there's any point."

Something in her voice or demeanour must have convinced him of her seriousness.
"Oh, come on, sweetie, back into bed," he said attempting light heartedness.

"Come on," he repeated, patting the mattress as she slipped on her shoes, "Hop in – and talk shop if you must."

"You patronising bastard." Darcy picked up her bag.

"Shit! What's with you Darcy?"

"It isn't working any more." She gave him a long hard look.

He frowned as though genuinely not understanding.

"But we agreed—"

"No involvement, no strings." she finished for him. "I know that Jonathon, but even friends listen, support one another when the going gets rough."

"But you can't just go," he protested, climbing out of bed and reaching for his dressing gown.

"Why not? We are as much strangers now as the day we met."

"I had no idea. You're not giving a guy chance to—"

"Goodbye Jonathon."

Darcy closed the door quietly as she left.

TEN

Jonathon made no attempt at contact. This, Darcy told herself, was a relief, as emotional entreaties might weaken her resolve. Another week passed by without word from Caro. Frank Kelly made no further mention of St. Gildas man, and took care not to give Darcy an opening in which to raise the matter. He kept her busier than ever before, but all of it mundane and routine, and frustration at being taken off the case still rankled. She sat at her desk, staring moodily out at an April sky changing from cloud to sunlight and back again within minutes, mirroring her mood swings With a sigh, she turned back to the computer and tried to drum up enthusiasm for a mediocre piece on the infamy of certain Timeshare companies.

The trilling of the internal telephone provided a welcome excuse for postponement.
"Darcy West."
"Hi, Darcy. Ed here – photography. That film you dropped in for developing."
Darcy's face brightened. Given the spate of work and taboo subject matter she had forgotten.
"It's ready?"
"Yes. But sorry – one or two didn't turn out."
"What was the problem?" Her tone conveyed her disappointment.
"Under exposure I guess. I'll drop them into your mail tray."
"Okay. Thanks, Ed."
It seemed, Darcy thought replacing the receiver, St. Gildas Man was a non-goer from the start.

Taking a mid-morning break, she collected coffee and photographs and returned to her desk. During the walk back to her office, she resisted the urge to slip the prints from the envelope. With each step, optimism and excitement grew, because one of her rare hunches had buzzed in her solar plexus. What if Ed was mistaken? What if something appeared on that print which was meaningless to him? For instance the bluish vapour rising from the body at the post mortem. For a moment, it seemed she smelled again that elusive blend of resins and spice that filled her nostrils and enthralled her mind. It was just possible that the aura around the body had been captured on film to be interpreted by Ed as a fault.

Barely able to contain her impatience, she forced herself to sip her coffee before putting it aside to pick up the envelope. The first photograph showed the facade of the Town Hall fronted by lime-spattered statues of Albert and Victoria, the feathered culprits pecking, strutting and being fed crumbs by passers-by. There followed shots of the chairman of the Local Business and Rate payers Association who had lodged the first complaint; a harassed-looking City Treasurer leaving the building, and various counsellors with pricey new cars.

Patience, she told herself dropping the prints onto the desk. To rush in now would be to tempt fate, and cause the coveted prize to disappear. An image of herself posing as Cat Woman at the Save the Children Fancy Dress Ball taken by Frank – Ed probably laughed at that one. She felt a familiar buzz in her solar plexus. She picked up the next print and, anticipating a revelation, sucked in air loudly as she scanned the picture. St. Gildas Man stared up at her from the operating table, green eyes accusing her of forgetting, his body still swathed and as yet not violated by Dr. Piper's raised scalpel. However, that was all. No sign of any effulgence, no bluish aura offering proof of the experience. Her shoulders sagged beneath the weight of disappointment, and tears were ridiculously close. Her hunch had felt so positive, but she had lost her touch; luck had deserted her leaving her as vulnerable and exposed as a snail with its shell crushed underfoot.

Mechanically, she sifted through the remaining prints, her confidence at lowest ebb. Ed, she discovered, was right: the last couple of shots were marred by shadows. Without expectation to sharpen perception, she almost missed it. At first glance, it was just another under exposed photograph. As she laid it on the desk next to the other two suspect prints, her heart beat faster. The progression from shadow to figure could be traced. Mistrusting her judgment, she took it over to the window for scrutiny by cold daylight. The dim interior, shot with light from gaps in ruined walls, and enriched with ochre and umber hues, was reminiscent of a Rembrandt painting, but the shadow superimposed on the chancel wall had form and substance. Something that could be a hint of armour showed as a gleam of greenish light leached from sky and sea.

Returning to her desk, she sat there for several minutes, staring at the image and striving to cope with a maelstrom of emotion. A sapling, its branches threshing and set singing by a high and changeable wind, she swayed from elation to fear, from certainty to doubt and back again. This thing has to be controlled, she told herself sternly, playing Canute to the tide of emotion. It must be kept in a professional pigeon hole where it belongs. For starters, Frank should know, then surely he would allow her to carry on her investigations.

She was halfway to his office when doubt began to gnaw at her courage like woodworm in ancient cloisters. If Frank was telling the truth, the decision no longer rested with him but with someone at the top of the hierarchy, maybe Max Dearden himself. The door of his office was looming, and it was too Late to changer her mind. With a fatalistic shrug she raised her hand and knocked. Frank would find a way, he would back her again once he saw the photograph.

Darcy stared at him aghast as he tossed the picture contemptuously onto the desk.
"I see nothing unusual," Frank Kelly repeated, correctly interpreting her expression.

67

"But it's there, look." She held up before him, tracing the outline with the tip of an index finger. He leaned back on his seat and watched her intently for a moment.

"Ever been given the Rorschach test?"

"No, why?" She frowned and looked puzzled.

He stabbed the air between them with his cigar.

"Because you soon will be if you keep this up. 'Look at the pretty inkblots and tell me what ghosts and monsters you see'. Standard procedure, I believe, for shrinks treating nuts with obsessions."

"Frank Kelly you're a bastard." Her face drained of colour, even her lips were white.

"And you're fired." He rammed the cigar butt into his mouth, turned away from her and clicked on the computer.

Stunned, she stared at him as the panic rose from her stomach, but he studiously ignored her presence.

"I'm sorry, I should not have said that."

"No you bloody well shouldn't." Still he didn't look her way.

"Did you mean it?"

"Mean what?"

She knew what he was doing, hated herself for submitting to humiliation, but knew her job was on the line.

"Am I really sacked?" she pleaded.

"Christ Darcy! I let you take some bloody liberties." At last he swivelled round and met her gaze.

"I know. Sorry, Frank." With a sense of relief she felt the tide turn in her favour.

He sighed with exasperation and clicked on 'suspend'. For a moment he glowered at her over his cigar, then shrugged his bear-like shoulders.

"Okay – get yourself over to Karen Benson – she's finally agreed."

"Thanks, Frank." Then puzzlement ousted relief and she frowned. The City Treasurer's secretary had steadfastly refused to be interviewed.

"What changed her mind?"

"A telephone call or two to her home. A hint about being an 'unwitting' accessory, though with her record of holidays and expense accounts, that's something of a euphemism. Anyway it seems she's ready to squeal on her boss if her own neck is at risk."

"You mean she's been harassed and intimidated." Darcy, her precarious position temporarily forgotten, threw him a look of challenge.

"You squeamish?" he accused, pointing his cigar at her.

"As a method it's suspect."

"So is the way her bosses are playing with rate payers money. Fat contracts for favoured contractors – in exchange for yachts moored off the Greek islands. You can't get much more 'suspect' than that! Save your pity for the poor buggers they're ripping off."

"Like us, you mean," she said dryly.

He moved the cigar from one side of his mouth to the other with an expert contortion of teeth and jaw.

"Now you have it, girl. You know the questions to ask: overheard telephone conversations, flights, hotel bookings, the lot, but make her feel safe so she'll talk. Plug 'public duty' and all that crap. Now go."

Darcy paused, then daring his eagle eye, snatched the photograph from under his nose and moved for the door.

"Darcy – you're not still playing with that one behind my back?" he asked in ominous tones. She turned to face him, and felt a sense of shock on seeing the concern behind his bullying manner.

"It still rankles," she evaded.

"Look," He rested his hands on the desk and clasped them tightly so the flesh over his knuckles turned white.

"Take a bit of advice Darcy, and leave this thing well alone." He glanced round nervously and lowered his voice: "You could end up in a pile of shit – and I won't be able to dig you out."

Darcy felt a sudden chill; this guy was not kidding.

"I won't involve you or the paper – I promise."

He watched her in silence for a moment, then nodded.

69

"Fair enough. But if you come unstuck, we never had this conversation, understand?"

"Absolutely." She hesitated then decided to risk a pitch. "But if I was fool enough to go in alone, can't you give me at least a hint of what I might be up against?" She paused, gauging his response. "Like the Home Office, for instance."

Apart from blinking once, he gave no sign of being perturbed.

"Look," he said, meeting her gaze. "Just because some ministerial toes are proving sensitive, there's no need to get paranoid, is there?" he said evenly.

She smiled briefly at this neat confirmation of her suspicions.

"Thanks, Frank. I owe you one."

She walked back to her office with a lighter heart. At least her hunch about the Home Office was correct, and Frank was right about the photograph, there was a rational explanation. At best her mental image of St. Gildas Man had been strong enough to materialise, and the thought-form register on film. The technique was well-known and documented; both Russia and the States used it in spying exercises. At worst she was seeing what she wanted to see, rather than what was actually there. It was a warning to chill out, she had almost lost it back there with Frank. The realisation that she had almost forfeited her job forced a decision. Frank had compromised, allowing her to back off without losing face, next time she would not be so lucky. On reaching her office she tore up the print and let the pieces drop into the waste bin. It was time to let Caro know she was dropping the case.

ELEVEN

The sun warmed Darcy's face as she walked down the tree-lined pedestrian way to Langdale, one of the four colleges that made up the Hilldean University campus. The groups of laughing and chattering students and the characteristic smell of beer and hamburgers as she crossed the cobbled courtyard brought a rush of nostalgia. How simple life had seemed when the chief worry in life was Finals; or whether the current boy friend would be The One or the romance be snuffed by the arctic wind of pre-examination nerves. All that had been a lifetime ago.

At least there was one familiar face approaching. Her ex-tutor, sporting a beard now but otherwise looking much the same, paused to speak.
"Hi there, Darcy – how's things?"
"Professor Jackson! Fine thanks," she replied, returning his smile.
"I see you have your own column now in the News."
"That's right."
"Excellent. Great to see you around again. Signed up for your Masters?"
Darcy shook her head. "Afraid not, just visiting Caro Stevens in Archaeology."
"Pity. Never mind, one day perhaps . . ." and with a smile and a wave he was gone.

Thoughts of Caro caused a cloud to dim Darcy's sun as she walked to the entrance. Still there had been no word, no promised photograph of the crypt. The previous evening she had telephoned Caro at home to suggest a meeting for today. Caro had been evasive, claiming to be very busy: extra lectures due to a colleague being on sick leave which was probably true,

71

but her voice had betrayed tension and reluctance. The most likely cause was the conflict with Dr. Piper. Caro, Darcy guessed, was suffering from split loyalties, but once the decision to drop the case was revealed to her, the problem should be resolved.

General Office had confirmed that Caro would be on campus all day. Darcy pushed through the group of students that thronged the foyer and climbed the stairs to the first floor. The door of the office was ajar and Caro was seated at the desk. "Hi, Caro."
Caro raised her head and anxiety flared in her eyes.
"Darcy!" She half rose then sank back on her seat. The flush of surprise faded leaving her face pale. "What are you— I mean, I'm rather busy."
She isn't going to believe this, Darcy thought wryly.
"Had to come out this way to an interview – thought I'd call in on the off-chance."
Caro gave her a sceptical look, seemed about to challenge this then smiled instead.
"Sure. I mean, nice surprise." Apparently regaining composure, she gestured to a chair. "Park your bum a minute, must finish marking this essay."
"Go ahead." Darcy chose a battered armchair out of the semicircle of seats arranged about the seminar area.

Surreptitiously, she looked around as Caro bent over her papers. The poster about having booked a nervous breakdown was admittedly a trifle dog-eared, but still in its place on the wall and made Darcy smile. Next, Darcy scanned the titles along the bookshelves whilst Caro scribbled some notes.
"Sorry about this, it has to be in by end of today," Caro apologised.
"No problem." Darcy's attention was suddenly caught by a folder on the shelf below the computer work station. It was secured by a couple of elastic bands, and the label bore the words 'St. Gildas Man'.

As though sensing her focus, Caro looked up and

simultaneously pushed aside the papers on her desk.

"Fancy a beer?"

"Can you spare the time?" Darcy could not help saying.

"Of course I can. Half an hour do?" Caro flushed with embarrassment, and something, Darcy thought, like guilt.

"Fine." Darcy stood up and watched her slip on a jacket, then impulsively reached out to touch her arm.

"What is it Caro?"

"I don't know what you mean."

"You're different; something isn't right."

Caro fiddled with the silk scarf that draped her shoulders and looked away.

"No really, I'm fine. Just
pressure of work."

"Okay." Darcy followed her to the door. "But remember,
you can trust me."

"Let's go get that beer." Caro's smile was strained.

Langdale bar heaved with chattering students who all looked very young and unfamiliar to Darcy. The décor had changed a la Française with wrought iron tables, reproduction fin de ciècle wall lamps and Toulouse Lautrec, Monet and Mucha posters, and there were no familiar faces behind the bar.

"Smart – but I prefer the peeling paint and tatty seats of my day," Darcy commented as they sipped beer and ate cheese sandwiches.

"It's called nostalgia." Caro smiled.

Darcy shrugged. "I guess," she said glumly then grinned. "Remember falling over a stool and getting thrown out because they thought you were drunk?"

"Most unjust. I hadn't even finished my first drink." Some of the strain left Caro's face as she laughed. "I can top that: Gilbert Arnold – philosophy, remember? You came in late, and tripped over that metal waste bin on the top of the lecture theatre stairs."

Darcy grinned; it was her turn to look embarrassed. "Could I ever forget? I watched it roll and clang down every step to the bottom."

"And Gilbert Arnold's face when it came to rest at his feet."
"Hysterical." Darcy laughed aloud at the memory. "All the kids were rolling in the aisles. He gave me a bollocking that made me feel two inches high. Most unfair – stupid place to leave a bin anyway."
"What were you like!" Caro shook her head slowly. "They were good times though, Darcy."
"Weren't they just."
"So, have we come to the end?" Darcy sobered and pushed aside the second half of her sandwich.
"All courses end sometime." Caro flushed and fiddled with a fingernail.
"I'm talking about our friendship, Caro."
"No, of course not, silly."
"Then why are you keeping me at arm's length?"
"I'm not—,"
"Caro – watch my lips, this is Darcy speaking."

Caro sighed, and her shoulders sagged.
"Okay, it has been difficult." She looked around and lowered her voice. "There's been pressure."
"To do what?"
"To shelve the project," Caro confided, her voice sinking to a whisper.
"Shelve St. Gildas Man?" Darcy stared at her in disbelief.
"Crazy isn't it, but it happened."
"But why? It's the find of the century."
"Search me." Caro shrugged. and pushed aside her barely-touched sandwich. She shook her head as though still unable to make sense of it. "This thing would have put Hilldean on the map. Our knight was probably a crusader – analysis of pollen grains and stomach contents – sorry Darcy," she apologised with the ghost of a smile as Darcy grimaced, "would eventually tell us. One minute David Watson – our Head of Department, you remember – was acting like a kid on Christmas morning, and full of plans for an exhibition and publication of my report. Then even before the radio carbon dating comes through, he goes cold on me. Just like that," she snapped her fingers to illustrate the point.

74

"Mumbled something about allocation of funds and the time not being right. Ever heard anything like it?"

"Yes," Darcy said, nodding grimly. "From Frank Kelly."

"You are joking." Caro frowned as she pushed aside her glass.

"No, I've been taken off the story."

"What's going on here?" Caro turned pale.

Darcy fiddled with a beer mat, and used it to mop the wet rim left by her glass, then reached into her pocket and drew out an envelope containing the black and gold cigarette end.

"I found this in the chancel. Could a crew member have left it?"

Caro looked round nervously before taking the envelope.

"No way. Smoking on site is forbidden. Even off it, I don't know anyone who uses these!" she said, peering inside. She handed back the envelope. "Is it significant?

"I don't know," Darcy confessed, replacing it in her pocket. "Do you have a copy of Dr. Piper's report yet?"

"No, but surely you don't suspect a link?"

Darcy shrugged. "It's the only lead I have. Tell me," she leaned forward and lowered her voice, "do you have access to personal data bases?" Darcy said lowering her voice, "the kind that might give a clue to Piper's background, his religious and political leanings for instance."

"Not legit. but I know someone – leave it with me."

"Great." Darcy drained her glass and put it down decisively.

"But what good will it do? I thought you were off the case."

"I am – officially. But there's nothing to stop me nosing around on my own account," Darcy disclosed, her resolve to back off forgotten. "Someone is mighty interested in our medieval knight, Caro."

"So it would appear."

"There's something else you can do." Darcy dropped her voice to a whisper. "Find out if David Watson received a call from the Home Office recently."

"I'll try. But what goes?"

"I discovered that our editor-in-chief, Max Dearden, received one the day before Frank took me off the case."

"But why should anyone at the Home Office want
to suppress the story?"

"I don't know." Darcy shook her head. "But it's my
guess that someone who read that piece of mine in the paper
was aware of the dead knight's identity." Frustrated, she tore
the sodden beer mat into pieces and dropped it into the
'Guinness' ashtray. "If only we had something to go on."
Caro looked cautiously around the room before bending to take
something out of her tote bag.
"Maybe this will help," she whispered, slipping it onto Darcy's
lap under cover of the table. "The inscription is incomplete, but
it gives you a starting point."
"You're taking a risk," Darcy warned as she slipped the packet
into her bag.
"I feel strongly about this. And I've—"
"Yes?" Darcy prompted as Caro faltered to a halt.
"Nothing. It doesn't matter." Caro stood up and draped her
fringed shawl over her shoulders. "I have to go."

Darcy started to rise, but Caro raised a hand in a
forbidding gesture.
"Better not be seen leaving together."
"There's something else, isn't there?" Darcy pressed as she felt
Caro retreat behind invisible shutters.
"I'll be in touch."
"You were going to come up to the cottage for the weekend,"
Darcy pressed.
Caro paused. "As I understand it the site has been closed, tidied
and abandoned. Perhaps I'll visit you anyway."
"Make it soon."

Darcy watched, frowning as Caro made her way to
the door.
"Wait!" Darcy stumbled against a stool in her hurry. "If the
vault is closed," she said breathlessly catching up with her
outside, "then where is our crusader – not reinterred I take it?"
"I guessed you'd get round to asking that sooner or later," Caro
sighed. "

"So?" Darcy demanded.

"I asked the same question myself. David Watson told me the body had gone to the British Museum, that it would be held there until its future was decided."

"But you don't believe him," Darcy said flatly.

"I think there's more to it," Caro confessed, looking ever more distressed and casting anxious looks up at David Watson's window as though he might be witness to her defection. "I heard whispers of a private museum."

"That's terrible!" Darcy stared, appalled. "I doubt it's even legal."

"Probably not. " Caro began to fidget, tap one foot.

"Then why not speak up!"

"I want to keep my job."

"You've been warned off?"

"The hints were plain enough." Caro shrugged. 'Staff co-operation will be appreciated," she continued, grimacing. "Especially in these difficult times of cut-backs and redundancies."

"Is this happening? Or have I got galloping paranoia?" Darcy breathed, pushing her hair back from her forehead.

"Both of us? That's unlikely! No, there is a cover-up and David Watson is simply 'following orders'. This comes from way up the hierarchy – and is dangerous. So take care, Darcy," and with this she hurried away without a backward glance.

Walking back to the car, Darcy found herself viewing the University from a very different perspective. Each tutor passed was seen as a potential conspirator, or at the least – like Caro – a collaborator by virtue of his or her silence. The walk across the Square and past the Administration Quarters brought the irrational desire to enter, demand to see the Vice Chancellor and insist on knowing why he was flushing Hilldean, success and the Archaeology Department, down the pan. Fat chance she had of gaining access, she thought wryly, never mind answers.

As the Square and main buildings were left behind

she found herself casting frequent glances over her shoulder, watching with a tight stomach as a man approached from the opposite direction. She heaved a sigh of relief as he passed, intent on his own business. In vain, she told herself to keep the thing in proportion. However, the sense of being watched, of something sinister dogging her footsteps, would not evaporate to order. The sun was eclipsed by marauding cloud, and the new foliage of the trees, previously a warm apple green, now assumed a cold metallic blue. Branches swayed in a rising wind, whispering suspicion and casting shade across her path and, she couldn't help thinking, presaging a shadowing of her life. Suddenly her beloved Hilldean had become a sinister place.

The knowledge unnerved and upset her, and caused her stride to lengthen. A figure glimpsed from the corner of her eye brought her stomach leaping towards her throat. On whirling round, there was nobody there, but apprehension remained. It was with a sense of immense relief that she reached the car. Fumbling in her bag for the keys, she cried out as a hand gripped her shoulder. Swinging round she gazed into the ruddy face of an elderly car park attendant. He released her and pushed back his peaked cap.
"Visitors shouldn't be parking here, miss."
"I'm not a visitor," she lied without exactly knowing why.
"You're not showing your student disc," he accused, wiping a dewdrop from his nose with the back of a hand gnarled by arthritis and reddened by cold.
"I left it at my digs."
"You could have been clamped."
"I'll remember next time," she said dully, too demoralised to protest.

Absurdly, tears stung the back of her eyes. She felt like an exile, rejected by the place that had once been her home. Sadly she watched him walk away, one foot scraping the floor slightly as he went. Compassion suddenly flared; the old boy was only doing his job. On impulse she ran after him and ignoring his protests, slipped a couple of one pound coins in his pocket.

"Why thank you miss, very kind. No offence meant. I'll save a place for you next time I'm on," he promised, pathetically eager now to please. I doubt there will be a next time she thought sadly, driving down the winding private road to the exit at the base of the hill. For the first time in her life, it was a relief to be leaving Hilldean. But something positive had emerged from that sad little encounter. The car park attendant's limp had brought to mind Daniel Piper, and a resolve to make further contact.

TWELVE

On her return to the flat, Darcy took Caro's envelope from her bag and drew out the photographs. The first was a shot of the vault, empty and showing the lining of sandstone and aspects of archaeological interest. The next – obviously taken earlier – showed the coffin prior to its removal from the tomb, and the skeleton of the unknown woman lying alongside. Darcy felt an emotion she could not name: was she his wife; had they died together, or had her locks been shorn whilst she was still alive – and if so, why? As a symbol of devotion it seemed to have more in common with a gothic novel than the political marriages of medieval aristocracy.

The next picture made her draw breath sharply. This was worth the wait. The inscription cut into the red facing stone was eroded and largely indecipherable, but as Caro had said, it was a start. To her frustration, the dedication was inscribed in Latin, which she should have anticipated given that he had been interred by the priory brethren. Well there at least was the obligatory *requiescat in pace,* recognisable despite missing letters, though somehow she doubted that either of the occupants had rested in peace.

The name – presumably this, given its position and grouping of the remaining but worn letters – was a disappointment, as it gave no immediate clue to his identity. There was an 'A' followed by several illegible characters and ending with what looked like an 'N'; then a two letter word, badly eroded, but given that the nobility of the period were mostly of French descent following the Norman invasion, this must be 'de' something or other. It appeared to begin with a 'B' with a medial 'M'. The date took some working out, as Roman numerals had been left behind a lifetime ago along with gymslip and schoolbag. At last she had 'thirteen hundred and something' – the last number being missing – which confirmed Caro's estimate.

The final photograph showed a stone carving of a sword and what remained of a distinctive cross, the arms having splayed ends. A caterpillar of knowledge stirred in the chrysalis of her mind but retreated again, insufficiently formed for metamorphosis and flight. She dredged her memory for cues, but came up with nothing that fit. At least now there was something to go on, a launch pad for her research. And tomorrow she would contact Dr. Daniel Piper and beg, steal or threaten from him a copy of his report.

****

The following morning, she took a second cup of coffee over to the telephone and dialled the number of the Whitecliffe County Hospital. On asking to be put through to Dr. Daniel Piper in Pathology she was informed by the switchboard operator that nobody was answering on his extension.
"Put me through to his secretary then please," Darcy requested, and waited again, to be told by his secretary that Dr. Piper was not available and no, she had no idea when he would be back.
"Is he on vacation, or sick leave?" Darcy persisted.
"Who is it calling please?" came the response, and Darcy became aware of reticence creeping into the other woman's voice.
"Hilldean University," she lied without shame.
"Maybe a member of his team could help."
"I doubt it. Unless they would know if we should have received a copy of his report by now."
"And which is that please?"
"An autopsy report – on a preserved body brought in a week or so ago."
"I'm sorry, I can't help you."
The tones were clipped and precise; the line went dead.

Momentarily at a loss, Darcy drank her coffee almost without tasting it and sat with her chin resting in her hand. Something was wrong. Was Piper on holiday, away on a course – or sick? Finding out proved ridiculously easy, all it took was a call to Central Administration. Introducing herself as a new locum to cover Path Lab for the duration of Dr. Piper's vacation, she elicited the information that there must be some mistake, as he was not listed on the holiday rota for that week. A second call to Male Surgical Admissions under the guise of being a relative brought another negative response. Third time lucky: Male Medical Admissions, after some close questioning (she claimed to be a niece recently returned from overseas) confirmed that they did have a Dr. Daniel Piper, admitted to Ward 4, room E26, but that they were unable to divulge information about his condition. Darcy, not wanting to risk running foul of further questions, smartly replaced the receiver.

Of course, it was absurd to link this illness with the post mortem, or Dr. Piper's worried countenance with the donning of that surgical mask. A glance at the clock made her grimace. Frank would be chewing on his cigar. No contest. This was too important to chicken out, even if her suspicions turned out to be groundless and it meant facing the sack. Grabbing her coat and bag, Darcy left the flat and closed the door on her doubts.

****

The desk at the hospital reception area seemed like an enemy fortress to be stormed in order to reach her goal. She gave a false name and claimed fictional kinship to Daniel Piper. The receptionist scanned a list of names on a sheet of paper attached to a clip board, then looked up with an inscrutable expression.
"Please take a seat; I'll fetch a member of the medical staff."
"Thanks, but there's no need," Darcy said quickly, "I'll just pop in and see him for a moment. A flying visit I'm afraid."
"Please take a seat," the receptionist repeated reaching for the telephone, her manner as cool and starched as her white coat.

82

Darcy retreated from the desk, and melting into the crowd that milled around the seating area, slipped round the back and through the double doors. A stream of uniformed personnel passed along the corridor, and due to her guilt, each seemed to eye her with suspicion. However, periodic glances over her shoulder told her that no-one was in pursuit. A progression of signs and arrows guided her, unchallenged, down a branch passage to the left, and past an unmanned nursing station to Room E26. A sign on the door read 'Isolation Unit –No Unauthorised Entry' and the metal name slot contained no card. She hesitated, then the inbred reporter's contempt for rules and danger made her reach out to the handle and slowly turn it.

Heart pounding, she slipped inside. The room in which she found herself had pale pink walls and floral curtains. The rays of a sickly sun filtered across grimy rooftops and onto a tiled rubber floor. This attempt at homeliness stopped short at the bed where chrome, glass and plastic made their clinical statement. The ventilator had bellows and a ridged tube with a valve for attaching the tracheostomy from the patient's throat to enable the lungs to be filled and emptied. The expected odours of sick room and antiseptic were absent. They were replaced by a warm spicy smell with overtones of the sea that transported her instantly back to the post mortem examination. In the present context, it made her gag with sudden fear. The bed had been stripped of linen to expose a plastic-covered mattress.

Darcy whirled round as footsteps sounded immediately outside and the door swung open.
"This isolation sign Staff, can I take it—," the voice ceased abruptly as the woman dressed in what Darcy took to be the uniform of an auxiliary nurse, bustled in and stopped on the threshold.
"Oh excuse me, I thought it must be staff nurse," the woman's eyes narrowed with sudden suspicion, "Who are you? What are you doing in here?"
"I was looking for my uncle."

The other woman's expression softened slightly.

"I'm sorry, but I must ask you to leave this room immediately."

"He's dead, isn't he?" Darcy said, striving for the demeanour of a shocked and grieving relative.

"If you'll come with me, I'll get a member of the medical staff to have a word."

As Darcy was about to respond, a second female voice erupted from the doorway.

"This woman is not a relative!"

The nurse frowned and looked from Darcy to the other woman and back again.

"How do you know, Frances?"

Darcy stared at the dark hair scraped into a pleat, and the gold spectacles from behind which a pair of earnest and angry eyes regarded her, and wondered where she had soon them before. Her heart sank as she recalled the girl behind the reception desk the day she had met Caro. This martinet launched into attack.

"When I came back from my coffee break Paula reported a 'visitor' who had been asked to wait but had disappeared. I came to check it out. This woman," and she pointed an accusing finger at Darcy, "booked in at reception the day of Dr. Piper's last P.M. examination. She is from the press!" she announced with such a note of triumph in her voice that Darcy felt like smacking her smooth, perfectly powdered and blushed cheek.

The nurse's expression showed conflicting emotions in rapid succession: initial anger was replaced by something that looked suspiciously like panic.

"You attended that post mortem?" she demanded, already moving towards a button set into the wall.

"Yes but what—"

As Darcy moved for the doorway, the other two women, as though at some prearranged signal, blocked her path.

"Excuse me," Darcy said in icy tones, attempting to push her way past. "Get out of my way," she demanded as they made no effort to move. As the three women jostled in the doorway, a male voice broke in.

84

"What's the problem?"
Darcy found herself being escorted down the corridor between two burly security officers.

She sat in the examination room telling herself this could not be happening. A complete lack of response had stemmed her spate of questions, and all she could do now was wait. A female nurse, masked and gowned, hovered nearby, watchful. A male counterpart similarly attired remained by the door. He had not actually restrained her from leaving, but when Darcy attempted it had taken her arm, and whilst speaking in persuasive tones about 'Ministry of Health regulations', and 'regretful but necessary precautions for her own wellbeing' had 'guided' her back to the stool.

A white-coated doctor entered, stethoscope slung around his neck and an impersonal mask for a face; there was no name-tag attached to his breast pocket.
"Just a routine precaution," he assured her, requesting that she undress in the curtained cubicle behind her and don the gown in preparation for X-ray and a routine blood test.
"I most certainly will not," Darcy protested, attempting to rise. He pushed her down again, albeit gently, and spoke in reassuring tones.
"A customary check – it will take five minutes, that's all. Nothing to worry about; a female nurse will be in attendance at all times."
"And if I refuse?" Darcy demanded giving him a direct look.

He shrugged, and glanced quickly at the nurse.
"Under the Public Health Act we could obtain the necessary authority. But it will take time; you could be here for the rest of the day, overnight even. Why not be sensible Miss West? There is nothing sinister going on here, a full explanation and report will be sent to your G.P.," he finished smoothly, but his gaze slid away from her face as he promised the latter.
"Piper is dead, isn't he?" she demanded.
"As I said, routine precautions."
"What was the cause of death?"

85

"We shall do everything to see you are comfortable
and keep inconvenience at a minimum."
A female doctor entered next and added her persuasion,
reassurance and honeyed request for cooperation. In the end,
wearied by pressure and anxious to be away, Darcy reluctantly
agreed.

"I wish to leave immediately," she demanded after
returning from the X-ray department and submitting to the
taking of a blood sample. Feeling exposed and vulnerable, she
pulled the regulation blue towelling robe closer about her for
protection. A female nurse clad in mask and gown was writing
'Darcy West' on the label that she had stuck on the vial of
blood.
"Do you hear me?" she demanded of the nurse who was
placing the vial in a rack.
"Won't be long now, Miss West," she said cheerfully,
flashing a Maclean-white smile.

She handed the sample to the male nurse who pressed a
switch set into the wall. A few minutes later, a knock sounded
at the door. He admitted a female who, given her youth and
white overall, was probably a junior technician. He held out the
vial in its tray. "Path lab – for immediate testing and result."
The assistant left with the sample.
"This is appalling!" Darcy persisted.
"You consented, and nobody forced you to stay." The nurse
peeled off surgical gloves and dropped them into a waste
disposal bin.
"No, you just removed my clothes from the cubicle," Darcy
accused.
"Doctor will tell you when you can go."
Darcy sighed with frustration.

He returned some twenty minutes later with a clipboard
to which a chart was affixed.
"No problem, Miss West. Blood test and X-ray are both fine,"
he pronounced, scanning the data.
"So what were you testing for?"

86

He strode to the door and paused. "You may get dressed now and leave. Thank you so much for cooperating."

"When will my G.P. receive a report?" Darcy demanded, giving him a look of disgust. The door clicked softly to as he left.

THIRTEEN

Late afternoon was giving way to evening by the time Darcy arrived back at Manchester. An early edition of the Cumbria Evening News, ordered via the Internet on leaving the hospital, was waiting on her desk. Impatiently she flicked over the pages to the section on 'Marriages, Births and Deaths'. Scanning the names, her finger came to rest on the only 'P' in the column. And there it was: 'peacefully at the Whitecliffe County Hospital, Dr. Daniel Piper, following a short illness,' and ending with the usual thanks to nursing staff and family names, a masterpiece of brevity and non-information.

Rustling back through the previous pages, Darcy checked every item. Nothing. No headlines, no small news item and nothing in the 'stop press'; no mention at all of the sudden and hitherto unexplained death of a county coroner and prominent local figure. Thoughtfully, she pulled away the strip of plaster from her arm and stared at the puncture mark left by the syringe. What sort of blood test had they done? Had they called in everyone who attended that fateful post mortem? Probably, she decided, realising that everyone bar herself would be known to Dr. Piper and his team, and would therefore be easy to trace. Her dual domicile in both Cumbria and Manchester would have confused the issue.

So, have they tried to track me down via Caro? she wondered, distractedly pushing back from her forehead an unruly lock of hair. A quick check of her e-mail brought no answer. A flick of the intercom switch and a word with Janet confirmed that Caro had telephoned, and left a message for Darcy to contact her when she arrived home. Darcy frowned: obviously Caro was distrustful of the office communication network, and feared interception. It seemed Brant Kennedy had called also and left his name and number but no message. Intriguing, but business first, she decided. He had not exactly rushed to get in touch. There was also a note in Janet's handwriting on her desk. Apparently the press secretary of Clare Cabbala, the celebrated clairvoyant who was currently visiting Manchester, had telephoned inviting her to interview Madame Cabbala at her hotel suite.

Darcy turned the paper over and put it thoughtfully down. It could be of interest she supposed. Clairvoyance, fake or otherwise, meant guaranteed readership. It seemed there was a built-in need for sceptics to scoff and the credible to reinforce their beliefs. Prior to St. Gildas Man she would have placed herself firmly in the first category, now she was less sure.

Frank Kelly, when she answered his summons, was obviously struggling between fury at her disappearance, relief that she was back and curiosity about the reason for her absence. However, as Darcy launched into an explanation and complaints about her treatment, his face became impassive. "Well aren't you going to say anything?" she demanded, leaning forward with her hands on the edge of his desk. "Frank – the man is dead."
"Unfortunate, but hardly a tragedy."
"It might be."
"I doubt it." The cigar moved from left to the right side of his mouth.

Darcy stood erect, and briefly closed her eyes whilst struggling with frustration.
"I was detained, for God's sake," she tried again. "Screened for some disease. Doesn't that worry you Frank, because it sure as hell worries me!"
"You're over-reacting." Frank moistened his fingers and used them to slick down his unruly thatch.
"It's a cover-up. I feel my rights have been violated; you should back me Frank, the Paper should go public."
"It wouldn't be appropriate." Frank scowled and his chin jutted.

"It couldn't be more so! There should be an enquiry, and if you won't shout for one, then I'll contact the Ministry of Health and Home Office to demand action."
"You'll be wasting your time."

Darcy felt the chill of premonition and fear.
"What makes you so sure?"
"They've slapped a Public Interest Immunity Certificate on it."
"They can't do this!" Darcy recoiled as though he had flung a glass of ice-water in her face. She crossed to the window and looked out without seeing, then returned to confront him.
"How did you find it out?" she demanded.
"I take it that was a purely rhetorical question." He examined his finger nails then gave her a quizzical look.
"You knew!" Her mind struggled to absorb the implications of his bombshell.
"Not until a short time ago." He shrugged his shoulders and spread his hands.
"You let me walk into it."
"Be sensible Darcy. I didn't even know where you were."
"So what now?" She swallowed hard and hitched her bag onto her shoulder.
"Nothing. Whatever is going on is strictly under wraps and not for us."
"I don't believe I'm hearing this."
"Look Darcy," Frank sighed and rumpled his hair. "You've checked out fit and well – so go home and forget about it."
She gave him a hard look as if seeing him for the first time.
"You think I have a personal agenda."
"Dead right I do."

"What happened to you, Frank? Has the whisky quenched your thirst for truth and justice?" she said with bitterness in both voice and expression. She waited, expecting him to sack her for real this time, but he simply looked at her with something like sadness in his brown eyes. Fighting back the tears, she threw him a last look of contempt and stormed from his office.

Arriving at her flat, she let herself into the hall, checked the rack for mail and stuffed the couple of bills behind the clock before going into the bathroom. She threw back her head, and let the jets of steaming water sluice away the sense of contamination and corruption. Her skin was reddened and stinging and still she stayed in the shower. The water was too hot for comfort, but not hot enough to cauterise the wound of betrayal. A cup of coffee and a sandwich later, she felt more composed and remembering Caro's message, picked up the telephone.

Some twenty minutes later, Darcy leaned back against the cushions of the settee nursing what was left of a large brandy whilst struggling to make sense of the latest developments. From Caro, she learned that during their lunchtime meeting her room at the University had been turned over. The door had not been forced and, as she had watched Caro lock it as they left for the bar, it had to be an inside job. To compound the mystery – and throw Caro deeper still into her loyalty-conflict – the master key was held by David Watson, the departmental head. His case was not helped in Darcy's book by his failure to call in the police, preferring to let the University's own security people deal with the matter.

Upon being pressed, Caro also divulged that she had been sent to hospital for screening and yes, the authorities had asked about 'her reporter friend'. When asked about other members of the late Dr. Piper's team, Caro reported two falling ill and pretty sick on admission, but now off the critical list. Reluctantly she acknowledged that bacteria could lie dormant and be reactivated, and that in the case of a body as well-preserved as St. Gildas Man, this was entirely feasible. On hearing this Darcy was overcome by queasiness, especially when Caro listed old enemies such as plague and tuberculosis, and 'God knows what unspecified infections that were rife in those days.'

Darcy shuddered involuntarily, and took a warming

sip of brandy to ward off the chill of fear. However, as Caro had reassured her, incubation dates since exposure at the post mortem were now well past, and any contamination would have shown up in the test results. Swirling the honey coloured liquid round her glass, Darcy stared thoughtfully up at the shadow-patterned ceiling. Then Caro had dropped her bombshell. Following the break-in, the only thing missing from her room was the file on St. Gildas Man.

FOURTEEN

So, she thought putting down her glass, somebody has effectively stitched up Caro. She could prepare another draft of the missing report but with no documentation or photographs to back-up it up, and without the support of her head of department, there was little point. More significantly. there was nobody to substantiate her find. Resolving to check out the British Museum at first opportunity, she picked up the telephone to return Brant Kennedy's call, but put it down again as a deeper implication struck. It was asking a lot of coincidence that the break-in had occurred on the very day she had visited Caro at Hill-dean.

So, could it have been a warning, not just for Caro but also herself? If somebody knew of her plan to be there (Caro's distrust of the office telephones now made sense) then what better way to target them both. This, combined with the screening and Public Interest Immunity Certificate, confirmed that some agency of power wanted St. Gildas Man not only buried but forgotten. A heady cocktail of fear and excitement buzzed along her nerves.

She had neglected to check for telephone calls during her absence, but saw now that the 'message' light was lit up on the answering machine. A touch on the 'play' button brought forth Frank's voice demanding to know where the hell she was; then Janet reporting that Frank was threatening unspeakable things, but she would do her best to keep him happy.
Suddenly, Jonathon's voice, warm seductive and cajoling, filled the room, and for once the half-mocking tone was absent. He had two tickets for the Royal Opera Company's Turandot on Saturday night, was missing her unbearably, and would she care to come. Seemingly of its own volition her hand reached

93

for the receiver. Don't be a fool, her inner voice warned. He only wants you to ring so that if you decline he has time to invite his interior designer or one of his other floozies. But he might just mean it this time, a second demon voice added. And she would give up a by-line for those tickets.

She wavered, desire warring with integrity. Despite Jonathon's undeniable selfishness, it wasn't fair to flick the emotional switch on and off at a whim. On the other hand, the dissolute voice tempted, she could wear her oyster silk, have her hair done by Angelo and go out on Jonathon's arm feeling a million dollars. Here was a chance to put intrigue and danger behind her for a couple of hours, and lose herself in pomp and passion, spectacular drama and the soaring notes of *Nessum Dorma*. Shit, who the hell needs integrity. Perhaps it was fate that the ringing-out tone sounded repeatedly but Jonathon's voice did not answer.

Time to make a return call to Brant Kennedy. Taking out the slip of paper on which she had scribbled his number, Darcy dialled and waited.
"Hi," she supplied when he answered: "Darcy West here; returning your call."
A few minutes were spent on pleasantries and breaking the ice, then Darcy felt an urge to share her concern and recounted Caro's trauma.
"A bit wacky isn't it, for a University room to be broken into?" he said, sounding puzzled.
"I suppose."
"Anything taken?"
Darcy frowned as she wound the flex around her finger. It may have been her imagination, but it seemed there was a significant pause before that last question, as though he was aware of showing too keen an interest.
"Nothing of material value, and it's too early to say whether any papers are missing," she replied smoothly, regretting her previous impulse to confide. It wasn't safe to trust anyone,

especially perhaps Brant Kennedy with his proximity to the priory and obsessive need of privacy.

"About that visit to the observatory – if you still want to that is," he ventured.

Darcy smiled. The slight inflection at the end of the sentence betrayed his wavering of confidence. In this otherwise self-assured man it was somehow endearing.

"Of course."

"Good." His voice took on a heartier note. "So, how about this weekend?"

She thought on her feet. A trip to the cottage and a date with Brant Kennedy – albeit an educational one – would place her beyond the reach of temptation and Jonathon's invitation.

"That will be fine."

"Right. I'll meet you Saturday, twenty hundred hours, the Priory Arms."

She grinned at his military precision.

"Yes, sir!" then added to break the ensuing silence: "Do I tog up in hiking gear?"

"There's a track to my place – no bother to a Land Rover."

She sighed. The starch was back in his manner: God what a touchy man.

"Actually I hadn't realised you meant an evening visit," she ventured, recalling the isolation of his farmhouse.

"That's when the stars come out!"

"Of course. 'Till Saturday then," she agreed, feeling foolish. After replacing the receiver, she remained seated and thoughtfully wound a curl around her index finger. It struck her that to go alone to that cliff-top house was to place a lot of trust in a virtual stranger, and that this was contrary to her previous intention. But that was the stuff of reporting, and faint heart never won good story, as Frank was fond of saying.

The thought of Frank made her frown as the hurt returned. How could he betray her that way? She might just as well trust Brant Kennedy. At a guess, his pride would not allow

95

him to take what was not freely offered, and with a bit of luck he might know something about St. Gildas Man. For a moment she was back in that bare hospital room, smelling again the scent of sea and spices. Safe now in familiar surroundings, she dismissed the experience, putting it down to stress and imagination. Her scepticism received a serious jolt as she prepared a milk drink to take to bed. About to mop up a spill, she paused with the cloth suspended in mid air. One of the tiles on the surface by the sink bore strange characters, words in some unfamiliar language. Crazy thoughts of higher dimension communication flashed through her mind. Experimentally and with great care she touched the letters – white on green tile – with the tip of an index finger. They did not rub off as expected but were firmly fixed to the ceramic surface.

Fear, confusion and fascination warred within. Her distracted glance fell upon a plastic bag containing half a loaf; the plastic was slightly puckered as though from contact with a source of heat. Common sense struck her between the eyes. Snatching a small mirror from off the wall, she held it next to the 'cryptic' message. *Baked in the traditional way.* The mundane message mocked her panic. She laughed aloud, and despite the absence of a witness cringed with embarrassment. It showed how easy it was to be taken in.
"Let that be a lesson to you, Darcy West," she scolded herself. Clutching her drink, she made for the bedroom. She smiled to herself as she lay on her back in bed. It was so simple. She had placed the bag on the spot where the hot milk pan had stood, causing the plastic letters to adhere to the tile and appear in reverse. It just went to prove her own maxim: there was always a rational explanation for so–called psychic phenomena. The smile still lingered on her lips as she drifted beneath the bridge of sleep.

But in the strange world in which she found herself, that maxim seemed not to work. The sound of rollers breaking over sandstone and draining through shingle came clearly to her, as did the keening of thousands of gulls. The priory walls were wreathed in mist and a black sun scorched the desolate landscape. The rays penetrated the lancet window, and touched the face of the man lying in the vault.

Only he was not dead. Decomposing and terrible now to look upon certainly, but lifeless - no. As twentieth century air wreaked its destruction, he moved within the coffin, his skin splitting and suppurating as it stretched. Darcy broke out in a cold sweat as he stretched out his hand. His flesh was now black as that terrible sun. She shuddered, recoiled in fear but was unable to withdraw. He pointed to the stone which bore the inscription, but the letters were reversed and made no sense. Her attempts to decipher them were thwarted as, frustratingly, they disappeared. The blank face of the stone sparkled with droplets of moisture as the mist closed in. If only it would clear then she would understand.

He opened his terrible mouth then and spoke, saying his name aloud. Despite the dripping of mucus and rotting of flesh, the voice was not cracked and sepulchral but as deep and resonant as it must have been in life. She heard and understood, gave her commitment in a whispered vow. He nodded and closed his eyes. A great stirring of the air behind her head made her start and duck. With a guttural croak the raven swooped and perched at the head of the vault; she heard the rasp of talon on stone as it landed. A massive claw was slowly raised, tucked close to the black-clad body, then lowered again. It turned its head, the better to survey her and she was first to look away as techno-wise deferred to ancient intellect. Raven, master of the Scavengers' Guild, blinked and shifted, anticipating the imminent feast. Sickened, she turned and walked away before beak and talons began their gruesome work.

She awoke with her forehead and upper lip beaded with perspiration, his face imprinted behind her eyelids. The memory of his speech was clear, but not a word could she recall. Pulling herself up against the pillows, she struggled with words of a different order, the language of a Dream-world that defied interpretation. Nonsense, she told herself. It was simply her subconscious mind working on the problem of his identity. There was no name because it had not yet been found; her apparent failure to remember was a way of dealing with this. Dreams work like that, she told herself, and this was a vivid one, hence the false feeling that something bound them together. There was no mystical union, no bond between one with a quest for the ultimate story, and one with such a story to tell.

FIFTEEN

The following morning, Darcy summoned Janet.
"Email a request, please," she said looking up as Janet breezed into her office wearing a daffodil-yellow dress. "Central Library – reference section, ditto the Harris at Preston. We'd best cover the local ones too – try Whitecliffe and Carlisle. I want the genealogy of medieval noble families of Cumbria, like yesterday."
"St. Gildas Man?" Janet asked, pencil flying over the page of her notepad.
"Affirmative. And whilst you are at it, buzz the British Museum – find out if they have the body."
"Sure. But you can't always hurry these people."

"Sort it Jan." Darcy picked up the mail from her in-tray and sifted through it. "Then see if you can get a report on Dr. Piper's death and the date of the funeral, and Janet—"
"Yes?" Janet paused at the door.
"On the Q.T. We don't want to give Frank a coronary. Arrange an appointment for next week with that woman, Cabbala to keep him happy."
"No problem!" Janet gave her a nod and wink and was gone.

****

That evening, Darcy sped along the motorway towards Cumbria. As she steered the car up and round to the parking area of Mistletoe Cottage, the silence, unbroken except by the hoot of a tawny owl in the wood, embraced her like an old friend. The twin beams of the headlamps ricocheted from boulder to tree, then back again, causing shadows of giant pines to leap from hiding, bow in the spotlight then retreat into darkness. The sense of security was fleeting. In that split second, the whiteness of a face was picked out and transfixed between the massive trunks. The scream was forced from her throat without conscious intent. It was the briefest of glimpses, but long enough to note the slash of the eyebrows that gave the owner an expression of permanent surprise. The same brows and white face she had seen on leaving the Priory Arms.

Her hands were shaking as they grasped the steering wheel. Self-preservation kicked in. and with the flick of a button she sealed first the windows then the doors. She sat for several minutes, unable to step from the car into suffocating darkness – and whatever lurked there still. Her eyes ached from staring into the shadows but nothing moved and nobody molested the car. The desire to be within stout walls forced her into action.

Groping in the glove compartment, she found a torch, clambered from the car and, slamming the door behind her, ran for the cottage. The erratic beam swept the shrubbery but revealed no stalker lurking there. The moments spent fumbling with key in lock were amongst the worst of her life, but the expected hand clamping her shoulder or encircling her throat failed to materialise. As the door creaked open, the sensation of being watched made her spin around and spray the surrounding darkness with light. The only thing she surprised was a solitary hedgehog shuffling through the previous year's dried leaves. A sob caught in her throat as she stumbled over the threshold, slammed the door shut and bolted it against the night.

The porch lamp and the light above the kitchen door were now switched on, and semi-circles of light nibbled at the darkness. The interior of the cottage brooded, with only a small lamp in the hall switched on to relieve the gloom. Torch at the ready, Darcy sat by the sitting room window, watchful and alert to any movement in shrubbery or garden. Periodically, she rose to peer from kitchen and bedroom windows before returning to her station.

An adrenalin-buzz shot through her system as something moved by the camellia bush. Her sigh of relief misted the glass of the window: a roe deer taking a midnight feast of sticky buds and tender new leaves. Forgetting her fear for a time, she watched, enchanted, as it browsed until, sensing her presence perhaps, it moved without panic away from the light. This told her that there could now be no stranger lurking in the vicinity. Five minutes or so later, she abandoned her vigil, made a hot toddy, went to bed and eventually slept.

****

The following morning, she rose early and made coffee then sat at the kitchen table to drink it. The room faced east, and sunlight streamed through the window and bounced off the whitewashed walls. The terror and vulnerability of the previous night now seemed like a bad dream. Could she have imagined it, that face peering at her from out of the trees? She shuddered involuntarily and decided not. If, she told herself watching leaf patterns dance on the walls, there was a threat of real danger then surely whoever it was would have persisted and broken in. A poacher perhaps? A nosy neighbour, or resident of the village surprised in keeping an eye on the place in her absence? More than likely, she decided rinsing her mug and taking a plate of scraps outside for the birds.

She wandered amongst a riot of lilac, hawthorn and apple blossom and sniffed appreciatively. The heady floral perfume was complemented by a roving clematis that wandered through their boughs, scenting the air with chocolate and vanilla. A resident blackbird hopped close, keeping a watchful eye on her movements – and the contents of the plate in her hand. She placed it on a tree stump and retreated to watch the feeding ritual. The sound of a vehicle accelerating over a rut in the lane caused a sudden whirring of wings, as the birds abandoned their meal and took to the air.

101

On investigating, Darcy found a van bearing the name of a Whitecliffe florist was parked in the lane, and a young man about to knock at her front door.

"Yes?" Callers were rare and annoyance sharpened her voice.

"Delivery for you miss."

"There's some mistake."

The lad shook his head. "This is Mistletoe Cottage, ain't it?"

"Yes, but—"

"And are you Miss West?" he called from the rear of the van.

"Well, yes."

"Then these are for you."

Darcy gasped as an enormous bouquet of red roses was thrust into her arms.

Inside the cottage, she read the card again, unable to believe her eyes. '*I think I love you – Jonathon.*' She bent over the perfect blooms, breathing in deeply until she could taste the perfume. But how had he known where to send them? Then it clicked into the place: the message she had left on his answering machine, declining his invitation because she had made arrangements with a friend to spend the weekend at the cottage. Panic fluttered briefly in her stomach. Jonathon was unaccustomed to rejection; to respond like this he must be serious. After ending the relationship, she had expected the famous shut-down not this touching declaration. It was difficult to know what to think, except that this was one complication she could do without.

That evening, she set off for the Old Priory Arms and found Brant Kennedy waiting for her in the bar. He was wearing cords and a denim shirt topped by a Guernsey sweater. It had been difficult to know what to wear for this unusual date, but it seemed she had pitched it right with her calf length skirt, cashmere top and caped Barbour coat.

"What would you like to drink?" he asked once the formalities were out of the way.

"A G & T would go down nicely," Darcy responded, smiling.

Tom brought over to their table a gin and tonic and a pint of local bitter for Brant.

"Thanks, Tom – and yourself," he said, obviously not encouraging their patently curious landlord to linger. Tom's hide, it seemed, was as thick as the local Herdwick fleece.

"Having an evening out then are we?" he pried, vigorously polishing the table between their drinks. Luckily, they were saved from having to answer by a shout from the bar.

"'Ere Tom, 'ave we to dee of thirst doon this end, lad?" so that Tom, grumbling under his breath about 'folks wi'out a minute to spare', moved off to take the disgruntled farmer's order.

"You'll be the talk of the village tonight," Darcy teased.

"I already am." Brant said and shrugged it off.

"Really?" Darcy tried to look ignorant of his failed marriage and reputation for misogyny.

He gave her a hard look. "On account of being seen with a smart city girl."

"Oh I see." Darcy, realising her mistake, coloured slightly.

"Good old Tom." He laughed wryly. "I take it he told you about my disastrous marriage."

"He simply said your wife had left."

"How tactful. Tom and the other folk here in the village are usually more generous, what they don't know they add from their own imaginations."

"Isn't that a bit hard?" Darcy commented, frowning.

"Maybe." He drank deeply from his pint glass. "I suppose you think I'm bitter."

"I think you've been badly hurt." Darcy gave him a direct look.

He stared at the beer in the bottom of his glass.

"You don't pull the punches, do you?" he said at last.

"Neither do you," she said recalling their first meeting.

The sudden smile softened the severity of his expression.

"Fair enough. And yourself?"

Darcy swirled the remaining gin around her glass.

"What about me?"

"Is there a man? Anyone special I mean."

"No."

"You said that very decisively."

"That's because there was someone, and now there isn't."

"It didn't work out."

"No."

"I take you don't want to talk about it." Brant looked faintly amused.

"Not really. I just discovered there was nothing there to work out. Do you want to discuss your marriage?" she challenged.

"No."

"And I won't press you."

"Point taken. Let's go," Pushing aside his empty glass, he stood up. Darcy slung her bag onto her shoulder and followed him to the door.

****

The Land Rover crept over the cliff top towards the Priory. Darcy suppressed a shudder. The wind ravaged shrubs that ringed the ruins resembled long-dead brothers-in-prayer. She wound down the window, admitting the distant swish and whisper of sea on shingle, and the rustle of wind through sedge and grass. She stiffened, aware, as on that first visit, of the sensed-but-not-heard chanting of ancient voices. A violet gauze had settled over cliff and fell, distorting lines and blurring edges and transforming reality into magic. Trees evolved into beings that crept across the horizon, and the ghosts of ancestors mutated from granite as shadowy legions marched the distant fells. An involuntary shiver ran through her body.

Brant turned to look at her. "Are you all right?"

"It's just that I feel like an intruder," she said with a self-conscious smile.

"So, you will." He smiled briefly then added, "This is the mystical hour."

"What do you mean?" Something about him, his strangeness, and even the whiteness of his teeth in the darkness, suddenly made her a little afraid.

"It's neither light nor dark, day nor night, but an in-between time when nothing is as it seems. What you feel is the soul of the mountain stirring."

"How beautiful you make it sound."

"Here, science and magic walk hand in hand." He touched her arm. "We have to acknowledge our debt to the past." He resumed his grip on the steering wheel as the Land Rover lurched and dipped over uneven ground.

They continued without speaking until Darcy broke the silence.

"I know what you mean, but I find it hard to trust my senses. You know, when they touch something half-real and almost recognised. I try to hold on to it, but its like trying to grasp the smoke from a snuffed-out candle."

"Or recall the face of someone you once loved." Brant Kennedy's voice had been matter-of-fact but she sensed the buried pain. As he pulled in at a pair of white gates, she risked a glance at him, saw that his face was white, and his lips compressed.

"I've never been in love," she confessed, caught out by descending night, the sense of unreality and the poignancy of his last remark.

He stopped the vehicle, switched off the engine and turned to face her. "But maybe you could be, one day?" he said watching her face intently. Darcy held his gaze, aware of the unspoken question. Aware too of the tension and something else that had burgeoned between them, the knowledge that they were somehow familiar strangers.

"Maybe," she agreed with a slow smile, allowing him a glimpse of possibility and hope.

He nodded as though satisfied with her answer.

"Look, the first star," he said with an abrupt change of subject that jarred, "we've been blessed with a clear night." He seemed not to notice her lack of response as she struggled with her emotions, and turning on the engine expertly pulled the

Land Rover back onto the track. "I'll take you to the observatory first, then we'll come back here to the farmhouse for supper."

"Fine," she said, recovering her composure and feeling she must have misinterpreted his previous mood.

Darcy gripped the sides of the seat as the Land Rover lurched and swayed, nose pointed at the heavens, as it tackled the steep climb over Sheep Howe. As they crested the summit, she drew in breath sharply. The dome of the observatory – invisible from the other side of the hill – rose like a giant jellyfish from a sea of grass. So incongruous, so alien did it appear that she almost expected to see it pulse with life. It gleamed dully in the light cast by stars and a fat, though not quite full, moon. It was, she decided, a metallic creature borrowed from an episode of the X-files.

The Land Rover bumped and swayed to the bottom of the rise. Brant jumped down and she joined him to stand at the padlocked gate in the chain link fence which protected the perimeter. He selected a key from several on the ring, and turned it in the lock.

"Come on." He grabbed her hand and led her inside, and Darcy wondered if the uneven ground was simply an excuse. Whatever the reason, her hand felt at home in his: there was warmth and security in that handclasp. There was something else too that made her blood sing and zip around her body, so that she was sorry when they reached the door of a smaller structure annexed to the dome.

"The office and store," he explained, releasing her in order to unlock it with an electronic device taken from his pocket. He clicked on a light and gestured for her to enter.

"And this," he said with pride in his voice, "is the observatory." The sliding metal door which separated the dome from the office slid silently shut. He flicked switches, and clicked rapidly on a keypad and a row of dim red lights glowed around the interior. Darcy walked round the dome feeling she must have walked in on a Sculley and Mulder scenario.

"This is incredible." She paused to peer at a bank of computer screens displaying constellations and galaxies - a map of the whole damned universe. Brant deftly touched some keys and the screen before her shimmered and danced with fire-bursts, segments of blue, green, purple and red that blazed and faded in turn. Darcy watched in fascination.

"What is that?"

"The surface of Pollux in the Gemini constellation."

"And the colours?"

"Electrical impulses. A sort of tracer of the varying intensity of light being transmitted. We can see the changes second by second."

"It's a universal kaleidoscope," she commented, shaking her head in wonder. His smile was genuine rather than patronising, so she smiled in return.

An involuntary shiver ran through her. It was chilly, damp almost so that the skin of her cheek felt soft when she touched it and the air was redolent with the scent of moss and peat. The dome seemed to mushroom from the ground, more an extension of Earth itself than a man-made building.

"This is really something." She stood looking up at the telescope gleaming on its circular platform at the centre of the floor. A monster of metal and cable, it reared its head to the apex of the dome.

"I'm glad it's quiet out there – a good time for viewing," Brant commented, busily clicking away on a keyboard so that the fiery images on screen changed with lightning rapidity. "If there is atmospheric turbulence," he added turning to her, "the reflected light from stars and planets – the images that appear on the monitors here – is distorted. Outside to the naked eye, it appears as a twinkling effect, but when magnified to this extent the stars leap about on screen like an ancient fireworks display."

"How do you focus it?" Darcy asked, consumed with curiosity, "and target the stars you want to observe?"

He moved to the work station arranged around a section of the dome.

"All the data – the various constellations, major stars and planets and the relevant sectors of the hemisphere for plotting their positions – is already programmed in. I need only tap into the constellation or galaxy I want to study and the telescope will align itself accordingly."

"Amazing."

"Watch." He pointed to the metal sheeting above them and tapped several keys. A sliver of night sky appeared at the centre of the dome as it slowly split like an oyster. The gap grew wider, the two sides separating until they finally disappeared.

"Magic!" Darcy breathed. There was nothing above their heads now but a swathe of stars and a fat moon against an indigo sky. She gazed in silent wonder at the milky mass stabbed at intervals by spurts of planetary fire. A low pitched whirring sound made her start and turn her head. The telescope was rising on its platform, tilting due north then homing in a few degrees west, adjusting to its programmed instructions. It continue to rise until the head cleared the shell of the dome. Darcy laughed with excitement and pleasure.

"It's like the set of a Bond film!"

"You wouldn't make a Bond girl."

"Gee, thanks." She turned indignantly on him, but it was too dark to properly judge his expression.

"Far too intelligent."

"Very diplomatic." She laughed aloud. "You're a survivor!"

He laughed softly in the darkness, and a warmth crept through her despite the chill of the night. She liked this man. Liked the way he refrained from making a grab the minute they were alone up here; liked the laid-back humour, the unhurried approach and the absence of toe-curling flattery. A refreshing change from city-slickers who moved too fast, men who were wealthy but didn't spend time on a girl, unless she was a cert in the sack. Brant Kennedy was an enigma and he had her intrigued.

"Isn't the light we are seeing now non-existent in

a sense?" and she pointed up at the myriad stars overhead. "You know, by virtue of having taken thousands of years to reach us."

"It's variable," he replied. "The light from Andromeda for example takes nearly two million years to reach Earth but Proxima Centauri, our nearest star, is only about four light years away. The computer takes it all into account in its calculations."

Darcy caught the animation in his voice, sensed his delight in sharing his knowledge and obvious passion.

"Does that mean it can show us past and future?" she asked, turning to him.

"Clever girl." It was said with warmth and sincerity rather than being patronising, and Darcy smiled in the darkness. Brant Kennedy, she decided, was not over-burdened with political correctness.

"See," he clicked the keys and the screen before them changed: "this shows the shape and pattern of the Universe a hundred thousand years ago." He clicked again, "and this how it will look thousands of years from now."

Darcy nodded. "I'm impressed. But it is only theory, projections."

"Amazingly accurate nonetheless. When computer results from light analysis are compared to existing records of known conjunctions – the positioning of two stars on the same degree of longitude – they correlate exactly."

She smiled. "I'm a bit lost here."

"Well, if models of past states are that precise, then we have no basis for doubting predicted ones."

"I see. I think."

Brant grinned. "Come on, you need feeding."

He closed the dome, shut down the computers, dimmed the lights and led her from the building.

"I thought," she challenged as he started up the Land Rover, "that you were involved in assessing weather conditions."

"I am if anyone asks!" Far from looking embarrassed by this admission of subterfuge, he chuckled aloud at Darcy's indignation as she tutted and shook her head. "And especially," he added provocatively, "when asked by a city-slicker journalist! But seriously, the Ministry is interested in what is happening out there in connection with space programmes, that sort of thing." He halted as though reluctant to divulge more. "I'm an astrophysicist," he said finally as though admitting a dirty habit.
"You can't help it; I won't tell anyone," she said solemnly, making him laugh.

"But come on, you were buzzing back there," she skewed round on her seat to see him better and watch his reaction, "forget the official version and tell me what really turns you on." He half turned, gave her a searching look then appeared to make up his mind.
"The use of astronomy to date historical events."
Darcy turned her head to give him a searching look.

SIXTEEN

Their supper of stuffed field mushrooms served with baked potatoes dripping with melted Camembert had been slowly cooking in the Aga during the trip to the observatory. They ate at the scrubbed wooden table in the kitchen after Brant had shown her around the house. The rooms were clean and lined with old paintings, spode-filled dressers, and pottery so ancient that the glaze was crackled and browned with age. Each room, Darcy noted, was free of feminine clutter. They dined by candlelight, though not, it transpired, of necessity. "I didn't think there would be an electricity supply out here," she remarked as he switched on a light above the work surface in order to serve the food.

"Nor was there. Courtesy of the observatory – and the Ministry," he replied then added, "Have you enough mushrooms?" effectively forestalling further questions.

"You're a good cook," she commented now, raising her glass in salute.

"I have to be."

"How long since your wife left?"

"Four years."

"Do you still see her?"

"No." He rose and taking a metal coffee pot from the Aga hot plate, filled her cup, and then his own. Mab and Brock stirred in their basket and briefly opened their eyes as he passed, then slumbered peacefully on. "She agreed to meet once after leaving but," he pulled a wry face as he sat down again, "the encounter was less than amicable."

I'll bet, Darcy found herself thinking, and ten to one it wasn't all her fault; he would not easily forgive betrayal.

"I thought-," she began then hesitated.

He swirled the brandy round in his glass. "Go on, say it."

"The woman in the pub – Helen, was it? I thought she was maybe—"

"My ex?" He gave a short abrasive laugh, "No, a friend of Stephanie's though, and I'm sure she reports back to her. To ease her own conscience perhaps, Steffie would like to learn that I'm entertaining a string of women. She is destined," he added with a self-mocking smile, "to be disappointed."

"I'm relieved to hear it," Darcy said in a bantering tone, then gave him a direct look. "Do you still miss your wife?"

He picked up his glass, stared at the wine before drinking, then put it down again. "I miss having someone to share things with, a companion," he admitted at last, "and a lover," he added meeting her gaze.

"Sure." She nodded to show that she was not taking this as a clumsy come-on.

"I mean sex, yes," he continued encouraged by her gesture: "but more than that the intimacy, the knowing someone and being known by them in turn. There's no guarantees, but if it works the world must be a less daunting place."

"I think you have to let go of your bitterness first," Darcy risked saying.

"As I've said before, you don't pull the punches."

"Not with someone I like," she responded swiftly, "and when I see them beating up on themselves."

After a moment's hesitation he reached across the table and placed his hand over hers.

"I like you too, Darcy. I like you a lot." The silence was as audible as the ticking of the ancient clock in the corner. The silver of his watch against the tanned skin reminded her of the day they met. She was acutely aware of his thumb caressing the back of her hand, of the warmth and semi-darkness, the sense of being cocooned in a private world up here on the cliffs. The soft shadows that purpled the ceiling between the beams added to the deepening air of intimacy. It would be so easy, she thought watching the interplay of candlelight and shade across his face, no effort at all to respond to the invitation she saw there and stay the night with this fascinating and unusual man. But they were drifting into waters she was not yet ready to navigate. He wanted more than a casual affair, had been badly hurt and it would be cruel to cause him further pain.

"Have you lived here long? You don't sound like a native." Her expression softened, and the words were gently spoken to allay any suspicion of rejection. Nevertheless, he withdrew his hand and she silently cursed her clumsiness. "Yet that is what I am. When my mother died I was sent to public school and that took care of my accent. I returned to Cumbria after graduating from Oxford."
"That must have been tough, losing your mother and being sent away." Little wonder, she thought, his emotions are kept in a strait jacket. He shrugged, looked away and took a sip of brandy.
"Brant – I," she started to say, half-reaching out to touch him then pulling back.
"One survives," he said, signalling that the subject was closed.

"Tell me more about your research," she urged as the minutes passed and she sensed his deepening withdrawal. "Is it really possible to date ancient events by the stars?"
"Astronomy has a long history." He poured more coffee into her cup then recharged his own. "Records of astronomical systems dating to ancient Egypt, Babylonia, China, Greece and Rome have been unearthed. Your friend Caro would confirm this.
"Okay, but I don't catch your drift."
He leaned back on his chair and stared for a moment at the shadows playing across the ceiling.
"All right, try this: way back BC," he made a wavelike motion with his hand to indicate the passage of time, "a rabbi by the name of Abarbanel prophesied that a messiah would be born when a conjunction of Jupiter and Saturn in Pisces occurred." His voice took on the conspiratorial tones of the story-teller and as he leaned forward, elbows resting on table,

the candlelight imbued his dark features with a mysterious and compelling quality.

"So, in seventeenth century Prague, Johannes Kepler – court mathematician and astronomer – read of this prophecy and decided to check it out. He worked in his planetarium to determine whether such an event had in fact occurred at the alleged time of the historical Jesus' birth."
"And did he succeed?" Darcy's smile conveyed her scepticism. Brant held up a hand to stem her impatience.
"He theoretically turned back the heavens some 1,600 years, just as we did tonight at the observatory but with ridiculous ease given our computers. His calculations confirmed such a conjunction occurred around the accepted time of Jesus' birth."
"But it's based on a belief in omens and portents," Darcy protested.

"Granted, Kepler was something of a mystic," Brant stated with a shake of his head, " but these calculations were firmly rooted in science. Don't confuse actual configurations with the symbolic meanings humans attach to the them," he warned. "You don't have to believe the dogma - the shepherds or three wise men and so on - to accept written accounts of an abnormally fierce and bright star 'in the east' – or to put it another way, the conjunction of Saturn and Jupiter in the House of Pisces."
"You accept the historical Jesus then?"

"It's of no account whether I personally do or not," Brant declared with a sigh of impatience. "That a man of that name existed, and became a leader, is now widely accepted by historians. I'm merely quoting this as an example of how astronomy can be used to date historical events."
"I don't buy it as an example." She took the lighter and cigarettes from her bag and offered the packet to Brant.
"I don't use them." He made a dismissive gesture with one hand, as though impatient of the diversion now that he was paddling the safe waters of professionalism, rather than floundering in a whirlpool of emotion.

114

Ignoring his invitation to go ahead and smoke if she wished. Darcy dropped lighter and cigarettes back into her bag. At last she knew: if he was telling the truth, he could not have dropped the cigarette found at the crypt.

"I mean," she continued, "it was all such a long time ago, and fact is fudged with myth."

"Okay, try the Middle Ages then. Astronomy was used in Alchemy, to calculate and reproduce the required celestial conditions to carry out the work."

"Alchemy you say? Turning base metal into gold and all that?"

"That's the popular definition. There was rather more to it; a complete philosophical system for starters."

"Tell me."

He shook his head and smiled. "Not tonight. I'll hope you are now sufficiently intrigued to want to see me again!"

"I don't need any inducement," she said with a provocative smile.

He moved round to the back of her chair, and as she rose to meet him, drew her into his arms. The kisses were becoming heated, and suddenly it didn't seem such a bad idea to stay. Why not? she thought, as his hand tentatively sought and found her breast, and his tongue teased and tasted her lips. His kiss deepened, until she had difficulty breathing and felt light-headed. She leaned against him, swaying on her feet, overcome by a sense of unreality. His sweater smelled of heather and wood smoke overlaid with the salt-tang of the sea, and evoked disturbing feelings that eluded memory. The candles were still burning on the table at his back. Through half-shut lids she watched beads of ivory wax well up from the head, then slowly drip the length of the candle to form an orgasmic pool at the base.

She moaned softly as his fingers wound around her curls and eased back her head, forcing her to look him in the face. "There's plenty of room, if you would like to stay," he said, releasing her hair and gently pushing stray tendrils back from her face. As desire warred with uncertainty, her hand tentatively caressed his cheek.

"I have a feeling that staying means committing."

"It does," he said solemnly. He scanned her features as though trying to see beyond the fragile barrier of flesh to the person beneath. "I wonder which one of us is most scared?" he said softly.

"At a guess we're level-pegging."

He drew her to him, cradling her head against his chest. "I'm not going to rush you. I want you to be sure." Engulfed in this warmth and security, Darcy felt, was akin to being bathed by a warm tropical sea. The desire to slip down, into and under, to completely submerge herself in him, and feel his maleness lapping and sucking the core of her being was becoming too strong to resist. She felt a desire to open and close around him like an oyster responding to the tidal current. Weak with emotion she leaned heavily against him, transfusing him with her needs.

"Are you sure about this Darcy, because—" he stopped in mid sentence, his lips an inch or so from her ear. "Brant?"

He placed a warning finger on her lips then remained perfectly still, listening. A low warning growl rumbled in the dogs' throats. The warm tropical sea was ruffled by a chill of unease. She drew back slightly, then stiffened in his arms as there was a sound from outside like the crunching of feet on gravel. Mab and Brock growled deep in their throats, barked and leapt from their basket. Brant raised a hand and effectively silenced them.

"Wait here," he said to Darcy in a loud whisper. Releasing her, he moved with feline swiftness to the door and flung it open. "Stay Mab – Brock!" he commanded, and was gone.

Darcy ran to the window and by the light of the moon saw a figure flit into the shrubbery. Minutes later, Brant followed in pursuit. A shadow on the path close to the house caught her attention. Commanding the dogs to stay, she slipped outside and pulled the door to behind her. Mab and Brock whined, and scratched at the wood. Hoping they would do no damage, she ran to the object lying on the stone slab. Her hand went to her mouth in an involuntary action to stop herself from screaming. Gagging, she took a step backwards from the mess of blood and entrails spilling across the path.

SEVENTEEN

The rat, the size of a small cat and with spilled guts glistening in the moonlight, stared up at her with sightless eyes. It's demise had been recent, given the faint trails of steam that rose from the body to stain the cold night air. Gripped by bizarre fascination, her mind registered the coarse hair spiked with drying blood, and the long tail ringed like segments of earthworm but with the leathery strength of a whip. Unlike the pitiable butchered body, this tail still harboured a latent power, so much so that she had to stare hard then look away and stare again to convince herself it was no longer moving with a mystical life of its own. Suppressing the urge to vomit, she ran back inside and, pushing the dogs away from the door, banged it shut and rammed the bolt home.

Who had done such a thing, and why? She waited, heart pounding with anxiety, expecting signs of a struggle and then to see Brant emerge with the trespasser in his grasp. Or maybe he would not walk out from the shrubbery. Her hand went to her chest as panic constricted it and made breathing difficult. Whoever was lurking out there was either a sadist or maniac. Mab and Brock ran to the door and whined and scratched until she called them back to their basket. Why, she wondered, had he not taken them with him? It seemed the natural thing to do if one suspected the presence of an intruder. Perhaps he expected whoever it was to be carrying a gun and had left the dogs behind for their protection. A frightening thought as Brant was unarmed. Gun or no, whoever had butchered that rat had a very sharp knife in his possession. The minutes ticked by, and panic fluttered in her stomach and rose to tighten her chest as she waited by the window. He may, she worried, be seriously hurt, may not even return and she would be left here alone. What sort of lunatic left a gutted rat on somebody's doorstep? The sense of being trapped in a nightmare heightened with each passing minute.

She was still waiting by the window when a movement in the shadows at the edge of the shrubbery caught her attention. With a muffled cry of relief, she watched Brant emerge from the foliage. He was alone and given his laboured breathing, had obviously been running. He stood for a moment, peering from side to side, then apparently seeing no sign of any intruder, jogged along the path towards the house. On reaching the dead rat he paused and glanced at the kitchen window. Darcy, recalling that she had fastened the door, ran across and drew back the bolt.
"Brant! Are you all right?" she called instinctively.
"Wait inside," he said curtly, veering left towards an outbuilding. On hearing his voice, Mab and Brock set up a furious barking and were frantic to get out. By the time she had calmed them down and returned to her post at the window, the rat was gone and Brant, spade in hand, was walking back to the shed. Minutes later he strode into the kitchen. After being allowed a moment or two of ecstatic welcome, Mab and Brock were ordered back to their basket.

"What happened? Who was it out there?" Darcy demanded, trying to keep the fear out of her voice.
"I didn't see anyone." Brant kept his back turned as he scrubbed his hands at the sink.
"I'm sure I saw someone run into the bushes," Darcy protested.
"You were mistaken," he said shortly, but his eyes strayed to the window and he moved across to look outside.
"I wasn't mistaken about that rat."
"The dogs disturbed a fox with its kill – or a marauding cat from the inn or village," he said shortly. "This is the countryside Darcy, not Manchester," he added as she make a derisory sound in her throat, "Things like this happen here."
"Oh please, you can do better than that!" she flared, fear and tension finding release in anger.
"I'll take you back," he said grimly, drying his hands then flinging the towel onto the drainer.

"I want to know what is going on here," Darcy said standing her ground.

"Nothing dramatic. But it's managed to change the mood all the same."

"I'm not happy Brant."

"There will be other times."

She made a gesture of impatience with her hand.

"You know what I mean. Over the past weeks, someone has been stalking me. Now this, in a secluded spot. Either someone followed me here—"

"Or what, Darcy?" His eyes were hard and cold.

"Or you are involved," she said without flinching. "I have a right to know what is going on."

"I have no idea what you are talking about."

He glanced away and his expression became guarded.

"Don't talk to me about commitment." Darcy picked up her shoulder bag and walked to the door.

"What is it with you?" he demanded, his face darkening with anger. About to open the door, she whirled round to face him.

"This, Brant," she said tapping the side of her nose. "I'm a reporter, and can smell a cover-up at ninety paces."

"So what do you think is going on?"

"I'm not sure. But I do know it's connected to finding St. Gildas Man."

"You've been reading too many novels."

"And you are infuriatingly pompous!"

He raised a hand in apology. "I'm sorry. I didn't mean to sound insulting."

"No problem; you manage without trying! A man has died Brant, and nobody wants to say how or why, and his body was cremated with indecent haste and no available records." That disturbing piece of information had been passed to her by Janet minutes before leaving the office for Cumbria, and she wondered now about the wisdom of sharing it with Brant Kennedy.

"A man?"

"The pathologist, Daniel Piper. I was pulled in for screening, so was Caro. Nobody wants to explain why. I was taken off the case, then that call came from—," she stopped short on seeing his narrowed eyes and intent expression, and realised she had been skilfully drawn into telling what she knew. She cursed her ego, and the anger that had fuelled the need to justify suspicion. "Go on," he said smoothly, joining her at the door.
"It doesn't matter," she said quickly, as a frisson of alarm shivered her spine.

She stepped back a pace, felt the timbers hard at her back. "Why didn't you take the dogs?" she said to drive him off track. "At first I thought it might have been a poacher, and wasn't going to risk them being shot."
"A poacher up here?" she said incredulously.
"There are pheasants on the estate."
Unconvinced, she gave him a searching look but his expression told her nothing. Her unease lingered; to be out here alone with this man who was virtually a stranger was not a good scene.
"I'd like to leave now if you don't mind."
Immediately he became courteous and polite again.
"Of course. No problem."
As they walked to the Land Rover, Darcy noted the way he scanned the alternately shadowed and moonlit walls, barn and shrubbery, and sensed his relief at taking her away.

It was a strange journey, bumping over moor and fell at dead of night. The muted roar of the sea as it pounded the rocks at the base of the cliff receded, and occasionally Darcy heard the shriek of a barn owl on the hunt. Once the plaintive call of a curlew haunted the moor and tugged at her heart. The silence between them thrummed with tension and the closer they came to the village the deeper it grew. Light spilled out into the blackness from the matchbox below them that was the Priory Arms. As they drew nearer strains of laughter and tired music drifted from the inn like smoke from a recently snuffed-out candle. A few vehicles remained in the car park, presumably the property of the privileged few who drank after hours and behind closed doors.

Her anger had long since dissipated and misery skulked in its place. Should he ask to see her again, she knew what her answer must be. Personal reasons apart, it appeared he was somehow involved in whatever was going on, she rationalised. However, he would not be in a hurry to repeat tonight's experience. Letting the engine idle, he switched on the interior light and turned to face her.

"Forgive me, Darcy," he said, proving her wrong.

"There's nothing to forgive."

"I blew it."

"No. We both got a little fazed that's all."

"That's very generous of you." he said smiling, and touched her cheek.

"It wasn't your fault. That incident apart, it was a lovely evening."

He looked at her without speaking and the silence spoke louder than any cliché or compliment ever could.

"May I see you again?" he said at last. His arm lay along the back of the seat, and his fingers caressed the nape of her neck.

"I'd like that."

"When?"

"I'm only here for the weekend." She said hesitantly, not wishing to appear over-eager.

"Tomorrow then?"

"Come for lunch." She was conscious of feeling as gauche and clumsy as a teenager on her first date.

"Where?" He raised an eyebrow and grinned.

"Oh, sorry. Mistletoe Cottage." Briefly she gave him directions.

Drawing her into his arms, he kissed her. Not with passion this time but with a gentleness that brought her close to tears. Nobody had ever kissed her like that. He was tentative and tender, sensitive to the newness and the need to make amends. Scared by the intensity of the moment and looming commitment, she pulled away.

"I must go. Good night, Brant." Not waiting for his reply she climbed down from the Land Rover and walked quickly to her own car.

EIGHTEEN

Darcy checked the contents of the oven. She then ran a critical eye over the cream ware pottery and crystal laid out on the kitchen table, and twitching a napkin into place glanced for the hundredth time at the clock. Last night had been special, with star-gazing and supper for two in a remote farmhouse on the cliffs; today – gunmetal grey and threatening rain – Brant Kennedy may regret accepting her invitation and retreat like a bat to the eaves at dawn. Then there was that unsavoury incident with the rat, although by daylight his explanation of a cat or fox seemed more acceptable. Perhaps she had over-reacted, and he would harbour resentment. However, if that proved to be the case it would not bother her one bit, she told herself, but was unable to resist yet another anxious look at the clock.

The throb of an engine, and a moment later the slam of a car door, interrupted her reflections and set off an electrical charge from somewhere deep in her stomach. From the rain-spotted window, she saw the Land Rover parked outside, flanks splashed with mud. Involuntarily she glanced in the hall mirror on passing. When she opened the door in response to a tattoo on the knocker, Brant Kennedy was standing there with a bottle of Chablis in his hand.

After finishing their meal, they took their glasses and the remainder of the wine into the sitting room. Beyond the Georgian-paned window, rain could now be seen ghosting across the fell in drifts of silver; if it was an April shower it promised to be a lengthy one. Darcy tossed a log onto the fire and was glad she decided to light it. The flames and glow compensated for the greyness outside, she thought, trying not to think it was also more intimate. Brant was seated in tharmchair opposite, and she had to admit how well he looked there.

"Great lunch," he said raising his glass.

"Not quite up to your mushrooms," she admitted. "I tend to rely on the freezer."

He smiled, and it was plain from the look in his eyes that he had more than food on his mind. Their eyes met and the silence deepened. A flush of self-consciousness burned her cheeks. A pocket of resin from one of the blazing logs exploded in the heat with startling loudness. They laughed and the tension broke.

"You were going to tell me more about alchemy," she said curling one leg beneath her and settling on her chair.

"Nice try but I wasn't," Brant responded with a laugh. "I am determined not to hog centre stage today! So tell me, what do you think is behind the St. Gildas Man affair?"

Darcy shrugged, and hesitated before answering. However, if this relationship was to progress, then sooner or later she would have start trusting Brant Kennedy.

"I told you about Caro's room being ransacked," she began then, when he nodded, added with straight-gaze cool "but I forgot to mention that the only thing taken was the file on St. Gildas Man."

"Odd." His steady regard mocked her deception and to her annoyance she felt herself blush.

"Yes very." The ensuing quiet, she worried, had more to do with speculation than intimacy. He leaned forward and topped up her glass with wine before refilling his own.

"So, who would want that file?"

"I don't know." She watched him carefully: "but I do know the Home Office wanted the story suppressed."

He frowned and there was a wariness now in his expression.

"Who told you that?"

"A telephone call was made then I was told 'no story' and in no uncertain terms."

Brant rose and placed his glass next to the chinoserie clock that had belonged to Darcy's grandmother.

"Oh, come now," he said leaning against the mantelpiece to face her, "are you trying to say the Ministry levied its power against a Manchester paper and provincial reporter to block a story about a local dig? Sorry, Darcy, it doesn't pan out."

"Thanks a million."

"I wasn't trying to put you down." Brant sighed, though with exasperation or regret she could not tell.

"You do it very well without!" Feeling to be at a disadvantage with him standing over her, Darcy rose to her feet. "For your information, the Manchester News is a respected and widely-read paper."

"In London?"

"Actually, yes." The patronising smile infuriated her, but she replied with dignity. "As the definitive source of Northern news for the Nationals."

"Excuse me," he grinned, holding up a hand in concession.

"And secondly," she continued, ignoring the irony, "we are not talking here of a 'local dig' as you put it – this is a find of international significance. Has it not occurred to you that apart from his cultural value, St. Gildas Man is also priceless? Certain private museums would pay a vast amount for such a prize – and not ask too many questions."

"I can't help thinking," Brant said looking unconvinced, "it is the reporter in you wanting to believe there's a mystery."

"Then hear this: I asked my assistant to ring the British Museum as they are supposed to have custody of the body. It appears they know nothing about it."

"Security measures," he said dismissively. "Until results of radio carbon dating, etc. are available and they know what they are holding."

"You are plain bloody-minded!" Darcy said, flushing.

"And you are an incurable romantic."

"Are you trying to put me off the investigation," she accused.

"No," he denied, "but it sounds as though somebody is, so maybe you should leave well alone."

"No way."

Brant shook his head and sighed with exasperation

so that Darcy was reminded of that first meeting on the
fell. Then unexpectedly he laughed.

"I didn't think for one moment that you would. You are bloody
impossible, know that?"

"And you are intolerably rude and pig-headed," Darcy said
grinning, "– especially as I have just given you lunch."

"A direct hit. I apologise without reservation."

"Idiot." She ran fingers through her hair so that it flared around
her head in a dark halo. "Oh why do we fight all the time?"

"Don't you know?" he said, moving closer. "It's the
oldest reason in the world." His eyes teased, and his smile
gently mocked. "Take Anthony and Cleopatra, Rochester and
his Jane, Mr. Darcy and Elizabeth Bennet, the list is endless."

"So you put it all down to sexual tension?" she said
suppressing a smile.

"What else?"

"Thwarted love?" she parried.

"That comes later."

"Does it?"

He gave her a searching look. "I used to think so."

"And now?" she pursued, intent it seemed on a
lemming approach to the brink of the cliff called 'commitment'.

"I'm not so sure." He took her hand, and stroked the inside of
her wrist with his thumb.

Darcy closed her eyes. His hand moved to her face,
his fingers caressing the back of her ear. Behind closed lids she
watched spurts of coloured flame: yellow, green red and purple
flicker across her skin then upwards and outwards in an erotic
aura. Electrical impulses similar to those on Brant's computer,
tracing not vigour of light but intensity of desire. She was a star
burning with energy, pulsing with sensuality and emitting
sexual signals in response to his fingers on the controls.

"Why are you smiling?"

She opened her eyes. "Because now I know how Pollux feels."

"Excuse me?" He looked bemused.

"Those shooting lights, remember?"

"Ah, yes." His fingers caressed the back of her neck, the movement causing the glass of his watch to shine in the firelight. "What about them Darcy?"

"They are flickering over my skin."

"So what happens when I do this?"

He pulled her close. This kiss was not tender and tentative, but one that conveyed his passion.

"And this?" His hand moved down to her waist, slipped beneath the cashmere sweater and cupped her breast. She sucked in breath at the contact, saw mirrored in his face the pleasure at finding bare flesh.

"Sunspots and comets," she whispered into his ear.

"And this?" His fingers continued to explore her as he spoke, caressing, kneading and gently squeezing. She leaned against him, revelling in the sensations, feeling him hard against her. This she could handle: this light teasing prelude to sex that allowed bodies to sing but emotions the merest whisper. This was the way it had been with Jonathon: the freedom to indulge without having to pick up the tab, a fantasy game where everything goes but nothing is forever. It was puzzling though, given his reticence of the previous night and his insistence upon commitment. For some reason, she thought, surveying his face from beneath her lashes, he was acting too, playing the accomplished seducer, maybe because he was unsure how best to respond to her needs.

But then came the change. She actually felt it, saw the mockery leave his eyes to be replaced with tenderness and uncertainty. She was also aware of her own unwelcome response to his vulnerability. He was holding her now at arms' length whilst looking into her eyes with disturbing intensity, his forehead puckered with concentration as though he sought to look into her soul. With a sigh, he pulled her close and crushed her face against his shoulder, stroking her hair in an ageless gesture that conveyed the desire to protect. He whispered her name, and she clung to him for support as fear mingled with desire.

Something was wrong: it was never like this with
Jonathon. The game had stopped, Brant had abandoned
his role of light-hearted lover and she was in danger of
following suit. He had broken the rules, had touched her heart
with the gentleness of the rain that misted the fells.
Commitment was a risky and scary business. Immediately he
sensed her withdrawal.

"What is it?"

"I'm sorry." She placed her hands on his chest and pushed
gently. "I guess I'm not ready for this after all." She watched
him struggle with his emotions, wanting to kiss away the pain
of rejection, but finding her hands and body rigid and incapable
of the moves.

"I understand Darcy," he said, coming to her rescue. "Thank
you for being honest."

He released her and feeling wretched, she pulled her sweater
down over her hips.

"I'll make coffee."

"Good idea." He smiled and touched her arm briefly.

"Brant, it's not that I don't want—."

"I've told you: not until you are ready. I'm not looking for a
casual affair." With great tenderness, he kissed her forehead.
She was relieved to see the warmth return to his eyes. "Now, go
make that coffee whilst I visit your bathroom," he added,
pushing her gently towards the kitchen.

She knew something was wrong the moment he re-
entered the room.

"Is it your birthday?" Suppressed anger lurked beneath his
smile and bland expression.

"Excuse me?" She frowned and paused in pouring the coffee.

"The roses."

Oh shit! Darcy silently cursed her carelessness. She had divided
them between three vases, left them in the bedroom out of the
way and obviously – and foolishly – left the door open. The
bathroom was directly opposite and Brant could not have failed
to see them. In fact in his eyes, her bedroom must have
resembled a bridal chamber.

"No, just a gift from a friend."
"A very special one, I would say. Those will have cost the earth."

In the awkward silence that followed, the ticking of the clock sounded abnormally loud. Combined with the crackling of the logs she had placed on the fire it scratched along her nerves like fingernails dragged down a blackboard.
"Cream and sugar, or black?" she said milk jug in hand, and knowing the false brightness of her voice betrayed her guilt.
"You said there was nobody special," he accused, giving her a hard look.
"There isn't." Darcy replaced the jug on the tray.
"Those roses look very special to me."
"Aren't you taking an awful lot for granted?" she bluffed.
"What if I told you Caro sent those as a 'thank you' for putting her up?"
"Then I'd be very worried about you and Caro," he said dryly. His eyes held contempt. "Don't play girlie games with me, Darcy."

Darcy looked at him for a moment then sighed with resignation.
"Okay, they are from a man. His name is Jonathon, and he is the one I told you about. It's finished, all over."
"Of course, and the guy is so happy about that he sends you dozens of roses," he said sarcastically.
"Don't be smart Brant." She looked at him coldly.
"So tell me then – why did he send them?"
"I don't think that is any of your business, do you?" The second it was out and she saw the hurt and rejection in his expression, she wanted to take it back. Unfortunately, she reflected, words are like feathers tossed from a pillow and blown away: you can never put them back.
"You're right of course. It isn't."

"Brant, wait!" Se followed as he crossed to the door, opened it and marched into the hall. He paused on the driveway, his eyes as cold and bleak as a winter tarn.

"My apologies. I obviously didn't make it clear: I'm not about to get involved with a woman who isn't emotionally free."

"You have no right to assume I'm still involved with Jonathon."

"Right, no - as you have already pointed out, but certainly sufficient reason."

"You are making me pay for what your wife did," she accused, her face pale now with frustration and pain. Brant's features set into granite.

"Goodbye."

He climbed into the land rover and roared away down the drive.

Anger, pain and frustration boiled over. Darcy took the stairs two at a time and grabbed the roses from their vases. Oblivious to the pain as thorns pierced her hands, she ran downstairs again and rammed them into the bin outside the kitchen door.

"Thanks, Jonathon. Thanks a million for screwing up," she shouted, finding relief in venting her feelings. Only as she fastened the door latch did she notice blood trickling down her arms from the wounds inflicted by the thorns. After tending them, she sat by the fire half hoping Brant would return, but knowing he would not. Brant Kennedy was far too proud and pig-headed, she thought whipping up anger again to dull the hurt. Rising from the sofa, she finished off the wine and told herself it was all for the best.

NINETEEN

Montgomery, Montague, Parry, de Quincey . . . Back at the Manchester News, Darcy pushed aside thoughts of Brant Kennedy and sent the cursor up and down the list on her computer screen, settled on a name and once again accessed the data. Montgomery: French; 'mountain hunter'. Ancestral estate: Hawksmere House, Cumbria. Then the family tree and that tantalising possible lead: one Giles de Montgomery, killed in the Sixth Crusade during the battle to recapture Jerusalem, and the only evidence of a crusader in any of the genealogies so far studied. A family of power and wealth which might feasibly have had his body preserved and brought back to England in a lead coffin. But the name 'Montgomery' failed to correspond with the surviving letters inscribed on the sandstone block of the vault – and the dates were wrong. A letter from Caro had arrived that morning; radio carbon dating placed St. Gildas Man somewhere between A.D. 1250 and A.D.1300, in line with the dates gleaned from the vault, but too late for the Crusades.

Thoughts of Caro brought a sense of disappointment. It seemed that Brian was down with a 'bug' and she would not be spending the weekend at the cottage as planned. Instead she proposed lunch at the Boot and Shoe inn at Lancaster. Caro also suggested making contact with a Miles Standish, an accountant living near Coniston Water who was also a respected history buff and who had in the past contributed articles to the Cumberland Archaeological Society's journal. Attached to the message were a couple of shots of the tomb with its inscription. Darcy opened up one image and looked at it thoughtfully. If he was not a crusader, then what was the significance of the engraved sword and splayed cross? The latter still rankled; she had seen that symbol before but could not recall the context.

Suddenly the door opened, and she swept the photographs into the top drawer as Frank Kelly entered.

"What can I do for you Frank?"

His eyes narrowed as she hurriedly shut the drawer.

"That interview report on Janice Benson?"

"Yes?" Their relationship was still strained, and Darcy watched his face with apprehension, half expecting a reprimand.

"Nice one. We'll run it this week."

"Good of you to say so Frank." Her sigh of relief must have been audible.

"No favours. It's all good stuff, Darcy. I knew if anyone could get her to talk it was you." He leaned forward and peered into her face, "You're looking a bit peaky. So, go see the Cabbala woman. She does her interviews in a suite at the Midland. Then lose yourself until tomorrow."

"Thanks, boss." An afternoon off. A chance to visit the Central Library and do some research. As the door swung to after Frank, Darcy grabbed her jacket and left the office before he could change his mind.

****

Darcy shifted on her white and gilded chair and glanced around the luxurious suite of the Midland Hotel. Her fingers moved swiftly over the keyboard of her notepad as she took in the brocade drapes, chandeliers and Rococo furnishings of Clare Cabbala's boudoir. The celestial charts decorated with red and white dragons and a weird sort of snake arranged mouth-to-tail to form a circle would be of even greater interest to her readers, as would the spherical object shrouded by a black velvet cloth that could only be a crystal ball. All as phoney as a politician's word; debunking this myth was going to be fun.

"So, you are prepared to meet my challenge, Madame Cabbala?" she said with confidence.

Clare Cabbala drew on a long black cheroot, and

shifted her considerable bulk on the gilded chaise longue upon which she reclined.

"Of course I will meet your experts, my dear," she lisped, exhaling a thin trail of smoke. The slight accent, Darcy noted, hinted at Baltic origins. An elegant woman of sixty-something, Clare Cabbala was flamboyantly but expensively attired in flowing cream silk, and gold sandals upon her feet. A pronounced glide in the left eye added to her somewhat bizarre appearance.

"That's very generous of you. I'll make the necessary arrangements." Darcy closed her notebook and prepared to rise, but sank down again as the older woman raised a hand.

"I am happy to debate and discuss paranormal phenomena with them, but I shall not be performing their tricks."

So that was the catch. Darcy tried to conceal her disappointment and was annoyed with herself for failing.

"But why do you object to the Psi-test?"

Clare Cabbala smoothed a crease from her peignoir.

"Because it is irrelevant."

"Okay." Darcy nodded and held up a placatory hand. "But the University would like to try more modern approaches like displacement technique and remote viewing. That means sending a volunteer out to a secret destination and asking you to mentally track and locate them."

"I am well aware of what it entails."

"Of course." Darcy coughed and thrust her notepad into her satchel. "It could prove a powerful tool to demonstrate your psychic ability," she tempted.

"No. It would merely demonstrate how I perform party tricks under laboratory conditions. Party tricks – even if you do call them 'experiments' – have nothing to do with true psychic phenomena."

Deep stuff, this woman is no fool, Darcy found herself thinking with grudging respect. Her professional eye noted the woman's folded arms and compressed lips: persistence now would harden her resistance and prejudice future opportunities.

"Very well, Madame Cabbala, I'll inform my editor and get back to you."
Darcy picked up her bag, then froze. Madame Cabbala was squinting intently at her and in a way that, despite her scepticism, ruffled Darcy's nerves.
"What is it?" she asked more sharply than intended.

The woman closed her eyes and stroked her forehead with plump beringed fingers tipped with gold-leafed nails.
"I sense danger around you," she intoned.
"It's probably my boss on the war path." Darcy relaxed and grinned. Ignoring the flippancy, the Cabbala woman placed a forefinger to a mouth from which the lipstick had bled into the finely etched lines above her upper lip.
"Temporal. I am getting the word *temporal* along with a sense of authority. Could this be temporal power? Are you perhaps?" she added opening her eyes to squint disconcertingly at Darcy, "delving into religious matters? The past perhaps? Whatever – it is leading you into dreadful danger."
"Sorry, Madame Cabbala, I don't frighten easily," Darcy said with a crispness intended to discourage further comment. She stood up. The woman had obviously read the piece in the News about the finding of the body at the priory. An old trick and one that no longer impressed.

The older woman gave her a look of disdain.
"Foolish child! This is way beyond your puny little campaign against myself."
"Oh but that isn't—," Darcy began, flushing.
Clare Cabbala waived aside Darcy's embarrassment with a plump white hand.
"Leave alone that which lies beyond your understanding, my dear. You are a nice girl – despite your scepticism."
A further wave of the hand dismissed Darcy and terminated the interview.

****

Darcy walked away from the Midland Hotel struggling with an irritating riddle . No matter how hard she tried to suppress it one word sounded over and over in her head. *Temporal.* She hurried towards St. Peter's Square and the Central Library, puzzling over its meaning. The pavement teemed with people who tutted and turned their heads as lost in thought, she pushed her way through the crowd. What had that woman called it? That was it: temporal power – and as she understood it, that meant eccliastical power, not that it clarified matters.

She glanced up as a flock of pigeons rose to the air with a flapping and whirring of wings. With a sense of timelessness and displacement she watched them circle the dome of the library. White, buff and blue-grey flight-feathers blurred into a soft focus image. The birds rose and fell at the prompting of the group mind, shifting shape and suddenly breaking ranks before reforming again. The movement, the strange sense of cohesion and the quality of light combined with hypnotic effect. Darcy stood transfixed, oblivious to the push in the back or dig of an elbow as people jostled past. The associations came without effort of will: *temporal: transient and ephemeral; temperate: abstemious, self-restrained and sober: Temple: place of worship, church, sanctuary.* She watched the dome, pale grey against a lemony Manchester sky and veiled by a myriad wings, shift shape and location to become larger and grander with Vatican gold against Mediterranean blue.

The cloud of pigeons broke, scattered and formed again in kaleidoscopic symmetry, the blurring of wings obscuring the dome which when visible again loomed squat and heavily pregnant with secrets, the gold burnished by an arid Arabian sun. Heat-shimmer rose in waves creating a mirage effect, distorting and stretching the tower first to phallic slimness then the rarefied airiness of the minaret. Rome: the Vatican; temples: the Middle East. Her numbed mind struggled to bring disparate pieces together and make sense of the vision. Papal power, almost certainly, but what did that have to do with the temples of the east? She gasped and exclaimed aloud as the truth hit. The Holy Wars and Jerusalem – home to the crusades.

"You all right miss?"
Darcy started, turned then flushed with embarrassment on finding herself under the scrutiny of a young and bored-looking policeman.
"Fine, no problem." Embarrassed and disoriented, she added: "I was miles away," and on making her escape smiled at the secret significance of that remark. Despite her intention to visit the library, her pace unconsciously quickened as though to escape the disturbing experience. What had her subconscious (undoubtedly the culprit and forget any mumbo jumbo) thrown up? Temple, power, church, order and so the stream of consciousness flowed.

She stopped in the middle of the pavement, so suddenly that a man carrying a sheaf of documents and wearing the black three piece suit of a court-bound solicitor collided into her back. Mumbling an apology, she turned and retraced her steps. Because now she had the key, the one that unlocked the memory of that splay-armed cross. Her steps wavered, surely it could not be that simple. Well, this is the place to find out, she thought entering the library.

TWENTY

Darcy returned to the flat that evening and, whilst soaking in a hot perfumed bath, reflected upon the day's events. Her insight had proved correct; the answer leapt from the page of the fifth or sixth book she opened. At first she had been unable to note down places and dates because the hand which held her pencil trembled and refused to obey her brain. The sight of the red cross with its splayed arms, or rather the chain of events which had led her to it, had given her a shock.

In retrospect however, the whole thing seemed less uncanny and scary. It had to be a simple case of the intuitive right brain triumphing over the logical left one, she decided stretching her legs and pointing her toes so that they protruded from the foam like seals from ice-holes. The cross patée, the emblem of that most famous of military orders, had surfaced from the obscurity of a sixth-form history lesson. It had nothing to do with Clare Cabbala's cryptic utterances except, she allowed, for a chance word acting as a stimulus. This had provoked a spate of word-association and flight of ideas which in turn had brought that long-buried memory to the surface.

Reassured by this piece of rationalisation, she soaked away the stresses of the day. Yet doubt refused to be swirled down the plug hole as the water disappeared with a last gurgle of protest. What, she wondered, wrapping herself in a warm towel, were the odds against the Cabbala woman choosing that particular word with its specific associations? She smoothed body lotion over her thighs with long strokes to relax tight muscles, and the oils of lavender and cedarwood soothed her agitation. Regardless of how it arose, this had provided the first real lead, and pieces of the jigsaw were already locking into place. No wonder there was no mention of St. Gildas Man in the genealogies, the chances were this particular son would have been expunged from the annals. The family may even have changed its name. Little wonder either that odd circumstances surrounded his death. He had not been a crusader but a Knight of the Temple, and the legend of the Templars had ended in heresy, torture and disgrace.

The previous evening Jonathon had telephoned and persuaded her to meet him for a drink. At first she resisted, feeling it was unfair to offer encouragement, but Brant Kennedy's hostile silence since their quarrel, and her ensuing low esteem, had overcome her scruples. Jonathon, she decided, must look after his own emotions. Besides, it would be naive to interpret that bouquet of roses and 'I think I love you' routine as anything but a ploy to get her back between his sheets. So here she was at their agreed rendezvous.

****

However, Jonathon's expression filled her with remorse and something like panic. The silence was stretching her nerves, but words stuck to her tongue like feathers on treacle.
"How did you find this place?" she said at last, glancing at the Victorian wall lights, antique mirrors and enamelled signs advertising various brands of ale and stout. "Is it for real? It certainly looks and feels authentic," she added when he did not answer.
"Stop it, Darcy."
The sadness lurking in his eyes made her want to weep.
"Lighten up Jonathon!" she chivvied, softening the words with a smile. "Has someone whipped a juicy account from under your nose?" she teased, aware of the falseness in her voice.
He grasped her hand as she tried to withdraw it.
"You know what is wrong."
"Jonathon-,"
"I love you, Darcy," he interrupted, his voice low and intense. "I meant it, that message on the roses. But I wasn't absolutely sure, not until tonight."

The silence stretched to uncomfortable limits.

Darcy pushed back her seat and stood up. "Forgive me, " she excused herself, adding by way of explanation as he looked panic-stricken, "the toilets Jonathon." Feeling the ultimate coward, she made a temporary escape. She stood with eyes closed and back braced against the toilet door. This was not on her agenda. A few short weeks ago she would have been overjoyed to hear Jonathon's words, but now it was too late. Moving across to the wash basins she surveyed herself in the mirror but then the image arose of Brant Kennedy's face, eyes dark and unforgiving, accusing her of duplicity.

Briefly, she closed her eyes to shut it out. On opening them again, she saw the evidence of anxiety and strain in her reflection. Serve her right for scheming and plotting, for trying to manipulate the affair to her own advantage. This flash of remorse was followed by burning resentment. Men did it all the time and got away with it, so why did she have to be overburdened with integrity? Taking a deep breath and squaring her shoulders for the ordeal, she walked to the door.

****

There was now no denying that Jonathon's pain was genuine.
"But I love you – want to marry you, Darcy."
His obvious sincerity touched her, almost caused her to waver.
"It's been great, Jonathon, but I don't love you," she said bleakly, wanting to offer comfort but knowing that to do so would be cruel in the end.
"Is there somebody else?" he asked dully.
She shook her head, but even as she denied him Brant Kennedy's face came before her eyes, and there could be no denying her sadness that it was Jonathon and not he declaring his love.
"Say you'll still see me, give me a chance to prove I'm sincere." he pleaded, panicking as she pushed aside her unfinished drink.
"That would be dishonest of me Jonathon."
"But I love you," he repeated bleakly.

140

"I'm sorry Jonathon, take care." Pausing to touch his cheek she whispered, "Thank you for all the good times," and left before she could change her mind.

By ten fifteen she was back inside the flat. Pouring herself a brandy and Canada Dry, she kicked off her shoes, threw her jacket onto a chair and after switching on the C.D. player, dropped wearily down on the sofa. Life was so bloody complicated. She sipped her drink, consoling herself with the knowledge that she had acted with honesty and decency while also acknowledging a sense of relief. Leaning her head against the cushions, she closed her eyes, and as the music washed over her in waves, finally dozed.

The sound of the telephone shrilling jerked her back to alertness. She hesitated before lifting the receiver, intuitively knowing who it was before he spoke.
"Hello, Brant. No, that's all right, I've just got in."
Vanity made her lie as he apologised for the lateness of the hour.
"Oh."
She sensed his distrust, the tacit question that arose but would not be asked. Sure enough he glossed it, a skater on thin ice unwilling to test the surface.
"Same here. I was working at the observatory," he offered instead. Darcy ignored the slight pause which was meant to coax her into making a similar disclosure. "I didn't realise it was so late," he continued, "but I did try you earlier."

A little smile of satisfaction softened her mouth. Now that he had made first move she could, with self-respect intact, tell him what he wanted to know.
"I went for a drink with Jonathon. He is the one—"
"I know who Jonathon is." The chill was back in his voice, the words sharp as icicles.
"Yes." She recalled the flowers, his condemnation and abrupt exit and deliberately made him wait.
"He asked me to marry him," she said at last.
"I see."

141

A deathly silence ensued. Hating herself for making him suffer, but at the same time recalling that he had stormed off and taken his time in making contact, Darcy made him wait. However, if she expected evidence of his suffering it was not forthcoming.

"I wish you all the best then, Darcy." His voice was neutral, betraying only the slightest flatness of tone that might be taken for regret.

"I told him I didn't love him. That I would not be seeing him again."

The silence resounded as Darcy waited.

"Thank you for telling me."

The irony was unmistakable; he knew she had deliberately let him think she had accepted Jonathon's proposal. She made a conciliatory gesture with her hand as though he could see it.

"Does it matter?"

"It helps."

She smiled to herself. This man was an original.

He cleared his throat. "So, now that is out of the way, do you think we might try again?"

"Yes please." She almost laughed aloud.

"Good. This weekend – can you come up here?"

"Your place or mine?"

"Mine," he said firmly. "You seem to do marginally better there!"

"Fair comment." She did laugh at that. "About eight would suit if it's okay with you; I have someone to see during the day. Caro gave me the lead. A guy called Miles Standish. He lives in Cumbria too, over Coniston way. Do you know him?" Brant gave no immediate answer. Darcy frowned as the silence lengthened into several seconds.

"Not really," Brant said at last. "He's published a few papers on local history matters."

He sounded normal, and Darcy thought she must have been mistaken about his apparent reticence.

"See you at eight then," he added, "and Darcy—,"

"Yes?"

"Take care; you are rather special to me."

142

It was unexpected, and she was touched by the words from this taciturn man who, when it came to dispensing compliments or praise, made Scrooge appear generous.

"You too Brant," she said softly and replaced the receiver.

Wednesday arrived, and Darcy received permission from Frank to take a protracted mid-day break in lieu of extra time put in the previous night on a Public Opinion Supplement. She hummed in time to the music coming from the C.D. player as the car sped along the dual carriageway towards Lancaster, and her lunch date with Caro. There was reason enough to feel good: sunlight dappled the windscreen as she passed beneath overhanging foliage, and the hedgerows teemed with dog violets, flowering ground ivy and drifts of sweet cicely interlaced with stitchwort and creamy cow parsley. She had a lead on St. Gildas man, a pleasant hour or so ahead, and best of all, the rift with Brant was healed. For a change, all was right with her world.

****

The inn was popular with University staff and students, and despite being mid-week the car park was full. Darcy pulled into a space on the main road close to Caro's Volvo. She found Caro at a window seat, sandwiches and drinks waiting on the table.

"How's Brian?" Darcy asked, wiping froth from her lips after sampling the local bitter.

"Man flu! And convinced he has double pneumonia."

"Judging by your red eyes and nose, I'd say you were succumbing too," Darcy laughed and pretended to back off. "I don't want the 'flu, thank you!"

"Sun and flowers out early that's all," Caro gestured towards the window adding as Darcy looked mystified.

"Hay fever."

"Of course. Forgot you were a sufferer."

They indulged in small talk for several minutes, easing themselves back into the fabric of their relationship. Once comfortable with it again, the real talk began: when pressed, Caro reported 'no progress' with solving the break-in and expressed the view that there never would be. The incident, she explained, was being played down. Security had mechanically gone through the motions, but it was clear that nobody really wanted to know. Darcy's eyes darkened with concern as she put down her half-eaten sandwich to listen intently as her friend talked. The reticence and anxiety present at their previous meeting had returned. Caro's hands fiddled first with a beer mat, then pushed away her glass and pulled it closer again but clumsily so that it almost tipped over. She glanced out of the window and around the room whilst talking, as though fearing to be overheard. Something, Darcy worried, was eating at Caro's peace of mind. There was little point in pressing her for confidences as she was obviously not yet ready to give them.

Instead, Darcy imparted the latest feedback on St. Gildas Man.
"Of course! A Knight Templar – I should have thought of that myself," Caro exclaimed.
My own feeling exactly, Darcy thought, giving Caro a sceptical look. Given Caro's passion for history and the fact that she had discovered the body, her research must have taken her down every possible path.
"But can we be one hundred percent sure, solely on the strength of that cross?"
"Obviously not, but I would bet on ninety-five," Darcy shot back, worried at the way Caro was trying to discredit what she must know to be the truth. "This morning I sent an application for relevant facts to the Archives at Carlisle and the Temple Repository in London," she added quietly, while looking directly at her friend.
"I'm impressed. Keep me in the picture."

But Caro's expression betrayed something other than enthusiasm.
"You know that sun is really hot through this glass." Darcy slipped off her red woollen jacket and draped it over the back of

the chair before adding: "Could you put a request in for me with the History Department at Hilldean?"

"No problem." Caro's hesitation was almost imperceptible. She pushed aside her plate of half-eaten sandwiches and seemed about to say more, but turned instead to watch the steady stream of traffic beyond the window. Darcy waited for her to overcome this obvious reluctance to speak, and eventually Caro turned back to her.

"Did you," she said slowly, as though still struggling with whatever was holding her back, "look up Miles Standish?"

"I'm planning a visit Saturday."

"Let me know how it goes."

To Darcy's relief Caro now sounded and looked brighter and seemed to have reached the decision that whatever her reservations, it behoved her to speak out.

"It may be a dead end, but he has written several papers on the priory settlement. Something else occurred to me," Caro added, "there is a school of thought that claims Freemasonry is a modern extension of the Order of Knights Templar, that the ethos still exists through the Masonic lodges."

"Is there any truth in it?" Darcy probed, leaning forward. Caro shrugged and dabbed at crumbs with her index finger, watching them adhere then drop back onto her plate.

"Possible but not probable. It's asking a lot, that kind of continuity. It all happened so long ago."

Darcy mopped up some droplets of ale with the edge of a beer mat.

"There are precedents. Christianity for example managed to survive."

"True," Caro pursed her lips and looked sceptical, "but there is a difference. Admittedly the early Christians had more than their share of persecution, but eventually they were accepted by the Establishment. For the Knights Templar to have survived so long in secrecy is rather like claiming the Druids are still ruling Wales behind the Welsh Nationalist Party!"

"I've often wondered about those Eisteddfod bards!" Darcy quipped with a grin. "That freemasonry idea may be worth a look if Miles Standish proves a dead end."

"Absolutely," Caro agreed, smiling and appearing to relax.

"And now I have to go," she said with a grimace, "I have a two o'clock lecture to take."

"And Frank will be yelling if I don't show my face soon."

"Thanks for the lunch – and your help," Darcy added, squeezing Caro's arm affectionately as she followed her to the door.

Caro shivered as they approached the busy road.

"It isn't very warm out here," she grumbled, hugging herself as a stiff breeze nipped their faces and skittered amongst the litter in the gutter. "I wish I hadn't left my coat in the car."

"I suspected it wasn't hay-fever," Darcy said wryly; Caro sneezed then shivered again as though to prove the point.

"Take this – I'm plenty warm." Cutting short Caro's protests, Darcy draped her woollen jacket around Caro's shoulders. "Who'll look after poor Brian if you go down too?" she said, laughing.

"Anything to stop you fussing," Caro sighed, slipping her arms into the sleeves and pulling up the collar.

"Your bag is open," Caro warned as they waited at the kerb to cross the road. "Come on Darcy!" she added over her shoulder as a gap appeared in the stream of cars. Darcy bent her head to fasten the clasp of her shoulder bag.

"Coming." The chill of presentiment brought up her head. The sense of someone at her back, and the scent of salt-mist with a hint of cedarwood. A set of fragmented images flickered across her mind like pictures on a screen from a projector. The approaching car, the impact, Caro tossed in the air like a rag doll and free-falling in slow motion, her broken limbs flailing the air at unnatural angles. The final image was of Caro lying lifeless in the gutter.

Then the lights went out and the show was over.

TWENTY-ONE

It all happened so fast. Caro was about to step off the pavement.

"Caro – stop!" Darcy screamed. Caro, one foot already in the roadway, paused and turned to look at Darcy. The car that had appeared from nowhere pitched forward with a roar of its engine. Caro spun and fell. The vehicle disappeared in a cloud of dust and exhaust fumes; Caro was lying motionless in the gutter, just as Darcy had foreseen it.

Darcy screamed and pitched forward, dropped to her knees at her friend's side and shouted at horrified passers-by to run to the inn and telephone for an ambulance.

"And the police! Hurry, please!" she implored, turning back to Caro and wanting to draw her into her arms but knowing she must not for fear of compounding her injuries. "Caro! Caro can you hear me?" There was no response.

"An ambulance is on its way," a man shouted minutes later. A woman from the inn ran forward with a blanket which she draped over Caro's still form. Darcy, dazed with shock, stared stupidly at the widening pool of blood staining the tarmac. Red blood. Red coat. Despite her disordered mind the truth hit her like an assassin's bullet.

Caro was rushed to the Casualty Department of the local hospital where she was now under strict observation. Darcy, shaking with trauma, was guided into a cubicle, and a nurse brought her a cup of sweet tea. Twenty minutes or so passed with agonising slowness before the curtains were swished aside to admit the nurse-in-charge.

"Feeling better?"

"How is she?" Darcy asked ignoring the question, her face as white as sister's starched apron.

"Mrs. Stevens is comfortable; investigations are under way and we'll let you know if there is any change," came the standard reply.

"Thank you." Darcy sighed and rubbed her forehead. "I believe you have already given the details of next of kin to the receptionist."

"That's right, her husband." Darcy licked her lips and swallowed hard. "Is she going to be all right? I mean," she steeled herself to ask, "is there any danger?"

"It's too soon to say. Your friend is still not conscious, but we will do all we can. In the meantime," the nurse's voice became crisp as though to forcibly counter Darcy's despair, "do you feel up to talking to the police?"

"Yes."

"Good. This way please."

Darcy stood up as the nursing sister pointedly looked at the watch pinned to her starched front as though to say 'buck up now, I have other things to attend to', and led her from the cubicle to a nearby interview room.

Detective Sergeant Drigg as he introduced himself regarded Darcy with a world-weary, 'seen-it-all, done-it-all, worn the tee-shirt' sort of expression, and tired grey eyes whose whites were stained a nicotine yellow.

"We'll need a full statement later miss," he said sombrely, closing his notebook with a decisive snap.

"You are the main witness to the accident see," his constable added with the vestiges of a Welsh accent. By way of contrast with his superior, this man radiated the rawness and enthusiasm of the rookie. The fresh face was carefully blanked of expression, but his stance conveyed an assumed dignity and air of *savoir-faire* patently beyond that which he could legitimately claim.

"It was no accident, sergeant," Darcy said tersely, ignoring the constable.

Drigg scratched his stubbly chin and the minute rasping sound scraped along Darcy's nerves.

"Certainly the driver was either too scared or callous to stop. At present we can't infer more than that miss, but hit-and-run is a serious crime. We'll get the culprit – I promise you that."

Darcy sighed with impatience and frustration.

"You are not hearing me, are you sergeant?" She walked to the window, stared sightlessly out at the concrete paths and geranium beds that latticed the hospital grounds. "Caro was wearing my coat," she said, turning to face him again and speaking with slow deliberation. "I was the intended victim! Caro bought it for me!" Tears of guilt and remorse welled up, and Darcy blinked several times as they threatened to overspill. For a moment Drigg watched her through jaundiced eyes, then turned to the ward sister.

"Miss West is obviously still very upset. We'll give her a few minutes more before taking her statement."

Digging his hands deep into bulging coat pockets, he jerked his head at his companion and slouched from the room, constable in tow.

Darcy, her protests unheeded, was ushered to a waiting area whilst Caro underwent tests and X-rays. From the public telephone next to the drinks machine, she dialled Frank's number and tried not to mind when he pressed for a report of the incident, knowing it was for insertion in the evening edition. She gave him the details, striving for professionalism despite the hysteria that threatened to bubble up and constrict her throat.

"Don't worry about a thing, kid. Take all the time you need," he said, and she almost broke down.

"I'll be in tomorrow morning Frank."

"You don't have to—"

"I'll be okay."

"Good girl. Look," his fruity-rich voice deepened with warmth and concern, "how about I come and pick you up at the hospital when you're through?"

"That's good of you Frank, but I'll be fine," she said swiftly, both touched and alarmed by the depth of feeling his words conveyed.

"I thought you might need some company this evening – a bit of sympathy you know."

"I do appreciate your kindness, but I need to be alone."

"Okay Darcy, but if there is anything I can do", his voice thickened with emotion, "anything at all—"

"I'll let you know. Now I have to go."

The last thing she needed, Darcy reflected on replacing the receiver, was to become embroiled in Frank's marital problems.

The sister-in-charge refused her admission to the ward where Caro was eventually taken, but the young duty doctor, seeing her distress, took pity.

"Strictly speaking it should be relatives only," he warned, "so I can only let you have a few minutes."

"Thanks, doctor. How is she?"

"It's too early to say. Again, I should only give this information to relatives, but I will tell you there is a break to the right ulna, a fracture to the left tibia and a couple of cracked ribs. The good news is, there is no skull fracture."

"Thank God for that." Darcy let out her breath on a long sigh of relief, but then her eyes darkened with anxiety. "But has she regained consciousness yet?"

"No," he admitted with obvious reluctance. The houseman looked grave. "And that, rather than the peripheral injuries, is causing us some concern."

Darcy looked at the floor and struggled for control.

"So what does it mean?"

"It could be that she is badly concussed – if so she is one lucky lady."

"And if not?"

He shook his head and looked uncomfortable.

"We can't rule out the possibility of brain damage. A few minutes remember," he added, and disappeared before Darcy could question him further.

She sat beside Caro's bed, surrounded by impersonal plastic and chrome that winked beneath the cold glare of fluorescent lighting. Caro lay motionless as a corpse, her face as white as the bandages that swathed her arm and head. The room was filled with the clinical odours of saline solution and antiseptic, and resounded with the rhythmical shhh, shhussha-shush followed by a muted clunk from the artificial sighing of bellows attached to a ventilator.

"Caro?" she whispered, leaning as close as possible given that the bed was surrounded by machines from which protruded tubes inserted in Caro's arm and nostril. "I'm sorry, Caro. Sorry for getting you into this nightmare," she whispered, the tears running silent and unheeded down her face. "It should have been me – not you."

Caro might have been killed. That thought kept running through her mind, filling her with dread. As it was, she was lying here in a coma and may not pull through, or if she did, might suffer brain damage. Sunk in misery, Darcy started and whipped round as the rings of the curtains screening the bed rattled on the rail. Was Caro not safe even here? Heart and pulse pounding she stared at the man framed in the opening.

TWENTY-TWO

Several terror-filled seconds passed before Darcy let out her breath on a sigh of relief.

"Brian!" She was only slightly acquainted with Caro's husband and had not at first recognised the tall gangly man with sandy hair advancing towards the bed. His features, placid whenever she had seen him, were strained with worry and his skin, usually ruddy with the horticulturist's year-round weathering, had the waxy texture and pallor of the lilies he held in his hand. "Caro!"

Darcy cringed at the anguish in his hoarse whisper and was ravaged by guilt. The blooms were dropped and left disregarded at the foot of the bed as he bent anxiously over his wife.

Darcy touched his shoulder, saying as he turned:

"Here's my card, Brian. Please call me if there is any change. Day or night," she surveyed his face anxiously as though expecting to see anger and recrimination mirrored there, but then he did not know the facts. "You will, won't you?"

"Of course." He ran a hand through his hair in a distracted manner so that it stood up in spikes on his crown. "And thanks Darcy for being there for her, for waiting until I came."

"It was the least I could do." Darcy swallowed, choked by emotion.

"What about yourself?" Brian gave her an anxious look.

"I'm all right. The police, did they—"

"Hit and run, they said. The bastard. If she dies I'll—"

"Don't say that, Brian. Don't even think it!" Her gaze went to the bed and lingered over Caro's still form, then to the machine that was breathing for her and, it seemed, sighing a lament. "She has to pull through."

"You're right. We have to be positive. Thanks for everything." Brian squeezed her hand before moving to the chair at Caro's bedside.

As Darcy left him, she could not help wondering how he would react if he knew the truth, that Caro had been mowed down by mistake through wearing her friend's jacket. She hurried out of the ward, head bowed in distress. The C.I.D. officers were waiting as she entered the corridor.

"Are you ready now miss?" Sergeant Drigg asked lugubriously. Darcy, still sunk in her own thoughts, stared stupidly at him, then sighed as memory returned and wearily she nodded.

"Sister says we can take your statement in her office rather than at the station."

"Thank you."

"This way, please miss." The constable placed a hand on her arm; Darcy pulled away and followed him down the corridor.

"So, you're a reporter, are you?" he said conversationally as she took a seat.

"Yes." Only this, she thought wretchedly, is one scoop I would have given anything to have missed.

****

They had not believed her story. In vain she tried to convince them of the events that led to the attempt on Caro's life. The sense of being stalked over the past weeks, the repression of her report, even the mysterious death of Dr. Piper had been politely taken in, rationalised and explained away. There was nothing with which to counter their scepticism; she could offer only hints, hunches and suspicions whilst hard facts were their only consideration. No, she told them, she had not noted the vehicle's registration number, it had all happened so fast. Drigg did not fail to point out that it had been Caro's room and not hers that had been ransacked, so any premeditation would seem to be levelled at Caro rather than herself. Worse still, he had a point. In the end, she gave up trying to convince them and retreated to the solitude of her flat.

Wearily, she let herself in and dropping her bag onto a chair poured herself a large brandy and swallowed half. The spirit ran like liquid fire down her throat and into her stomach, briefly melting the icy ball of fear that had lodged there. Someone had tried to kill Caro. The rest of the brandy followed and marginally helped. She sat for a moment recalling how, on turning back, she had seen Inspector Drigg and the ward sister deep in conversation. Obviously her fear and suspicion had been dismissed as the result of shock.

Something else, less tangible but more disturbing, was causing her anxiety. The premonition, the flashes and images prior to Caro stepping off the kerb that had served to alert her and hopefully save Caro's life. That, and the by now familiar perfume, and the sense of somebody at her back. It was almost as though the long-dead Knight Templar had intervened with a timely warning. Crazy, but it was hard to dispel the feeling of a mutual back-scratching operation, a sort of 'I'll keep you safe to tell my story' routine.

Food was the last thing that appealed, but a wave of dizziness sent her into the kitchen. Falling apart was not the way to help Caro, she decided, and managed a bowl of soup followed by yoghurt. She had to keep up her strength in case Brian called in the night. An emergency – what a dreadful thought. She lowered her head on her arms then and wept, wiping her cheeks with the back of her hands when the tears were exhausted. The temptation to call Brant was strong, but she decided to wait until there was positive news. Somehow, to tell him now was to tempt fate. So much for the hard-nosed rational reporter intent on debunking myth. After wallowing in a hot bath she donned clean clothes and dumped duvet and pillows on the settee in preparation for the night's vigil.

Darcy slept fitfully on the settee, fully dressed and in dread of the telephone ringing. However, the night passed without the dreaded call from Brian. As did the next one, but unable to stand the waiting and inactivity any longer, she called Brian and asked him if he could arrange for her to visit.

Friday evening saw her back at Caro's bedside,

courtesy of the friendly house doctor after Brian had pleaded her cause.

"Five minutes," he warned, his look of severity given the lie by the liking that lurked in his eyes, an interest that had the circumstances been different, Darcy may well have been tempted to explore. Caro's condition was still 'critical'. Dark smudges underscored her eyes, as though someone had dipped their thumbs in purple eye shadow and smeared it beneath the lids. Her skin had the same waxy pallor, her face that sense of vacancy that said there was no-one at home. Brian had remained at her bedside day and night, apart from this brief respite, and even now
he had only gone for a stroll in the grounds and a cup
of coffee in the canteen.

"Caro," Darcy whispered, her voice breaking as she leaned over her friend, trying by sheer force of will to infuse the still form on the bed with some of her own vitality. "Caro, can you hear me? Don't leave us, Caro. "Please come back!"
The bellows sighed and softly clunked, and Caro's
eyes remained firmly shut, her mind in flight to some
alien world.

On returning to his wife's bedside, Brian took one
look at Darcy's face and told her firmly to take a
break over the weekend. "Go to your cottage and get
some rest. You can do nothing here, Darcy. They won't
let you visit again – tonight was a favour. I'm the only
one allowed in until she is out of danger." he reasoned.
"Oh but I couldn't—," she started to protest, but
Brian interrupted.
"Yes, you could, and you must! It won't help Caro if you drop from exhaustion. I promise I'll let you know immediately if there's any change."

Darcy wavered. It would be a relief to do something
instead of sitting around feeling helpless, and,
she remembered with a pleasurable buzz followed by
a pang of guilt as she glanced at Caro's lifeless form

155

on the bed, she was meant to be meeting Brant the
following night. The need to confide and seek comfort
in his calm, common sense was overwhelming.
But there was another powerful argument too: the
planned visit to Monk Grange and the mysterious
Miles Standish. The best way to help Caro now was
to track down her would-be assassin.
"Do it Darcy, it's for the best," Brian urged, as conflicting
emotions flitted across her features.

In the end she capitulated, and on returning to the flat
from the hospital, packed an overnight bag, threw it
into the boot and set off for the cottage. Driving at speed on the
motorway, then through the emptiness of a deserted moonscape
and on to narrow lanes engulfed in darkness all brought their
own brand of relief. But the journey eventually ended and there
remained the silence and loneliness of the night. Saved by
exhaustion, she dropped into bed and sank almost immediately
into oblivion.

****

The following morning brought typical Lakeland
weather that changed by the minute. As Darcy drove
from the cottage, brassy sunlight sped through the valley
flooding it with a light that, by contrast with the lowering sky,
seemed unnaturally vivid. Then armies of cumulus marched in
from the West and the sun was swiftly extinguished, and the
countryside plunged into gloom. The road which snaked up
and over the fell brought yet another change: storm clouds were
ousted by snowy cumulus above reaches of sun-bronzed
heather and bracken, and the treeless, uninhabited moor
seemed a friendlier place. However, as a misty sea came into
view and she dropped down to St. Gildas Bay, the sky lowered
once more.

Light and shade patterned the backdrop of cliff and
fell in rapid succession as though, she could not help

156

thinking, some mischievous cosmic joker manipulated
a dimmer switch at will. She drove through the village, past the
Old Forge on her left, over a level crossing and parked by rusty
gates bearing a faded plaque that told her this was Monk
Grange. Tall chimneys poked their heads above a tangle of
trees. The iron gate groaned and squealed as she pushed it
open. Her feet released the mingled aroma of thyme, lavender
and chamomile as they trod a path that also sprouted a myriad
daisies and dandelions. It led her through an overgrown garden
that once must have been magnificent but which now struggled
under neglect.

Even so, it was a riot of colour, with a tangle of
laburnum, hawthorn and lilac blossom all vying for light and
space. Swathes of dock and nettle choked the pink and blue
inhabitants of the herbaceous border. She paused, struck by the
poignancy of a crumbling stone cupid standing knee-high in a
sea of ox-eye daisies, but also because a sense of oppression
was creeping into the garden. Pushing aside sweeps of purple-
flowered clematis that wound its way through the gnarled
branches of an apple tree on one side of the path, and an
ancient plum tree on the other, she stopped to look and listen.
There were no signs of human habitation. The only sounds
were the buzzing of insects, drone of bees and the twitter and
chatter of countless birds. On drawing closer to the house, the
aura of unease deepened.

The Grange was a rambling Victorian house built of
local stone and Green Westmorland slate that. like the garden,
displayed signs of neglect with peeling paint and faded chintz at
the windows. It was not her idea of an accountant's residence.
Unconsciously, she had expected a well-maintained house
surrounded by clipped hedges, tidy beds and scrupulously
weeded paths, a property in keeping with neat sets of books
and precise rows of figures. Miles Standish could be elderly, she
mused, but Caro had not said that he was retired. Maybe he
was an eccentric, yet accountants and eccentricity somehow
didn't gel, were a contradiction in terms.

The ringing of the door bell brought no response so she pressed it again. There was no sound of doors opening or approaching feet, only a furtiveness that fuelled a feeling of being watched. Quelling a strong desire to run back to the car, she walked round the side of the house in search of another entrance. Country people did not usually use the front door, it followed that they probably paid little attention to callers who approached it.

The rear garden was brooded over by a dark yew hedge. An octagonal summer house was almost hidden by a rambling rose bearing a profusion of white blooms; more roses framed the back door of the house. After knocking and gaining no response, she peered through the old-fashioned bottle-glass panes but could see only a distorted image of table and chairs beyond. She rapped again on the panels, then walked round the house with the intention of making her way back to the path and the car. Pausing at the French windows she grasped the tarnished handle and turned it. To her surprise the door swung inwards at her touch. The sense of being observed was so strong now that she paused, reluctant to continue. There followed a moment of indecision, of nervous glances over her shoulder. However, the reporter's prime maxim 'never pass up an opportunity' propelled her over the threshold.

The drawing-room in which she found herself must once have been elegant, but now brought to mind dust sheets and over-blown roses at summer's end. A grand piano had settled beneath a mantel of dust, and the poppies adorning the paper above the dado had faded from red to insipid pink.
"Hello?" she called, but nobody answered and nothing stirred. A second try resulted in a similar lack of response. She wandered around the room, scanning the faded paintings that lined the wall. In the main they were Victorian watercolours of silver rose bowls on polished tables and children or small dogs held by females with ethereal faces posing under blossom-laden trees. One, however, stood out from the rest. She stopped before the sepia drawing of St. Gildas priory in the days before

it lapsed into ruin. What a pity Miles Standish was not at home to answer her questions about it.

Engrossed in speculation about the picture, the sound of a door opening at her back made her gasp and whirl round. A scream strangled by fear escaped from her throat. Petrified, like a rabbit caught in a poacher's beam, she stared at the man, and the gun in his hands.
"You!" she cried, backing away from the barrel until her spine bumped against the wall. Rheumy eyes regarded her from under brows that were hard to forget: black slashes on a white face that gave him an expression of permanent shock. She was facing the man who had stalked her since the day of the post mortem.

TWENTY-THREE

He was standing full square in the doorway, the shotgun levelled at her chest. Stupid, absolutely stupid, she silently berated herself: nobody knew her whereabouts and Brant did not expect her until eight that evening. And by then it could be too late, came the chilling thought.

"Who are you?" he snapped.

"You must already know so why ask?"

"Don't be smart miss!" The barrel inched up a few centimetres higher.

"Why have you been following me?" she demanded, then immediately regretted her aggression as he scowled and the hands on the gun shook with anger.

"I like to know who is sticking their nose in my business – and why."

Darcy raised a hand to run it through her hair, then cringed as he reacted by levelling the sights at her head. Nonetheless she managed a watery smile.

"Forgive me for barging in like this, but I did call out," she added in a conversational manner, seeking to defuse the situation. His eyes held a manic look: too much white and a fixed stare. This man knew I was here from the moment I opened the gate, she realised with certainty. Still he did not speak. "As I guess you already know, I'm Darcy West, a reporter with the Manchester News," she tried again, then added quickly as he recoiled and raised a hand as though to physically ward her off, "But I'm not here in my official capacity. A friend gave me your name. I'm interested in local history, especially the priory." She risked a glance over her shoulder at the picture to demonstrate that she recognised it and therefore was serious in her quest for information.

He watched her for a moment in silence, head to one side like an inquisitive bird, then snapped:

"What friend?"

Darcy thought on her feet. The chances were he would not know Caro, but may be acquainted with a county neighbour.

"Brant Kennedy."

The gun barrel dipped slightly. Darcy tensed herself and inching towards the French windows prepared to risk flight.

"You know him?" she persisted.

"I've heard of him."

Darcy stopped clenching her teeth in fear as he lowered the gun to his side.

"I've been longer than I intended. I had better be going – he's waiting for me," she lied, taking an experimental step towards the French windows, then sucking in her breath and freezing as the gun was raised again. The manic eyes narrowed and his pinched features took on a foxy look.

"You came alone."

"If you saw me, why didn't you answer the doorbell?" she demanded, frustration temporarily overcoming fear. "You could have spared us both this charade."

She closed her eyes and held her breath, waiting for the report of the gun. When none came, she opened them again and blinked hard, stunned by what she saw. He had leaned the gun against a mahogany bookcase and was smiling.

"Miles Standish," he said courteously, hand outstretched. "My apologies Miss West, but one cannot be too careful. Last week a house in the village was ransacked. A young woman played decoy to get the elderly lady to open the door for the scoundrels."

He is a liar. He is also mad, Darcy thought dispassionately, reluctantly taking the proffered hand. Darcy watched him, aware that his behaviour was volatile.

"Look, I'm sorry to have intruded like this, I'll go now." She took another backward step towards the glass doors then jumped and paused as he barked:

"Come back here!" in a voice that cracked across her nerves like a whip.

"But I—"

The mask of courtesy had momentarily slipped, but was swiftly tugged back into place and he was smiling again.

"My fault entirely. Not your fault – no." He paused and again that bird-like posturing of the head as he murmured as though to himself: "Quite right: should have opened the door. French windows, yes, how stupid." A worried frown creased his forehead and his fingers made a minute scratching sound as he stroked the stubble that shadowed his chin. "Come into the kitchen, I've just brewed a pot of tea," he said brightly. Darcy eyed him warily, but decided he was not out to do her harm. Given the sheen of perspiration over his face, and the way his hands twiddled nervously with the buttons of a cardigan enamelled down the front with dribbles of dried egg yolk, it was he who was afraid. But of whom or what? To leave now was to give up the chance of an answer.

"I can only stay a few minutes. If I don't meet Brant as arranged, he'll come looking for me," she added as a precaution.

The table at which they were sitting was littered with newspaper clippings and sheets of typed and handwritten notes. The air smelled musty and damp with a background odour of rotting vegetables, soured milk and stale sweat. Mouse droppings soiled the floor and sink.

"More tea?"

"No milk thanks," she reminded him, going along with the game whilst eying with distaste the cheesy mess of congealed milk in the stained bottle. Taking her mug he poured the untouched tea down a butler sink, the once-white enamel of which was streaked with brown stains, and refilled it.

Darcy reluctantly drew her attention from a page depicting a family tree: Montgomery and De Quincy were two familiar names that leapt out. They had been talking now for about half an hour, and she had learned much of the priory and its former inhabitants. She had also gleaned that Miles Standish was married but that his wife and teenage son and daughter had 'gone away'. Whether this referred to a holiday or something more sinister he did not say, but given the state of neglect that characterised both himself and the house, it was safe to assume the latter.

She covertly watched him dump the mug before her, spilling its contents over several of the papers. This was the last thing she had expected, this young-old man whose age was an enigma. Thirty something? The lack of grey in his mousy hair and the unlined skin seemed to bear this out, but the greyness of flesh and pinched cheeks suggested someone much older. Or was he prematurely aged by fear? Her reporter's nose told her he had something to give.
"Fascinating stuff, the history of the priory – but what I'm really interested in is the Order of the Knights Templar," she gambled. His reaction was startling: his hand trembled violently and tea slopped over the table; saliva dribbled from the slack mouth onto his stubbled chin.
"They have sent you," he whispered. He was deluded, and thought she was part of a conspiracy, Darcy realised. She rose and eased the teapot from his uncertain grip then placed a hand on his shoulder.
"No. It's all right, I promise." she soothed, distressed by his terror. "No-one sent me."

He looked up beseechingly, like a child seeking reassurance after waking from a nightmare. He rose abruptly and moving to a glass-fronted cupboard took out a bottle of whisky. As he poured some of the spirit into a mug and gulped it down, Darcy scanned the notes that littered the table. Her hunch was correct: they contained the lineage of the noble houses of the North.
"Sorry about that," he said, turning to face her again, his mask and accountant's precise voice back in place. "Stupid of me. Like some?" he added, brandishing the bottle. Darcy had been about to refuse but in time realised this may be taken as

163

rejection. The best way to get him to open up was to go along with the game but make sure he did the drinking. "A drop in my tea," she conceded, sitting down again and holding out her mug.

"You followed us to the farmhouse and left that rat outside the door, didn't you?" she said in a matter of fact way to draw him out.

"Meant no harm. Only wanted to frighten you off" he muttered, his eyes roving to door and window as though seeking a means of escape.

"Is that why you have been dogging me these past weeks?"

"Yes – no!" He wavered, about to say more but appearing as confused as Darcy was mystified.

"Go on," she prompted, seeking to understand.

"I hung about. The hospital, you know. Post mortem. Daren't attend. No, they were there, you see," he gabbled, the whites of his eyes showing more than ever. "Your name on the list. Thought you might help. No!" he shouted suddenly causing her to almost knock over her filthy cup, "One of them! Won't help poor Miles. She wants to kill him, shut him up for good." He covered his eyes with a forearm and whimpered like a hurt child.

"It's alright, Miles," she soothed, beginning at last to understand. His motives for stalking her had been as divided as his schizoid mind. Her presence at the post mortem and the report in the paper, coupled with his subsequent spying, had all revealed her preoccupation with St. Gildas Man. During paranoid episodes, he had thought her 'one of them' and had tried to scare her off; in his saner moments, she realised, he had followed her for a very different reason. In his fear and isolation he was desperate to reach out to someone who apparently shared his obsession, but lacked the courage to actually make an approach.

"There is a connection, isn't there Miles, between the body they found, the Knights Templar – and whatever it is you are afraid of."

164

He swallowed his whisky, then poured more into the cup and ignored her question. Suddenly she banged her fist on the table.

"Let's stop pretending here! My friend is maybe dying and I want some answers."

He leapt up and backed against the wall. As she also began to rise, he slid down it to the floor and sat there whimpering, reminding her forcibly of a baby bereft of loving attention. His head sunk to his chest and he raised his arms, covering his eyes with his forearms. His fingers clawed his shoulders in a desperate self-hug.

"Don't!" Darcy knelt beside him. "I mean you no harm, Miles," she soothed, moved and appalled by this extreme reaction. Grasping his wrists, she forced his arms from his face. "Come and sit down," she coaxed, standing up and extending her hand and thus offering help in a timeless gesture. "I promise to do what I can." Speaking reassuringly, she managed to guide him back to his seat. He watched her for a moment, his eyes fixed and owl-like, then fumbled in his pocket and brought out a battered pack of cigarettes and a lighter. Mentally she checked the brand: Marlborough - not Black Russian. His hands shook, and he dropped the lighter onto the table.

"That's right. You have a smoke and a drink," Darcy soothed, picking up the lighter and, clicking it, she offered the flame. "You'll find talking about it will help." Miles Standish's expression suddenly changed.

"You first," he said with a crafty look, "Tell me what you know and where you fit in."

Darcy's hesitation was fractional.

"No problem." He might trust her then and open up. She proceeded to relate the story, starting from Caro's finding of St. Gildas Man and omitting only the details of her quasi-mystical experience and her relationship with Brant. "So that's my involvement to date," she concluded, shaking her head as he proffered the packet of cigarettes and drew out another for himself. She stubbed out the previous one which he had left smouldering in the brimming ash tray; he cringed at the movement.

"Now you," she rapped, capitalising on his fear. Standish took another swallow of whisky and stammered.

"I'll try."

"Don't try - tell it!" She relented at his expression, fearful of initiating another panic attack. "Just start at the beginning, Miles."

Hesitantly he began to talk, then fluently and with growing confidence as the floodgates opened.

"And as you may already know," he continued, still eyeing her with distrust but speaking with a stronger voice, "the Templars were basically an order of monks, but a military order ordained originally to police the Holy Land at the time of the Crusades. Over the years they amassed immense wealth and power which placed them above the law of the land, and the rule of kings and queens. Eventually they were beyond even the jurisdiction of the Pope. They were virtually untouchable, and that is power indeed. How? Ask yourself how they could have achieved this."

Darcy shrugged. "I have no idea."

"No because it is the world's most closely guarded secret. The biggest cover-up since Adam's cock-up in the Garden of Eden!"

At this, Darcy suppressed a smile: mad he certainly was, but sexist he was not. His face took on a crafty, vulpine expression.

"I can tell you how though."

Whatever, he knows his stuff, she thought watching his face as he outlined years of research, countless 'lost documents' and frustrating denials from the world's reference libraries and museums in response to requests for information, and anonymous threats of violence when he persisted in that research. Either that or he possessed the greatest imagination since Tolkein.

"I don't believe it," she said at last, rising to her feet. "Not a bloody word of it!"

"Don't be naive," he snapped, suddenly lucid and

166

assertive. He tapped his cigarette so that the accumulation of ash at the end dropped onto the table. "I thought you were a journalist."

"So?"

"Yet you reject ideas just because they are controversial." Professional pride stinging, Darcy hesitated, then slowly sat down again.

"Let me get this right – you are asking me to believe that the Templars achieved their wealth through practising alchemy." She waited impatiently as Miles Standish lit another cigarette from the smouldering butt of the last one.

"It is an accepted theory. You have to remember that alchemy was not only the forerunner of modern Science, but also a spiritual discipline, a sort of 'alternative Christianity'. Remember, the Templars were basically a religious order. In order to release precious substances from Mother Earth via the basic elements of fire, air, earth and water, practitioners had to show great self-discipline. The laboratory was a shrine where they underwent inner changes."

"Like shamans in their caves?" Darcy scoffed.

Miles Standish scowled his disapproval.

"Don't mock what you do not understand. It has always been known that ancient sacred texts – even the Bible – contain encoded messages." He leaned forward across the table, his previously weary eyes alight with the fanatic's enthusiasm for his subject. "Processes used in planetary imaging are now being adapted to access ancient texts. The new technology has unlocked the secret but it is known to only a few."

"Planetary imaging?" Darcy repeated, recalling Brant's observatory. Coincidence – or something more? A comment Brant had made half rose from the depths of memory then sank like a stone, spreading ripples of unease but settling just beyond recall. He nodded, his expression manic and his fingers constantly sifting through the papers that littered the table. "For example, it is currently being used to interpret and decode the Dead Sea Scrolls of Nag Hammadi."

Darcy frowned and stared out of the grubby panes of the window to the gloom of the garden beyond.

"But," she said turning back to him with a frown, "given the interested parties apparently have the power to suppress Piper's death, then slap a Public Immunity Certificate on the contamination incident, plus dispose of a valuable preserved body, then we must assume they are in a position to access secret information. If so, why the fuss over St. Gildas Man?"

Miles Standish looked uncertain about the wisdom of divulging more. Then he shrugged his thin shoulders, and apparently deciding that he had already said enough for it to make little difference, continued:

"Because whilst the secret texts reveal much, one vital secret remains."

"And I think I know what it is," Darcy interrupted. Someone is wondering what happened to their treasure – and can't wait to get their hands on it!"

He smiled wanly. "A creditable effort. But even the Templar fortune dwindles to insignificance in the light of the real prize."

"Which is?

"The formula."

"Formula?" Darcy frowned and tried to suppress her impatience as he rose for the whisky bottle, splashed some of its contents into his cold tea and sat down again. "Oh, you mean for transforming base metal into gold?"

"That," he nodded, " and forming the Philosopher's Stone."

TWENTY-FOUR

The silence that followed was broken by a series of squeaks issuing from a dark corner. Darcy suppressed a shudder at a glimpse of a long, leathery tail disappearing through a hole in the skirting. "You speak with great fluency and authority for a mad man," she scoffed to cover her fear at both sight of the rat and this most bizarre of situations. Miles Standish's mouth puckered like that of a sulky child.

"Please yourself. You asked – and I gave you the answer." Darcy watched him in silence for several minutes whilst absently twirling the head of a matchstick in the pile of ash spilt on the table.

"Is it true? Does it really exist?" she said at last, throwing down the match in disgust as the stale stench of tobacco rose and offended her nostrils.

Miles Standish peered owlishly at her as storm clouds gathered beyond the window and the gloom inside the kitchen deepened.

"It is true to say that 'your knight' was a Templar, and that the Templars knew about alchemy and the transmutation of base metals to gold." The unpleasant smile implied arcane knowledge, "It is also true that there are those today who believe what you do not. Those who will kill to possess and keep the secret. And those now, as then, who have the power to suppress information. Gold is a beautiful but terrible mistress. She drives men and women to unspeakable things. You must know of the present scandal concerning Nazis, gold teeth and murdered Jews."

He smiled unpleasantly again as Darcy gave an in involuntary shudder. "Horrific isn't it? We cannot imagine human beings stooping that low. But they will – for the secret of how to 'make' gold. And it seems the Templars went beyond this, to discover the secret of tissue renewal and therefore, it might be said, of immortality. Their symbol for this was the Philosopher's Stone. What price would man pay for that?"

"It doesn't really matter if it exists or not, does it?" Darcy said in a low voice, "As long someone believes it does. That's enough to fuel the greed."

"Now you begin to understand." He spoke with growing confidence as though deriving strength from sharing the burden of his knowledge. "Ask yourself: the Templar's body – where is it now? Is anyone willing to tell you? You had better believe me Miss West, because you are in grave danger."

"It's the reason your wife left, isn't it? Darcy whispered as despair crept in. "And all this," Darcy gestured with her hand at the debris and filth that littered the kitchen.

"For being holed up here looking like a tramp?" he said bitterly. "Fear does that to people you know."

Suddenly he rose, his self control cracking like ice on a puddle beneath a jack boot.

"Get out! Go now and forget all you have learnt, before it does the same for you." He unbolted the kitchen door, opened it and peered cautiously to left and right.

"May I come back next week?" she ventured, pausing in the doorway. He shifted his weight from one foot to the other.

"I would like that," he said eventually, with an appeal in his eyes that moved her to pity. His shoulders slumped and he seemed to retreat within himself as he added with a worried look, "But in allowing you to come here again I may be responsible for your death, or mine – or both."

"I'm prepared to risk it if you are." She watched the conflicting emotions war in his face as he struggled between fear and the need for a confidante. Finally, he nodded.

"Next Saturday then."

"Thank you. Now before I leave, are you going to tell me Miles?"
That crafty look again. "Tell you what?"
"Oh come on! His name." She hid her impatience and gave him a pleading look adding "You know it, don't you?"

His face took on a closed expression and he folded his arms across his chest. "If I did, I wouldn't tell you and add to your danger. Now go!" he shouted as Darcy would have protested. Taking her arm, he bundled her with surprising strength through the door.
"Make sure you are not followed here."
Miles Standish's anxious voice followed her down the overgrown path, grew fainter and finally died.

The reason for not divulging the Templar's name was to ensure her return, Darcy realised with resentment. She pushed aside dripping foliage and waded through drenched undergrowth; the rain was driven by a north-easterly that needled her face and chilled her bones. Violet-brown nimbus threatened thunder, and the air crackled with static. Moisture-laden trees loomed over her, dark and threatening with a Company of Wolves feel, and in the distance the fells brooded, scowled and hunched their backs against a leaden sky. It was with a sense of relief that she passed through the gate, into the lane and quickly climbed into the car.

As she drove through the village and over the level crossing, she sifted her memory without success for the connection between something Brant had said and Miles Standish's story. In her time as a reporter, she reflected driving back to Mistletoe Cottage, she had never come across anything this bizarre. Miles Standish had to be either undergoing a breakdown or be suffering from paranoid schizophrenia. Yet there was a coherence to his story, and he told it with assurance and patent scholarship. Obviously, he had invested a great deal of time and effort in research. So, the ranting of a madman or the revelations of a scholar? The truth, she guessed, lay somewhere between the two extremes. The myth of the Philosopher's Stone had appealed to his deluded mind and taken hold, had become a symbol perhaps for the crazy, scary happenings that had disrupted a previously normal and ordered life.

The reality of Templar wealth and power was a matter of historical fact, and she could well believe that the search to locate the former and thus obtain the latter could still excite rivalry and greed. Not only in academic circles either, she realised, her brow furrowed with concentration as the car negotiated a hairpin bend and seventy per cent gradient in response to her hands on the wheel. Given the extent of the treasure, and also the mystique and rather sinister aura surrounding the Templars, it could be a very attractive acquisition for anyone seeking to influence others and incite fanaticism in their following. Such a quest may conceivably also breed obsession and ruthlessness in the seeker. So maybe there was some justification for the man's paranoia about his safety.

The car wandered to mid road as a devastating thought struck: had Brant Kennedy been aware of Miles Standish's condition, and if so had he deliberately kept silent about it? She pulled the car back on course. *Take care, you are rather special to me.* Suddenly the words that had given her pleasure now took on a sinister meaning. Take care because he knew she was walking into danger? She shook her head at the ridiculousness of the notion. Nevertheless, she would challenge him over dinner.

He met her as arranged at the Old Priory in St. Gildas village and they left immediately for the farmhouse on the cliffs. Throughout the journey, she covertly watched him, searching for signs of guilt about her visit to Monk Grange. He showed none, and given that he made no mention of it Darcy could only assume a complete absence of curiosity. As they neared their destination she broke the news of Caro's 'accident'.

172

"Why didn't you tell me before now?" Brant demanded as he ushered her into the kitchen and bolted the door.

"It all happened so quickly, then the longer I left it—," she faltered to a halt as he turned to confront her and she saw the pain in his eyes.

"Four, five days is it now? And no time to make a lousy 'phone call?" he accused.

"I'm sorry Brant," Darcy began looking stricken. "I didn't realise—"

"That I would want to be there for you?"

"I'm sorry," she repeated, realising he wished to be needed and she had succeeded in making him feel the complete outsider. "Please forgive me," she added miserably.

A minute or so passed, during which time he visibly struggled with his feelings but then he forced a smile.

"Okay, we won't fight about it." He touched her cheek briefly with a finger. "Let's have a drink then some dinner." He poured a gin and tonic and a whisky for himself and they sipped them while setting the table. From the Aga, Brant took a dish of pasta bubbling with cheese and fragrant with basil. When they had eaten, they carried wine and glasses into the sitting room to drink before a blazing log fire. The wood smoke was fragrant, the mood mellow and the setting idyllic but Darcy reluctantly knew it was time to speak.

"I visited Monk Grange this morning," she said casually, offering her glass for a refill as he held out the bottle.

"You saw old Miles then?"

"I did." The irony in her voice must have registered but he failed to react. He picked up a log from the basket and added it to the blaze.

"And was he helpful?"

"Oh very. Once he had overcome the desire to blow off my head."

Brant paused in dusting-off his hands on his denims and raised his eyebrows.

"Miles? We can't be talking about the same guy."

Darcy flicked a stray curl behind her ear and her eyes narrowed.

"You didn't know he was crazy?"

"No idea. The poor sod." He rubbed the side of his nose and looked away, unable to meet her steady gaze. "Tell me about it," he added, bending down to pick up another log. Behaviour, Darcy thought watching him and drawing on her experience with interviewees, that indicated he was lying through his attractive white teeth.

"You must have known," she accused, putting down her glass on the low table with a decided snap.

"No." He answered calmly and with a hint of amusement in his eyes. "Suspected something a tad odd maybe," he added. "One hears gossip."

"So you let me go in without so much of a warning!"

"Come, you're a big girl now Darcy. And in your line of work – well, I guessed you were intrepid enough to deal with any danger."

"I could have been killed Brant Kennedy!"

"I trusted you to look after yourself."

"Gee, thanks."

"That's enough."

His eyes lost the look of lazy amusement and took on the grey of an iced winter tarn.

"I was unaware of his true condition. If I had told you he might be well, unsound, you wouldn't have gone there."

Darcy was about to protest at this, then the truth dawned and she said angrily instead:

"Correct. And you couldn't risk going there in case you were seen, because that would have blown your cover. You were using me to get a report on Miles Standish and an update on the script at Monk Grange."

"I don't know what you are driving at," he said coldly.

"Don't try to tell me you are not mixed up in all this."

He shrugged, his face tight with anger.

"Our lines of research sometimes intersected."

"What research?"

"Keep out of this Darcy. Drop your stupid inquiry."

174

"Of course! Darcy clicked her fingers. "That's the
second reason you let me go there without warning.
To frighten me off. You didn't bargain on my staying
long enough for Miles Standish to spill the beans."
Brant's hands clasped her shoulders.
"And did he?"

She stared at him without answering, suddenly afraid at
the coldness and intensity of his expression and the way his
eyes had narrowed.
"Well did he?" His grip on her shoulders tightened and she
tried to squirm free.
"You're hurting me,
Brant."
"Answer!"
Self-preservation clicked into place.
"I don't know what you mean," she evaded, "he talked some
rubbish about alchemy and somebody being after him, but he's
obviously paranoid. God, the place looked, and stank, like a
midden! You couldn't believe a word the man said," she said
with a dismissive gesture.

She tried to hide her discomfort as Brant looked hard and
long into her face, then as though satisfied with what he saw
there, released his grip. He ran his fingers through his hair and
sighed.
"Whatever you may think, I was worried about you. As it
happens, it was partly your fault."
"How did you work that one out?" she said indignantly,
rubbing her shoulder.
"If you had told me earlier about Caro, I would not have let
you go to Monk Grange."
"You're a high-handed bastard!"
"Catch 22!" He sighed with exasperation. "I was uncaring for
letting you go there, and now high-handed for saying had I
known I would not have allowed it."

Despite her annoyance, Darcy had to laugh. Soon

175

he was joining in, and the tense moment passed. She desisted from pressing him further as the look he gave her made it clear he would tolerate no more of her third degree routine.

"After all that I need the bathroom."

"Remember the way?" he quipped with a grin.

"Sure." She touched his arm in passing to show there were no hard feelings.

Once upstairs, she ran a comb through her curls and sprayed her wrists and neck with Ghost. How far could Brant be trusted? she wondered, staring at her face in the mirror. He had not actually lied about his involvement but was certainly guilty by way of evasion and omission. It made no difference to her feelings for him, but neither was she going to quit the investigation.

As she descended the oak staircase, Brant emerged from the sitting room. Without a word he took her into his arms. Initially the pressure of his lips against hers was light, his hand as he stroked her hair gentle as was her response. Then, as though rebelling at being held in check for so long, their emotions exploded. He pressed against her, drawing her to him as though to absorb her essence, and she clung to him with equal force. They broke apart and gasped for air, then collided again in a second embrace. It seemed all the waiting and quarrelling served to intensify this moment. They broke apart again, then laughed together self-consciously. Then the smiles died. He searched her face before appearing to suddenly make up his mind. Taking her by the hand, he led her up the stairs.

TWENTY-FIVE

The bedroom was dominated by a Victorian brass bed. He pulled her close, so that her body slid against his own as they kissed; it felt hard and muscular and suddenly Darcy had difficulty breathing.

"Are you sure about this?" he asked, holding her slightly away from himself to study her expression. She slipped in close again and moulded herself to his body whilst her hands answered his question. They paused and briefly broke apart, and their laboured breathing was the only sound in the room. But there was a distinctive aroma – and a familiar one. It wafted on the air, a mere hint, yet as distinct and sensual as the elusive bitter-sweet scent of intermingled lovers, then stronger and unmistakable as the clean citrus top notes were deepened and enhanced by undertones of cedar-wood, frankincense and oriental spice. Precious oils from the Middle East perhaps brought back by a Knight Templar.

Darcy stared intently at Brant, studying his face in the light from the landing that filtered through the partially open door. The breath caught in her throat: for a second his face appeared to change, to have superimposed upon it darker and less familiar features. But not totally unfamiliar. She had seen the black hair, aquiline nose and high cheekbones before, on the operating table of a hospital theatre. Ice-water trickled down her spine.

"What is it?"

Brant's whisper broke the spell. The image wavered and broke like a mirage in the desert allowing Brant's familiar features to surface. But then it reappeared, distorted and fragmented, only to be overlaid and lost again as two personalities seemed to war for possession of the same body.

"Darcy – what is it?" Brant repeated, holding her now at arm's length. The depth of concern in his voice and expression jerked her back to reality.

"Nothing," she murmured, trying to still the trembling of her limbs. "Just a trick of the light."

They stood like that for a full minute or more, looking at each other with growing intensity. His eyes had deepened and darkened to the greeny-grey of a slatey pool. She shuddered as their potency increased so that he seemed to look through her, piercing fragile flesh and bone to touch her soul. The perfume teased her senses, swirled inside her head and consumed her with desire. Suddenly they came together as though by instantaneous and mutual consent. His fingers fumbled with the buttons of her blouse, hers with his shirt. Within seconds they lay naked beneath the quilt of the huge brass bed.

Their lovemaking had about it an ecstasy and intensity that both frightened and drew her, like a moth to the flame. She wept silently as he suckled her breasts evoking unbearable tenderness. He licked the tears as they rolled down her cheeks, tasting them with the tip of his tongue. Then came a complete change of mood, and her head threshed wildly from side to side on the pillow, tendrils of hair streaking her face as his vigour unleashed undreamt of power and uninhibited passion. Up and up she climbed, thinking this must be the peak, only to soar, then slide and begin the ascent all over again.

Yet there was a core of fear at the heart of this passion, a deep dark pit which was drawing her in like the centre-pull of a whirlpool.

"Brant?" she cried, at the top of her voice yet only a feeble whisper sounded in her ears. Whirling, down, down, down towards the centre, a dark hole that slowly changed colour on drawing closer. It burned now with a fierce glow, a red inferno coloured by screams and tainted with the flesh of its victims. Flames rose from the pit's centre, licking her arms and legs and face and blackening her body.

"No! No!" Her screams were locked inside her throat. Brant pushed on, his rhythm increasing, pushing her closer to the rim.

Her skin was seared by agony now, her world reduced to vibrant, hungry devouring red, a red shift in time that threatened to claim her now as it had then.

What was she thinking? Was she going mad? Using every last shred of will-power, she mentally pushed back from the rim, closed her mind to the redness and saw only black behind her eyelids. A cool, dark, soothing black that poured balm on her burns and wrapped dying memory in its shroud.
"Darcy! Darcy?"
His cry drew her back to consciousness, and she clung to him like a drowning child to a rock. She stared up at him without recognition, struggling to find in his face the person she knew. The skin was olive-smooth and taut, the black hair vital, the nose aquiline and giving him a haughty look - the eyes an impossible green. Love swamped her; it seemed all the poignancy and sadness she felt for the unknown knight was focused here in this bed. An awareness of the timelessness of events suffused her, and brought tranquillity. As Wittgenstein once said: *whereof one cannot speak one must be silent.* No more questions, but acceptance of things sensed but not understood.

"Brant?" Never had there been anything like this. For a moment she held back then, pulled irresistibly forward by the momentum, let go and allowed herself to be swept along on the tide. She felt the contraction of his muscles along with her own, the unbearable tension that gripped him as the pressure neared the point of explosion. He shuddered and cried out, his cry mingling with her own, and clung so tightly to her that it seemed her rib cage would be crushed. Then incredible peace, as they floated together somewhere beyond the pain, disillusion and ordinariness of the everyday world.

Slowly, she drifted down to a normal level of awareness. The memory scared her and she studied his face, seeking to understand the experience. Gently he pushed her hair back from her cheeks and forehead and smiled down at her.

179

"Are you back yet?"

"It was scary."

She blinked, and focused on his familiar features then nodded. He rolled onto his back and stroked her thigh with a finger.

"Most things worth doing usually are."

She stretched, her fingers coiling around the bars of the bedstead and finding them deliciously cool and soothing. How much of the strangeness had he shared?

"You reckon?"

"Absolutely."

He turned his head on the pillow to smile and touch her lightly on the nose.

"Remember your first ride on a big dipper? The first time you stood up to the school bully and bloodied his nose? And your 'first time'," he added his voice sinking to an intimate whisper, "when you defied your parent's curfew to make love with your first grown-up boyfriend?"

Darcy raised herself up on one elbow and stared down at him with a disconcerted frown.

"How do you know those things?"

He rolled onto his side pulling her round to face him.

"I now know everything worth knowing about Darcy West. I know you inside and out."

His eyes glittered in the twilight and once again she felt a frisson of fear. Fear of being this close to someone, but also fear of the unknown. Maybe it had been a delusion, an effect of her heightened emotions and the altered consciousness of lovemaking. It was comforting to believe so.

"Like a drink?"

"Love one."

He crossed to the wardrobe, his lithe body gleaming as he passed through the first shafts of moonlight seeping in at the window. Her hand flew to her mouth to stifle the sound of shock. As he moved, the shadow on the floor behind him was that of a man wearing a cloak and helmet. She blinked, and the image disappeared, was replaced by his normal shadow. Obviously, another delusion brought on by her heightened senses. Yet there was something pagan about him, something timeless and ageless that struck a chord within and brought her once more to the brink of tears.

"No," she said quickly, as he moved to draw the velvet curtains. "I want to see the stars."

He smiled and walked to the door fastening his silk dressing gown as he went.

She lay still, searching for the first stars. There: faint at first but the pinprick of light growing
stronger as she watched. Then another, and another.
Brant would know their names. A drowsiness overcame her, a delicious languor that made her limbs leaden and relaxed. Her eyelids drooped, and as she allowed her eyes to close, the images appeared behind them. She watched, too fascinated to feel fear. Gulls wheeled over livid cliffs and a stunted tree pointed the way with a spindly arm. Guided by intuition she focused beyond, rather than at, each image.

Immediately, colours became more vivid, shapes sharper and incredibly real so that it seemed possible to reach out and touch the grasses and flora of the headland, and feel the rough stone of the priory beneath her hand. Before her eyes spread a feast of form and colour, and slow deliberate movement as gulls wheeled overhead, and tall grasses swayed gracefully in the light wind. Another world had opened up, sharper and more real than the material one that receded from perception. No longer an observer, she was now a participant in this strange-yet-familiar world, moving into and through it, a part of its lavish colour and texture. The trick was to look deeper, to hold onto the images even as they shifted, searching ever deeper until peering through them to the one behind.

A bride. A bride in the snow, white veil spreading to be at one with the winter landscape. Fascinated, Darcy watches it float, dissipate, glide over the damascene snow, leading her on a mystical journey. A tree stump appears against the horizon, a charcoal-black smudge against the whiteness. Moving in closer, and what appeared as a stunted tree is really a man in a metal

181

helmet and burnished armour. He is holding a shield bearing a strange device: a dragon and eagle entwined round the splayed red cross of the Templar. His mouth opens and words spill forth, but scrambled like a police-encoded radio message. He mouths them again but she cannot understand them, only the desperate plea in his green eyes. *Tell them, tell my story.*

Moving in for a close-up now, as in some strange dream or slow motion movie, then passing by to the slab on the side of the vault and he points to the inscription. As she moves in closer, the marks can be discerned as words. Any moment now she will know his secret.

"Darcy?"

She starts, the unexpected noise giving rise to pain in her head. Not now Brant, not now when I almost have it. Go away, she wills as he speaks again, this time more sharply and her concentration wavers. The words are beginning to fade erased by her lack of attention. The unknown knight beckons, his mouth opens but his words go unheard.

"Darcy – wake up!"

Ignore the call. Don't let the words escape. A large and ornate 'A' like the illuminated initial letter of a monastery manuscript, followed by some smaller letters and a large 'd' followed by a smaller 'e' and a space, then a large florid 'B' and more letters settling
into a recognisable pattern from the photograph of the inscription.

A......De..B.......

"Darcy, what the devil—"

Someone was shaking her fiercely. Take no notice; concentrate and you have it. Don't let them slip away. A flurry of snow falls in slow motion, the wind swirling the flakes into drifts and eddies until the stone is covered, the words obliterated. He stands there, a tiny crease at the corner of his mouth that could almost be a smile and a light in the green eyes that endows them with life and brings to mind gratitude. I have it! she thought jubilant. You are no longer unknown, she adds as his image begins to fade.

Anton. Anton de Beaumont

I will tell your story, Anton, she whispered, I promise.

TWENTY-SIX

Someone placed a hand on her shoulder, and was shaking her hard.

"Darcy, for God's sake wake up!"

Stunned, she stared at his anxious face.

"Brant, I know what -," then she stopped, realising that she was about to blurt out the name. Brant would be bound to ask awkward questions and she could not even begin to explain. Safer to keep the vision or whatever it was to herself. So she said lamely: "I must dozed off and been dreaming."

"Dozing? I thought you had died on me!"

He stuffed a pillow behind her back, and when she struggled into a sitting position, handed her a glass of wine.

"Do you normally go into coma after lovemaking? Because if so – I would have appreciated being told beforehand," he said solemnly.

She laughed, and leaned her head against his shoulder.

"Only when I trip to heaven, and not having been there before, I could hardly warn you, could I?"

"Diplomatic little devil, aren't you?" He pulled a strand of her hair.

"I mean it, Brant," she protested, twisting round to face him. "Wherever we went, I have never been there before."

"Same for me, actually." He stroked her hair and kissed her forehead then added "May I book a return trip?"

"Anytime." Placing her half-finished drink on the bedside table, she slipped her hand beneath the covers and backed up her declaration with a practical demonstration.

****

"Can I take it you're not going back to the cottage

184

tonight?" he said later as they sat up in bed.

"You mean you don't fancy that long drive over
the cliff?" she teased, unsure of how to answer.

"I mean I want you to stay."

She realised this was a serious move, one he would not have
made without much inner searching. It was a safe bet that no
other woman had slept here since his wife left with her lover.

"I'd love to," she replied, dropping the bantering tone.

"That's settled then." He slipped on his robe, "I'll fetch the rest
of the wine – but," he paused in the doorway and raised a
finger in admonition, "no tripping out please whilst I'm gone."

Darcy grinned. "I promise."

She sighed with satisfaction and, leaning back against the
pillows, looked out on a velvet night and the vast sweep of a
Milky Way shot through with planetary fire. There was a
candle in a wax encrusted holder on the window ledge.
Obviously, a back-up for winter power-cuts, she thought, but
tonight it would add a touch of romance. Slipping out of bed
she put on her shirt, thinking there must be matches somewhere
nearby. When window ledge, dressing table and mantel all
proved negative, her gaze fell on the drawer of the bedside
cabinet. On sliding it open the first thing she saw was a box of
Swan matches. She was about to pick it up when a packet, half-
hidden beneath a map of the fells and a paperback book,
caught her attention. A chill of foreboding made her hesitate
before drawing it out. The pack was crumpled, the front
smeared with mud as though it had been dropped on fresh
earth. Opening it, she withdrew one of several cigarettes. It bore
the distinctive jet paper and gold tip of a Sobranie Black
Russian.

Her mind spun in crazy circles. Brant had said he did not
smoke, he also claimed never to have visited the priory ruins.
There could be no innocent explanation; the brand was too
uncommon for coincidence. The creaking of a stair followed by
footsteps along the landing made her turn and hover, packet in
hand, in an agony of indecision as to whether or not to confront
Brant with her find. Suddenly making up her mind, she stuffed

it back in the drawer and slid it shut as the door opened and Brant entered.

"Still awake I see," he observed dryly, putting down the wine bottle.

"Oh very droll," Darcy responded lightly whilst striking a match, and trusting heightened colour would not give away her agitation. Brant glanced at the matches and frowned then swiftly recovered his composure.

"A touch of romance," she explained, lighting the candle and placing it back on the window sill.

She frowned and touched a crystal ash tray that was partially hidden by the brocade curtain.

"I thought you didn't smoke."

"My wife did," he said easily.

"Oh." She moved back to the bed and perched on the edge with her drink. "Have you never indulged?"

"As a boy." He laughed and looked rueful. "At school it was *de rigueur* – or be ragged for a sissy. I never liked it though and remember thinking it most unfair when I was caught and suffered the caning without enjoying the crime."

Darcy smiled, and felt the ice of suspicion melting. The anecdote made him seem more vulnerable and therefore convincing which was totally illogical, she admitted, but then emotion and logic were fundamental strangers. She teetered on the brink of asking about the packet of Sobranie but then withdrew. She was in a fair way to being in love with Brant Kennedy and would rather not face the unpalatable truth. Yet it was impossible to resist a ploy, in the hope that he would volunteer an explanation.

"I've virtually stopped myself; the only cigarette I miss now is the post-coital one! Don't suppose you have an old packet of your wife's hanging around?" she gambled, mentally crossing her fingers at the lie.

"Afraid not."

"No problem." She struggled to hide her disappointment

at his failure to disclose the existence of the packet in the drawer.

He joined her on the bed and ran a finger down the front of her shirt, lingering between her breasts.
"I have other vices though."
"Really?" She managed a smile and provocative look. He took her glass from her hand.
"Would you like me to show you?"
"Brant Kennedy you're insatiable."
He pursed his lips and appeared to consider the matter.
"For you, I rather think I am." He slipped the shirt from her shoulders, "but I did request a return trip."
"Another?"
"I have a season ticket."
"So you have."
She fell back against the pillow. Brant's mouth, first at her lips then nuzzling her nipples, drove out any lingering worry and suspicion.

****

The following morning after breakfast, they packed a picnic lunch and walked along the cliff top. Below them white water creamed the rocks and sprayed the sun-filled air with miniature rainbows. Gulls of every description lined the rocky shelves, either merely resting or landing and launching like miniscule gliders riding the currents.
"I'm hot." Darcy had to raise her voice in order to be heard above their incessant squawking and quarrelling. She paused and pulled off her sweater, tied it at the waist and rolled up her shirt sleeves. Brant reached out and took her arm as she bent to pick up the basket containing the food.
"I'll take that."
"My turn."
"No need." He went to take it from her and she pulled away.
"Let me, Darcy." Seeing his expression, she shrugged and held out the basket.

187

"Be as independent as you like at work," he said
taking her hand as they walked. "but when I'm around
you get looked after, so get used to the idea, okay?"
"Bossy bastard!" She laughed, pulled away her hand
and raced along the path.

"What did you call me?"
"A first-class chauvinist!" she taunted over her shoulder,
laughing and stumbling in her haste as Brant's footsteps
pounded the earth close behind. Catching up, he grabbed her
around the waist and pulled her down into the heather.
"Chauvinist am I?" he goaded, rolling her onto her back and
pinning her arms above her head with one hand. "Now let's see
if you are ticklish."
"I didn't mean it!" she gasped, threshing about in an abortive
attempt to escape. "Pax! I take it back."
"Little coward." He grinned and lowered his head
until his lips were inches from her own.
"I am, I am!"
"So how shall I make you pay?"
Her eyes became slanted, her breath laboured as his hands
slipped beneath her shirt and found first her breasts then the zip
of her jeans.
"I'm sure you can find a way," she breathed.
"Believe it."

"Happy?" he asked later as they lay on their backs with
the warm sun on their faces.
"Yes." And she was, she told herself, listening to the rhythm of
the sea, the sucking and pounding of the surf which in some
strange way had served to heighten their lovemaking. Brant was
the perfect lover: back at the farmhouse that morning he had
been sensitive enough to rise first, leaving her to visit the
bathroom in peace and dress at leisure. Their intimacy was as
yet too new for her to be unembarrassed by bathroom sounds
and flushing toilets. Later she had been drawn downstairs by
hunger and the aroma of freshly-perked coffee and cinnamon
toast. The sole blemish on the face of their otherwise perfect
relationship was that damned packet of Sobranie cigarettes, she

thought, her eyes momentarily clouding. If only she could screw up courage to confront him with the issue. Brant was such a touchy man and would be bound to take offence.

"What is it?" he asked, acutely sensitive to her mood.
"I was thinking how perfect this is – and that I'll have to leave in a couple of hours," she improvised.
"Must you?"
"Caro." She nodded. Propping herself up on one elbow, she plucked a long stem of grass. "I want to call at the hospital. Just in case."
"I understand." She knew he was hiding his disappointment for her sake. "Let me know if there is any change. But now," he added firmly reaching for the picnic basket, "you need to eat before you drive."
"Sure. I'm starving." Determined not to spoil the last hour, she forced a smile.
"You can't be, not again," he said laughing, referring to the mound of toast she had consumed at breakfast.
"I told you: making love makes me ravenous. This wine is delicious."
"Here, have a tomato and wedge of cheese with it."
"Yes, and a hunk of that crusty bread – oh, and a hard-boiled egg please."
"I can see keeping you in food is going to be a major item," he said with a challenging look.
"You bet." She met his gaze and smiled. As short a time as a week ago, she thought, a similar hint at commitment would have made her turn and run.

They finished their picnic and sat on an out-crop to watch the sea creaming the rocks below. Darcy found her thoughts returning to Monk Grange, its bizarre occupant and the question of how far Brant could be trusted. Possibly she was over-reacting; the sole evidence against him was a crumpled pack of cigarettes in a drawer and the fact that he felt it too insignificant to mention or had forgotten they were there. The only way to get answers was to risk sounding him out.

189

"I was just thinking about Miles Standish," she said casually, picking up a pebble and throwing it over the edge. "Do you think there is anything in his bizarre theory about Templars and alchemy?"

She turned to find Brant regarding her closely and with a look that was difficult to interpret. He dropped the stem of grass he had been chewing.

"What do you know about the Knights Templar?"

Chilled by his expression, she hesitated then decided to take the risk.

"I know St. Gildas Man was one."

"And?" There was steel in his eyes and in his voice.

"That in popular belief alchemy was about turning base metals into gold, and," she added meeting his gaze squarely "that the Templars held fabulous and unexplained wealth."

"I see." Brant looked out to sea, the colour of his eyes deepening to aquamarine. He sat that way, without speaking or moving, for several moments. Darcy guessed by the crease between his eyes, and the tensing of the muscle at the side of his mouth, that he was working through some kind of conflict and so resisted the urge to interrupt.

"Let me show you something," he said at last. He rose and held out his hand and as she grasped it, hauled her to her feet.

"Where are we going?" she asked, watching as he packed bottle, glasses and litter into the rucksack.

"Sheep Howe," he replied, tossing left-over crusts to a fleet of swooping and fiercely combative gulls.

In contrast to the brightness and warmth outside, it was cool and dim inside the observatory. Darcy blinked once or twice, then pulled on her sweater as the chill penetrated her shirt. The metal door clicked shut and the wedge of light disappeared bringing a fleeting sense of panic. Then a series of clicks as Brant moved along the panel and the low-voltage lights glowed red. He moved surely amongst his equipment, flicking switches and swivelling dials. Instrument panels buzzed into life and monitors flickered with green light.

190

"Here it is."

"What am I looking at?" Darcy tried to make sense of the myriad stars and planets depicted on the screen.

"This." Brant clicked a laser indicator at the central light-mass. "Remember Abarbanel?"

Darcy looked blank and he sighed with impatience.

"Of course you do. Our rabbi and writer of sacred texts – I told you," he added accusingly.

"Ah, the 'star in the east' guy." Darcy grinned: this was like being back at school, unable to grasp the point quick enough for some erudite and impatient master. Her eyes suddenly widened and just in time she stifled an exclamation. Now she knew what had troubled and eluded her when Miles Standish had spun his incredible tale. On that first evening with Brant at the farmhouse he had talked about the stars being used to pinpoint events in history – and had alluded to alchemy.

"The conjunction of Jupiter and Saturn in Pisces," he corrected sternly. "Which he claimed would herald the birth of a messiah. And Kepler, you recall, calculated that this rare conjunction had actually occurred in the month of December in the alleged year of Jesus' birth."

"And I thought it an 'iffy' example." Darcy shrugged dismissively, " and not being religious with a capital 'R', I still do," she added.

Brant sighed heavily.

"Bear with me. Kepler has a respectable pedigree; his three laws of planetary motion provided the basis for Newton's work." He clicked the laser again and the images changed. "So, this is an exact replica of how the heavens appeared at the last known conjunction. This one," he turned to give her an intense look, "took place around A.D. 1136."

Darcy peered at the screen and frowned. "So?"

"In 1139 a Papal bull or edict was issued by the Vatican. In effect it made the Templars accountable solely to the Pope, thus placing them beyond the jurisdiction of governments and monarchs. That, Darcy, is power with a capital 'P' and one wonders what, or who, they knew in order to achieve it."

"I don't get the connection." Darcy turned from watching the screen to search his face.

Brant sighed and rumpled his hair as though in exasperation at her slowness.

"Okay. During the crusades the Templars were a handful of warrior monks with a brief to protect pilgrims in the Holy Land. A far cry, wouldn't you say, from an Order capable of making or deposing monarchs?" He flicked a switch on the consul, dimming the images on screen. "Henry the Third got twitchy over their power and wealth, and was unwise enough to threaten the order with confiscation. The Master of the Order publicly replied along the lines of 'up yours', and reminded Henry that he remained on the throne only as long as it pleased them. Not a squeak out of Henry after that. This, by the way, was not in some exotic eastern empire but right here in England. In fact the Grand Master of the Order was regularly invited to the King's Parliament. King John was a regular visitor in his time, and guess who was at his side at the signing of Magna Carta?"

"The Grand Master by any chance?" Darcy supplied dryly.

"Correct. So in answer to your question about the Templars, there has always been speculation about them and their meteoric rise to power."

"You mentioned alchemy once – what is the connection?" she dared.

"Now you are getting there! The stars and their positions were crucial to alchemical workings. The conjunction of Saturn and Jupiter would have been an event of unsurpassed magnitude. Following it, Templar wealth and influence multiplied and continued to do so. Some schools of thought link that power to the decoding of alchemical secrets. Certain people believe the formula still exists and will stop at nothing in their search. "

Darcy looked sceptical. "Surely not in this day and age, and within major institutions?" she protested as the Home Office came to mind. Brant stood watching her for a moment as though undecided about how much to divulge, then appeared to reach a decision.

"In mid west America there is a three million pound Advanced Technology Telescope. This is the Vatican Observatory based on Mount Graham in Arizona."

"Did you say Vatican?" Darcy asked looking incredulous.

He nodded and gestured for her to let him finish.

"It is manned by a team of eleven Jesuit priests. And I know what you are thinking," he added, "that this is some wacky American sect. Not so. Their vice-director is one Father Christopher Corbally from Ware-ham in Dorset. He taught physics in a Derbyshire school before going on to theology – and a Ph.D. in astronomy."

Struggling to make sense of all this, Darcy tapped her front teeth with a fingernail.

"So what exactly are they doing there?" she probed.

Brant moved round the dome switching off equipment.

"Father Corbally," he continued whilst logging off the main computer, "after years at the Vatican Observatory searching for evidence to support biblical 'events', has come to a radical conclusion. He believes that the so-called 'Star of Bethlehem' was not a star at all, but a rare conjunction of planets known to alchemists as a Conjunctio – the so-called sacred marriage."

Darcy stared at him without speaking, her features mirroring the internal fire of her thoughts.

"Abarbanel's prediction and Kepler's conjunction," she said slowly, shaking her head with lingering incredulity. "But surely there must be—"

"Father Corbally considered all the options," Brant interrupted, pre-empting her objection, "including the favoured one of a supa nova – a dying star which exploded shedding brilliant light – but he discounts it on time scale: the nova would burn for around twelve months, too long for the fabled Star of Bethlehem. He also discards the comet theory due to there being no mention of a 'fiery tail' like that described in ancient sightings of Halley's comet."

"Fairly convincing," Darcy grudgingly conceded.

"It's serious stuff," he corrected, standing by the exit. "I'm only telling you all this in the hope that you will realise it."

"I do," she reassured him, joining him at the door.

He smiled, and flicked one of her curls with a finger, a habit she found endearing.

"What exactly is this formula," Darcy asked, following him outside.

"It concerns the heart of alchemy: the Philosopher's Stone."

Darcy blinked in the glare after the dimness of the dome. "But it's just a myth."

"When you talk alchemy, think symbols," Brant advised, locking the gates. "The term 'Philosopher's Stone' is a way of summing up a very complex chemical and mystical process and end result. The substance produced was reputed to cure all diseases and impart eternal youth. Gold was central to the process and gold finings," he added leading her back to the Land Rover, "were known as immortal dust."

TWENTY-SEVEN

It was all too much. Outside, beneath a blue sky and a cliff top drenched in sunlight, the whole thing seemed incredible. Aware of Brant at her back, she faced the sea and briefly closed her eyes as the wind blew spray in her face. The salty aroma combined with that of herbage warmed by the sun, brought memories flooding in. The post mortem, her feeling that this was something momentous and there was no turning back, and now it seemed that premonition was justified. This was not the crazy obsession of a handful of cranks; here was something that learned and powerful people had taken on board, people like Brant, a scientist with years of training and research to his credit. Public bodies and government departments too, and if Miles Standish was to be believed (and according to Brant he had previously been stable and an ace guy) the libraries, archives and political institutions of Europe.

There were also two distinct and separate issues, she realised, and if sense was to be made of all this they had to be treated as such. The historical and undisputed reality concerning the wealth and power of the Templars must not be confused with the popular myths surrounding alchemy. Once she could see the fabled Philosopher's Stone as a symbol, a sort of shorthand for the alchemists' ultimate aim (maybe even pinnacle of achievement arising from centuries of study and learning), this sense of unreality and incredulity would disappear. The trick, she realised, lay in avoiding taken-for-granted ideas about what the Philosopher's Stone and romantically named 'immortal dust' actually were, concentrating instead on what they represented. Back there in the strangeness of the dome this had been difficult, out here in ordinary surroundings it was easier and her thinking less clouded.

Okay so far, but one aspect still seemed tainted by gross coincidence and superstition. Gulls keened and screeched overhead symbolising her turmoil. She swung round to face him.

"Why have we all come together in this? We all had separate lives then they suddenly seemed to converge, why?"

"Do you think I haven't asked myself that same question." Brant shook his head and rumpled his hair in the characteristic gesture that signified his discomfort. "I assumed I stumbled on all this by accident because of my interest in history and astrology. But the links are uncanny. Miles, Caro, and you Darcy, ripping through my life like a meteor in full flight. The only common denominator seems to be St. Gildas Man. I'm a scientist, yes, but I sometimes wonder." His eyes searched hers as though for the answer.

Encouraged by this shift, however slight, from scientific to mystical, Darcy impulsively decided to confide her vision of the previous evening. Afraid of derision, she spoke haltingly but need not have worried: Brant listened gravely throughout.

"And so now I know his name," she concluded, anxiously scanning Brant's face.

"You think you do," he corrected but not unkindly.

"No." Emphatically Darcy shook her head. "I know it in here." She touched the area around her solar plexus. "He is Anton de Beaumont, but I can't explain how I know." Her anxiety was plain in her expression.

Brant clasped his hands behind his back and stuck out his lower lip.

"Easy," he said, giving her a quizzical look. "You said Miles' kitchen table was strewn with papers – family trees and the like? And that you glanced through them when his back was turned," he continued as Darcy nodded agreement.

"Briefly."

"Then it's obvious to me that the name entered your subconscious without you being aware of it. Then, in the

196

heightened state of lovemaking it resurfaced, but in the guise of weird images, stream of consciousness and all that."

"I guess you're right."

"Does it matter?"

"I would find it hard to handle anything else," she confessed. "Facts are my forte, anything that smacks of the so-called supernatural gives me a problem."

"The facts are there; problems arise because of the way we interpret them," Brant contributed.

"And because of how we define 'natural' too I guess," she added.

"I'm impressed! You're beginning to show a decided philosophical bent!"

Suspicious, she gave him a swift look but the smile and tone of voice robbed his words of mockery. However, a sudden change of mood caused her to frown as he crossed his arms and looked grim.

"I suppose it's a waste of time asking you to drop this particular line of research?" he said roughly.

"Absolutely."

"I will stop you if I can." His expression hardened.

"If is the operative word."

"Okay." He turned away and his stance betrayed anger and frustration as he added over his shoulder: "but don't say I didn't warn you."

As he walked away, she followed.

"But why, Brant?"

He turned suddenly and grabbed both her arms.

"You can ask me that, after Miles Standish – and Caro?"

"You forget Brant," Darcy said brusquely, "I'm a reporter. I have to know 'who, how and why'. How can you ask me to back off now?"

He shook his head and looked up to the sky in exasperation.

"Because I love you woman!"

"What a romantic declaration," she could not resist commenting as he sighed and pulled her close.

197

"Shut up, Darcy!"
The pressure of his mouth on hers left no option.

The journey over the cliffs passed in virtual silence.
Suddenly, Darcy thought miserably, the farmhouse
seemed light years away from her pad in Manchester.
"Next week?" he asked as they stood by her car at
the Old Priory inn.
"Same time, same place?" she said, nodding.
He smiled. "We sound like the couple in Brief Encounter."
"I hope that's the only similarity," Darcy quipped.
"I'm not noble."
She laughed. "And I'm not married."
"That's settled then."
"Anyway I'm too young too remember the film,"
she teased.
"Cheek. I've only seen it on Golden Oldies."

He flicked one of her curls with a finger in the way she
found so endearing. But it was time to part and the bantering
ceased.
"Take care, and Darcy-,"
"Yes?"
"Trust no-one."
Chilled by the sudden gravity of his tone, she would have
pursued this, but he was already climbing into the Land Rover.
With a throbbing of engine and crunch
of wheels on gravel it pulled away.
"Remember," he added, sticking his head out of the window.
"whatever happens – I love you. "

Darcy, a frown on her face, stood pondering these
last words as he drove away. She sat for a while in her car
watching the Land Rover climb the winding track towards
Brant's farmhouse on the cliff. It grew smaller by the minute
and soon resembled an ant crawling along a vast dung hill. As
she drove away, the scene intensified her loneliness.

TWENTY-EIGHT

Ten minutes of visiting time remained as Darcy parked
the car in the hospital grounds and rushed along the corridor to
the side ward. The door was ajar, and as she approached, the
gap widened and Brian appeared.
"Brian?" She waited, fearful of hearing what he had to say.
"I was hoping you would make it today." He looked pale and
the shadows beneath his eyes were testament to his nightly
vigil. Darcy frowned, there was difference, an absence she
could not place.
"You have something to tell me?" Her breath caught in her
throat and she hardly dared listen as he began to speak, albeit
incoherently.
"Been waiting for you. Phoned last night, the cottage, but you –
no answer - already left."

Darcy groaned aloud. Caro had needed her and she
had been in Brant's bed. Overcome by guilt she tried to peer
past him.
"Caro?" she whispered, seized by dread.
"It was yesterday – about tea-time," he babbled, "I was sitting
there, talking to her you know, as I do, well you know, hoping
somehow—"
Darcy wanted to stem the fateful words, because once they
were uttered Caro's death would be real and irrevocable, but
shock had rendered her speechless.
"It didn't register," Brian rushed heedlessly on: not at
first—"
"Wait, please Brian. I can't take it yet." Unable to carry
the burden of guilt, Darcy covered her face with her hands.
"But Darcy—"

"Who is it Brian?"
At the sound of that weak but recognisable voice,
Darcy unceremoniously pushed Brian aside and rushed

to the bedside.

"Caro!"

"I was trying to tell you she opened her eyes," Brian
said from the doorway.

"You could have got it out sooner!" Darcy said, but with a
weak smile.

"Hi. What kept you?" Pale and weary looking, but
very much alive, Caro smiled weakly up at her from a
bank of pillows.

"Thank God," Darcy took the hand that lay on the
coverlet and gently stroked it, mindful of the drips, supportive
frames and biofeedback electrodes that were still in place.
Suddenly she knew what had registered earlier: there was no
sighing of bellows and artificial breath – Caro was breathing for
herself. With her free hand, Darcy brushed away a tear.

"What are you at Mrs. Stevens, giving us such a
fright?" she said gruffly to hide her embarrassment.

"Sorry. Most inconsiderate of me wasn't it?"

That whispered attempt at a joke wrung Darcy's heart.
She glanced up, saw that Brian was standing at the foot of the
bed, smiling and obviously deliriously happy.

"You two have the last ten minutes together," he said
moving back to the door. "I'll go square it with Sister, then nip
back before I leave." he added with a loving look for his wife.

"Don't let her talk too much, Darcy," he whispered in passing.
"It's early days yet, and she has to avoid getting over-tired."
Darcy nodded her understanding and satisfied, he left.

Caro, the strain of excitement apparent in her drooping
eyelids and laboured breathing, lay with her gaze fixed on
Darcy's face. She moistened her lips with her tongue and spoke
with obvious effort.

"Darcy, you have to stop blaming yourself."

"It was me they were after." Darcy shook her head and
sighed. "It was my fault for involving you, and insisting you
wear that bloody coat," she said miserably.

"Listen, to me Darcy. We only have a few minutes," Caro whispered. The urgency in her voice made Darcy fall silent and lean closer in order to hear.

"Have to help them," Caro paused to take a deeper breath and a shuddering sigh escaped.

"Don't talk any more for now," Darcy urged, suddenly afraid.

"Must," Caro whispered. "Tried to tell you, night of the post mortem."

Darcy frowned then recalled the nightmare, the scene in the spare bedroom and Caro's obvious terror. Then the persistent feeling that Caro had wanted to confide some secret. "What has been troubling you?" she urged gently as Caro's eyes closed, and for a moment Darcy feared she had slipped from consciousness back into oblivion. But at her words the purpled lids flickered and eventually opened. The distress apparent in Caro's eyes chilled Darcy and made her almost wish the question had been left unasked.

"It gives me no peace." Caro's fingers plucked at the sheet and sweat beaded her forehead.

"Don't let them drug me again Darcy; I have to stay awake." Her eyes were huge in her pale and waxy face, and her head moved from side to side in agitation.

"It will be all right, just tell me," Darcy urged, trying to ignore the snowball of fear that constricted and chilled her stomach.

"It's there whenever I sleep." Caro's voice sank to a hoarse whisper, and fear stared out from her face.

"What is?" What do you see?"

But Caro now seemed to have slipped back into her own private world. Her speech was incoherent and the babbled words made little sense.

Darcy's throat became dry with fear, but she had to know more if Caro was to be helped.

"Tell me about it, lovey," she whispered. The vacancy of Caro's expression as she struggled to answer made Darcy want to weep.

"Nightmares." Amongst the garbled phrases the one word sounded clear. Gradually the absent look was replaced by one of fear which at least, Darcy thought with a strange flash of objectiveness, meant Caro was back at home. "But then they become worse than real. I watch them leaping into the pit," Caro whispered, her eyes becoming huge and her skin stretched over her cheek bones. "Then it is my turn. It is me, Darcy, I am the one burning to death in that hell hole. I feel the indescribable agony as my skin crisps and curls from the bone." The whisper trailed away and her eyes closed, but then the eyelids jerked open again as though the horrors they concealed were too awful to contemplate or contain.

"Easy now," Darcy soothed, taking a moist tissue from the pack on the locker to wipe Caro's forehead. "Caro you must tell me: who is it in your dream?"
"Yes, must tell you," she repeated, urgency seeming to add new strength to her voice as footsteps approached along the corridor. Darcy leaned closer as the door was pushed wide.
"What, still here Miss West!"
Darcy turned to see the martinet of a sister accompanied by an embarrassed looking Brian.
"Sorry sister. I was just going."
"I should think so."
"It was my fault sister—," Brian started to say but was summarily over-ruled as her narrowed eyes took in the distressed state of her patient.
"What on earth has been going on here! Out please!"

She glared at Darcy who reluctantly rose to her feet. "Now!" she added, without raising her voice but in tones that prohibited argument. "Right Mrs. Stevens," she turned a disapproving eye on her patient, "time to rest; you look exhausted," and moving to a tray holding items of medication, she picked up a hypodermic and began filling it from one of the vials. The mute appeal in Caro's eyes wrung Darcy's heart, but there was no option but to squeeze her friend's hand and leave.

"We'll talk again soon," she promised, giving Caro a meaningful look from the door and receiving in return one of mute despair.

TWENTY-NINE

The following morning, Darcy rose early and, ravenous despite a night of broken sleep and disturbing dreams, sat down to a breakfast of fruit juice, boiled eggs, toast and coffee. It was a lie, she thought stacking the used crockery on the drainer of the sink, that love and sex put you off your food. Would Brant mind if she got fat? Somehow she doubted it and recalling his mock look of disgust as she helped herself to a second egg during their picnic, smiled as she emptied the coffee dregs down the sink.

The smile died on her lips as Caro and her nightmares intruded. The agitation that had kept her awake during the night returned to churn her belly. The gape of the flame-red pit the night of her lovemaking with Brant would not be banished. Coincidence maybe, but perhaps there was a connection between that terrifying experience and the burnings of Caro's nightmares. It was all so improbable but that, she recognised, was why it was so unnerving. Give me facts any time, she thought shrugging her jacket onto her shoulders.

However, there had been a problem with the Philosopher's Stone until she had viewed the thing from a different perspective. Once she had seen the words as pointers to something rather than taking them literally the problem disappeared. So maybe there was a rational explanation for this too. For instance, there was that day in the library when the Templars had first come into the frame – and she had read the gruesome account of the burning of Jacques de Moliere. Given her profession and current topic of research, Caro would also have come across the disturbing story. Feasibly, it could be triggered by stress to arise spontaneously from their respective subconscious minds and be played out in different scenarios. All very logical and reasonable; yet the ridiculous notion that the long-dead Anton de Beaumont was trying to tell them something would not completely vanish. She gave a sigh of frustration, picked up her bag and left the flat.

****

At the office, she made a determined effort to consign thoughts of Caro and Anton de Beaumont to the back burner and push on with her report on the Council Corruption case. When the post arrived, she sifted through the pile and was about to consign it to the 'see to it later' tray when a handwritten envelope addressed 'for the personal attention of Miss Darcy West' caught her eye. Ripping it open, she pulled out the single sheet of folded paper and frowned. The paragraph it contained was headed 'for insertion in tomorrow's personal column' and read: 'Would Miss Austen's hero (should the man of business fail to keep his appointment and be sent to the wall) be drawn by his pride into prior ruin to save the family name?' and was signed 'Abarbanel'.

There are some fruit cakes around, Darcy thought, and not for the first time since joining the Paper. Yet that was an odd pseudonym, and one that itched irritatingly at her memory but just beyond where it could be scratched. Why on earth should anyone send a personal ad. to her direct? Someone perhaps who read her column every week, felt they 'knew her' in a personal way. It did happen. She shrugged and put it to one side for Janet's attention.

A half hour or so later, Janet's voice came over the intercom. "There's a guy on the outside line, won't give his name but reckons you'll speak to him."
"Some crank probably," Darcy groaned. "Upset by my piece on the Council."
"He said to tell you: 'all that glitters' if that makes any sense."
"Not much. Get rid of him." Darcy's hand hovered over the intercom switch. "No, wait." Her forehead furrowed as the words registered. Why that covert reference to gold? "Put him through," she amended.

205

Miles Standish sounded even more distraught than when they had spoken over the weekend.

"I have to see you."

"I'll come Saturday as arranged."

"No, I mean now."

"I cannot get away."

The silence sent a shiver of apprehension along Darcy's spine.

"Tonight. Be there – or you'll never know."

"Miles, wait!" she almost shouted as insight struck between the eyes. "Did you send me a cryptic message, a small ad?"

"I may have."

"But what does it—"

"Tonight."

There was a click, and the line went dead. Picking up the 'ad' again Darcy folded the sheet of paper and stuffed it in her pocket.

A knock sounded at the door, and Janet entered carrying a cup of coffee.

"How is Mrs. Stevens?" she asked, placing it in the space that Darcy had cleared by pushing aside a sheaf of papers.

"Making good progress, thank God."

Janet gave her a searching look. "Don't wish to pry, but you look a tad stressed."

"Just tired."

"Well, there isn't a lot on this morning, the preliminary hearing on the Council case is adjourned until next month."

"Good." Darcy glanced at the door and lowered her voice, "Can you cover for me tomorrow, Janet? Something has cropped up and I have to go north."

"No problem, leave Frank to me."

"Thanks. Anything in yet on the Templar Repository in London?"

"Sorry." Janet shook her head.

"And the various archives and libraries?"

"Negative. Responses vary but the message is roughly

the same 'requested data unavailable' or rather," Janet smiled wryly, "classical stonewalling."

"I see."

Darcy sipped her coffee; Miles Standish's complaints about a conspiracy to withhold information were seeming less fantastic by the day. And this morning he had sounded on the brink of desperation. It was inconvenient and would probably cost her a rollicking from Frank, but the planned weekend visit to Miles would have to be brought forward to tonight. The telephone bleeped and at a nod from her boss Janet picked up the receiver, listened for a moment then saying, "One moment please, I'll see if she is available," flicked a switch and put the call on hold.

"Madame Cabbala," she said, eyebrows raised in inquiry.

"I'll take it," Darcy said with a grimace, relieving Janet of the receiver. "Darcy West here, Madame Cabbala. What can I do for you."

Immediately, the professional, Darcy leaned back on her seat and despite being preoccupied with Miles Standish, stitched an attentive look onto her face.

"A compromise you say? One that will satisfy your scruples and integrity. Of course. Yes, we can certainly discuss that possibility with you," she soothed, picking up a pencil and doodling on the message pad. "That will be fine, thank you for calling."

Replacing the receiver, she looked up at Janet. "Will you see her for me, Jan? She's insisting on tomorrow at two."

"Great. Thanks, Darcy." Janet's eyes were shining and her cheeks had gone pink with pleasure at this evidence of her boss's confidence in her abilities.

Darcy waved aside her gratitude.

"Hear what she has to say, then I'll see her to firm things up if it's a goer."

As Janet closed the door behind her, Darcy's attention was caught by the doodle on the message pad, that of a snake swallowing its own tail. With a derisory sound that said 'Darcy you really have lost your marbles', she tore off the sheet and was about to screw it up and toss it into the waste bin when something prevented her from doing so. There came a tug on the strings of memory, but not hard enough to drag it into the light of awareness. She stared at the image, leaned back on her seat and half closed her eyes. Where had it come from, and what had dredged it up from the primal mud of her subconscious?

Leaning forward again she idly drew a circle around Clare Cabbala's name and time of appointment. Immediately, she was transported to the clairvoyant's suite at the Midland Hotel and, without warning, a piece of the jigsaw clicked into place. Her mind's eye ranged over the spheres and celestial charts and there it was, the snake swallowing its tail, the image she had seen first in that hotel room, and just now had unconsciously reproduced on the pad. All that remained now was to crack its significance. An astrological or alchemical symbol? She didn't mind betting it was one or the other – and her money was on the latter.

That evening, she telephoned Brant but there was no answer, and she decided he must be working at the observatory. Restless, she rose and crossed to the window and watched a group of children kicking a ball about in the park over the way. Her attention was claimed by a young couple strolling hand in hand through the mauve shadows and butter-gold of evening. Oblivious to all but each other, they paused and kissed before moving on again, and Darcy was overcome with longing for Brant. Moving away from the window, she browsed through the collection of compact discs, selected one and placed it on the player. The haunting sound of pan pipes and the theme from Picnic at Hanging Rock brought yearning and a frisson of unease. Sinking down on the settee, she brooded over Caro's dream-induced fear, and what could be done about it, and Miles Standish's weird behaviour and what her impending drive north might reveal. Glancing at the clock, she decided to try Brant one more time before leaving.

This time he answered immediately, and once the initial greetings were over, Darcy told him of her planned visit to the cottage. Almost, she confided her intention of stopping off first at Monk Grange, but something held her back. And that something, she reflected on replacing the receiver, had to be the lack of complete trust. Yet Brant had acted only mildly surprised by the fact of a mid-week visit, and though she listened attentively for any nuance of voice which might betray anxiety or suspicion, detected none. She announced Caro's recovery, but withheld her admission of fear, deciding that it was a confidence between friends and therefore she need not feel guilty. Maybe she would tell him over lunch when they met the following day.

Recalling Mile's warning to be sure she was not followed, Darcy glanced both ways along the street before emerging to put her overnight bag in the car. The scent of philadelphus blossom in the park drifted in at the car window. Orange blossom for lovers. Driving off, Darcy realised she was desperate for Brant to be innocent of any sinister involvement in this affair. During the drive to the motorway, her gaze constantly went to the mirror. Following a left turn onto the dual carriageway her heart beat faster; the twin glare of headlamps, visible before the turn-off, were still reflected there. At this hour there was little traffic going into town, so it was easy to identify and track the car. A detour for milk and a bottle of wine from the off-licence, and another to the garage on the pretext of needing the air line, confirmed her suspicions. So they knew about the flat. The chances were they also knew about Mistletoe Cottage. The prospect of lying alone in the darkness and silence of the countryside brought a chill of fear. No friendly orange glow of street lamps there, no muted hum of passing traffic to comfort and reassure.

Nothing to gain by working herself up into a panic either, she told herself. A cool head was needed here, and a plan of action to deal with the situation. Despite her resolve, panic threatened to overspill in dark waves. It would be unthinkable to place Brian and Caro at risk again by going to their house, or anyone else's for that matter, so friends were out. Leaving the garage, she saw with a stab of fear that the lights of the car behind were still reflected in the mirror, an anonymous threat undiminished by distance. Making a lightning decision, she swung off the by-pass and took the route for the city centre. The safest place right now, she decided, was her office.

The lights behind the glazed frontage of the Manchester News tower glared with reassuring brashness against the night sky. Parking up in a well-lit area close to the entrance, Darcy resisted the urge to run and entered the foyer without a backward glance. After an hour or so of abortive watching, her pursuers would maybe assume she was on the night shift, give up and drive away. She flashed her card at reception, and risking a glance over her shoulder to check that no-one had followed her indoors, mingled with reporters, cleaners and clerical staff and made for the lift.

As Darcy waited, the lights on the panel winked on and off in descending order and the lift sighed to a halt. The doors opened and a man of forty-something with thick wavy hair, and wearing a red bow tie and harassed expression, stepped out. His shirt sleeves were rolled up, and he carried a sheaf of newspapers under one arm. The distracted look was replaced by one of pleasant surprise.
"Darcy! What the devil are you doing here?"
"Hi, Nick." She smiled at the night editor. "Long time no see. I just want to check something out in my research files for tomorrow."
"Now there's dedication." Nick Carter grinned.

Darcy pretended to hitch her bag further up on her shoulder while casting a furtive look back at the foyer. Reassured, she turned back to him. "Nothing so noble; I have to eat."
"You okay?" he asked frowning.

"Sure."

"Come on. You don't fool me," then added as Darcy looked at him in dismay, "I know naked ambition when I see it – and a high flying reporter."

"Right. Got you." Darcy relaxed.

"You're looking tired and kinda stressed Darcy," he commented, still frowning. "Tell that Frank Kelly from me he's working you too hard!"

"Frank's okay," Darcy said with a smile, "It was my own idea to drop in tonight."

"You need looking after. Not hitched yet?"

"No-one will have me," she quipped, grinning.

"Not surprised. You'd make a lousy wife – cooking up the next story instead of the poor guy's dinner." He turned as a male voice hailed from down the corridor. "Okay, okay Jack, I'm on my way! See you, Darcy – take care."

"Sure, see you Nick."

The lift doors began to slide to and Darcy watched Nick Carter hurry away down the corridor.

For a moment there, Nick's kindness had almost caused her to weaken, she reflected as the lift whirred into motion. She had been tempted to confide her fears of a stalker waiting outside the building. Yearning for Brant swept over her, a longing to be encircled within the safety of his arms. Please don't let him be mixed up in all this, she prayed for the hundredth time as the lift sighed to a halt.

She paced the floor of her office, sat down for a minute or so then paced again, pausing to peer out of the window. The lights of the city pierced the night and deepened the shadows of empty doorways and semi-deserted pavements. She stood for a while watching the flash of neon signs frizz and spray the dark with brazen and unabashed colour. She shifted uneasily and searched the ground below. The car park was out of view from this side of the building so there was no way knowing if her pursuers still lurked there. After glancing repeatedly at the clock she decided to visit the staff canteen for coffee and some company.

The lights, chatter and bustle of the cafeteria promptly raised her spirits.

"Hey, Darcy!"

Darcy turned. A girl with vibrant red hair was waving from a nearby table.

"Fran – it's been an age!" Darcy carried her cup over and sat down.

"Too long girl! So how's things – have they transferred you to nights too?"

"I popped in for some data I need," Darcy said, shaking her head.

"Pity." Fran looked glum. "I miss the laughs."

"We were a good team," Darcy agreed, grinning. "Remember the day we rigged a call from the Press Complaints Commission? Frank threw a big one."

"And we nearly swelled the ranks of the unemployed," Fran responded, her green eyes sparkling with fun.

"Seeing anyone special these days?" she added, stirring a mini pot of cream into her coffee.

"Hey, what is this?" Darcy exclaimed, pretending to look indignant. "I bumped into Nick Carter and he asked me much the same thing."

"Well, you are knocking on a bit, aren't you," Fran said with an innocent look.

"Bitch! Whose your latest anyway?" Darcy laughed. Instantly Fran leaned forward and her expression became animated.

"Had I met Matt last time I saw you? He's real cool, a great guy," she rushed on without waiting for Darcy's reply. Cursing her mistake in asking, Darcy sighed and resigned herself to a litany of the unknown Matt's virtues which she knew from experience to be both forthcoming and lengthy. However, it did allow her to switch off and simply nod at intervals or look suitably impressed whilst a plan took shape in her head.

"Anyway, this is the one Darcy – I can feel it."

"Great, hope it works out," Darcy responded, doing her best to look interested.

"I'm pretty much in the same situation myself," she added, making her opening move, "in fact I'm on my way north to see him." She paused and pulled a wry face. "only I have a bit of a problem. Don't suppose you could help me out?"

"Spit it out and we'll see."

"Whilst I'm up there I have to check out the scene of my last report. Problem is, I wasn't too welcome last time round and my car will be recognised. Don't fancy the lynch mob so I wondered if we could swap vehicles for tonight?"

"Sure. No problem." Fran shrugged.

"Great. Thanks, Fran, gets me out of a corner."

Darcy resisted the urge to grab Fran's hand, squeeze it and offer profuse thanks. Play it cool and Fran would not suspect anything odd, reporters in a hot spot frequently swapped cars to avoid recognition. Then conscience stuck a pin in her balloon: Fran would be exposed to danger by driving a marked car. Darcy agonised for a moment or two, then recalled that Fran would not be leaving before daybreak, so even if the stalker was still around, he could hardly mistake this flame-haired Amazon of a woman for Darcy West. They chatted some more over a second coffee, then Darcy ventured onto the car park to remove her overnight bag. She lodged it with reception for picking up later, rather than immediately placing it in Fran's car. This, she hoped, would avoid alerting the stalker to her plan. Back in the canteen, they exchanged car keys before parting with a promise to meet up again soon.

Darcy returned to her office and took from the closet a military style raincoat kept there in case of unexpected showers. Putting it on, she tied the belt and, crossing to her desk, picked up an elastic band. Scraping back her curls, she used it to secure them at the crown of her head. A pair of shades from her bag completed the disguise. A glance in the mirror assured her that even Brant would have a problem identifying her now. Nervously jangling Fran's keys, she made her way to the foyer and collected her bag.

It took all her nerve to walk towards Fran's car with an air of calm and confidence. After a surreptitious surveillance of the car park, she slipped behind the wheel, swiftly located lights, wipers and indicators and pulled out of the space. Frequent glances in the mirror revealed nothing sinister, but a stalker would hardly try something nasty on a busy car park outside a well-lit office block. Her heart missed a beat as a man wearing a Mafia style suit stopped beneath a street lamp to light a cigarette. The lamp was faulty and the deep red glow suffused the scene with an element of the surreal. The match flared, casting the hollows of his face into shadow whilst highlighting the bones with evil effect. Seconds later, he tossed aside the match and entered a waiting taxi. Weak with relief, Darcy pulled out onto the road.

Her heart pounded and her mouth went dry as the cold and unblinking stare of some giant beast stalking its prey was reflected in the mirror. Her immediate reaction was to press down hard on the accelerator, but that would tell her nothing. Stomach cramped with fear, she forced herself to a steady pace and watched the headlamps draw closer. The winking of the offside indicator brought forth a sigh of relief. The car overtook and sped away with a friendly flourish of tail lights. A detour to the off-licence convinced her that her pursuers had given up. Turning onto the dual carriageway, she headed out of town and towards the motorway.

Cumbria at last, and a mere ten miles or so from St. Gildas Bay and Monk Grange. A glance at the clock in the dashboard showed the time to be 12.10 a.m. The question now was whether to go straight to the cottage and call on Miles Standish the following day, or carry onto Monk Grange despite the lateness of the hour. The chances were, given his agitation and insistence on an immediate meeting, he would still be up and awaiting her arrival. Ignoring the turn off that would lead eventually to Mistletoe Cottage, Darcy took the coast road and headed for St. Gildas Bay.

Leaving the car at the end of the lane, she pushed open the gate and entered the overgrown garden of Monk Grange. The memory of Miles Standish's evident distress that morning made her pause on the path. Tonight, or it will be too late he had insisted. He was expecting trouble, and it was possible that somebody else had got here first. Her stomach lurched at the thought, but no vehicle was parked nearby and the house skulked in darkness. She stood perfectly still, watching and listening, not daring to switch on her torch, then cautiously moved on.

Nothing stirred around the house save some nocturnal creature in the undergrowth disturbed by her arrival. The screech of an owl and a ghostly white shape gliding overhead momentarily checked her progress. The garden, imbued with a bygone charm in daylight was by night a place of sinister enchantment. Flowers were bleached by moonlight to eerie silver, and Tolkienesque trees with dreadlocks of honeysuckle and clematis dipped spindly arms to clutch her hair as she passed beneath. The stone cupid leered at her from a sea of moon-daisies, his chipped face mocking her fear.

A rap or two at the panels of the front door brought no response. Keeping to the shadows by the wall, she crept round to the rear where white roses clambering over the derelict summerhouse glowed eerily against a sombre backdrop of yew. Darcy's unease grew as no light shone forth from the kitchen window, and the French windows when tested proved to be locked. Knocking produced no response. After a precautionary glance round the moonlit garden, Darcy took a strip of plastic from her pocket and slid it into the catch. The resultant click sounded frighteningly loud in the stillness of the rural night but at last she was inside.

Risking her torch, but shielding the beam with her hand so that light trickled through her fingers and made them glow red, she stood for a moment and listened. There was no sound save the occasional creak old houses make as they settle back on their haunches to slumber.

"Miles?" she ventured, raising her voice to add when nobody answered: "It's, Darcy. Are you there?" Silence pressed against her ears and scorned her timidity.

Growing bolder, she removed her hand and allowed the beam of the torch to range over walls and furniture. An involuntary gasp escaped her as it revealed the slashed chairs and upturned drawers and pictures hanging drunkenly from their hooks. Each room told the same story. The mattress in the bedroom obviously used by Miles had been slit and the carpet turned back. This was no random break-in, whoever was responsible was after something specific. She grimaced in distaste at the stale smell of alcohol, sweat and urine. The upturned tumbler, the empty bottle by the bed, the ashtray brimming with stubs beside the crumpled cigarette packet, the flotsam and jetsam of a ruined life brought a rush of compassion. Whether the chaos was due solely to the frantic search or evidence of a struggle Darcy could not tell. Whatever, Miles Standish was not in the house.

Downstairs in the kitchen, moonlight spilled in at the uncurtained window onto the marked and faded linoleum. Papers littered the table and lay scattered across the floor. Miles may have fled, possibly to join his wife and family in their hideaway, taking his secret with him. Whilst puzzling over what to do next, she picked up a couple of sheets, scanned them with the aid of her torch and dropped them again. Family trees, historical dates and genealogical details were all meaningless when out of context. Frustration gnawed at her insides but something else was nudging her mind into action. Family trees: the phrase repeated itself in her thoughts, and adrenalin buzzed in the region of her solar plexus as awareness struck. *To save the family name,* that line from Miles' weird message. It might refer to Anton de Beaumont and some secret he took to the grave. And that bit about *should the man of business fail to keep his appointment:* Miles as an accountant was a man of business, and he had failed to turn up tonight.

A rummage inside her bag brought forth the folded sheet of paper on which it was written. Sweeping aside papers with nibbled corners and littered with rat and mouse droppings, Darcy sat down at the table and nervous still of turning on lights, used her torch instead. Ten minutes or so later, the rest of the message was still a mystery. Rising, she wandered listlessly around dredging her mind for inspiration. Dispirited, she made her way back to the drawing-room intending to leave by the French windows.

"I hope you are safe, Miles," she whispered, her gaze moving sadly over the desecrated room. Her nostrils flared with distaste as they detected dust, mustiness and a disturbing scent that was hard to label but which suggested residual fear. Moonbeams filtered in through the window and dappled the wall, silvering one of the crooked pictures with eerie effect. About to step through the doors she paused, feeling as though she had been struck by lightning. Moving back inside, she stared again at the drawing of the priory ruins and, moving swiftly now, took it down from its hook. *And be sent to the wall and drawn by his pride into prior ruin.* What had seemed meaningless drivel now made sense. The line was a cryptic reference to this picture. Fired by success, her brain made connections, associations that brought further revelations making her wonder how she could have been so blind. That reference to Miss Austen's hero for example, and *...by his pride* could only relate to Pride and Prejudice and Mr. *Darcy.* In short, the message was addressed to herself. The previously puzzling signature now took on significance. Abarbanel, she realised with mounting excitement, was the name of Brant's ancient astronomer.

She pried back the old-fashioned metal clips that held the picture's backing in place, splitting a fingernail in the process. Her hands shook as she removed a folded sheet of paper. Elation was short lived. Here in her hand lay the object of a determined search and whoever had been responsible may well return. Putting down her torch and fumbling in her haste, she stuffed the paper into her bag, then replacing the back on the frame, she restored the drawing to its hook on the wall. One backward glance then she was outside again in the moonlit, watchful garden. Moving like a shadow, Darcy ran down the path to the gate. In pulling it to she noticed the gleam of gold on the ground. The buzz in her stomach told her what it was before she stooped to pick it up. The Sobranie cigarette stub felt to be scorching her palm.

Once back in the car and pulling away from Monk Grange, Darcy's numbed mind began to clear. So they had got to him first. She drove through the village and saw the lights of the level crossing glowing ahead. Somehow it seemed like a frontier: Once it was crossed danger would be behind her and sanctuary lay ahead. Good, all was quiet, the barriers raised and the way clear. Level crossings were not her favourite feature, there was something sinister about them that was hard to put into words. It was, she thought approaching this one, rather like a legalised game of 'chicken'. No matter how remote the odds there was always the chance that something could go wrong. Machinery might fail at the last minute causing the automatic barrier to jam or, due to human error, train times be confused.

A slight tingle along the nape of the neck always accompanied a crossing, and tonight was no exception. Halfway over, and the half-expected onrush and clamour and lights of the hurtling metal missile had not materialised. She was about to emit a sigh of relief when her feet instinctively stamped the brake pedal and her eyes started in fear and disbelief.

THIRTY

The figure wavered before her eyes, leaving a fleeting impression of a white surplice bearing a splayed red cross. This was no wraith, no insubstantial vapour. The man before her appeared physical and real in every respect for the second or two in which his figure darkened the windscreen. It was over in an instant. Her head was filled with the squeal of tyres and ear-hurting screams which eventually she recognised as her own. She braced herself, knowing there was no chance of avoiding impact. The back end skewed round as the car went into a skid and teeth clenched, Darcy closed her eyes in terror.

The bone-shaking jolt brought them wide open. Desperately afraid of what might confront her, she stared into the pool of light shed by the headlamps. The dreaded mangled body and splatters of blood were not in evidence. The car had nosed into one of the barriers with little discernible damage. Climbing out, she moved to the bonnet and steeled herself for the gruesome find, but discovered nothing. No prostrate figure bled beneath the wheels or lay spread-eagled upon the ground. Bemused, she stared to left and right of a moonlit track that stretched into barren infinity. There was a metallic taste and smell to the air, as though something cataclysmic had erupted: a thunderbolt or lightning ball or some other freak of Nature. Yet nothing disturbed the silence of the night save her own erratic breathing.

Trauma put logic to flight. Later, when the shaking of her limbs had subsided and her mind cleared, she would want to laugh at the insanity of searching for the apparition's body. Leaning against the bonnet, she swayed on her feet as dizziness and nausea swept over her in a wave. Pull yourself together Darcy West, she exhorted herself, ashamed of her weakness. Eventually self-preservation took over, that and the need to place as many kilometres as possible between herself and Monk

Grange. There had been nothing ethereal about that cigarette end, or the way in which Miles Standish's home had been ransacked.

About to climb back into the driving seat, she paused, one foot raised and a hand on the door and the other grasping the steering wheel. A freeze frame occurred, a second or so when reality slipped from her grasp and the air shuddered with shock. The movement, the figure and splash of red on white, shattered normality before disappearing.
"Wait! Stop!" she cried, leaving the car door gaping to clamber over the barrier and drop to the other side.

Cloud buffeted along by a light wind briefly obscured the moon and she stood hesitantly, body tense, eyes strained and feet unsure in darkness combined with unfamiliar surroundings. Maybe her imagination was focused by danger and fired by shock. A half minute or so passed in which this explanation held good, but then her head swung round as her eye was caught by a blur of grey, a brief movement that found an echo in her solar plexus as every nerve in her body jerked. Fear and something else, a reverence perhaps for something sensed but unknown, kept her silent. Stumbling in the dark, and cursing her stupidity for leaving the torch at Monk Grange, she attempted to follow, her feet snagged by the brambles and bindweed that choked the embankment. Danger now threatened from two sources. Her ears strained for the clacking of wheels over points, and her eyes ached from searching the darkness for the pin points of light that would warn of an approaching train.

She quickened her pace, then some three hundred yards from the crossing stopped, recalling with a jolt that she had left the car in a dangerous position. A disturbance ahead, a scrambling of the light that reminded her of the device used by television studios to hide the faces of interviewees, deterred her from turning back. The fragments of whatever it was shivered and shimmied with energy before disintegrating.

Something was irresistibly drawing her onward. Cloud blotted the moon plunging her into darkness.

Disoriented, she wandered too close to the line and, catching her foot, stumbled. Steadying herself, she cursed beneath her breath and saw what appeared to be the limb of a tree. All she needed now was to sprain her ankle or worse, and with this in mind remained motionless waiting for cloud to disperse. The freshening wind did its work, and the face of the moon was briefly revealed before being partially covered again. Disclosed in that instant was a scene as bizarre and disturbing as any Salvador Dali painting.

No cry was wrenched from her throat, no impetus for flight carried her forward. It was simply beyond belief. A tableau so awful and improbable that it must be a figment of her disturbed state of mind and disordered imagination. She stood numbly, staring unseeingly into the darkness, willing the delusion to be gone before the next pitiless onslaught of light. A chill was creeping through her body. She cringed, and without conscious thought her thighs contracted, forcing together knees and ankles to avoid contact with any object lying on the ground. Seconds passed as slowly as eons during that terrible wait. The wind gusted, bending tall grasses into submission and whipping cloud into shreds. The healing, concealing, darkness was replaced by a fitful haunting light.

Darcy stuffed a fist into her mouth and bit her knuckles until the salty taste of blood made her stop. The limb her foot had caught against was not covered by bark but mangled fragments of cloth and skin. The whiteness of bone gleamed obscenely in the half-light; limbs and fragments of torso littered the railway lines. Retching uncontrollably, Darcy now tasted fear as well as blood. Sightless eyes watched her distress. On the opposite side of the track lay Miles Standish's severed head.

THIRTY-ONE

Somehow, she made her way back to the car. Sitting motionless behind the wheel, fighting the trembling and nausea that wracked her body, Darcy slipped into denial. The whole incident was a delusion. Things like that just did not happen to people like herself and not in real life. Hugging herself, curling up in the driving seat into foetal security she managed to convince herself that Miles was safe somewhere with his wife and family. The obscenity on the track was expunged from her mind, blanked out by shock and necessity. Reason had taken a holiday; the compulsion to leave this place was purely mechanical. She turned the key in the ignition, engaged first gear and released the hand brake all without conscious thought and drove away with as little emotion as a factory robot.

Except, that is, for the tell-tale squeal of tyres as the car leapt forward. Robots had no unconscious fears to threaten the cover-up process. A robot had no need to flee with the speed of a greyhound out of the trap. Confusing thoughts. Half thoughts. Confusion rules O.K. Nothing wrong, just keep driving and don't let the memory of something-that-never-happened rise from its grave.

Climbing the road up to the moor now and surfacing into midnight-space studded with stars and blessed with isolation; an emptiness that matched the void inside her head. It all helped: the spinning wheels, humming tyres, the comforting purr of the engine. But the silence outside was greater. So was the midnight sweep of infinity stretching to the horizon, the place where now meets forever. An eternity of stars and ice-blaze of planets reproached her retreat from reality. The feeling of being alone in the world but part of something bigger, touched her soul and restored her senses. The engine stalled and the car lurched to a halt scraping an outcrop of rock in the process. Unable to sustain the pretence, she allowed the full horror of what she had witnessed to wash over her in choking waves. Still grasping the wheel, she supported her head on her arms and sobbed without restraint.

Eventually, the paroxysm ceased to be replaced by an awful calm and rationality. Nothing could help Miles now. That was the bottom line and nothing was going to change it. Whoever had done this terrible thing would be long gone from the area – because no way was his death an accident. The guy had been living in abject terror, had probably known it was on the cards for tonight. *Tomorrow will be too late*, and his words came back to haunt and fill her with pity. However, putting her own life at risk by becoming involved would serve no-one. So there would be no reporting the grisly find, no statement made to the police, nothing to connect her with the incident. It would be discovered soon enough. Granted her fingerprints would be everywhere at Monk Grange, but could be accounted for by her earlier visit. A call on a local historian by a reporter doing a piece on a local find would be accepted as normal.
"I'm so sorry Miles," she whispered, turning on the ignition. Would she tell Brant? That question burned her mind as she dropped down from the moor and headed for Mistletoe Cottage.

The darkness in the valley was complete. For once it was unrelieved by the friendly glow of a farmhouse porch, or a shaft of light from a barn window as a farmer tended sick stock or a difficult birth. Granted it was late, but there was always a light on somewhere in the village. The white walls of the inn loomed to her right, but the all-night bulkhead above the entrance was dead. The absence of artificial light could mean only one thing: a power failure. Faults were common out here, the blame usually being shared by adverse weather conditions and antiquated equipment.

It could be worse, she consoled herself, turning down the track to the cottage. It could be mid winter when the darkness could be cut with a knife. As it was, a milky opalescence lightened the sky to the north, the residual glow from the Northern Lights. Even so, braving it would be an ordeal. The darkness had the effect of compounding the silence so that it pressed against her mind, demanding to be kept unbroken. She found herself easing shut the car door; to slam it would be to anger the Fates and make her even more vulnerable to danger. For the second time, she wished she had not left the torch back at Monk Grange.

The flutter of panic was hard to quell. Reaching the front door was going to be a gauntlet-run. They have no idea you were at Monk Grange tonight, and therefore do not know you are here now, she consoled herself over and over whilst feeling her way forward. Nevertheless, her legs felt as though they were about to give way. She paused, spun round and peered into the gloom. The shadows shifted, trembled and settled again, though whether in response to movement within them, or merely her imagination, it was hard to say. The corresponding leap in her stomach subsided, but the feeling of not being alone remained.

Dense shrubbery, and the shadows cast by inky pines towering a hundred feet and more presented perfect conditions for any intruder, she worried. Shock buzzed along her nerves as the ghostly white form of a barn owl glided overhead, its ghostly screech muffled by a fug of threat and shadows. As she fumbled for the key, the darkness pressed at her back and silence dinned in her ears. The sensation of being watched was growing by the minute. Desperately, she tried to control her breathing and thus the upsurge of panic. At last the dark rectangle shape of the door loomed ahead. Relief propelled her through those last few steps to where safety beckoned. Her fingers felt for the metal keyhole. Instead, they found something warm and soft and alive. Her cry exploded into the night, ricocheting around the pines and circling her head like Edvard Munch's 'scream'.

THIRTY-TWO

Darcy's body froze in terror, then adrenalin pumped into her bloodstream mobilising her limbs for flight. She spun round but the hand she had touched shot out in restraint.

"You're late."

Her legs sagged, and she slumped against the door jamb.

"Shit!" she stared at the shadowed figure with eyes that were wide with shock.

"Sorry, Darcy. I didn't intend to startle you." The hand eased its grip on her arm.

"Startle me," she exploded, relief finding expression in anger, "Brant Kennedy, you almost gave me a coronary!"

Ignoring this outburst, he brushed past her to open the door and usher her inside.

Despite herself, his touch buzzed along her nerves and disordered her heightened senses. Forgetting the power failure, she automatically reached for the light switch. A second click brought a beam of light which sliced through the darkness of the entrance.

"You had a torch," she accused. He raised his eyebrows but did not answer. His continuing silence, and the way his gaze flicked over her hands then lingered on her shoulder bag, brought a frisson of unease. "Why didn't you use it back there?" she demanded, "instead of frightening me half to death."

"I didn't recognise the car." He closed the door and smiled apologetically. She had forgotten the swap with Fran. Darcy's emotions wavered, the compass needle trembling between suspicion and acceptance: she settled for compromise by committing to neither.

"It belongs to a colleague; there was a minor problem with mine."

The cool officiousness of his manner changed.

"Hey, you're shaking," he said, sounding concerned.

225

He placed an arm about her shoulders, "What you need is a stiff drink." Pushing open the door to the living room, he drew her inside, a move she approved as the tiny hall had become too cramped to hold herself, Brant and the tangle of her emotions.

"Brandy? Candles?" he demanded, setting the lamp down on the mantelpiece.

"Brandy-," confused, she stroked her forehead. "Cupboard-, over there." Her hand shook as she pointed, "and the candles. No they're not, they are—," she faltered, sinking into the mire of reaction but forcing her mind to surface, "yes, kitchen cabinet, top shelf - with matches."

"Good lass." His voice controlled her; she responded to its tones in the way of a lost or injured beast. "We'll get those first, shall we?" When he picked up the lamp and moved to the door waves of panic broke over her head.

"Only dark for a moment, Darcy," he soothed, disappearing into the kitchen.

Darkness smothered her, whispering warnings of isolation and vulnerability and bringing to mind dreadful pictures of Miles Standish's mutilated body. It was Brant moving about out there in the kitchen, she reminded herself, and so there was nothing to fear. Better not to dwell on that Sobranie cigarette on Mile's path, or the packet in Brant Kennedy's bedroom. The sound of match striking against box was followed by a shifting of shadows and leap of light that retrieved her from the brink of hysteria. Brant entered with two candles stuck on saucers. The flames danced, flattened and rose to peak in a thin trail of smoke as he placed one on the sideboard, and the other on the mantel above the grate. Like Darcy's unease, the flames gradually settled.

"Now for that brandy." Taking a bottle and two glasses from the cupboard, he poured two generous measures and handed one of them to Darcy. "Drink up – all of it," he ordered.

The fire trickled down her throat and warmed her

stomach, reviving her spirits and calming her nerves. She frowned as certain facts gelled: a glance at the clock showed the time to be past 3 a.m.

"Have you been waiting out there all night?"

"I love you Darcy, but not that much!" he said with an ironic smile. She rolled her glass between her palms.

"So how did you know what time I would arrive – or even if I would?" she said without looking at him, then glanced up sharply to catch his expression on answering.

"It was easy enough to calculate." He returned her stare with a bland look

"I guess." The finger of suspicion wavered again; he was not supposed to know about her visit to Monk Grange. There was also the delay caused by her office detour to take into account. To make it fit, he should have been waiting out there for something like an incredible three or four hours.

"So how long were you waiting?" she asked.

"A while."

She saw that his jaw had a clamped look that made the muscles protrude and knew there would be nothing more forthcoming on the subject. He motioned for her to drink up, then as she complied, took her empty glass.

"Did you find anything?"

It was said casually enough, yet she gained the impression he could wait no longer to ask.

"I don't follow."

"At Monk Grange," he said smoothly.

Darcy stared at him without answering. How could he possibly know?

"I took it you would call there first." The slight smile mocked her, as though he had read the thought. Her hand automatically went to her mouth as though to prevent any indiscretion from escaping.

"Why would you? Why should I go there?" The slight smile and deliberate silence were more intimidating than words. She was acutely aware of the submerged force that had both attracted and daunted her from the day they had met. It seemed he was sure of his own power and therefore felt no need to display it for others; but it was there, a whirlpool swirling beneath the unruffled surface. She found herself wondering if it was also evil, after all she knew very little about him.

"Did Miles make contact?"
"No," she said automatically, then wavered beneath his steady gaze. "Well yes actually, he did," she admitted, wondering how much to disclose.
"Stop playing games, Darcy."
His voice cut through her defences, and in the flickering half-light Brant appeared more than a little sinister. Instinctively Darcy took a backward step.
"He's dead," she said dully, her defences crumbling beneath his stare. Covering her face with hands that shook she began to weep.

She huddled before the fire which Brant swiftly kindled, hugging a glass containing a second dose of brandy that he had pressed upon her when she had finished confiding her story. But nothing about finding the paper in the back of the picture. Acutely aware of her omission and its significance in terms of trust, or rather a lack of it, her hand instinctively went to the strap of her bag which was still slung over one shoulder. Brant's gaze registered the movement and compassion was tempered by steel.
"And?" he prompted.
"What?"
"You've not told me everything."
His gaze seemed to bore through her and into the back of the chair.
"Somebody murdered Miles. Isn't that enough?" she said bitterly. He was watching her carefully, his eyes narrowed as though in deliberation before responding.
"Or he killed himself," he said then added in response to Darcy's look of outrage, "it is possible."

She rose and paced the room in her agitation before pausing to round on him.

"It was not suicide," she asserted, her eyes dark with emotion against the pallor of her face. "You know how he was living; the man was being hounded ."
"He was crazy. You said so yourself."
Anger boiled and threatened to overspill: Brant's attitude seemed like a betrayal of Miles. Darcy stood facing him, her hands gripping the back of the chair.
"Crazy with fear maybe. But I do not believe he would contact me, ask me to meet him, then lie down on a railway track to die. Have you forgotten Dr. Piper and Caro?" Moving forward she bent and grasped the arms of his chair so that her face was inches from his, "I tell you Miles Standish was brutally murdered and nothing you say will change that."

"Sit down, Darcy." It was said quietly, but his expression made her aware of her threatening pose and the need to withdraw.
"I did not," he said, as she sat on the edge of her seat, "say he had killed himself, only that it was a possibility given his disturbed state of mind. But whatever the truth, you and I should not be falling out over it Darcy." He rose, and taking her hands, drew her up from the chair and gently kissed her. "Poor girl. What an awful thing to find," he murmured into her hair whilst patting her back as one might do for a troubled infant. His compassion broke down the defences that had been holding in her fear and distress. Now she clung to him, and did weep like a child. He held her for several minutes, then as though judging the worst to be over, gently set her from him.

Picking up the glass containing the remains of the brandy, he put it in her hand.
"Finish this off, then try to sleep. And Darcy—"
"Yes?"
"Be sensible and stay out of this from now on."
"That's a bit high-handed isn't it?" Her nerves were raw and she snapped without thinking.
"Maybe, but do it." He looked up and sighed as if struggling with impatience.

She wanted to stem the retaliatory words before they were spoken but seemed powerless to halt the down-hill rush to disaster:

"Just because we slept together once," Cruelly she stressed the word and with it the brevity of the relationship, "that doesn't give you rights of ownership." The hurt that flashed across his features and darkened his eyes made her instantly sorry but the words, like feathers from a slashed pillow, had already escaped and could not be taken back.

"Where are you going?" she asked, striving to keep the panic out of her voice as without speaking he walked to the door.

"To do the necessary," he replied, pausing on the threshold, and Darcy cringed at the coldness of tone and manner. "The authorities and so on; I don't want you involved," he added."

She took a step forward, then faltered on seeing the hardness of his expression. Suddenly the desire to be held was overwhelming.

"Brant – I didn't mean—,"

"Forget it."

"I'm upset, stressed out by what happened tonight."

She stroked her forehead distractedly, an unconscious and timeless gesture conveying her confusion and distress, "I didn't know what I was saying," she added, only this time it was a deliberate attempt to use Miles' death to excuse the inexcusable. And he knew it. The look he gave her brought a flush of shame to her cheeks.

"I think you did, Darcy." He gave her a searching look. "This is the last time I'm going to ask you this question; think carefully before you answer." His gaze intensified, and his eyes darkened to midnight pools, though whether from desire or hostility it was impossible for her to know. He watched her in silence, allowing the import of his words to sink in before speaking again: "Did you find anything at Monk Grange?"

Darcy dropped her gaze, and her hand instinctively tightened on the shoulder strap of her bag. The pause was infinitesimal, but she saw it register in the flicker of his eyelids.

"No," she said at last, forcing herself to meet his look without flinching.

"Very well."

The severity of his expression filled her with apprehension; he might just as well have added 'on your head be it, she thought with conflicting feelings of fear and outrage.

As Brant abruptly quit the room, the flames of the candles wavered, peaked and subsided, threatening to plunge her into darkness. The sound of the door closing, and minutes later, the throb of the Land Rover's engine and sweep of headlights across the window brought a surge of pain and loneliness. *I should have told him.* Suddenly weary, she sank down on the settee and held her head in her hands. But she held back, and now it was too late. In being afraid of taking the risk, her faith in him had failed the acid test. To survive and flourish love had to be nourished with trust; whatever had burgeoned between them was over. Hot tears burned cheeks that were chilled from fatigue, distress and shock. But, she thought minutes later, there were more serious and far-reaching issues at stake.

Thoughts of the paper still lurking in her bag brought a surge of adrenalin that dispelled fatigue. Whatever her personal problems, there was no question of going to bed until it had revealed its secret. Carrying one of the candles into the kitchen, she lit four more and stuck them on saucers with gobbets of melted wax. Then putting the kettle on to boil, she gave silent thanks for the calor gas stove. Five minutes later, she was settled in the sitting room, candles arranged around her and a mug of black coffee to hand. Her find was also on the table and, as though to concentrate her mind, the gold of the Sobranie cigarette stub gleamed dully in the candlelight. After taking a sip or two of scalding coffee, she unfolded the sheaf and discovered several sheets of notepaper covered in Mile's handwriting.

And there it was, amongst the collection of strange diagrams and symbols: Anton de Beaumont, the name of the knight as she had somehow foreseen it after making love with Brant at the farmhouse on the cliffs. The 'mummified' body with its distinctive features, leathery flesh and faded eyes now took on a new dimension. As though this indisputable proof of his personality had brought him to magical life, his image took on a new realism and vitality. *Anton*. Darcy played with the name, saying it over and over softly to herself like a sacred mantra, relishing the intimacy after weeks of anonymity. As she read on, it became clear she was right about something else too; here was a man with a compelling story to tell. And now, due to Miles' ultimate sacrifice, she knew why Anton de Beaumont had died.

THIRTY-THREE

Her intuition about Anton de Beaumont being a Knight of the Temple had been correct. He had joined the order of soldier mystics despite being forbidden to do so by his father. It was not hard to imagine: a handsome young knight fired by an ideal and driven perhaps by a mission not yet understood by the mind, but fired by the heart and undertook by the soul. Staring into the fire. the scene came alive. Embers and half burned logs turned into turrets as he rode from the castle into an unknown dawn. At the brow of the hill, he paused to look back as the sun rose, birds sang and mist wreathed the valley below, his heart feeling as though it must burst as he looked down on his home for what he instinctively knew was the last time, knowing he was deliberately cutting himself off, and that his father would have no choice but to disown him.

And how poignantly that was expressed. The image behind her eyes sharpened and clarified as facts and imagination fused. There was no differentiating the two, only insight. The sun-sparked shield that he carried was bare of device, his chest as plain as the surplice of any foot soldier. No family coat of arms, no crest or motto to offer protection and support. This more than anything else underlined the enormity of his decision. Empathy flowed, and for the first time it seemed she knew him as a person. A log burned through and collapsed in a cascade of sparks, and the fire in the hearth returned to being just that.

She exhaled slowly, then sat back with her head resting against the cushions of the settee and watched shadows flicker and leap across the ceiling. The lateness of the hour, the candlelight and silence all heightened the sense of unreality. She raised herself up on the cushions and shivered involuntarily. The temperature had dropped, the fire burned sluggishly and she found herself idly wondering if she had dropped some green logs into the basket by mistake. The flames in the grate burned a sickly and unnatural blue as though starved of oxygen and about to die. A chill was creeping around the walls and breathing damp air down the back of her neck. Her head whipped round, and she stared wide-eyed into corners that seemed to contain more than inanimate shadows.

One of the candles flared and spluttered, bringing her upright and tense on the settee. Why had this come her way – and what was she supposed to do about it? Her mind ricocheted from one possibility to another like a ball off the pins of a fruit machine. Rising, she paced the room then sat down again, forcing herself to quell the rise of panic and paranoia. At length the adrenalin ceased to pump and she sagged with weariness against the cushions, overwhelmed by events and feeling powerless to effectively deal with them. A migraine threatened, and her eyes smarted from smoke and fatigue. Brant was right: this was not something to dabble in; from now on these bizarre incidents would not be her concern. In fact it would be a pleasure to be reporting cosy Council corruption and debunking the myth of Clare Cabbala. Snuffing all but one candle that lit the way up the stairs to bed, she checked at the bedroom window for any sign of movement in the shrubbery below.

Moonlight froze the scene in a still from another world. A medieval world, with unfurled banners of cloud that trailed ragged ends across a midnight infinity, and Lady Moon swelled with pride and bestowed upon Earth a smile that was almost sinister. The wash of argent sharpened the webbed silhouettes of flittering pipistrelle bats, and deepened the purple and indigo shadows that shrouded the base of the pines. If anyone lurked in this fabulous realm they would be well hidden from view. Darcy was about to twitch the curtain back across the window when a movement caught her eye. Heart thumping in her chest, she paused like that, one hand in the air and her gaze fixed on the shrubbery below. For a second or so, impossible images strayed into her vision: the gleam of armour burnished by moonlight and a white robe with the familiar splash of scarlet. A fantasy as illusive and fleeting as the dance of the pipistrelle bats, yet one that infused her with guilt. The wordless clamour accused her of betrayal, and the abandonment of a promise made. Her hands shook as she covered her ears to shut it out and alleviate her distress. "Go away," she whispered distraught, "Leave me alone – I cannot help you." A soft moan escaped her lips and she closed her eyes in despair.

When she dared to open them again only purple shadows inhabited the shrubbery. A white shape sailed past her line of vision, followed by a spine-tingling shriek. She cried out and shrank from the window before realising it was a barn owl on the hunt. With all that had happened, her nerves were shot. Yet so real had that figure seemed, that for one wild instant she suspected Brant of hiding out in the bushes, wearing a sheet with a red painted cross, pulling some cruel and macabre trick to frighten her off the case. She opened her mouth intending to call out Brant's name, but discovered the silence was too profound to be broken. Besides, in her heart she knew it was not Brant. No, that figure out there had been a fantasy, a figment of her disordered imagination. *It had to be.*

Raising a hand that still trembled, she absently massaged a spot above her left eye, then realised that the earlier threat of a headache had hardened into a dull and persistent pain. And that was the answer, she told herself: it was simply a bizarre example of the visual disturbance that so often precedes a migraine. She yanked the curtain across the glass with a savage movement that caused it to snag and stick. Tears of frustration and reaction burned her cheeks as she struggled to release it. Whatever the truth, her life was a mess, and peace of mind a rare luxury. Weariness overcame her, and she collapsed fully clothed onto the bed.

Sleep eventually came but not oblivion. Smoke and the acrid smell of burning stung her nostrils, that and a sweet underlying odour that defied recognition but made bile scald her throat. Billows of smoke were ushered away by a westerly wind, revealing a sight from Bosch's Hell. The fiery pit belched and spewed its flames to stain the morning sky with blood. A lark briefly soared singing out its heart, then as the heat and miasma rose to meet it, fell silent and dropped like a stone. People – men, women and children – were being herded by soldiers to the brink of the pit. The stench of fear was added to that of charred flesh, but the people kept coming, resigned and unresisting like cattle to the slaughter.

"No! No!" Darcy screamed, sweat glistening in beads on her forehead and upper lip as she moved closer to look and protest.. Unbelievably, and with gut rending obedience, they leapt into the glowing, searing, roaring fire below.

She covered her ears with her hands to shut out their screams, and the whimpering of children next in line and clinging for life to their mothers' skirts.

"Bastards! Stop it! Stop it!" she screamed at the stony-faced soldiers prodding with sword and pike as they drove their victims into the fiery chasm. A geyser of sparks crackled and fell as the flames received their human fodder. Slipping now out of bed and safety and into that scene from hell. Teetering now on the brink, knowing there was to be no escape, feeling the heat rise through the ground to burn her feet, and hot breath rise to sear the skin from her face. Wild-eyed, she cast around for a last sight of his beloved face, but saw only anonymous ones above the uniform of the King's troops.

The soldiers were ushering forward the next consignment to the flames. Mutely, obediently, she took a step forward with her companions as though part of a group mind. No point in resisting, came the silent message. This was their greatest gift to the faith but paradoxically the ultimate revenge. The faces of knights and foot soldiers said it all: set in marble, features immobile and eyes deader than the poor wretches who were turned to ash in their thousands. How else could they look? Only by seeing their victims as mindless beasts could they carry out their terrible duty. A lifetime and beyond of torment would haunt their souls and deny them rest. Could she find it in her soul to forgive them? No! No! Never! her heart cried out in denial as the next rank of men, women and children clung together, murmuring aloud their prayers with awful dignity before making the fatal leap.

The belch of flames exploded in her face bringing to her nostrils the stink of singed eyebrows and hair. She looked wildly round, afraid to call him by name. Their secret must lie cooling with her ashes once the agony was over. Oh, God let it be quick, she prayed as her skin reddened, stretched and blistered in the fiery eruption. The press at her back inched her closer to the inferno. She closed her eyelids, half-crazed by pain and heat, ready to let her weight carry her forward.

"This one!"
The whiplash recoil almost snapped her neck as somebody grabbed her from behind and hauled her back from the brink.
"Anton!" Her heart knew it was he; the name left her lips before she turned to face him.
"Leala."
The agony was there in his eyes at sight of her poor blistered face.
"Do as I say, Leala," he said in an urgent under-voice then he shouted to the guards: "Her parents have repented – she has been granted one last chance."
Her arms felt to be wrenched from their sockets, then oblivion came as they hauled her clear of the death-pit.

Darcy sat bolt upright in bed whimpering with terror and writhing in pain. Throwing back the duvet, she lurched to the dressing table and reached for the overhead lamp, forgetting the earlier power cut. It must have been repaired because light flooded the dark corner. Afraid of what the mirror may reveal, she squeezed her eyes tight shut. Would she be disfigured? and more frightening still, whose face would be reflected? Plucking up courage, she risked a look. Her face stared back at her, wild eyed and pinched for sure – but un-scorched and deathly pale in its terror. Confused, she stood with hands pressed to her unblemished cheeks, then stretched out her arms and minutely examined them. The flesh gleamed pale and wholesome in the subdued light from the lamp.

Minutes later in the bathroom, the shock of cold water splashing her face and arms cleared her mind and dispelled the illusion of scorching pain. From the cabinet above the sink, she took a bottle of paracetemol tablets and swallowed a couple to ease the ache at her temple. Returning to the bed, she sat for several moments on the edge, unconsciously stroking her left arm with slow soothing strokes. This, she guessed, was similar to what Caro had suffered the night she stayed at Mistletoe Cottage, and prior to that too, probably from the day the coffin was unearthed - given Caro's edginess at the post mortem. The chances were it had been recurring ever since. The realisation brought a wave of compassion. Poor Caro must have feared for her sanity, so no wonder she had appeared preoccupied and remote.

Responsibility weighted Darcy's shoulders. Whatever the truth of her 'vision' in the shrubbery and the terrifying nightmare, one thing was becoming increasingly clear: there could be no backing off from the investigation, no breaking of her rashly made promise if peace of mind was to be restored. Exhaustion overcame her in leaden waves. Leaving the bedside lamp switched on to dispel the shades, Darcy lay down and drifted into uneasy sleep.

The terrible screams were still ringing in her ears. She should not be able to hear them now, Anton had dragged her clear of the pit and out of that pitiful crowd. On and on it went. Her head tossed to and fro on the pillow, and finally Darcy opened her eyes, striving to make sense of a sound split between recurring dream and reality. The source registered: the telephone on the bedside table was shrilling. Blinking away the remnants of sleep, she reached for the receiver and mumbled first her name, then as her head cleared and recognition hit,
"Brant?" as she hauled herself up against the pillows.

"Whose turn is to apologise this time? I just forget," he said cheerfully. She had to smile. The nerve of the man. But one who could warm her simply by the sound of his voice could not be all bad.

THIRTY-FOUR

Sunlight slanted in gold bars across the kitchen floor and bird song drifted in through the open window. How, Darcy wondered pushing aside her untouched breakfast, could everything be so normal after the horrors of the previous night? After making coffee and toast she boiled an egg, but on smashing the shell to slice off the top had pushed it aside, being unpleasantly reminded of Miles Standish's severed head. The authorities would be involved by now. She tried to picture the scene by the railway, the police cars and grim-faced officers, cordons of tape whirring in the breeze, the photographers and forensic team and was sickened anew. And afraid. She could only hope that Brant's assurance of keeping her out of the enquiry was grounded in fact.

But that in itself was worrying, she thought with a frown. Because if so it begged questions about the degree of power he held in his ministry position. It crossed her mind that he was ideally placed for a key role in this affair – and on either side. He had persuaded her to have dinner with him that night, and the fact brought more comfort than she cared to admit. Meanwhile, she intended to spend the day in research at the library in Carlisle. On her way to the car, she paused to search the shrubbery where the figure had appeared the previous night. No broken twigs or crushed leaves, no footprints on the dewy earth. Making a firm resolve not to dwell on the implications, she walked briskly to the car.

Late afternoon, she drove back to Mistletoe Cottage in a mood of elation and with a pad bursting with notes. So much now made sense. Her research verified the mass burnings experienced through her nightmare. She now knew that the girl in the dream was a member of the Cathars, a pious religious sect declared heretics and burned in their thousands. The Templars however had refused to participate in their persecution and had offered support, even going so far as to enlist members of the sect to their ranks. There was now no doubt in her mind that Anton de Beaumont had fallen in love with a Cathar, and that the skeleton found beside his coffin was that of the woman named in her dream as 'Leala'. It followed that the hair found draped across his chest also belonged to her. One thing was sure: in loving Leala he had risked his life and alienated himself from the order by breaking his vow of chastity. Somehow, Anton had saved this Leala from the flames. The mystery of how they came to be buried at the remote priory remained unsolved.

But not for long. As she read on, the reason was elegantly revealed. It appeared the Order of Knights Templar had become too powerful for their own good. In October of 1307 someone betrayed them to Philip the Fourth of France who, consumed by envy at their wealth and power, had stormed their Paris headquarters in a dawn raid. The accounts of charges, torture and burnings had made gruesome reading, she reflected soberly on turning into the valley. Reading it had led her into a world shadowed by heresy, corruption and barbarity. And again Brant's claims had checked out: the sect had indeed been accused of consorting with dark forces, of involvement with esoteric doctrines, occult practices and bizarre initiation ceremonies. That such a high profile person should be buried at the priory now seemed all the more remarkable.

Gradually all became clear. On 22nd March 1312 Pope Clement the Fifth issued a bull declaring the Order of Knights Templar be dissolved. An item which, on recalling how Brant had disclosed the fact that the Templars enjoyed the pope's protection and, being answerable only to him were therefore above the law of the land, raised a further mystery. Why had the Pope finally deserted his powerful protégées? Had he in fact been the one who betrayed them, and if so why? But leaving this new conundrum for later, she had turned her attention back to St. Gildas Bay.

241

Philip of France it appeared. had tried to enlist the support of Edward II to undertake a similar purge in England. Initially Edward had refused, but being in a politically sensitive position, had appeased Philip by agreeing in principle, but had compromised by treating known Templars with leniency. It appeared the most popular sentence was a couple of years spent in retreat at a remote monastery – and here, to the disapproval of a hovering librarian, Darcy was moved to impulsively cry aloud 'yes!' This, she thought in triumph, explained the presence of Anton de Beaumont's body at a priory on a remote Cumbrian cliff top.

What it failed to explain however, was the inclusion within the crypt of a female member of a sect denounced as heretical. Another thought struck, and Darcy frowned as she spun the wheel and urged the car up and round and into the parking space behind Mistletoe Cottage. If Anton de Beaumont had indeed been sent to St. Gildas Bay to repent for his sin of being a Templar, then why had his body been preserved and buried in such an elaborate manner? His fatal injuries and manner of death also remained a mystery.

After showering and dressing ready for her dinner date with Brant, she sat down to unwind with a cup of tea and the Telegraph cryptic crossword begun that morning at breakfast. Half an hour later, only one elusive clue remained unanswered. *Clasping holds the answer rather than chasing it.* Nine letters, first one is an 'O', third a 'b' and ending with 's'. Absently she sucked the end of her pen and wondered why Clare Cabbala suddenly come to mind. She searched for a connection, then tutted aloud with frustration when nothing gelled. Okay, forget association of ideas and go for syntax – and cheating. Switching on her pocket-sized electronic puzzle solver, she tapped in the letters.

There was only one possible word, and that one so obscure that it meant nothing. A dip into the dictionary filled the gap in her education. As it hit, the simplicity and cleverness of it made her exclaim aloud in admiration. So, clasping holds the answer. O.K. An asp is a serpent, right? – as we all know courtesy of Cleopatra. The word 'asp' is 'held' between 'cl' and 'ing' which together make 'cling' which is why 'clasping' can be said to hold the answer. So the clue was about a snake clinging-to rather than chasing something – and as the saying goes, we chase our own tail, so that 'something' had to be just that. A snake holding its own tail – the ouroboros.

The name was new to her, but she had seen the symbol before. At Monk Grange maybe, amongst the sigils and signs on Miles' papers. Certainly she had seen it in Clare Cabbala's hotel suite. That, Darcy recalled, had been determined the day she had doodled the snake symbol on her telephone pad. It seemed this snake motif had been clamouring for her attention all along. Flushed with triumph, Darcy stood up, paced the carpet, then sat down again as the implications hit her with a force ten on the Beaufort scale. Either this was the most amazing coincidence, or Fate was taking a hand by manipulating the physical environment. 'Fate' because it was too bizarre to suppose that some residual force from Anton de Beaumont, and his eventful life, was bending the rules to guide her steps by means of bizarre connections, dreams and visions. Her mind whirled into orbit, then plummeted to Earth as the Land Rover drew up outside.

****

Brant drove her to an elegant Georgian country restaurant built of sandstone and set in immaculate grounds. Fortunately, Darcy had chosen to wear a dark green skirt with matching jacket and a cream silk shirt that did not look out of place in these grand surroundings. How typical of Brant not to warn her in advance, she thought smiling to herself as the waiter cleared the debris of a first class meal washed down with a bottle of Moet. When she asked him what they were celebrating, he replied 'a weekend retrieved from disaster'.

They retired to the coffee lounge where, despite the mildness of the evening, the obligatory log fire blazed.

All had gone well. They had enjoyed each other's company, she reflected, watching him over the rim of her cup. In fact, revelled in it would be a more accurate description. They had smiled constantly at each other across the table, their talk accompanied by seemingly insignificant little movements of hand and body but each mundane action magically transformed into an intimate gesture. Along with an underlying tension, these had built up into a tacit and mutual invitation and acceptance.

Only one thing marred the perfection, Darcy worried. No mention had been made of the events of the previous evening, and given their magnitude, this rendered the situation totally unreal. Miles, and any related topic, had been studiously ignored, she thought, smiling absently at the amusing anecdote Brant was relating; rather like the unpardonable practice of ignoring a senile person or a handicapped child at a social gathering, only not out of embarrassment here, but fear that the dam would burst and the weekend spoil beyond retrieval.

But there was something she had to ask.
"Brant," she began decisively, replacing her cup on the saucer and shaking her head as the waiter hovered with coffee, "what is an ouroboros?"
His hand poised in mid air, cup half way to saucer.
"An ancient symbol; a snake holding its tail in its mouth. Why do you ask?" he added, replacing the cup and looking at her the way he had done so the previous night, as though suspecting her of having unearthed more information.
"Crossword – last clue," she said airily adding by way of explanation as he gave her a speculative stare. "It was driving me mad."
"I see."
The tone said it all; he didn't believe her but she pressed on.
"Is it an astrological symbol?"
"Not exactly."
"What then?"
The hesitation was marked, that and his reluctance to answer.

"It was used in alchemy."
So, she mused, he knew the subject in some depth, another pointer towards his involvement.

He watched her closely as she made no comment. "Have you come across it before? Other than your crossword I mean."
"At Miles' house in the—, in his notes," she amended quickly, flushing on realising she had almost disclosed the existence of the hidden papers. She shifted uncomfortably on her seat as his eyes narrowed and took on the slant of a cat on the hunt. "I didn't know its name though, or meaning," she prompted with a look of inquiry. He did not answer immediately, but continued to watch her, his expression grave and unsmiling.
"It is a symbol of wholeness."
"Pardon?" She gave him a blank look. There was however no smile in response.

"In The Gold Making of Cleopatra – written circa A.D. 100 – the Ouroboros, or circular serpent, accompanies the text "One is the All.", he explained but reluctantly as though unsure about the wisdom of speaking out. "The roots of alchemy lie in the notion of a natural base material. Gold, and even the ultimate Philosopher's Stone, evolved from this prima material - or base matter. It is already in there and emerges via alchemical knowledge and processes. Hence the concept 'All is One'."
"So what is this primal matter?" she pressed.
"That, my girl, is alchemy's greatest and most closely guarded secret," he said dryly. "Maybe a base metal, or earth containing certain minerals – who knows." He finished his coffee and pushed aside the cup. "By the way, Caro's recovery must have been one big relief. How is she, and what did she have to say?"
It was said innocently enough, but nevertheless he had abruptly, and Darcy suspected expediently, changed the subject.
"She was very weak and Sister-in-Charge was just the opposite," she said lightly.

"Ah. Threatened to turn you off the ward if you exhausted her patient."

"Absolutely." Darcy folded and re-folded her table napkin to avoid his gaze. "Actually, she did say something odd before the accident," she lied without blushing. "About the last known conjunction of Jupiter and—,"

"Saturn," he supplied, as she struggled to recall the second planet, which despite that frown and failure to meet her gaze was better, Darcy decided, than being met with blank refusal to participate in the discussion. "What about it?"

"She said it was time, perhaps, to do a little research into when the next conjunction might be."

"Brandy?" His gaze met hers in a hard stare.

"Last time we were at the observatory, you insisted there was an on-going interest from certain academic quarters. Are you also saying then that this conjunction thing could still be of importance to someone?" she persisted.

"I'm saying it's time to order brandy," he said firmly.

She made a gesture of refusal and sighed with frustration, aware that he was declaring the subject closed.

"Later perhaps?" He signalled for the waiter to bring the bill. Darcy pretended not to know what he meant.

They crossed the car park together, the crunch of feet on gravel sounding loud in the stillness of rural night. She decided to risk reopening the apparently taboo subject.

"That conjunction thing, It's just that it was all so long ago. It's asking a lot to believe it signalled the right planetary aspects for the Templars to crack the secrets of alchemy, or that anyone today could still be interested in all that crap. "

"I'm not aware anyone is asking it of you, but to many people it is far from crap," he said frostily, still without looking her way.

 "You accept there is something in it then?" Darcy demanded, halting in her tracks. Brant carried on walking towards the Land Rover.

As they drove away from the restaurant, it seemed Brant was determined to change both mood and subject.

As though in complicity with his intent, Nature contrived to provide the perfect props to his act. The magical scents of wild thyme and sea pinks drifted in through the open windows and like lost souls in search of a resting place, the silver shapes of gulls wheeled silently overhead. They drove through shadows that had the quality of velvet and an almost full moon eliminated the need for headlights. Removing one hand from the steering wheel, he stroked the inside of her wrist in a seemingly insignificant gesture, but one which nevertheless made fire leap in her womb.

"My place – for that brandy we denied ourselves?" he asked.

She nodded, heard her voice saying:

"I don't see why not," and knew herself to be lost.

****

They lounged on the rug before the log fire that Brant had kindled on their arrival at the farmhouse on the cliffs, their backs against the bank of cushions heaped on the floor. Darcy breathed deeply and allowed herself to relax. The fire, the cognac she was sipping, the aroma of wood-smoke and the feel of Brant's body next to hers nurtured an aura of warmth and security. As did the fire-glow on copper jugs and horse brasses, and the dappled shadows dancing between the roof beams. Brant touched her glass with his forefinger.

"Another?"

"It would send me to sleep," she purred, smiling.

He took it from her hand. "We can't have that Miss West – not yet."

She made no protest as he drew her close.

Like a child recovering from a nightmare, she gave a long shuddering sigh and rested her head against his chest.

"Poor girl," he soothed, stroking her head. "You've been through so much. Foolhardy too: you mustn't take such risks." What luxury to bask in his support after feeling the whole world was against her. The strength and firmness of his body at first soothed and reassured then inflamed her to passion. For a second the spectre of a Sobranie gold tip darkened her pleasure but as his kisses became more insistent she gladly relinquished her doubts and suspicions like captive wasps from a jam jar. From somewhere in the back of her mind came the knowledge that they would return. But not now. Not as his hands brought joy back to her body and made it sing. Unembarrassed, she helped him with the buttons of her shirt, and the fasteners of skirt and underwear until she lay naked against the cushions, firelight warming and lighting her breasts, belly and thighs.

He smiled down at her. "Wanton, that's what you are," he said softly, tugging at a perfect pubic curl. She laughed aloud with pleasure, glorying in her womanhood as she watched him remove his clothes.
"And beautiful," he added.
"You too."
And it was true, she realised with a sense of detachment. In his nakedness Brant was Timeless. Firelight licked his chest and loins, and burnished the dark wavy hair to auburn where strands were highlighted by the flames. They gilded too, the tips of his pubic hair whilst casting the flat planes of his belly into aching purple shadow. Stripped of the trappings and signature of a particular age he could have come from any. Could easily be Anton de Beaumont, a realisation which brought Anton closer whilst Brant seemed ever more remote.

Their lovemaking too had a timeless quality. Less Hurried, yet just as intense as that first encounter, it seemed as though each were tasting and savouring to the full and in perfect synchronisation. Her hands and tongue explored as joyfully and boldly as his, their bodies matched in every move of the dance. The tempo quickened, the beat became insistent and hypnotic. Darcy uttered an animal cry, knew she was going and leaving Brant far behind.
"Take me with you!" The urgent whisper told her he had sensed her silent departure.

But Anton was with her, she vaguely realised, before

rational thought and speculation ceased. Holding back whilst resisting the pull with difficulty, she reached out and drew him inside, led him through the labyrinth to darkness and the secret warmth of the cosmic womb. No fires of hell to scorch her this time, but an inner blaze to light the way. She let go of the present, felt his body shudder, his mind and soul fuse with her own.

"Anton, Anton," she whispered, and it seemed she heard him reply *Leala, my love* before the illusion fled. Brant's lithe body gleamed in the light from the fire. Like some arcing, flashing fish from the deep or a merman from magical legends of old, he delved and thrust his way upstream to spawn. Darcy clung tightly to Brant, their arms, thighs, groins and souls so intertwined that it was difficult to say where he began and she ended.

"Darcy."

Was it a trick of her imagination, or was there a nuance at the end of the word implying doubt? Questions tumbled about in her mind like acrobats around a circus ring. Yet she dare not ask. Something held her back, an intuitive knowledge that some things could be silently shared but had to remain unspoken; such things dwell beyond the boundaries charted by words.

They sat by the fire watching the flames leap in the grate and cast living shadows on wall and ceiling. Sensing Brant observing her, she turned her head. The expression in his eyes, the way he held her gaze made her suspect he may be about to speak out, to force her to confront their relationship and define it. There was a limit, she sensed, on how long he would be willing to drift along without benefit of direction or destination. He had somehow managed to convey a tacit understanding of marriage. That surely should lay to rest any lingering doubts about his integrity? But as his wife I should be alone with him here, and thus virtually in his power. The fleeting suspicion filled her with self-revulsion, and was immediately dismissed. But the question had arisen and would have to be addressed before making a commitment.

"Brant," she forestalled him, seeing he was about to speak, "If I ask you something, will you give me an honest answer?"

"If possible." His eyes, heavy-lidded from love-making, veiled his thoughts. Darcy took a deep breath and hoped desperately that he would give the right response.

"At the priory ruins I found a Sobranie Virginia cigarette. Did it belong to you?"

"No."

Hope left her body on a sigh, leaving her empty and the future bleak.

"But there is a packet in the drawer by my bed."

Her head shot up and she could not conceal her joy. He had volunteered the information and that surely must prove his innocence.

"Why?" she persisted, forcing her voice to remain calm, "You don't smoke."

"I found it on the cliff top path. It was rare enough to keep, given recent events."

"So, why did you not tell me before?" she demanded, pushing back her curls in a gesture that conveyed mingled relief and frustration.

"You never asked." Brant looked amused. Then, as she began to protest he added: "you only asked if I smoked, remember?"

"You guessed – and let me go on thinking the worst!"

"I must confess, I wondered how far you would take it."

"Brant, I thought—"

"I know very well what you thought and it wasn't very edifying."

"'Forgive me?"

"For doubting my honour and branding me murderer? Sure, don't give it another thought." However, he was smiling and the light had returned to his eyes.

"But on one condition," he added with mock severity.

"And that is?"

"That you tell me everything you know." All signs of amusement had disappeared. She wanted so much for the suspicion between them to be erased like footprints by the incoming tide, yet still she hesitated.

"Look Darcy," he said taking her chin in his hand and turning her face to his, "it is obvious to me that you are not going to take the slightest notice of my warning to drop the investigation. So," he released her and sat back against the cushions in order to observe her expression, "I suggest we pool resources and work together instead of against one another. That way I get to keep an eye on you and give you some protection. What do you say?"
"I have told you practically all I know," she evaded.
"It's the 'practically' that worries me!" he said, sighing. "It refers to what you found at Monk Grange."

Startled, she searched his face for a moment then made up her mind.
"All right." She nodded, and felt relieved at succumbing to recklessness and the inevitable. "I found Miles' notes."
Briefly Darcy told him what she had gleaned from her find: confirmation of Anton de Beaumont's identity and his status as a Knight Templar. She also confided that he had fallen for a Cathar girl and broken his vow of chastity, thus incurring the wrath of the order. Without actually lying, she managed to create the impression of having gleaned this from the same source, thus avoiding the embarrassment of recounting her nightmare. The chances were, Brant as a scientist would not believe a word of it, despite the supporting evidence of her research into Templars and Cathars.

Darcy lapsed into silence and sat watching firelight play on the planes of his face.
"Okay." She sat upright and threw him a look of challenge. "Your turn."
"Pardon?"
"You declined to answer back there at the restaurant, but now it's time to give. Do you believe all this is still of interest to someone?"

"Opportunist." He coiled one of her curls around his finger and tugged.

"You said pool resources. Now tell."

"That's only fair, I guess. Okay, academics have long speculated that the Templar fortune and documents chronicling their secret knowledge are still to be found."

"So who might be involved? Individuals, a society or what?" Brant shrugged. "Ask yourself who would go to great lengths to suppress the St. Gildas Man story – and why."

"Not some fusty University don that is for sure; I realise it has to be somebody pretty powerful," she said slowly, watching his face. "As for why, I guess to prevent what Miles did, and what we are doing now: asking questions, digging around and coming up with answers that might just lead us to them."

"And this they do not want," Brant said dryly.

"So, it is a group or sect of some sort," Darcy said swiftly and took his grave-faced silence as confirmation.

"Then let me get this right," she said, skewing round to face him squarely, "are you saying this secret sect is after locating the Templar hoard of gold?"

Brant gave her a long hard look, as though once more debating whether to hold back. "That is perfectly possible," he said at last, then added: "But 'power syndicate' rather than sect might be a better description today."

"Or are they after the secret texts – the results of Templar alchemical discoveries?" Darcy asked, her eyes half closed in concentration as she pursued her line of thought aloud: "Is the coveted prize not so much the treasure but the possibility of creating gold from your prima-whatever."

"That would depend on who was involved," Brant replied, but with obvious reluctance to divulge anything further. However, in response to Darcy's inquiring look and encouraging noises which made it clear he was not off the hook, he added by way of explanation:

"Well, academic high flyers would rate finding the Templar documents on a par with locating the holy grail. So would wacky new-age extremists who take it literally and believe they contain the secret of eternal life and making gold. However, political or military factions would be thinking of the influence and power the Templar treasure could buy. It all depends on your perspective."

"So, where are you placing your bet?" Darcy asked with a direct stare.

"Your guess is as good as mine." Brant shrugged non-committally.

"I don't think so. I think you know who is involved."

"I have some ideas."

"Okay, give," she said impatiently when he failed to disclose them.

"The deal was I tell you what I know: I've done that, anything else at this stage is speculation. More to the point, have you disclosed everything you found in Miles' notes?"

"Well yes," she said slowly, frowning.

"But?" he prompted.

"There were things I couldn't decipher – symbols and signs and the like."

"Okay." He lowered his head and massaged the back of his neck as though striving for patience.

"I'm sorry, was that important?" she said looking contrite, then her eyes widened as insight struck. "Could they have been alchemical formulae – or," she added excitedly as the train of ideas gathered momentum, "symbols relating to the whereabouts of the Templar hoard?"

"I think you need to let me have a look at these documents Darcy." She tried to give the answer he wanted but the words stuck in her throat. "I'm tired right now Brant, let's go to bed," she said rising to her feet.

THIRTY-FIVE

The black dog of doubt and guilt worried her mind and held sleep at bay. Why, she fretted listening to his regular breathing in the darkness of the bedroom, had she not agreed to let Brant have the documents? He had known she was holding back, that much had been clear by the narrowing of his eyes and the tightening of minute muscles around his mouth. If he was as innocent in all this as he claimed and she still refused, it would ruin their relationship. How could he love her knowing she did not trust him; and a thought which made her even more wretched, she would not deserve to be loved. But maybe he was involved in some conspiracy and therefore was not trustworthy, she worried drifting uneasily towards sleep.

To dream once more of Anton de Beaumont. This Time, on waking, something struggled for recognition, an anomaly she had been vaguely aware of in the past but which had not risen to the surface. The Anton of her dreams was unlike the Anton found by Caro's team. Awareness of the critical difference hit her with waves of shock. Why had that not struck them on seeing his body? The chin had been shaved of the internationally recognised badge of courage: the beard that as a Knight of the Temple he had been forbidden to cut.

The following day was spent quietly at the farmhouse. Brant brought her breakfast in bed: boiled egg, toast and marmalade with a pot of tea on a tray with an antique lace cloth and a rose from the hedgerow. He reappeared carrying his own tray, and perched on the bed to eat as though unable to bear her absence for any length of time. As sunlight slanted through the leaves of the rowan outside the window, and dappled the patchwork quilt on the bed, Darcy was superstitiously afraid of happiness at a time when security and safety, let alone joy, could no longer be taken for granted.

All too soon, it was time to leave. On the journey to Mistletoe Cottage they talked of the weather, the sunset that fired the bay, the latest Merchant and Ivory film, anything except the imminence of parting. At the front door of her cottage, she said with false brightness:
"Coffee?"
"It will just make this harder," Brant said shaking his head. "Plus I want you to get back before dark." Her then added with an abruptness that betrayed his intensity of feeling, "So are you going to let me take care of Miles' document?" Her hesitation hurtled around their heads threatening their relationship. Darcy looked long and hard into his face before finally nodding in agreement. He seemed satisfied and even relieved.

"Good. I want to study it of course, but I'll also feel better when it is out of your keeping."
There was no need to ask what he meant. Holding on to it would make her the target of the organisation that, she was now convinced, was behind the killings and intrigue. But can Brant be trusted? The thought filled her with guilt, so she drew the parchment out from her mattress and handed it over despite her misgivings. In any case, she reasoned as the Land Rover roared away, what harm could it do? Brant already knew its contents. The devastating answer came from herself. If he wasn't trustworthy, he could pass on the specific configurations to the dubious party interested in the alchemical and astrological content. She shrugged and closed the door, deciding there was little to be done about it now except hope her doubts proved groundless.

With Brant gone, the cottage echoed with loneliness and foreboding. Like a sand spit eroded by the encroaching tide, her courage and confidence dwindled. Trying not to dwell on the possible dangers awaiting her in Manchester, she packed an overnight bag and left.

After leaving Fran's car at the office, she drove away in her own vehicle and headed out of town. The moment she

255

entered the building it was apparent that something was wrong. A sort of sixth sense tightened the muscles of her stomach and solar plexus, and warned her to be prepared as she inserted the key and opened the door to her flat.

THIRTY-SIX

"Oh no! Please God no!" was all Darcy could say when faced with the devastation. The state of the living room made her recoil in horror. Every drawer, cupboard and anything that remotely resembled a container had been systematically turned over. Dazed, she stood ankle deep in papers, cassettes, compact discs, magazines, cushions and anything that could be flung to the floor. The settee was turned upside down along with the armchairs. She stared at the mess, her mind temporarily refusing to function. What to do? Who to contact? The owners did not live on the premises; the lease had been arranged through a glossy uncaring estate agency and she knew none of her neighbours other than to greet in passing, each like herself being wrapped in his or her career. There was nobody. No-one to ask what they had seen or heard, or what to do next.

Pull yourself together girl, she told herself sternly. The first thing on the agenda was to ensure that no-one still lurked in the flat. She stood motionless and listened, head to one side and heart thumping. Leaving the front door open she snapped on the light and quickly crossed to the kitchen. Her stomach heaved. The contents of cupboards, drawers and refrigerator had been thrown on the floor. Spaghetti spirals floated on pools of milk, and coffee granules stained the jellied mass of broken eggs a faecal brownish black. But – thank God – the room was empty.

Something made her pause outside the door of the bedroom. The kitchen had felt empty, and there had been little fear of entering, but here she became aware of something that made the hairs on the back of her neck stand on end. A hated presence, an alien intrusion. Paralysis claimed her and stole her breath but she could not stay here all night. Back pressed to the wall and inching forward until the door to the bedroom was direct left, she paused, listened and took a deep breath.

Necessity and movement simultaneously exploded within. Turning the handle and kicking the door wide in one fluid action, Darcy snapped on the light. Waves of shock charged through her system as her gaze swept the room. Then relief that turned her knees to water and made her sag against the door jamb. Chaos reigned in the bedroom: her clothes were strewn about, her bed had been stripped – but nobody jumped her or skulked within. She slumped on the bedside chair and allowed the tension to drain from her body. Gradually anger started to burn, scorching the fabric of her fear until it blackened around the edges and burnt to ash. How dare they! The bastards! How dare they violate her home this way. This same anger scoured her mind and focused attention. She must call the police. For one heart-stopping moment she feared the telephone wires had been cut, but then, as she lifted the receiver, came the reassuring tone.

Having reported the break-in, she searched amongst the debris and finding an unbroken bottle of brandy, poured herself a stiff shot. It was whilst awaiting the arrival of the police that realisation hit: apart from food being thrown on the floor, no damage had been done. The door was not splintered, the lock remained in place and the windows intact. The furniture had not been slashed nor, at a quick glance, did anything appear to be missing. The stereo and video were still in place, as was her lap top and cappuccino maker. This was no bored young thug looking for a buzz and some easy cash. Neither had her clothes been ripped or, worse still, defiled with excrement or semen, excluding a sexual motive. Far from being reassuring, all this chilled her to the marrow. There was a professionalism about it, a coldness and ruthlessness that depersonalised both herself and her belongings. Whoever had done this was looking for something in particular, had carried out their search systematically and devoid of passion. And she knew what it was they wanted. Thank God she had handed Miles' document over to Brant.

****

258

Darcy stared at the young and obviously junior detective with ill-disguised contempt.

"I had one small brandy to steady my nerves, acceptable I think, given the circumstances," she said icily in response to his query. He shrugged and replaced the empty glass on the table.

"Of course, miss." His smirk, she thought inwardly fuming, said it all.

"You're sure your boyfriend hasn't been round and got upset? A lovers' tiff maybe?" his senior colleague suggested, watching her face intently.

"I have already told you, that was not the case."

"We have to be sure, miss." His tone turned warm and conspiratorial and he moved closer, "I can understand it, you know, the need to get even with him. But better to not let it get any further than this."

"Watch my lips officer. There is no boyfriend involved here - but unless you are prepared to do something constructive, your superior officer will be." Darcy threatened, holding his gaze. He gave his junior colleague a look that said 'we've got one here all right!' but said with reluctance.

"I suppose there's enough to go on to justify a S.O.C.O.," albeit in a tone that conveyed both scepticism and reluctance. "That's a Scene of Crime Officer miss," he added with a patronising smile.

"I am familiar with the term."

"Ruth Rendall fan are we?"

"Actually, I'm an investigative reporter," she replied with a disparaging look.

"I see. You'll know the procedure then. The S.O.C.O. will look the place over for prints and the like." He cast a glance over the tiled kitchen visible through the doorway, " and bring an electrostatic lifting-device for that floor – to reproduce any shoe marks, but you'll know all about that too, no doubt," he sniped with a sidelong glance at his grinning junior. "In the meantime, miss, no cleaning till he's finished, and we'll take a statement if you're ready."

"I'm ready," Darcy said wearily, already knowing it

to be a waste of time.

She had no illusions. This investigation would be no different from the one into the break-in at Hilldean, or the events surrounding Caro's near-fatal 'accident'. Nevertheless, she answered their questions and did her best to ignore the expressions of incredulity. Once they, and the reluctantly summoned S.O.C.O., had left, she tried hard to suppress suspicions about corruption and conspiracy, and picking up the receiver dialled Brant's number.

The ringing-out tone droned on and on, but nobody answered and she finally broke down and cried. It seemed Fate and the whole damned world was against her. A drink was in order here, but then she thought I'll end up like Frank if I don't watch it, and pushed the bottle aside. Instead it was jacket off and sleeves of her sweater rolled up. If she was to stay the night in the flat (and it was imperative that she did, otherwise she would never be able to sleep there again and good pads in prime locations were hard to find) there was work to be done. Systematically she set about cleaning, disinfecting and tidying every room.

At around half past two in the morning the machine whined and thudded to a halt after washing and spinning the last of her clothes and bedding. The rest, still warm from the tumble dryer, sat on the kitchen table in neat sanitised piles. And now, she thought checking each door and window for the third time, I think I can stay the night.

Propped up against the pillows, she tried Brant's number again before settling down to sleep. Just another three rings, she told herself, and waited for six more before replacing the receiver. He should be there for her when she needed him so badly, she thought whilst silently recognising the injustice of this given he was unaware of her circumstances. Even so, it was difficult to quell the suspicion that his non-availability might be connected with the fact that he now had the parchment. Given his professed worries for her safety surely he should have telephoned, or at least stayed in the farmhouse, until he knew she was home. In his part of Cumbria his mobile 'phone was useless due to the fells blocking the signal, but come to think of it, she did not have the number anyway. If he was not going to offer it, then sure as hell she was too proud to ask.

The thought that she might have been used chilled her to the bone. Brant wasn't exactly helping to build up trust and allay her suspicions. At least he could not be responsible for this episode, she thought, then came a devastating thought. He could have set off for Manchester direct from the cottage: that way he would have arrived before her. However, it did not make sense. The object the intruder wanted was already in Brant's possession. None of this made sense. Her head reeled like the spinner in the washing machine, until finally exhaustion brought sleep. But she slept fitfully, and with the bedside light left on as a concession to the night's traumatic events.

THIRTY-SEVEN

The following morning brought a message from Frank received via a telephone call from an unknown secretary. Janet Darcy surmised, would be working in his office. In essence it told her to report in A.S.A.P. which at first puzzled then exhilarated Darcy. On the way to the office the scenario unfolded itself in her mind: Frank was coming round to her way of thinking. He had realised what an ace reporter he had on his staff, the importance of the story and the chances of netting a scoop with St. Gildas Man. Maybe, she thought swinging into the car park of the Manchester News, promotion was in the offing. She would be generous, would not rub his nose in it or complain at the time it had taken for him to come to his senses. Frank was pleased, and that was all that mattered.

Yet as she entered the building, the same vague feeling of something being wrong assailed her, as it had on entering the flat the previous day. Which was simply a reaction, she told herself, smiling broadly at Bob the doorman as she passed him with a cheery greeting. Bob had not deliberately looked the other way; it was just that he was distracted by the rep who was trying to sneak his way past and into the building. The fact that there was a new and unknown face behind the reception desk did momentarily throw her, but that was just coincidence and she smiled on her approach. Yet it was odd, the way he avoided her gaze then regarded her with a mixture of what seemed suspiciously like shame and defiance.
"Er, Miss West?"
"That's me." She paused on her way to the lift.
"I'm afraid I can't let you go up there." He rubbed his neat black moustache twice with the crook of one index finger.

"I beg your pardon?" Darcy stared at him dumbfounded.
"I'm sorry miss – orders."
"Whose?"

"I'm to give you this, miss," he said ignoring her question and holding out a brown envelope. Darcy wavered between curiosity and an impulse to head straight for Frank Kelly's office; curiosity won and drove her across to the counter. People she knew stared and hurriedly looked the other way on meeting her gaze. The foyer of the Manchester News was not the place for a confrontation. In silence, she took the envelope, ripped it open and took out the single typed sheet. Her eyes widened as phrases filtered through the veil of disbelief: '. . . *absent from duty without leave...use of company car without authorisation ...serious breach of discipline...came to my attention of late...*and then the killer sentence: *'regret your services no longer required...three month's salary in lieu of notice.'*
The letter of dismissal was signed by Max Dearden.

Anger exploded like a grenade when the pin is pulled. "This is ridiculous – some kind of joke," she raged, turning on the po-faced man behind the desk. "I want to see Frank Kelly – like yesterday, do you hear me?"
"Sorry, miss. Mr. Kelly is unavailable." The man, now that she had lost her cool, spoke with infuriating smugness. He stroked his moustache with a new confidence and a sleazy sensuality as he watched her fume.
"We'll see about that." Darcy moved swiftly to the stairs and was half way up them before her tormentor had recovered from the surprise. She glanced over her shoulder without slowing her pace. He dashed from behind the counter and wavered, obviously assessing his chances of catching his quarry, then returned and pressed the buttons of the intercom instead. Despite the nightmare scenario, she derived a degree of triumph from his defeat.

By the time she reached her office it had dissipated. This could be the end of all she had taken for granted, her place on the News and the privileges of her favoured position. Surely not. She half expected the door to be locked but it yielded to her touch. Obviously, management had not anticipated her revolt.

She paused on the threshold, numbed with shock. The office was bare, except for a couple of boxes crammed with books, software and files. The room buzzed and echoed with the ghost of her working self. The computer remained on the otherwise empty desk. The sound of heavy footsteps pacing the corridor made her move. The screen lit, shuddered and settled and she tapped in her personal key-word. The words leapt at her from the screen: *Access denied. Unauthorised key-word.*

"I have to ask you leave miss."
She whirled round. The two security officers were stationed either side of the door, arms folded and peaked caps pulled forward to almost conceal their eyes, the embodiment of anonymous and sinister power. Darcy stood her ground.
"I rather think that is my line. This is my office."
"Not any longer."
The burliest of the two had spoken. She scanned the face beneath the peaked cap for possible signs of compassion but saw none in the brutal, thin lips and pugnacious chin. No purchase to be had there.
"Do you want to do this the hard or easy way miss?" he taunted.

Ignoring him, Darcy turned and appealed to his companion whom she knew slightly. He opened her office door with his pass key when she was accidentally locked out.
"Jackson?" she repeated. He avoided her gaze and seemed uncomfortable, but seconds later his jaw-line took on an angular look and his lips compressed before he spoke.
"Sorry miss."
She sensed that he really was, but that he would not, or could not, help.
"Just let me see Frank Kelly," she pleaded.
"Forget it." It was the other man who had spoken. "Now if you don't mind." He looked pointedly at the door and took a threatening step forward.
"Won't you take me to him Jackson?" she insisted, hating herself for begging.

"I can't Miss West. You really must leave now. Nothing personal you understand."

"Cut the crap, Jackson," his companion snapped adding: "and you lady – out the door."

"That's enough Brewster." Jackson glared at the offending guard. "The lady," and he emphasised the word, "is just leaving." He pushed the door wide in an unmistakably final gesture. "If you don't mind, Miss West. Please don't make this any harder on yourself."

Darcy stared him out for a moment then moved to the door, shoulders slumped in defeat. Like the man said, no point in making things worse, a noisy scene would only result in loss of self-respect. Later she would track down and confront Frank Kelly, approach the union and Nick Carter the night editor and ask them to act on her behalf. Oh yes, there was plenty she could do.

"I really am sorry, Miss West," Jackson said, escorting her down the corridor.

"It's not your fault," she allowed, taking pity on him. "Jackson. Just tell me, where's my assistant, Janet?"

"Not your problem."

Jackson ignored his companion's growled response.

"I did hear she had been transferred miss."

"Where to?" she pressed, making for the stairs. No way would she enter a lift with that bozo, despite the presence of Jackson.

"Sorry – can't say."

"Jackson!" his companion warned. "You know our brief. No questions, no answers. Now move it, okay?" he said with a menacing step forward.

"You've been watching too many cheap U.S. export movies," Darcy said scathingly, descending the stairs with shoulders back once more and head held high.

The foyer seemed to be a mile long, the exit a million strides away, but she stared straight ahead and made it. Ignoring the curious stares and whispered comments, Darcy quit the building – minus a job but with dignity intact.

THIRTY-EIGHT

Which, as the hours wore on, felt like little or no consolation. The rest of the day she spent mindlessly walking around department stores and sitting in the anonymous chrome and Formica coffee bars and twice, in a moment of panic and confusion, unable to recall whether she was in Debenhams, Littlewoods, Marks and Spencer or some other place. Eventually, she wandered around Whitworth Park simply to avoid a return to the flat where silence and solitude would force her to confront the situation. On impulse she entered the art gallery. The timeless quality of portrait and landscape soothed and distracted her mind for a time, but on emerging an hour or so later into the unforgiving world, worry and anxiety flooded back. Ignoring this awful development would not make it go away; a plan of action was needed. It was time to go home.

The first thing she did on arriving at the flat was make a strong cup of black coffee as an instant reviver. On the way home there had been time to calm down and reflect. Viewed from within the context of recent events her dismissal was not extraordinary. In fact it should have been anticipated. If she had been warm enough to have her story on Anton de Beaumont blocked at the outset, by now she must be red hot. Some big noise had pulled strings, but Frank should have warned her instead of vanishing like the proverbial rat. Pulling the letter from its envelope she read it through again.

Three months salary in lieu was excessive, given that a month would have been generous if management were confident that the alleged breach of discipline would stick. They were buying her silence, she realised tossing aside the sheet of paper as though contact with it would contaminate. At the time she had not bothered to inspect the pay cheque, but did so now. She gave a low whistle of disbelief. They wanted her silence all right – and how. The amount on the cheque was much more than the sum stated in the letter. Here was an obvious if unacknowledged pay-off.

So what had they told Janet? Reaching for the telephone she dialled the number. The monotonous tone told her the number was no longer available. It had been stupid to try, Darcy thought replacing the receiver and suddenly feeling very alone. It would have been part of Janet's deal: new job, flat and telephone number in return for a fat salary – and no contact please with Miss West. And Janet had bought it. Bitterness flooded Darcy and tears threatened. But it was unfair to condemn Janet. According to Miles, there were some powerful people behind all this. Janet may have been told anything, for instance that her boss had been secretly promoted to a political or legal section handling classified material, and that communication between them was no longer permissible.

A frightening thought struck, and despite having used it moments before, Darcy's hand shot out to the telephone. The dialling tone gave instant reassurance. For now – but how long before her own telephone became mysteriously disconnected? That would surely be the next step in what she now saw as a systematic plan for her isolation, and ultimately perhaps, her disappearance without too many questions being asked. There seemed to be no escape route. Given their reaction to date, there was no point in going to the police. If she persisted with her complaint of a conspiracy, they would likely bang her on a section and have her hospitalised as a paranoid schizophrenic.

In a moment of panic, she dialled Brant's number but nobody answered. The worm of doubt gnawed her insides. It was as though Brant was part of her enforced isolation. From there it was but a step to assume that he was in on the plan. Oh, Brant please get in touch and prove me wrong, she pleaded, then jumped violently as the telephone shrilled as though in response to her plea. However, upon picking up the receiver she realised it was not Brant but Caro.

"Caro, where are you? How are you feeling?"

"At home, and fine but neglected."

"Caro, I'm so sorry. I hadn't forgotten you, honest. It's just that things well—"

"What's wrong Darcy?"

"Nothing."

"You always were a rotten liar."

"Okay, so I lost my job today. It's not the end of the world."

"What happened?"

Darcy thought on her feet. Better to play this low key, Caro would still be convalescent and it was unfair to put her under stress.

"Oh, my face doesn't fit anymore, that's all."

"A row with Frank Kelly?"

"No." Whilst knowing this laconic reply in place of the usual, and therefore expected, tirade would alert Caro, Darcy could not help being lost for words.

"That settles it. Get over here like yesterday Darcy West!"

"What!"

"You heard." Caro's voice was stronger than it had been for ages. "It's time you stopped bullshitting me. I might be on crutches but there's nothing wrong with my marbles. We have to stop chatting and talk."

"You are beginning to sound like Frank," Darcy quipped, despite her distress. "Okay, give me an hour."

"Granted. See you."

Secretly relieved at being told what to do, Darcy replaced the receiver.

Within the hour, Darcy and Caro were talking over a bottle of wine in the sitting room of the stone-built house about a mile from Hilldean University. Caro was more mobile than Darcy had expected, the hairline fracture to her leg being well on the way to being healed. Darcy asked if it still gave her pain. "Can't feel a thing. Aches a bit when I'm tired, that's all," Caro replied cheerfully. Crepe bandaging had replaced the plaster cast, but her arm was still rigidly encased.

"I'm becoming quite an adept at left-handedness," she quipped, proving the point by pouring wine into their glasses without spilling a drop. "Which is perhaps rather appropriate given the subject of your inquiry," she added with a shrewd look. Darcy let this covert reference to superstition, or arcane knowledge depending upon one's perspective, pass without comment. In response to Caro's prompting, Darcy embarked on a version of the day's events. It was difficult to judge how much it was safe to divulge, but Caro cut in on the expurgated edition.
"I said no bullshitting Darcy. Any fool must know what happened to me was no accident. I have a right to know – even the nasty bits."

Darcy gave her friend a long hard look then nodded.
"Fair enough." She proceeded to relate the full story including the murder of Miles Standish, Brant's cosmic and alchemical revelations and the break-in at the flat followed by her dismissal. Finally, she revealed the identity of Anton de Beaumont. As Darcy finished her account Caro, was frowning.
"You feel sure about this alchemy thing?"
"You don't believe me."
"I accept that the Templars were practitioners of the art and that alchemy was an internationally accepted movement in the Middle Ages." Caro frowned, and elbow on table, supported her chin on her hand. "I also accept that the Templars went underground, and that their ideology was carried on by movements such as the 17th century Rosicrucians," she said slowly, thinking it through. "But I have a problem accepting the claims of alchemy, and the belief that the Templars cracked the mystery of the Philosopher's Stone. I doubt it even existed, and more so that Anton de Beaumont died guarding the secret. Even harder to take is the notion of a present day secret sect bent on using it to gain power. It's the old world-domination theory straight from a Bond film!"

Darcy leaned forward, her enlarged pupils and pallor of face betraying her intensity.
"But as Brant says, what matters here is that somebody – a secret organisation or whatever – has the power and means

269

to make such a claim convincing. Even more worrying is their timing. Think of it Caro, they have chosen the most fertile era possible. The western world is aware of the global mess. People feel betrayed by Establishment, let down by religion and are ripe for accepting a fringe alternative."

"Scary stuff." Caro nodded and looked sombre. "Okay, so we start from the base that the truth of this alchemy stuff is not at issue, its about what people can be manipulated into believing." Darcy shrugged, and some of the intensity evaporated. "Either that, or it is just a blind and the real issue is the location of the Templar fortune. There has to be loads of contenders for that one – and you don't have to be wacky or swallow bizarre ideas. And that brings us back to square one," she concluded glumly. "Bottom line – it could be anybody, motivated by either scene!"

Darcy took a sip of wine and thoughtfully twirled the stem of the glass in her fingers.

"Caro, you never finished telling me about your nightmares."

"No."

"I think you should be telling me now."

"I guess so." It was said reluctantly as Darcy raised her eyebrows and made it clear that a response was required.

"Still getting them?" she prompted.

Caro swallowed and looked through the darkened pane of the window as night gathered outside, then shook her head.

"Not for about a week."

No, because I am now taking them for you, Darcy thought, and the relief which accompanied this insight was profound. At least she could take that one away from Caro who had endured so much on behalf of her friend.

"Let me make it easier for you," she offered as Caro fiddled with the pendant around her neck and obviously had difficulties in broaching the subject.

As plainly as possible, and without emotive language, Darcy recounted her dream then encouraged Caro to do to the same. It was as she suspected: Caro's nightmare had

270

been similar to her own.

"What does it mean?" Caro asked quietly, her face looking white and pinched. Filled with remorse, but then absolving herself from blame on the grounds that Caro's trauma was less harmful for being shared, Darcy sought to reassure her friend. "At least you know you are not ready for the psycho ward," she quipped, forcing a smile despite the trauma of recalling those horrific scenes of the flaming pit and the screams of the victims "Or put it this way, if you are then so am I!"

"But why should we both have the same nightmare?"

Darcy shrugged and shook her head.

"Perhaps with all our high-tech advances we still haven't grasped the reality of Time. Maybe some grave wrong was done and Anton de Beaumont's need for justice transcends conventional time. I can't answer your question Caro, but I believe that Anton de Beaumont fell in love with a Cathar girl, broke his vow of chastity and so incurred the wrath of the Order."

The distress was melting from Caro's features; by showing it to be a shared experience, Darcy had opened the door to her solitary prison and set her free.

"So how and why did he die?"

Darcy stuck out her lower lip and looked thoughtful.

"I don't know yet. Maybe it was down to some arcane knowledge he carried, perhaps after all he did carry the secret of transforming base metal to gold."

Darcy became aware of the ticking of the station clock above the door, of the green, herby scent of dried flowers and the friendly glug-glug-glug of water travelling through an antiquated system of pipes. A backdrop of normality against which their conversation seemed even more bizarre.

"Maybe there really is something in this alchemy thing, this immortal dust," she said to herself. At this Caro looked up.

"How did you know about immortal dust?"

Darcy rose and paced the floor of the kitchen.

"Brant," she said shortly. "He said that in alchemy it symbolised eternal youth and prolonged life."

271

"He's in on this?"

"I'm hoping not."

"You love him." Darcy shrugged and looked miserable. It was a statement not a question and required no answer.

"Could you make anything of the signs and symbols, or remember any of them?" Caro asked, obviously aware of Darcy's distress so diplomatically changing the subject. "In Miles' documents," she supplied as Darcy looked blank. "Only the obvious ones like the sun and moon – oh, and the ouroboros. I managed to unscramble scraps from the samples of Latin text. Some sort of working hypothesis involving the heating of metals and elements, to be carried out at specific times by the astrological calendar."

"Sounds about right," Caro agreed. "The trouble is alchemy is not expressed in literal terms but in visionary and metaphorical language. Very difficult to understand."

"So how does the death of Dr. Piper fit in?" Darcy said frowning. "It seems at odds somehow with universal panaceas and prolonged life."

"I'm working on that one. Pour the coffee, will you?" she said, pointing to the cafetière, and Darcy knew from experience it meant 'subject closed for now'.

"Okay," she rose and poured coffee into two cups placed ready at its side. "Any ideas then about the organisation behind all this?" she said placing cafetière and cups on the table before sitting down again. Caro leaned forward her expression tense.

"Two possibilities come to mind. For one, Nazi Germany. Hitler was heavily into medieval knighthood and the mystery of the grail."

"Hitler!"

"I know it sounds crazy but it is true," Caro insisted. "In the Autumn of 1936 a poster was issued showing Hitler as a grail knight! As with alchemy, Nazism was not just a political ideology but a religious one. If you don't grasp that you'll never understand the phenomenon, the demonic fanaticism that fuelled the movement. Believe me, Hitler knew what he was doing in activating the religious instincts of the German people."

"Hitler as high priest?" Darcy's expression of scepticism hardened.

Caro failed to return her challenging smile. "Absolutely. In essence, that was the powerful persona he projected." She paused to refill their cups with coffee before continuing, "And instead of scoffing, consider the Nazi use under his direction of religious props: special lighting, nocturnal settings, ritual and perhaps most potent of all, chanting of the mantra *zieg hail!* Stir that heady brew with Wagnerian elevation of the German spirit via his stirring music and we have deliberately-induced altered state of consciousness. The Nuremberg Rallies are a classic example. Study old footage, Darcy. The faces are rapt, the expressions ecstatic."

"He hardly turned the other cheek," Darcy commented wryly.

"There's more than one brand of religion," Caro replied with a look of reproof at her presumption about its roots. "Nazism was actually hostile to Christianity; rather it drew upon ancient Germanic paganism."

Darcy nodded, signifying acceptance. "Okay, I can go with that." She sipped her coffee then cradled the cup in her hands whilst studying Caro's face. "But you said two possibilities."

Caro nodded. "I did, but in actual fact I've already mentioned aspects of the second. The Nazis borrowed the use of symbolism from Freemasonry. The ceremonial daggers, weird rituals and so on, but that is the only connection. I didn't go for it then, and I don't now, but thought it worthy of elimination. Personally I plump for the Neo-Nazi theory. Read what C. J. Jung has to say about the Nazi psyche, and I'm sure you too will be convinced."

"I'll take your word for it! Darcy pulled a wry face. "But where is all this leading?" she added.

"Back to the Templars," Caro promptly replied.

Coffee splashed the table as Darcy almost dropped her cup.

THIRTY-NINE

"You have to be joking," Darcy breathed.
"No. I touched upon the subject as part of a 'Psychology of Conflict' project. It all came back. How in setting up the S.S. – his elite 'priest-hood' if you like – Hitler was influenced by various secret societies: most notably the Order of New Templars."
Darcy picked up her cup then put it down without drinking.
"I don't believe this."
"You'd better!" Caro smiled grimly. "They were active during the 1820s and the period shortly after the first World War. Himmler – the S.S. Colonel-in-Chief – modelled himself on the Jesuits who in turn were derived from the Templars. So the links are there and far from tenuous."

"It's bizarre but you've convinced me; I'll follow it up," Darcy promised, taking the cups to the drainer and turning on the hot tap. "Now it's time I went home."
"But we haven't sorted your personal problems!" Caro protested. Darcy squirted some lemon washing up liquid into the steaming bowl and breathed in the refreshing fragrance.
"What personal problems are they?"
"Your job, for one!"
Darcy grinned over her shoulder. "Ain't got one to worry about."
"And Brant?"
"After the mega-issues we have just talked about? Like I said: what problems?" Darcy said lightly, sniffing again as the citrus-infused steam rose to her nostrils.

"There," she said slipping the last plate into the drainer rack and dropping clean cutlery into the holder before wiping foam from her hands. "Now I'm off. Don't worry about me," she said, crossing to Caro and applying gentle pressure on her shoulders to dissuade her from rising. "I can see myself out. I'll give you a bell to arrange an up-date soon," she added, holding up a forefinger as Caro would have protested. "No argument!"

"Okay. Take care, Darcy."

"I'll be fine. And thanks, Caro."

"For what?"

"Supper – and for dropping my own whinges into perspective."

"This Nazi thing – any leads?" Darcy asked, pausing at the door. Caro frowned with the effort of concentration. "You could try Schmidt – Ernst Von Schmidt. He eventually settled in Britain, but no idea where. There was a whiff of 'war crimes' but it never went to trial. He might be worth a bit of research."

"Thanks, Caro, you've been great," Darcy said, giving Caro a hug. However, as she closed the front door and stepped into loneliness and darkness, Darcy's bravado faded and died like the flare of a shooting star.

****

Hamilton-Smythe, Ernest: Parc y Meirw, Powys. A far cry from Ernst Von Schmidt, but despite the quintessentially English name it had to be the same guy. The age at 82 years was right, as was the profession listed as 'professor of European history'. Military and War history? Could be. And political connections were spot on too, the links being with public figures on the far right. She clicked off-line and shut down the computer whilst blessing the fact that she still had access to certain privileged research files. At his age, she wondered dubiously, would he still have influence and a vested interest in wealth and power? Well it was good enough for Pinochet and others like him, so why not. How, if at all, he fit the alchemical jigsaw was a little harder to perceive.

He was a disparate piece surely, with all the wrong angles for the vacant space between Anton de Beaumont, alchemy, and the Order of Knights Templar. Then she recalled Miles Standish's reference to the gold teeth scandal and the Nazi lust

275

for gold. Not so tenuous a link after all. In her own pad by the light of day, it all still seemed depressingly improbable. But there was no place else to go; this was her only lead. Heading for the kitchen with coffee and sandwich in mind, she paused halfway, decided against it and returning to the telephone dialled Ernest Hamilton-Smythe's number.

It was easier than anticipated, Darcy reflected as Chester was left behind, and the car sped along the A483 through a Welsh landscape that became increasingly rural and remote. The past humility of a threatened war crimes charge had obviously left Hamilton-Smythe still raw and – lucky for her – eager for a voice. It had taken several minutes to talk her way past a dour and pompous housekeeper and gain access to her octogenarian employer. The voice that came over next took her by surprise: strong despite its owner's years, it bore no trace of his Fatherland only a precise and dated 'BBC accent'. Neither did it betray any hint of senility. Articulate and urbane but cautious, he had made her work hard to obtain her goal. By means of a toadying that made her cringe, and the lie that she worked for a far-right magazine, and hinting at fascist tendencies on behalf of both herself and the paper, she had managed to procure an interview on the promise of a sensitive and sympathetic account. She consoled herself that in this case, the end did justify the means if some monstrous plot was foiled.

For a time, Darcy concentrated upon driving and route-finding until first Oswestry, then Welshpool, were left behind. Then, as the road cut through the lonely Cambrian mountains and the pace slowed, Darcy found herself wondering what had possessed Hamilton-Smythe to settle out here. Obviously, a need for secrecy and seclusion, she answered herself as the car progressed through a wilderness of lakes, velvet-green forests, emerald valleys and high, windswept moorland. At journey's outset, she had donned sunglasses to protect against the glare of the late spring sunlight. Now however, she removed them as sombreness draped the mountains and mist shrouded the moors. Here winter-bronzed bracken and heather still slumbered, and bare spindly trees clawed the wind, refusing to give premature birth to their embryo leaf-buds. Spring would be late here in the so-called Desert of Wales. Named thus, she recalled from her Reader's Digest Road Atlas, not because of its lack of colour but on account of its emptiness and wildness. An apt description, she reflected, as rain lashed the windscreen and ghosted across the mountains.

Eventually, she reached the desolate Gors Lwyd wetlands near the head of the Elan Valley, north of Rhayader along the old coach road from Devil's Bridge. Here, in the upper reaches of the Efan Elan and Efan Ystwyth water surged everywhere. From the outflow of these two rivers, it seeped through the peat beds of the moors and trickled, chattering and grumbling to weep onto the track that passed for a road. She stopped for a moment and let down the window. A plaintive mewing like that of a cat puzzled her at first, until she saw the broad-winged buzzard sail majestically overhead. Desert indeed. But one with a wild Celtic magic that challenged the twenty first century and the preconceptions of the urban visitor. An involuntary shiver crept along her spine and she closed the window. Within a few miles of this wilderness, Ernst Von Schmidt, masquerading as an English country gentleman, lived with his memories and nightmares. Putting the car into gear she took a deep breath and continued her search for the house named Parc y Meirw.

Built of stone and Welsh slate, the neat mansion lurked at the end of an unmarked drive, the entrance to which she passed by twice before deciding this had to be it as there was no other dwelling for miles around. An avenue of ancient yews clasped gnarled and twisted arms above the driveway, creating a dark tunnel which added to the pervasive gloom. Oak, chestnut and a couple of magnificent lawn-sweeping cedars surrounded the gardens, whilst Scotch and Douglas pines provided a sombre backdrop and cast the house in shadow.

She rang the bell and waited at the pillared and wisteria-clad entrance, nervousness gnawing her stomach like a hungry rat at a week-old carcass. She was about to raise her arm to ring again when the door opened a couple of feet. A formidable figure dressed in tailored black surveyed her with a mien to deter the casual caller.

"Yes, what is it?"

No sign of a Welsh ancestry there, nor in the thin closed features. When making contact, Darcy had toyed with the idea of an assumed name, but given that she would probably be checked out by Von Schmidt's network had abandoned the idea. Her credentials as a journalist would have to stand up if the interview was to proceed, and no doubt these had already been checked via the Internet. The problem of the 'far right mag' would have to be addressed later.

"Darcy West. I have an appointment with – Mr. Hamilton-Smythe." The hesitation scarcely happened, yet the older woman's eyes – she was probably sixty-something – perceptibly narrowed and she subjected Darcy's features to intense scrutiny.

"You had better come in," she said pushing the door wider, then begrudgingly adding, "Follow me," as Darcy stepped over the threshold.

The scene in the drawing-room was as quintessentially English as Hamilton-Smythe's assumed name. As the housekeeper announced her and ushered her forward, Darcy became aware of the mingled scents of polish, wood smoke and a heady perfume, the latter emanating from a glass pitcher in which cherry blossom and lilac spikes were artfully arranged. A grand piano, mahogany sideboard, walnut bureau and various occasional tables glowed with beeswax in the blaze from a log fire. From the depths of a leather armchair beside the fireplace, the owner of Parc y Meirw surveyed her with unblinking stare.

"Thank you, Mrs. Bates. A tea tray I think."

"Very good, sir."

Bates left the room and the door shut with the obligatory country-house creak.

Given her crow's garb and sinister air, Darcy would

not have been surprised if the woman's name had turned out to be Danvers. Certainly the house fit the bill for Manderlay. Was there perhaps a mistress somewhere in its rooms and was her name Rebecca? she wondered, then recalled the web-site information that Ernest Hamilton-Smythe was a bachelor. As he rose from his chair to greet her, Darcy was struck by the Englishness of his appearance: the tweed suit and moss green shirt with woollen tie, and the brown brogues glowing with polish in the light from the fire. She stared at the outstretched hand, and grasped it just in time as a flicker of annoyance contracted his angular features.

"Miss West. So you found us."

So perfect an English accent.

Doubts assailed Darcy. Maybe she was wrong about his identity. On the other hand it was too perfect; like this room and the stereotypical housekeeper and the whole carefully orchestrated 'English' ambience. Her 'nose' told her to go with intuition. The hand that held hers was dry and cold. Like parchment, or the dead skin of its victims, the thousands of lives it had signed away. Despite the heat from the fire and the background central heating, Darcy felt a chill creep into her bones.

"A lovely place you have here," she said, pulling away her hand and refraining with difficulty from wiping the palm on her jacket.

"It suits me." Hamilton-Smythe gestured for her to be seated. I bet, Darcy thought sitting on the chair at the opposite side of the fireplace. It was the perfect retreat for a man with secrets.

A china-laden tea tray was brought in by the Bates woman and placed on a low table. Once again Darcy was struck by her resemblance to the imaginary Mrs. Danvers, until that is she turned to leave the room. The plastic butterfly clip, predatory teeth interlocked at the nub of her upswept hair, provided a modern and incongruous touch. Now she and Hamilton-Smythe were alone. Tea had been poured, scones consumed, pleasantries about travel and weather exchanged, and the interview was under way. Cautious at first and constantly watching her responses, Hamilton-Smythe gradually succumbed to enthusiasm and the luxury of being given a voice. "Did you ever meet Himmler?" she ventured at last, inwardly cringing as she feigned the reverent tones of a far-right reporter from a fascist rag.

"Many times." One gnarled finger stroked the clipped, military-style moustache. "I worked with him on merging the whole German police service – of which he was head of course – into the S.S. and Gestapo." There was no mistaking now the pride in his voice.

"You were an S.S. officer?" Darcy forced a note of admiration into her voice.

"I was a deputy commander of the Totenkopfverbande." That sickening note of pride again, as though he had just announced himself head of the Red Cross or Amnesty International.

"Which means?"

"Death's Head Units. They guarded the camps."

The papery eyelids did not so much as flicker, Darcy noted whilst struggling to hide her disgust.

"The concentration camps?"

"Of course. They were also under Himmler's control." As though picking up on her disgust, he leaned forward on his seat, hands grasping the silver knob that topped his ebony walking cane. "The world never understood. Such ignorance and lack of vision! We should have been lauded for our efforts instead of hounded and reviled. But it was beyond the grasp of ordinary minds."

"What was?" Darcy felt a thrill of premonition.

"The truth. Our enemies thought it purely a military movement."

"And it wasn't?"

He tilted further forward, knuckles showing white on the gnarled hands as his grip on the cane tightened.

"Much more. A crusade. You might say Himmler and his generals were the Fuhrer's black-clad priesthood."

"So it is true they were modelled on the Jesuits?" she ventured, daring to draw him out. She waited, unconsciously holding her breath as he frowned and gave her a searching look.

"You have done your research, my dear." He seemed to deliberate, to hover between suspicion and respect for her knowledge, but finally gave her a look of approval.

Darcy breathed again. "And they," he continued, "in turn, honoured the Knights Templar."

"A powerful order in their day."

"And a force still to be reckoned with," he responded with a sly look.

"They still exist in some form?"

"Their ideology does, my dear, and who knows what else?"

"Templar gold perhaps?" Darcy dared.

He stared her out in silence, and fearing 'too much too soon', she carried on smoothly whilst inwardly cringing: "And the Fuhrer? What of him?" With effort she made it sound like an enquiry about the nature of God. To her relief the awkwardness of the moment passed and he chose to ignore her indiscretion.

"Not just Kaiser but shaman! A Grand Master of the finest order," he enthused, as though mollified against his will.

Darcy decided to risk another sensitive question.

"What was it about the Knights Templar that fascinated the Fuhrer, made him emulate them?"

"Their mysticism and zeal, the single-minded purpose."

"But they were a Christian order," Darcy objected, "as such, to serve God, not an earthly ruler, surely was the object of that purpose."

"Foolish girl, you know nothing!" But the smile he gave her was one of indulgence. "Their knowledge predated Christianity; they dared move beyond it"

"To what?" *Alchemy?* she wondered but dared not say.

"The secret of Life itself of course." The brows knit over the bony nose and he paused, patently aware of revealing too much. "But none of this concerns you."

Sensing that he was about to terminate the interview Darcy changed tack.

"Do ends ever justify means?" she ventured, toying with her empty cup and fragile saucer. His glare told her she was right to be nervous.

"There can be no doubt. The purification of a master race is necessary to its development. Inferior beings drag it down, suppress its full potential."

Ethnic cleansing – it's always been with us. Darcy swallowed the rising nausea.

"To rule the world?" and she failed to omit the tinge of irony.

"Next time, my dear. Next time."

The smile which failed to reach his eyes chilled Darcy's heart.

"Do not waste your pity on slaughtered cattle," he added sharply, as though becoming aware of her growing disgust. "They fulfilled their destiny. Besides, the lower orders feel little, are unaware of the subtleties of suffering. "

As revulsion seeped through her guard, his demeanour visibly changed. The eyes became hard and focused, sharpened by a gunmetal glow. Steel behind the eighty-odd years recalled the younger man, the scourge of Naudhausen, Belsen and terrible Auschwitz where four and a half million died. As she scanned his features the skin turned the texture and colour of ash: the flaky-grey of the ash that had rained down from the chimneys of death, covering the streets of Auschwitz with eternal and indelible shame.

She saw again the museum erected by the Polish Government and visited as part of her never-to-be-forgotten assignment. Saw again the millions of shoes, the swathes of hair in glass cases, and perhaps most poignant of all the piles of luggage: the cases in which they brought their lives, a last journey and one-way ticket to death to which battered leather and cardboard bore pitiful witness. His eyes were now twin moons, possessing no light of their own but lit by the shameful fire of the furnace. No longer the rheumy semi-opaque of respected age, but dark, fathomless pools of one who has cared too little and seen and done too much. In the absence of soul they mirrored her strained white face.

"Is anything wrong, Miss West?"

She picked up the sharpness of tone, the inherent suspicion in the cold eyes and cursed her carelessness.

"I'm overawed, sir," she offered and saw to her relief that he was nodding and looking pleased. Darcy scribbled the words *vile fascist bastard* on her pad and drew some comfort from the covert gesture.

"Is it true that S.S. officers were encouraged to copulate on the graves of illustrious forbears?" she side-stepped, aware that she had almost blown her cover, and was unable to trust herself further down that particular route. He waved aside her tacit but palpable accusation of crankiness and obsession.

"Do not discount what you cannot understand or explain," he said severely, leaning forward so that his knuckles showed white again as his weight rested on the cane.

"Essence is not destroyed by physical death. Vibrations, higher thought patterns, superior trait, all these are distilled. They remain and seep into the elements of stone and earth – and into the waiting womb. Orgasm is an alchemical instant, the Conjunctio, the marriage of what is above with what is below. Wonder at the child conceived in such a place!"

Darcy's heart leapt at this triumph of fanaticism over discretion. So the Nazis were aware of the Templars' preoccupation with alchemy. She assumed the blankness of innocence as she faced Von Schmidt which was the only way she could now think of him.

"Alchemy? Is it about turning base metal to gold?"

The set features unfurled in a brief, patronising smile.

"And much more," he seemed unable to resist adding.

It all came flooding back, every reference that had come her way over the years: art treasures shamelessly appropriated. The

National Gallery even now was self-investigating works by Cezanne and Monet, she recalled, acquired in post-war Europe and without provenance or written validation. Then there was the hoards of plundered currency. In essence, the Nazi greed for gold. Ostensibly appropriated to fund The Cause; in reality much of it claimed by Hitler and the officers of his corrupt inner enclave.

Somehow, this catalogue of evil, looting and theft was connected to her quest.

It was then that she first became aware of the prickling at the nape of her neck, a sense of familiar presence. The scent of ocean spray, cedarwood and spices teased her memory and nostrils. Anton. She became aware of a prickling along her nerves, and with it the fleeting sense that he was endorsing her insight. The Templars had been formed to protect the weak and wage war upon injustice, and genocide was the same whether waged in the thirteenth or twentieth century. Unconsciously she had been searching Von Schmidt's face for clues.

"Heil Hitler." He spoke in little more than a whisper, in the cracked and aged voice of undying vice and corruption. Nevertheless, it ripped through her consciousness like the cry of a ravening vulture stripping human flesh of dignity and meaning. "It is not over, you know." His smile brought to mind a grinning death-head. "He will rise again."

As his voice rose, droplets of moisture sprayed the air and clung to the hairs of his nicotine-stained moustache. "Remember – Eternal Youth. And now, Miss West, I think you had better go."

The words *whilst you still may* irresistibly sounded inside her head. Did he mean this in a literal sense? Was he referring to the Hitler Youth Movement and the Neo Fascists of the present day? More than likely, but it echoed with something else too, like Templar secrets from long ago.

"I have heard more than enough." Darcy rose from her chair and backed towards the door, too distressed now to worry about blowing her cover. His sunken cheeks glowed with twin hot coals, two spots of livid colour on grey flesh.

"That is because you, fraulein, are stupid," he spat, the Anglicised BBC accent lost to a guttural German one. "What can you know in your closed little world? It is happening now, right under your inquisitive nose." He rose, and savagely stabbed at a bell push on the wall. "Make no mistake, fraulein. The spirit of the Fuhrer will live again."

"Forget this charade," Darcy snapped, indicating the stately room, furniture and hangings with a scornful sweep of her arm, "You will always be Ernst Von Schmidt."

She was about to make her own way out when the door was opened by the woman in black. He began to laugh then, a low chilling laughter that followed her from the room and down the hall to the front door. As the housekeeper, Mrs Danvers as Darcy could not resist mentally calling her, showed her to the door Darcy paused to ask:

"What does it mean – Parc y Meirw?"

The other woman's hesitation was slight but noticeable.

"Field of Death," she said finally, face impassive as she stepped back and closed the door.

As Darcy hurried towards the sanctuary of her car, the woman's words echoed through her mind. Never, she thought sombrely, was a place so aptly named.

FORTY

It took a bath followed by a scalding shower to rinse away the sense of evil and contamination. Later, Darcy picked at a plate of pasta washed down by a glass of red wine that she found at the bottom of a previously opened bottle, and the events of the past week careered through her mind like an out-of-control juggernaut. From this session of soul-searching one truth emerged: Von Schmidt may be mad but he was not alone. In isolation his threats could be dismissed as the ravings of a crank, given the sequence of events he became the latest link in a conspiracy, a chain forged by fascism and fired by a lust for power. There could be no doubt that Von Schmidt was involved in some nasty political faction. Furthermore, much of what she had learned at that harrowing meeting substantiated Caro's theory: that the impulse for the original Nazi movement was not political or military but a dark mysticism which slotted neatly into the bigger picture of the principles of alchemy, the Templars and St. Gildas Man.

Darcy shook her head and leaned back against the cushions to stare at the ceiling. It was unbelievable. Here she was, dropped in the middle of the biggest thing since World War Two and nobody wanted to know: the ostrich syndrome running amok. It was inconceivable that those in power either did not know or did not believe what was going on. And at the lower end that included Frank Kelly. He had abandoned her to social isolation, ostracism and possible extinction. Well, he was not going to get away with it. A glance at the clock as she rose from the settee told her in Frank Kelly's terms, the night was still young.

A slow crawl past the detached brick house on the north side of town confirmed her suspicion that he was not at home. His treasured sixties Daimler Dart was not parked in its usual spot beneath the carport and the house was in darkness apart from a porch light. No problem. She knew where to find him. Turning the car with an angry squeal of tyres and, annoyingly, a crunching of gears she drove back to the main road and into the car park of the Wheatsheaf Inn. She saw him at once, propping up the bar and chatting to the barmaid.

"Hello, Frank. 'Thought I might find you here."

He swung round and the colour drained from his cheeks. "Darcy!" The bloodshot eyes were testament to the quantity of whisky he had already consumed. To drown his guilt, Darcy thought with a rush of anger.

"Surprised to see me?" she said icily. "Come, come Frank, I'm sure you have been expecting a visit."

Frank Kelly looked furtively around him at his fellow bar-proppers who were looking interested in a scene that promised a whiff of scandal to enliven their late, and solitary, drinking. The inquisitive barmaid hovered waiting for more, but then shrugged and moved away from the challenge of Darcy's narrowed eyes.

"Look kid, I know what you must be feeling—"

"You don't Frank, not for a moment." She made no effort to lower her voice.

"For Chris'sakes, Darcy - what do you want?" He cast an agonised glance around.

"Justice - and some answers."

Frank moved closer and spoke in a undervoice.

"Look," he wheedled, "I've enough problems already with my wife, without this little lot being misunderstood. If it gets back to her – well, it will give her an excuse to leave."

So it's true his wife is messing around.

"That's tough, Frank," she said forcing herself to be ruthless and raising her voice a decibel or two, "because if you don't agree to talk to me, I'm going to park my car back on your drive and wait until she returns."

"Bitch!" he said softly, then added with an agitated gesture as Darcy turned to leave, "At the News. The car park behind the pumps."

"Okay. But Frank—,"
"Yeah?"
"Be there." She left the 'or else' hanging over Frank Kelly's head and left.

Driving onto the car park of the Paper brought an upsurge of bitterness. A short time ago she had been the rising star of the stables, and was now forced to keep a low profile for fear of being recognised by the night crew. The hand brake rasped in response to the angry jerk of her arm. Though to be fair, not only her job but her life had been on the line from the moment of her involvement with St. Gildas Man; it had been her decision to go it alone. The realisation made her greet Frank Kelly when he arrived with a modicum of tolerance.
"Get in, Frank," she said gesturing, then could not resist adding: "Be quick, or one of the bosses may see and you'll risk your job as well as your marriage."
"Lay off Darcy." He sat heavily in the passenger seat and slammed the door shut. "I came, and losing my job won't help you any, will it?"
"No, but speaking up for me might have."
"Negative."

He pulled a King Edward from his inside pocket, stripped off the cellophane wrapper, and lit the end of the cigar with a gold lighter.
"Nothing could have made a difference." He blew a stream of fragrant blue smoke through the gap in the passenger window.
"Did you try?"
"As a matter of fact I did. To the point of Max Dearden suggesting I might like to draft an ad. for a replacement features editor."
Conscience-stricken, Darcy stared at him. She had expected excuses, not this.
"Thanks for that, Frank."
He shrugged and took another pull on his cigar.

"Like I said – made no difference. Someone with clout wanted you out of the way, the decision was made even before I was summoned to their lousy meeting."

"You could have warned me, rather than let me walk in on the humiliation."

"You were out of town, Goddammit. Besides, I have been warning you back from the edge for weeks, only you were too bloody-minded to listen." He shuffled on his seat and ran fingers through his mane so that it stood up in spikes.

"Oh, shit. I'm sorry it happened kid, but now do yourself a favour and quit this crazy investigation."

He gave her a half-smile as her eyes widened in surprise. "Yes, I know you've been carrying on behind my back, but now is the time to stop. They scare me, Darcy – scare me rotten. Not the jerks who run the paper but the bastards pulling the strings. That's real clout. It may be more than your job next time." She surveyed him in silence for a moment.

"What do you know Frank?"

"Enough to shop you to the authorities for your own good if you don't see sense," he threatened, skewing round to face her.

"Nice try. But I haven't broken the law – yet."

The cigar moved from one side of his mouth to the other, depositing a plug of ash on his front due to the force of the movement.

"Shit! What does it take, Darcy? Look, I got problems, but I ain't tired of living yet. I do know the organisation backing this one goes back a fair way. Which is where your crusader or whatever he was comes in. For some reason they wanted your story blocked. That's all Max Dearden told me. But I'm not dumb. I have some ideas of my own and they check out."

"Fair enough," Darcy said with ill-concealed impatience. "But you need to take this on board. This isn't confined to a few British civil servants and bureaucrats." She recalled with a suppressed shiver Von Schmidt's perverted nationalism. "This organisation is big, very nasty and extends into Europe possibly beyond."

"You don't need to tell me."

She looked full into his face, saw the gravity and weariness there and knew the truth of his words.

"Okay. So you know that this is not so much about cranky formulas for making gold as the manipulation of frustrated and power-hungry people. And you must also know how dangerous that can be. Somebody has to do something Frank."

He exhaled the huge sigh that Darcy from long experience recognised as one of resignation.

"What do you want of me Darcy?"

"Two favours."

"Only two?" The dryness of his smile, and accompanying prune-wrinkled face brought memories of past confrontations and a lump to Darcy's throat. But this was no time for nostalgia.

"Time – and credibility."

"Go on."

A new wariness had crept into Frank Kelly's voice and expression, so she chose her next words with care.

"A couple of interviews. If anyone calls to check me out, you must back me up by confirming I'm still on the News."

"Now I know you are crazy." Frank snorted and almost lost his cigar.

"Give me a break Frank; I'm out on my own," she pleaded.

He sighed heavily again, sat back and surveyed her from beneath puffy eyelids.

"Who are they?"

"Our Madame Cabbala—"

"And the other?"

"Ernst Von Schmidt." Darcy moistened her lips and stared straight ahead.

"*What!*"

"Will you do it Frank?"

"Yes to the first—"

"And Von Schmidt?"

"The short answer is 'no'."

"He's vital."

"I have another epithet for him. Forget any idea of interviewing that bag of shit."

"I already did it Frank."

He looked at her for a long and heart-stopping moment before speaking.

"Darcy, you don't know what you're getting into here."

"I do. And that's why you have to back me up if he or one of his fascist lackeys make contact."

"What did you tell him, Darcy?" Frank audibly groaned.

"That I freelance for a far-right mag," she said with a confidence she was far from feeling. "He will check me out for sure, and sooner or later the trail will lead back to the News."

"Even if I did agree, and I've not said I will, what will you get out of it?"

"Like I said, time. Plus, if they think I have some hard backing," she paused and fixed him with a direct stare, "they'll maybe think twice before putting out a contract on me."

"Christ, Darcy."

"You don't have to tell an outright lie," she said pressing her advantage as he wavered. "Just give the impression I freelance – but am based at the News."

Frank withdrew his cigar, thoughtfully surveyed the end and stuck it back between his teeth.

"Okay. I'll back you on these two – no more mind."

"I understand." It was Darcy's turn to let out a long sigh. "Thanks Frank," she breathed.

"I guess I do owe you one," he said gruffly. "I shouldn't have let you walk in on that shit."

"Stop beating up on yourself, Frank. It wasn't your fault."

She could see he was basking in her gratitude, enjoying the role of benefactor rather than villain.

"Just don't ask for more; I have difficulty saying 'no' to you." He patted her arm, and let his hand rest there a moment too long and his bloodshot eyes misted with sentiment.

"Maybe we could do one another some good," he said softly, the whisky fumes heavy on his breath. "I've always had a thing about you Darcy."

"I'm too dangerous to know at present, Frank. Besides, you've got problems enough without me," she added, letting him down lightly.

"Some other time then, eh? Maybe when all this shit is cleaned up." Unfounded hope had softened the lined and cynical face, stirring pity and a deep affection in Darcy.

"Do me a favour – stop drinking yourself to death. Go home instead and sort that wife of yours out," she said, adding quietly: "She's the one you really want."

He sat in silence, legs apart, staring at the floor between his size elevens, then sighed heavily and nodded.

"You could be right."

"I am. Go talk with her Frank – not *at* her mind – before it's too late." Leaning forward she kissed his bristle-shaded cheek. His eyes were moist as he climbed from the car and rested an arm on the roof whilst peering in at her with a grave expression.

"Now you take my advice, Darcy, and get away until it cools." She pursed her lips whilst thinking about this, then conceded with reluctance:

"I could join my parents for a week or two in France."

"Do it, Darcy – do it for me."

"Sure thing, Frank," she said nodding.

"You know, this is the rummest lark I ever came across." He shook his head like some great puzzled bear.

"Want to hear something funny?" Darcy laughed, a dry cynical laugh that sounded hollow and mirthless.

"Could sure do with it."

"O.k. I know this is about power, greed, politics and you name it. But know what Frank—"

"What's that Darcy-girl?"

"I think it's really the old one. The bit about Good and Evil."

"I ain't laughing Darcy." His expression conveyed something other than amusement. He rammed his cigar, burnt- out end turning cold, further into his mouth and started to walk away. Then he turned to face her again.

"You hear me? I'm not laughing." Still chewing on the dead cigar he disappeared into the darkness.

FORTY-ONE

The first thing she did on arriving at the flat was to reach
for the receiver and dial Brant's number. Depression hit her like
a stone as the tone continued to ring out but nobody answered.
There was no Brant, with his common sense approach to quell
the rising tide of panic and isolation. No support, nothing. On
the verge of tears, she slumped against the cushions of the settee
knowing there was nothing for it but to carry on. How and in
what direction was another matter. Thoughts whirled around
her head like fallen leaves in the wake of a passing car. As the
vortex settled, one notion floated free and persisted, the same
hunch that had prompted her to add a certain name to that of
Von Schmidt when asking her favours of Frank. Alchemical
symbols, astrological signs, a flock of pigeons and visions of
Knights Templar did have a common denominator. Clare
Cabbala – and the woman had tried to warn her off the
investigation.

The more she thought about it the more credible it
became. The Cabbala woman was no seaside entertainer
but an internationally renowned clairvoyant. As such she was
'on the circuit', accepted by the elite, the powerful and the
wealthy. Celebrities and cabinet ministers were known to be
amongst her clients and, rumour had it, that a minor royal had
summoned her to the palace for consultations. If there was any
truth in her fears of a Neo-Nazi up-rising in Europe fuelled
– as was Hitler's Germany – by debased spiritual fire then Clare
Cabbala must be amongst the first to know of it. As Brant had
pointed out, however improbable it all seemed people would
believe what they needed to, and right now many were in
spiritual poverty and hungry for revolt.

She half-rose in excitement then subsided again on the
cushions as her promise to Frank struck: lying low with her
parents at their holiday home in Provence was a boring

prospect. Resolving to defer a decision until daylight, Darcy made her way wearily to bed.

****

One final visit to check out this hunch, then down to packing and travel arrangements was the decision by light of day. Restored by sleep and the prospect of positive action, she crossed to the telephone and dialled Clare Cabbala's private number entrusted to her by Frank. On the pretext of setting up a meeting between the clairvoyant and a panel of experts from the fields of physics, philosophy and parapsychology she secured an immediate appointment.

Buoyed by daring, Darcy entered the house on the edge of town that had been leased by the clairvoyant for the remainder of her stay. She was ushered into the drawing room by Madame Cabbala's companion, a nondescript woman of around thirty as thin as her employer was stout. Her hair was scraped back in an uninspiring bun and her pale face devoid of make-up. A deliberate foil, Darcy guessed, to set off her mistress's opulence and flamboyance.
"Miss West for you, Madame." The voice was resonant and seemed incongruent with the frail frame.
"Thank you Jennings; you may bring refreshment."
From her chaise longue Madam Cabbala waved a plump white and beringed hand in dismissal then turned to Darcy.
"Come here, darling girl, come here," she purred, indicating a gilded Louis sixteenth armchair close to the chaise.

Jennings reappeared carrying a tray laden with coffee and petit fours, laid it on the table then discreetly left. Darcy outlined the plan for the bogus meeting. Her companion listened with eyes half-closed as she exhaled a thin stream of smoke from what appeared to be a thin black cheroot in the habitual elegant holder.
"You will have to await my consent," she said, after Darcy had concluded her account, "until I have your paper's assurance that my clients' anonymity will be preserved. Only then can I

295

let you use their case histories as examples of my achievements."

"I understand," Darcy responded courteously whilst feverishly searching for a way of approaching the real reason behind her visit. She watched in fascination as smoke caught in a haze of sunlight and dust motes then spiralled towards the chandelier and ornate plaster rose on the ceiling. A way to direct the conversation into pertinent channels now presented itself, a way moreover that would also serve to put Caro's alternative theory to the test.

"Your agent has done you proud with this house," she commented, launching her plan. "Tasteful rented accommodation is not easy to find"

"That is true, and I do require beautiful and harmonious surroundings."

"Isn't that what they call egg and dart mould," Darcy asked artlessly, indicating the plaster ceiling rose.

"I believe so." Madame Cabbala squinted at the emblem, then back at Darcy with a faintly puzzled expression.

"I read somewhere that the patterns held secret significance for the craftsmen. Masons I guess they were."

"Yes, I suppose they did." The older woman's eyelids scarcely flickered.

"There are parallels, I think between yourself and the freemasons," Darcy ventured.

"Why do you think so?" Cabbala's voice turned silky, and her eyes narrowed with suspicion.

Darcy leaned forward and placed her empty cup and saucer on the low onyx table.

"Well you are into symbolism too, aren't you?" She glanced at the framed astrological charts and paintings of dragons and other alchemical beasts that lined the walls.

"An interesting thought; how clever my dear." It was said with a patronising smile, but Darcy did not miss the stroking movement of the plump white hand over the white satin peignoir, as though Cabbala was attempting to smooth away creases in her composure. "But I assure you," she added with an arch look that sat ill with her huge frame and lined face, "I do not belong to any secret society."

"Of course not," Darcy murmured setting her trap, "I suppose they employ bizarre rituals to bind members to their vows." She eyed the opposition and decided to up the ante. "I'm sure you have no need of such things. I guess they are the ones with real power, so they need the mystique as a safeguard."

"Nonsense!" Clare Cabbala's plump cheeks were suffused with the pink of indignation. "Mere puppets." She frowned and shifted her bulk on the chaise in evident agitation. "But is this for your feature?"

"Heavens no," Darcy exclaimed beginning to reel in her victim, "Rest assured you won't read a word of what we talk about today in the Manchester News," she added with truth if also deviousness. The older woman gave a sigh of satisfaction.

"I think you are a good girl Darcy West. And a clever one. It is stimulating to talk with you like this. I get to see no-one here."

"Jennings?"

"Is like the majority of my clients, ignorant of true esoteric knowledge." In support of this denial of her companion's intellectual ability, she shook her head and the ringlets bounced on her forehead.

Darcy slid into the proffered opening.

"I know little, Madame, but am honoured by your interest and would love to learn more," she fawned whilst inwardly cringing, but it seemed to be working.

"Then forget the masons," Cabbala snapped. "Oh they dress up and have their little secrets like signs and rituals, and then make the mistake of thinking themselves important. But really they know nothing." Darcy almost smiled in triumph.

"But you know, don't you Madame?" she said shrewdly, sensing the need behind the woman's voracious ego. "You move in exalted circles and must have been amongst the first to know."

"To know what, my dear?" Again the coyness sat oddly with her maturity and bulk; fear and excitement mingled in her face as Clare Cabbala wilfully flirted with danger. Darcy played a desperate ace:

"The truth about Anton de Beaumont."

Clare Cabbala blanched and stared at Darcy in shock and disbelief.

"I'm sure I have no idea of what you are talking about," she blustered, then added in a whisper, "Who are you?" Sensing an advantage, Darcy went for gold.

"I am not at liberty to say."

"Of course not." Perspiration glistened on the hairs above her top lip; taking a handkerchief edged with lace from a pocket in the peignoir she dabbed delicately at her mouth.

"I am here on my own account."

The glide in Cabbala's eye became more pronounced as she stared at her adversary.

"I don't believe you." Evidently deciding to call her bluff she heaved her bulk off the day bed and moved with surprising speed to the bell that would summon Jennings. In order to forestall the action Darcy fired into the dark.

"I could hardly be one of them, could I?" She met the other's gaze without flinching. "I'm enormously flattered, but I ask you – would they bother with someone like me, so lacking in wealth, knowledge and power when they have illustrious members like yourself?"

The inspired shot hit its target dead centre of Cabbala's ego. Hesitating, finger on bell, she turned and squinted at Darcy then to her relief, smiled.

"Very true, dear girl, and very sensible of you to admit your lowly position. I admire you for it," she said in condescending tones, moving away from the bell and back to the day bed. "But it lies within my power to change all that."

Darcy contrived to look suitably impressed.

"It does, Madame?"

"But of course," Cabbala patted the back of her coiffure and continued to watch Darcy through narrowed eyes. "I think you have potential. It is not easy to penetrate the Inner Circle and its secrets, you have done your research well. When the time comes to broadcast the news here in Britain, it must be through the Establishment and handled by someone with boldness and intelligence." Cabbala's plump face crumpled into a coyness that made Darcy want to retch, "Someone like yourself, Darcy," then, as Darcy would have obligingly gushed her thanks, the other woman held up a cautionary hand. "But can you give me one good reason why I should not have Jennings show you the door?"

"Because I obviously know something – and you don't know how much or whom I might tell."

Cabbala looked as though she might explode, then suddenly smiled and nodded agreement.

"So I would do better to recruit and nurture you. I do not have the power to appoint you myself, but my recommendation would, shall I say, be conclusive." The smile then cast her way filled Darcy with sudden foreboding. "If I like you enough."

"I should be very honoured and grateful to be considered." Darcy's hands tightened their grip on the arms of the chair and agonised: this over-dressed crank had not yet divulged anything of value but the price – if the sickly smile and abandoned pose were anything to go by, was rising. May as well make it pay.

"Tell me about Herr Schmidt," she pleaded, feigning reverence.

If Cabbala was shocked by this revelation, she hid it well. "A true visionary. He has worked so hard for the Cause."

"You have heard him speak?" The temptation proved too tempting for Cabbala to resist.

"I have enjoyed that privilege," she crooned, preening the satin over her plump breasts in the manner of some bloated pigeon.

"It is only fitting for someone with your gifts," Darcy flattered, toes curling within her shoes: but now for the kill. "I could never hope to attend the rallies."

"It could possibly be arranged." The older woman peered coquettishly from under creased and shadow-streaked eyelids. "I like you Darcy," she breathed, allowing her peignoir to fall open and reveal white and lardy thighs topped by a hint of pubic hair. "Come here dear girl and give me a little comfort."

Darcy cringed as her suspicions were confirmed with regard to Jennings' true role. Much as she wanted to crack the truth, playing sex toy to Clare Cabbala was not on her agenda. "Madame, I am so sorry," she said, forcing coyness into her voice, "but I have another appointment. I assure you I should love to stay," she lied. Cabbala sighed and pouted, making no attempt to hide her disappointment.
"Next time, yes?" Her piggy eyes and puffy face took on a crafty look. "Becoming personally acquainted will help me to judge your suitability as my protégée – and potential P.R. officer to the Movement," she added craftily. Darcy lowered her head implying modesty but it was a ploy to hide her disgust. "Good, good." The big woman stroked her thigh and all but purred. "I know how to make you feel good too, Darcy. My knowledge is considerable."

"You mean I shall get to hear Herr Schmidt too?" Darcy said in reverent tones, deliberately misunderstanding.
"An innocent, how charming." Cabbala smiled her indulgence. "Of course, if you please me."
"Oh, but when?" Darcy forced herself to reach across and touch the other woman's leg as though in an unguarded and spontaneous moment. Momentarily flustered by the contact, Clare Cabbala flushed then glanced at the chart on the wall which mapped the signs of the Zodiac and their constellations. "When the sign appears, of course."
Darcy hurriedly withdrew her hand as Cabbala tried to grasp it and thrust it between her thighs.
"I am so ignorant Madame," she said despondently, deliberately being ambiguous.
"The thirtieth, child, the thirtieth," Cabbala chanted with an indulgent smile. "The date of the Conjunctio."
This at least was familiar. Darcy grasped at her scanty knowledge of alchemy.
"Of course, the sacred marriage." Judging it time to be gone she rose to her feet. "I really must go Madame Cabbala. Until next

time then—" She left the tacit promise hanging on the air and ignored the other woman's demand for a farewell kiss.

"Very well," Clare Cabbala pouted, "I shall send for you soon." Flipping back the lid of a carved wooden box she took out what Darcy at first took to be another cheroot and fitted the gilded end into her diamond-studded filter. Suddenly Darcy's gaze focused and Cabbala misinterpreted her fixation.

"Would you like to try one, my dear? They are a gift from one of our illustrious members."

Darcy declined, mumbled her thanks and backed up to the door, still unable to drag her gaze from the box containing Sobranie Black Russian cigarettes.

FORTY-TWO

Driving through the city centre on her way to the flat, Darcy marvelled at her good fortune: her intuition about that last minute visit had been spot-on. *They were given to me by one of our members.* The source of the Sobranie cigarettes and therefore the killer of Miles Standish could be traced via Clare Cabbala, providing she could crack the meaning of the sign the woman had mentioned. It had to be either an astrological one like Pisces or the Gemini twins, (both 'double' images and therefore possible candidates for the 'sacred marriage') or an alchemical symbol such as the dragon or ouroboros.

Still deep in thought, Darcy drew to a halt at the traffic lights and stared absently past vehicles strung bumper to bumper to the streams of workers hurrying through their lunch break. Once she had been amongst them with an office and job to return to; now she was an outsider and completely alone. Bitterness welled at this disastrous change in status and the resolve to clear her name hardened. Turning her attention back to the lights she saw they had turned to amber and prepared to move off, then froze. A Volvo saloon, two cars ahead and in the offside lane, caught her attention. It was something about the passenger and the way he held his head. The man turned to speak to a person in the rear.
"Brant!" Her hand hit the horn and she let down the window. The driver in front turned and glared, convinced that he was the target. With an angry gesture at the lights which had that second turned to green, he pulled away at a snail's pace as though to curb what he saw as her impatience.

Frustration made her reckless, and to the accompaniment of a blare of horns she overtook, keeping her gaze riveted on the Volvo in the next but one lane.
"Brant! Brant, stop!" she shouted, then kept her hand on the horn but to little effect. Sick with frustration she saw the

Volvo's right indicator flash. He was about to escape. Switching lanes and dodging in and out to a second blast from angry drivers, she tried to force a way in. The driver of the Volvo, professional-looking but sinister with his black suit and tie and reflective shades, glanced in the mirror and the car picked up speed. He knows I am on to him Darcy agonised, convinced now that Brant was suffering from selective deafness and blindness. Another set of lights loomed offering a second chance, but the Volvo swung right on amber. An automatic response to the red light made her hit the brake. She had a split second to decide. Ramming her foot on the accelerator, with a squealing of tyres she swerved into a right turn.

The angry blare of horns receded, and it seemed she had made it. The Volvo was several cars ahead and picking up speed. Her foot squeezed the accelerator then relaxed the pressure. A groan escaped her as the blue light flashed and was reflected in her mirror. Desperate as she was to catch Brant, she was not stupid enough to ignore a police car, and with a sigh of resignation pulled in.
"You went through a red light there, miss."
The officer unbuttoned his top pocket and drew out a notebook and pen. By the time Darcy had produced her licence, and concocted some outrageous story about a life or death lead-story whilst flashing her press card, the Volvo had disappeared.

On arriving at the flat, she told herself she could be mistaken and rushing to the telephone dialled Brant's number. The ringing-out tone sounded monotonously but nobody answered. And now she knew why. There was no mistake about the man's identity; there had been that other trip to Manchester when he had been 'too busy' to look her up. No longer able to ignore the implications, she sank onto the settee and covered her eyes. He had led her to believe that he would be staying at the farmhouse and working at the observatory. Anger blazed; they were lovers weren't they, and supposedly working together.

She rose and poured herself a drink then returned to the sofa. She had been stupid enough to fall for an honest face and boyish smile but it seemed honesty was not one of Mr. Kennedy's attributes. There had been no time to note the Volvo's number, therefore no way of tracing Brant. Her shoulders drooped beneath the weight of despair; had Brant proved true, nothing would have crushed her resolve. Yet to give up now was unthinkable. Justice for Miles Standish and Caro had been amongst her reasons for going on, but there was one other. It took the form of Anton de Beaumont, a ghostly yet real presence. It was the one about herself in search of the ultimate story, and the guy with that story to tell.

And now, amidst the pain and disillusionment of Brant's betrayal, came awareness. Her obsession with Anton went deeper than the excitement of solving the mystery of his life and present significance. Fascinating though that was, Anton spoke to her in a far more personal way. She saw now what had prevented a deeper involvement with Jonathon. For her ordinary love was not enough. Not for her the two-point-five kids, the staying together for 'the sake of the children' followed by the quickie divorce as they grew up and their parents grew apart. No, it had to be a towering all-consuming passion, one like that of Anton for Leala: a love that could defy death and survive the grave, a love that in his case empowered him to transmit his need over centuries, and paint pictures with his yearning. It had to be a love for which she would die or kill, one that despite the battle scars and passing regrets would prove as eternal as the Universe itself. A passion preferring hatred to a lesser love, but which could never embrace indifference.

Images of a silver dome, energy flares and star-dances filled her mind. They say each soul on Earth is incomplete, that somewhere each one has a mate. Brant's awareness and intensity, the expansiveness of his vision had inspired her to hope that he, like herself, was in search of that missing half. The full impact of her pain burst inside her chest, and the fragments flared and stabbed like spurts of planetary fire. She had thought to find such a love with Brant.

Realisation, and an accompanying sense of foolishness for daring so to believe, drained her of hope and energy. Her head lolled back against the cushions and tears of bereavement – for a lost love, or rather one that had never been – wet her cheeks. It seemed that the familiar scent of haunting cedar-wood, salt-rose breeze and mystical frankincense that she now associated with Anton crept into the room to mock her sadness. When she closed her eyes, he was there, the cross of the Templar emblazoned on his armoured chest, an image on the screen of her mind, drawn with longing and despair. He had the body and persona of a long-dead knight but the face and bearing of Brant. As she watched, the features faded and dissolved in the luminous oval. The end of a vision and the death of a dream at its birth. If it seemed a far-off voice called to her from within advising her to keep faith and stand firm, Darcy chose to ignore it. There lay false hope and eventually more pain. Better by far to let go now.

Eventually rousing herself from the pit of hurt and self-pity, she tried to plan ahead. Her escape to France must wait for a day or two; a quick review of facts and probabilities convinced her of the need to stay. Clare Cabbala held the key to the 'celestial sign' and the rally scheduled for the thirtieth of the month at some secret location. So where did Brant and the Neo-Nazi league fit in? Astronomy and astrology linked Brant and the Cabbala woman, but how did they slot into an organisation responsible for a new fascist rising? Surely Brant could not be involved in anything so sick. She forced her mind to scan possible connections: astrology used charts, dates and conjunctions, and astronomy also employed them to date events in the past. There was a bell ringing somewhere, but no it had gone. Frustrated, she rose and paced the floor then was suddenly sure of her next move. The answer lay somewhere on those computer screens and Brant was away in Manchester. Now was the time to pay a second visit to the observatory but this time alone.

A couple of hours later she was in Cumbria and on her way to the observatory. The wind tore and sucked at her lungs leaving her breathless as she hurried along the cliff-top path, having left the car at the Old Priory. From time to time, she turned to look over her shoulder convinced that she would see the Land Rover bouncing towards her across turf and heather, or Brant – hair dishevelled by the wind and face like thunder – pursuing her on foot like some latter-day Heathcliff pursuing a faithless Cathy. But Brant was miles away and in any case would never expect to find her up here alone. Gulls, the only sign of life, wheeled overhead and screamed at her folly and daring. She pushed on, hair streaming back and cagoule flapping and crackling as though struggling to escape from her shoulders. To the left, surf creamed like saliva around sandstone fangs hundreds of feet below. At last it loomed in her view, the hill that hid the observatory from the casual walker.

At the iron gates she brought a bunch of skeleton keys from her pocket and glanced nervously over her shoulder. The last time she used them had earned her a 'serious reprimand' from Frank. She half-smiled as the key slipped in. A gesture of course, to give the impression the Paper cared how its reporters got their stories. A click and the iron loop of the padlock swung free. A second lock on the inner door proved harder to crack but eventually yielded. The familiar damp green odour of earth and secrecy assailed her nostrils. How stupid of her to not bring a torch; the switch on the console was somewhere to the right. Her fingers groped and found it, and a row of lights glowed redly in sequence around the perimeter of the globe. Not relishing the idea of being shut inside with no glimpse of sky she left the door ajar to admit some light.

Recalling the procedure Brant had used to vitalise the dead, grey screens, she activated the power switch on the computer terminal and set about pressing buttons that would bring the celestial maps to life. So absorbed was she in scanning energy fields that the slight change in atmosphere failed to register. Tense with concentration she leaned closer to the monitor. Feverishly her fingers worked the keys, moving the programme forward. The fireworks display of planetary energy flashed across the screen igniting memory traces. The use of astronomy to date the past. Once again the phrase arose to tease and elude. And there, at the centre of it all the explosion of light, the fusing of constellations.

Then it hit. Involuntarily glancing around her she suppressed a cry of excitement. Abarbanel was the link. The ancient astronomer, mentioned on several occasions by Brant and used by Miles as a pseudonym in that fatal cryptic message. The Conjunctio – Alchemy's sacred marriage – had to refer to the union of Saturn and Jupiter in Pisces. This, she recalled, was the big one; the conjunction rumoured to be the 'abnormally fierce and bright star to the east' recorded at the time of the historical Jesus' birth. Emotively loaded and symbolic of hope and a new age. And the last conjunction of Saturn and Pisces occurred in the Middle Ages and according to Brant, was used by alchemists in forging the universal panacea of the Philosophers Stone. Clicking on icons like fury now, she suddenly stopped, straightened up and gave a smile of triumph. Because there it was: the next conjunction was scheduled for the thirtieth of the month.

This, combined with the body of St. Gildas Man, must provide the New Order with the most potent of symbols. Rather more striking to the imagination than a red rose, she thought ironically. What better motif for the union of mysticism and politics? Crackpots and megalomaniacs they may well be, but given the involvement of the Home Office, plausible ones and a real threat to democracy. Symbols, rituals and hysteria worked for Hitler to the point of genocide, she reflected sombrely, closing down the computers. And they said it could never happen again. But the power of the collective psyche was an awesome engine when mobilised. And Hitler wasn't the only one to target the religious impulse of a nation. Single-handed and without military or political backing, the Ayatollah Khomeini had fuelled the zeal of a people, then used it to destroy the Shah of Iran's sophisticated regime.

But there was an example closer to hand and therefore infinitely more chilling, she thought as September Eleventh and the Twin Towers inferno came to mind. She shivered and hugged herself in distress as the implications made impact. What more terrifying testament could there be to chaos and destruction wrought by fanaticism? Now, thanks to fundamentalist extremists, suicide bombers and terrorist attacks were an ever-present evil and threat to civilisation. In the wrong hands, ideology and even more so religion, were powerful weapons. And therein, she realised, lay the peril: the majority could be inflamed by the zealous few.

And now it could be happening in Europe: the Nationals all carried stories of Neo-Nazi demos and atrocities in Jewish communities. The date for the rally disclosed by Clare Cabbala had obviously been chosen to coincide with the date of this major celestial event to provide a backdrop of drama for Von Schmidt's warped dream of a Nazi revival. What she needed now was the location, which meant following the Cabbala woman on the thirtieth. Plus – and this was the big one – to convince Frank Kelly and through him the Establishment, and so gain the necessary clout to smash the conspiracy.

She frowned as the change in atmosphere increased and infiltrated her consciousness. Heart thumping, she took her hands from the keyboard as the monitor died. The row of red lights slowly faded to extinction. Panic rose as darkness descended. What else had changed? The hairs at the nape of her neck prickled as realisation struck. She was no longer alone in the dome. The sense of human presence was unmistakable. As she waited in the darkness, motionless and sifting her senses for information, her nails dug into her palms. Instinctively, she began to move to the sliver of light filtering through the partially open door. Her heart skipped a beat: the opening was diminishing with each step. A dull thud echoed around the metal dome as the door slid shut.

Darkness wrapped her in suffocating folds. She stumbled forward bumping into cables and terminals on the way. A twist of the handle and a couple of hard pushes with her shoulder told her the metal slab was not about to yield. Fighting down panic Darcy groped for the power switch. It clicked several times beneath her finger, but to no effect. In desperation, she crawled from wall to computer console, feeling cold metal and unsympathetic plastic beneath her hands, and pressing any button they touched. Eventually the panic of a trapped animal was replaced by reason. It could not be Brant because he was in Manchester with no way of knowing she would be here. The hit man who had murdered Miles Standish then? Access would be no problem given their contacts and level of operation. The thought of being at the mercy of someone capable of doing what was done to Miles brought a sheen of perspiration to her forehead. She was safe for the moment: if he wanted her dead he would have finished her there and then. The comfort brought by that thought was brief. *Until he makes sure the cliffs are free of walkers in order to dispose of your body*, a voice within warned. In that case, her potential assassin would return. She shivered and, standing motionless, listened and waited but heard nothing. The tension at neck and shoulders relaxed a fraction.

A more immediate worry arose to gnaw like a rat at her confidence. If he did return, would he do so in time? She tried to recall from the days of an Outward Bound team-building course the length of time one could survive without food and water. Such calculations were interrupted by an even more pressing thought about the air supply in the dome and how long it might last. Maybe the plan was to leave her sealed up inside and let events take their natural course. A regrettable accident; and taking place in a top secret location like this, how simple to arrange a cover-up.

As though in response to her fear, the darkness appeared to thicken, smothering her mouth and nostrils and stifling breath. Claustrophobia, once a remote concept, was now a terrifying reality. The walls were contracting, and the ceiling pressing down on her head, bringing to mind an Edgar Allen Poe chamber of torture. The air inside the dome became thicker and denser. Would it soon carry the smell of a Sobranie Black Russian?

"God help me," she whispered, sinking to her knees as the pressure increased.

She had no idea how long she cowered there on the ground, but eventually innate courage and common sense came to the rescue. Given the size of the dome, there must be sufficient oxygen to keep her going for hours she reasoned, and whilst total darkness was somewhat unnerving it was not life-threatening. It was all a question of preparation, self-protection and keeping control in her head. The element of surprise would give her an edge.

She shuffled along the floor, coming to rest with her back against a unit, and tried to fill her mind with positive thoughts. Reaching up onto the work surface she felt about for a potential weapon but nothing came to hand. Striving to stifle fear that threatened to spin her out of control, she slid along to the next bench. Her hand explored but found nothing. At the fourth attempt, she rejoiced as her fingers closed round a heavy oblong object, at a guess some sort of remote control console. Sliding along on her stomach commando style, she made her way round the edge of the dome to the door and settled down to wait.

Something jolted her out of torpor. In her estimation a couple of hours must have passed, her watch was not luminous and therefore could not be read in the blackout. She stiffened and stared at the adjacent wall; a crack of light had appeared. The fissure grew an inch or so wider, as though someone had opened the door and was watching and listening before pushing it further. She held her breath as the gap widened inch by inch. Afraid that her captor would hear the thudding of her heart, she pressed her free hand to her breast as though to stifle the sound. Her other hand tightened its grip on the improvised weapon. A figure appeared silhouetted against the daylight. Darcy took a deep breath and, raising her arm, prepared to smash the skull of the intruder. As the figure passed by then paused to listen, she struck. She screamed as the man swivelled on his heel and seconds before impact grabbed her wrist. His grip tightened like a vice and the weapon dropped from her hand. Darcy, succumbing to shock after weeks of strain, slumped to the ground and lay still.

FORTY-THREE

A warm sea engulfed her, cradling her exhausted body in swimmy-green dimness, the amniotic fluid of the universal womb. Her limbs obeyed instinct, and she slowly began to rise, floating towards a circle of light above her head. The sense of weightlessness gave way to one of pressure. Black spots swam before her eyes as she spiralled upwards, tadpoles that wriggled and squirmed before her vision. Shot through like silk, the circle of light was diffused, and yes, confused – because now there were two of them and she was staring into a pair of compelling green eyes.

A muted cry escaped her and bubbled towards the surface; the face above her was that of Anton. A youthful Anton with dark locks that sprang back from an unlined forehead, and spread across the surface in Medusa-like coils. The green eyes urged her on, compelling her to rise from this sea of unknowing and tell his story. His mouth began to move, a black hole at the halo's centre that spread on the ripples to engulf and swallow her whole. The thoughts, feelings, sensations of his entire existence swamped her, driving out self and filling her with his need. She was bathed, cajoled and seduced by the irresistible power of his psyche. Nothing existed but this seductive darkness to which she was about to succumb. Pinpoints of light reappeared, rapidly grew, pulsed and merged into one, a gateway to reality. Preferring the womb-like darkness her mind resisted, but her body rose to the lunar pull. She gasped and blinked on breaking the surface-tension.

The brilliance of the light hurt her eyes. She whispered his name, but the face above her was not, after all, that of Anton. The hair was dark and virile, but the eyes staring anxiously into her own were not green but a formidable slatey-blue. "Brant?" Her limbs felt heavy and water-logged and the weight of them defeated her struggles to rise. She closed her eyes as the lights in the dome came up to full strength then cautiously opened them again and tried to rise.

"Remain still." The calm voice of authority did much to restore a sense of normality. Gradually memory seeped back; she shrank away, unsure of his intentions. He was down on one knee, head bent in a curiously knight-like pose but when he spoke again there was a marked absence of chivalry.

"Darcy, what the hell are you doing here?"

Unable to speak, she shook her head and fought back the tears.

"Come on," he ordered, standing up. "You need a stiff drink." Hauling her none too gently to her feet, Brant Kennedy steered her to the door.

It was dark when he parked up at the rear of the farmhouse. There was a nip in the air and the stars seemed unusually large and bright against a cloudless sky. The stillness was unnatural: not a leaf or blade of grass stirred as though the wind was waiting with bated breath for the next scene in the drama to unfold. Darcy stared at him from across the kitchen table, the brandy in the glass before her untouched.

"You locked me in," she accused.

"Don't be ridiculous." But he could not look her in the eye.

"I know it was you," she persisted.

"You can see in the dark, can you?" He lifted the lid of the Aga and placed a battered kettle on the hot plate.

Fear touched her with a cold hand as he turned to face her again. This was not the Brant she had left behind a mere week ago. This man was remote, possessing a hardness and professionalism that chilled. But not exactly a stranger, she realised, there had been something of this quality about him the day they met when he challenged her on the cliff.

"Don't play games with me Brant," she said in a low voice, beginning to doubt her judgment in the face of such absolute assurance. "Who else could it have been?" Her fear must have shown; a sudden smile relieved the severity of his expression.

"Drink up, Darcy. You've had a nasty shock," he said and reached across the table to take her hand in reassurance. She withdrew, shaking her head with vehemence. "Don't try and make me doubt my sanity Brant."

He gave her a long hard look, seemed about to speak again then hesitated as though having had second thoughts. He stared down at the worn and scrubbed surface of the table then met her gaze. Darcy thought she detected shame and compassion in his eyes, then decided he was weighing the pro's and cons of levelling with her.

"Very well. I was there." The words seemed to intensify the ensuing silence.

"Why Brant?" she whispered at last, her gaze scouring his features as though in the hope of finding justification. She covered her face with hands that shook as reaction set in. Swiftly he moved to her side.

"I didn't know it was you, Darcy. You could have been armed, been one of them."

She wiped tears from her face with the back of one hand.

"You left me in the dark. Where did you go?"

"The village, to inform the authorities."

Her eyes widened with incredulity.

"You could have 'phoned from here."

"Lines can be tapped," he said, shaking his head. "Nobody knows that better than yourself. I didn't want a hit man getting here first as with poor Standish."

"So where are the police?" she demanded.

"I saw your car as I reached the Old Priory and realised there was no need to involve them."

Before or after you locked the observatory door? Darcy could not help wondering. If the former, it would explain the seemingly extraordinary coincidence of Brant turning up there at the same time she entered the dome. He had guessed where she was, and followed.

"When I realised it was you in there, I went straight back to let you out," he added as though sensing her suspicion.

"I tried the power switch; it didn't work," she accused. "There's a master switch in the panel by the door. I turned the power off when I entered the first time, then switched it back on when I returned," he explained smoothly.

"It was a nightmare; I believed I was going to die."

"I am truly sorry Darcy. But to be honest, for a moment back there I wasn't sure about you." He half-smiled as though in shame. "Terrible admission, isn't it? But you see I could think of no valid reason for you to break in." The emphasis on the final two words was slight, but sufficient to make her feel guilty and fortify his position. Suddenly he was the aggrieved party and she the transgressor. To be fair, on many occasions she had harboured the same sort of doubts about him. It lent credence to his story yet, she worried, there was something wrong. it was all too glib and convenient.

So, when he leaned forward to kiss her forehead Darcy withdrew. But she was exhausted, shocked and badly in need of the comfort of his embrace, so when he pulled her to him her resistance was token. His voice in her ear was warm, deep and the colour brown like the bed of a mountain stream; the fibres of his sweater smelled reassuringly of dogs, heather and bracken. "It's too late for you to be driving back." He held her at arms length and critically surveyed her face. "And tonight you need looking after. Will you allow me to tuck you into bed with a bowl of broth and a hot toddy? Will you let me do that Darcy? Will you?"

His voice was low and persuasive, almost hypnotic. A part of her knew this to be deliberate, a learned technique to render her pliable and quiescent, but the ticking of the antique clock in the corner soothed her fears and the warmth of the kitchen was strangely soporific. She followed unresisting as he led her through the door and up the stairs. When she had finished her toddy, Brant joined her in the Victorian bed. Her body – greedy for contact after the fear and isolation of the dome – responded instantly to his touch. Sensing her need he caressed her face and hair with tenderness rather than passion. Love swathed her in layers of purest silk, the folds floating on air and suspended in light before drifting down to veil her insecurity. Despite her resolve to reject him, her womb opened to receive him without reservation. With renewal came the courage to share, in a gesture of deep and age-old giving, a symbolic surrender that is all about trust and nothing at all to do with submission. A gift which is known to each woman in love whatever her age, race, creed or occupation. He paused as though sensible of her bequest, his face unfathomable by the light of the solitary candle.

"Whatever happens in the days ahead, remember I meant this." When she nodded but did not speak he urged: "Give me your promise, Darcy."

"I promise."

As he held her close, Darcy shivered. Brant had allowed fear to creep into the bed.

****

Darcy awoke to the drumming of rain against the panes of the window. She lay still for a time, staring at the grey light of dawn and puzzled by her surroundings. Gradually the events of the previous night flooded back. The rain, she realised, had not been the cause of her waking but rather the coldness and emptiness at her back. She turned to find Brant dressed and standing by the bed, looking down at her with a troubled expression.

"Brant?"

"Good morning, Darcy." His voice was constrained and remote as though he were consciously striving to distance himself from her, and she sensed not only in an emotional sense. Suddenly alarmed, she raised herself up on one elbow. "Where are you going?"

"I'll be back this evening." He placed the mug of tea he was holding on the bedside cabinet

"You haven't answered my question." She pulled herself up against the pillows.

"Drink your tea before it gets cold. And forget work for a day or two, Darcy, you need a rest."

Darcy, startled and disturbed at the authoritative tone, knew it was time to test his honesty.

316

"I lost my job Brant."

"When? What happened?" He managed a look of surprise. She made a dismissive gesture with her hand.

"It's history now. I 'phoned several times to let you know but got no answer. Were you here all the time?" she asked, hating herself for laying the trap.

"Of course, here or at the observatory."

She almost groaned aloud. If only he had told her the truth, admitted to being in Manchester. She watched the steam from the tea rise in fantastic coils and streamers, thinking that their love of the previous night was now as cold and lacking in comfort as the air in the bedroom.

"Shame about the job, but something better will turn up. You can tell me about it later. At least now," he added, "You won't need to go rushing back."

"I'm sorry, Brant," she said, wrapping a sheet around her nakedness as she clambered out of bed, "I really can't stay."

"I'm afraid I must insist," he said firmly. His back was rigid, discouraging protest as he left. Even before she ran to the door and tried the handle, Darcy knew it would be locked.

FORTY-FOUR

She sat on the edge of the bed, hoarse from shouting and knuckles sore from pounding the panels of the door. There was no further point in trying to shame him into setting her free; the front door had slammed shut and the cough and rumble of the Land Rover's engine had died away. Yet even though her heart felt squeezed of life, she had to put her mind and energies to escaping before his return. A survey of the room revealed a Thermos of coffee and plate of sandwiches beneath a cloth on the marble-topped wash stand. The adjoining dressing room at some stage had been converted to a bathroom and the door to this had been left unlocked. Rather than consideration for her needs, she saw these measures as evidence of cold-blooded premeditation. Anger replaced the previous panic and reinforced her determination to escape.

The prospect from the window offered a drop of some thirty odd feet without benefit of ledge, outhouse or drainpipe to assist descent. There was only one way out of here. Feverishly she searched the room for her bag. Had it been on her shoulder still when Brant had brought her here, shocked and dazed by her ordeal? Closing her eyes, she pictured her movements as he led her to the bed. Lifting the valance she gave a sigh of relief; her bag lay where she had dropped it, and the skeleton keys were inside.

Once in the hall, the proximity of the door and freedom lent her courage. He had shown her his study on her first visit to the farmhouse and she entered it now. Ignoring the computer. she sifted through the piles of documents, maps and charts that littered the desk. Nothing at first to cause excitement, then his diary was unearthed. Eagerly, her fingers leafed through the pages to the thirtieth of the month. *Conjunctio* The word leapt up at her from the page. It was followed by the initials J & S in P for Jupiter and

Saturn in Pisces, and then the location she sought: Edgeway
Hall, Alderley. No need now to risk detection by following
Clare Cabbala, this must be the location of the forthcoming
secret gathering. Alderley Edge, she recalled, was in the
remoter reaches of Cheshire.

She was about to close the diary when an entry for two
days previous caught her attention. The name of Riva Dubois
the French Minister for Foreign affairs and President of the
European Federation. Following her name was the memo:
FEU Congress, London. Darcy closed the book and stood for a
moment deep in thought, aware of a mounting excitement. The
Federation for European Unity Congress was a key event in the
Euro calendar. There may be no connection between the
conference, Von Schmidt and the Conjunctio, but a little voice
inside was telling her there was, and that Brant had for this
reason marked it in his diary. What if Von Schmidt and his
cronies were using the venue as a smokescreen for their real
activities? An opportunity to meet and plan, or put into action
more mischief. The suspicion grew and took hold. Despair
banished hope into exile. Even if it were true, she could not
hope to convince the authorities, and certainly not in time.
They would as likely write her off as insane. But this was not
the time or place for speculation, it was a long walk back to the
Old Priory Inn and her car, and Brant might have an attack
of conscience and decide to return early.

The temptation to stop off at Mistletoe Cottage made
her waver en route to the motorway, but common sense
prevailed. The one-time haven was known to Brant, and as he
was obviously working with the opposition it would also be
known to others. There could be no immediate escape to
France either, given the suspected events of the thirtieth of the
month. The hope of successful intervention seemed remote, but
someone had to at least try. The muscles of her stomach grew
tight with apprehension as the car came to a halt outside the
flat. However, everything was in place and there was no sense
of intrusion. After making strong, black coffee she sat on the

settee and switched on the television to catch the lunch time news.

She watched in desultory manner, distracted by a tide of bitterness and pain over Brant's betrayal, but eventually the newsreader's words registered: reports of disturbances resulting from a rash of Neo-fascist rallies throughout the country and the rest of Europe honed her concentration. *"Governments and Police Authorities at home and abroad have declined from official comment,"* the newscaster went on to say, *"but information leaked from internal sources hints at a growing fear that fringe groups are being coordinated by a powerful organisation."* Which fits, Darcy thought grimly, switching off the set. Ernst Von Schmidt with his links to the far right was obviously behind this little lot.

****

During the days that followed there were more reports of demonstrations ending in riots and deaths within various Jewish communities. Yet strangely, it seemed to Darcy, the scheduled FEU Congress was given limited coverage by the media and with no mention at all of the venue. Obviously they were playing it down for reasons of security, as heads of state would be gathering in one building. In the past these conferences had been one of Frank's favourite 'beefs'. Acting on impulse Darcy moved to the telephone, hesitated a moment, then dialled his number.
"Can you talk?" she asked when he answered.
"What the—? Shit, Darcy you can't be calling me up like this!" Then a sigh of resignation and, "Give me a sec." and a series of clicks on the line and a more relaxed Frank speaking to her again. "We're O.K. now but be brief."

"The FEU Congress Frank."
"That crap. What about it?"
"It's like the biggest event in the Euro calendar gets hardly a mention."

320

"Never does – media black out. High-ranking bastards carving up the world to suit don't want us to knowing about it!"

"I can go with that. But this time it's not being held at some remote French chateau, Spanish hacienda, or in the wilds of Scotland. It's London."

"That so? How the hell did you find that out?"

"A lead. But with such a high-profile locale, how can they hope to block it"?

A silence ensued during which she could picture Frank manipulating his cigar and scowling over the enigma.

"It's a scam," he said at last.

"What?" Despite the seriousness of the issue she smiled at his rampant paranoia and penchant for conspiracy theory.

"First off, forget the 'Awareness in Europe' arena and the 'Support for the Euro Parliament from Commerce and Industry' agenda – that's the official crap. Translate as; mega bucks and names wanted to finance our operations. I'm not sure who is behind it but I have my ideas."

"Like Riva Dubois maybe?"

"Bloody hell – just what have you been up to? You're getting in deep girl. Anyway the Conference has come in for a lot of flack the last couple of years, with rumours of secrecy and conspiracy. Quite right too. I don't like it, Darcy, when industrial barons and big-league banks meet with Eurocrats to do the Business."

"You're saying the London meet is a blind?" Darcy said, thinking aloud.

"As three mice. For 'Business' read crash economies, create trouble spots and plunge the Third World into debt. A lot think like me Darcy, so maybe they want to look like they've sanitised their act. Get me? So, what do you know Darcy?"

Frank's voice was harsh. She hesitated, sensing excitement overlaid with anxiety and maybe even fear.

"What's the street talk on Fascist demos?" she side-stepped.

"The Government is shitting itself. 'Defused and under control' is the buzz phrase, but 'Six' and the F.O. are wondering who is behind them."

"Von Schmidt?"

"Undoubtedly, but he is a pawn and the game is first league," Frank said snorting his disdain.

"And Riva Dubois, does she command a high transfer fee?" she probed, opting for an oblique shot.

"More than possible. But keep your nose clean, we could be talking Big Time."

"World domination, Bond style?" she scoffed.

"Not funny. Like I said, what do you know?"

"Thanks for listening Frank." She replaced the receiver and for several minutes sat looking out of the window.

Reports of demos and civil disturbances continued to dominate media space. The nationals led with the story of a jeweller's shop in Germany being burned to the ground. The living accommodation above the premises also was destroyed and two members of the Jewish family – father and daughter – perished in the fire. As the scheduled date drew nearer, the FEU Conference was plugged, discreetly at first then more up-front, with the main news carrying cameos of leading Euro politicians. There were daily reports too of a crisis for sterling and an increasingly troubled British economy linked to financial problems in Europe.

Was she, Darcy wondered, succumbing to Frank's paranoia and conspiracy fever or were these key issues linked? Civil unrest continued to dominate headlines and fuel her suspicions. And all this, she thought folding up The Times and dropping it onto the table, had been set in motion by the finding of St. Gildas Man. A centuries-old body with a spirit as potent today as in medieval times. Momentous events, yet it was her personal pain that she felt most keenly now. Crossing to the window, she gazed out over the park.

The trees were already tinged with Autumn, their leaves taking on the colour of gold and the texture of old parchment. A light mist smudged the edges of branch and building, and she was overcome by nostalgia and a nameless yearning. The first man she had really loved had turned out to be a con-man and liar, maybe even a killer. The worst part, she acknowledged, was that knowing this did not automatically erase that love or the pain that went with it. But her personal troubles had to be put aside. Riva Dubois' visit to England was only two days distant, and a couple of days after that the 'rally' would be staged at Edgeway Hall.

FORTY-FIVE

The drive to London came as a welcome escape from the flat which since the loss of her job had taken on the aspect of a prison. A golden haze softened hills, buildings and trees and the warmth suggested an Indian summer. With the window down, breeze lifting her hair and a Vanessa Mai CD playing full blast, she was able to shake off the despair that had dogged her since that last day at the farmhouse. As the traffic snarled-up her mind tussled once more with the problem of how to penetrate the FEU Congress. Beyond the arrival of Riva Dubois at the Savoy for the start of the conference, the events of the day were an unknown quantity and she would be obliged to play it by ear. However, it was in a mood of optimism that she entered the City and negotiated the streams of vehicles that moved with a corporate will towards the Centre.

The original plan had included trying for a sight of Madame Dubois, the designated President of the Federation, as she arrived for the Conference. However, according to the Radio 4 newscaster the proceedings were already under way. In any case, Dubois had arrived the previous evening and in the absence of the expected invitation to stay at number ten, had opted for a suite at the Savoy, the chosen venue for the conference. Which amounted to a snub, Darcy thought, raising her eyebrows as she listened. The official explanation of 'not wishing to upset other Euro members by appearing to single out individuals' did nothing to quell the buzz of speculation, the newscaster concluded.

Darcy switched off the radio, and concentrated on dodging in and out of the traffic. In view of sensitive British beef negotiations, and the delicate relationship between Britain and France, it had been taken for granted that the President of the Congress and the British Prime Minister would show a united front to both media and public. So this slight smacked of deliberate distancing strategy by the British government. Providing of course, Darcy checked herself as she left the car park, that Dubois really was a covert leader of a fascist faction in league with Ernst Von Schmidt, and that the government held her under suspicion. Here against the booming voice of the City where dusty sunlight softened old buildings and gilded the Thames, it was so much harder to believe. As she slipped into the cosmopolitan crowd of visitors, obligatory cameras slung around neck as they strolled the tourist-trail, it seemed even more preposterous.

To while away the hours until the conference closed for the day, Darcy also played the tourist. Taking the underground to Westminster, she gazed at the Houses of Parliament and wondered if anyone in there was aware of what was really happening in Europe. If so, they were playing it close, she thought strolling towards Poets Corner and on to the Abbey. After pausing to buy a newspaper, she found a bistro and ordered lunch. The Times made depressing reading. Economic crisis loomed in Europe with the lire devalued and the pound threatened as it struggled against the French franc. Typically the British Government and Bank of England were laying the blame at the door of currency speculators, but the truth she suspected of being rather more sinister. Last week the German mark had plummeted, but the Banque de France was aggressively in support and an upturn in the German economy seemed certain. It was too much of a coincidence that France and Germany were both thriving whilst the rest of Europe floundered. Speculation about Von Schmidt and Riva Dubois ousted appetite, and she sat lost in thought, the food on her plate untouched.

Albeit the only thing against Dubois so far was the appearance of her name in Brant's diary, but the gut feeling that she was linked to Von Schmidt and implicated in fascist activities persisted. Her position as a high-profile politician who in terms of orientation had frequently sailed rather too close to the flourishing Right would make her a powerful and dominant ally. The suspicion that France had deliberately sunk the mark, then organised its recovery via the extreme German Right, was not only possible but probable. If so it meant Dubois and her party were in control of the economy and therefore of the government. The French Minister for Foreign Affairs was also President of the Federation, and the Banque de France was now supporting the mark. Definitely a little too much for coincidence, Darcy decided, struggling to eat at least some of her lasagne and side salad in order to keep up her strength for whatever lay ahead.

At least, the goal for today was now clear: to be alert and observant and hope that in some way Riva Dubois would betray her allegiance to Von Schmidt and his Neo-Nazi nightmare. How Anton de Beaumont fitted into all this was still a mystery, she thought folding her newspaper. Maybe that was the real coincidence: chance links with Europe, a secretive sect with a combination of wealth and power and only her fertile imagination to actually string them together. Whatever the truth, the only option now was to see it through, she decided on leaving the bistro.

A couple of hours window shopping, exploring Harrods and making minor purchases – the latest Dior perfume and a Chanel lipstick – served to both pass the time pleasantly and relieve her tension. Pausing to hitch up her sleeve and view her watch, she was jostled by a swelling stream of pedestrians which had notably increased both in speed and impatience denoting single-minded purpose. The traffic was also thickening, the blare of horns becoming more evident and belligerent by the minute as the onset of the rush-hour threatened. This was it then, she thought making for the Underground to Charing Cross. Tourist role-play was over for the day. As the tube picked up speed and she swayed to and fro with the rhythm, her stomach churned. It was, she judged, time to be in the vicinity of the Savoy.

A crowd was already gathering outside the hotel. People jostled, pushed and pressed forward hoping for a sight of the EEC celebrities. Outside broadcast units lined up, adding to the air of anticipation and excitement. A cordon of police officers posed a problem and Darcy was forced to think on her feet. The press had been allowed beyond the barrier to wait with notebooks, cameras and woolly microphones bristling, forming a highly competitive group at the entrance. Adopting a blasé attitude to cover her nervousness Darcy flourished her press card and smiled confidently as an officer examined the photograph and studied her face. He indicated with a jerk of his head that she could pass, and Darcy breathed again.

Minutes later she was amongst the privileged reporters being ushered into the lobby of the hotel. That card, she thought with a touch of irony as she elbowed her way to the front, had been her passport to more exciting situations of late than ever it had whilst valid.
"Sorry," she murmured, on receiving a glare from a girl wearing a cashmere suit with silk shirt and tie. Obviously a prodigy from one of the Nationals, Darcy thought dismissing a pang of envy as unworthy.

A lull of some thirty minutes left her restless and with nerves frayed. Then suddenly there was a buzz of excitement as a couple of patently British plain clothes officers appeared through the double doors and fastened them back. They were followed by a multi-national group of heavies, pan-faced and brutish bodies ill-concealed within elegant suits, who swarmed into the lobby and took up their positions as personal bodyguards. The knot of reporters surged forward, and Darcy was carried along by the momentum then just as swiftly forced back by the bulldozing sweep of official arms.
"Come on now, we don't want to have to send you back outside," a uniformed sergeant chivvied. He and his fellow officers turned their backs on the crowd to face the doors through which the delegates began to emerge.

They were led by Hess, the German Chancellor who was looking happier than of late which, Darcy thought cynically, probably had more to do with the recovery of the mark than the outcome of the day's talks. A fireworks display of cameras flashed. His jowls creasing in a smile, and portly figure exuding good will, Hess stretched out an arm and ushered to his side the Danish delegate, a handsome woman of mature face and youthful figure. To his other side he drew a thin olive-skinned man whose lugubrious expression reflected the points dropped by the lire at close of dealing, enabling Darcy to recognise him as Morel Lorenzo the Italian Minister for European Affairs. Delegates flooded the lobby: a sea of faces recognised from the media, but no sign yet of Riva Dubois.

Surely, that could not be it. Darcy repeatedly clicked the button of her Schaefer fibre tip pen with an aggressive motion that mirrored her frustration. She had taken it for granted that the Frenchwoman would appear.
"Have Britain's options regarding the single currency issue been agreed Minister?" The high pitch of the female voice rose above the buzz and welter of questions being hurled at the politicians.
"Has the P.M. made concessions on timing?" a man shouted from the rear as Hess made a non-committal answer.
"We have made good progress." Hess simpered for the cameras and microphones that vied to catch his every word and gesture, despite the official format phrases that tripped from his tongue. For the sake of authenticity, Darcy clicked away at her camera, scrabbled some shorthand notes on her pad and, swallowing her disappointment, turned to leave.

Then froze as a woman followed by four bodyguards emerged from the double doors, and with Thatcheresque confidence advanced to front the group of delegates. The Chanel suit hot from the catwalk, and Cardin-styled hair epitomised French chic and identified her as Riva Dubois. As the group parted like the biblical Red Sea, and she was ushered to the fore with seemingly communal consent, Darcy drew in her breath sharply. The woman's blouse of burgundy silk provided the perfect foil for the pendant and chain around her neck. The coils of the ouroboros were wrought in gold and the serpent's eye glowed with the fire of a ruby.

The snake that swallows its own tail: Darcy tensed

with excitement on recognising the alchemical symbol. After all, Dubois could hardly be expected to flaunt a swastika badge, but here was the sought-for link. Whilst the ouroboros in itself was a symbol innocent of racism or evil, Darcy acknowledged whilst clicking away at her camera with the rest, its use in this present context undeniably tied Riva Dubois to the Cabbala woman and therefore Von Schmidt. There was now no doubt in her mind that this woman was indeed the head of a fascist party set to wreak havoc in Europe. Despite the elegance, poise and charm the square chin and steely eyes betrayed a formidable strength and determination.

For some reason Darcy's attention was caught by one of the four members of the President's personal escort. A frown creased her forehead as memory raced on a loop. The square pugnacious features and the bulging biceps beneath the sharp black suit kept it focused. There was something familiar about the set of those shoulders, the carriage of the head on the bull neck, a sort of backward tilt that gave him an air of amused arrogance. She frowned in concentration, striving not to stare for too long for fear of attracting attention. Then it arose, an atavistic memory from her subconscious, an image so dark it resembled a negative with light and shade eerily transposed. She saw again those shoulders, that head – behind the wheel of the car.

A cold sweat broke out on her forehead and along her spine as the slow-motion replay unwound, and Caro collapsed like a stringless puppet at the roadside. The involuntary sound Darcy made was swiftly disguised as a cough. Appalled, she openly stared as he stood to attention behind Dubois, hands respectfully clasped in front and feet slightly apart. Standing before her was the man who had attempted to murder Caro.

FORTY-SIX

He was staring straight at her, and Darcy found herself looking into the coldest eyes she had seen outside of the shark tank at the zoo. Hoping he had not yet recognised her, she shrank back into the group of reporters. Thankfully, the press call was at an end and the delegates began to file from the lobby, Madame Dubois and her loathsome bodyguard included. Time to get out of here. Darcy, about to make for the foyer doors, froze in her tracks. The man had returned. Obviously now off duty, he was standing head bent, lighting a cigarette. Darcy turned away as he looked up and through narrowed eyes scanned the people milling around the lobby. With a stab of fear, Darcy slipped deeper into the crowd, realising he remembered her face and was now seeking her out.

She watched him approach and speak to the girl on reception duty who shook her head as though in response to a question. With a Gallic shrug of his massive shoulders, he stubbed out his cigarette in the ashtray and left the hotel. Hardly daring to breathe, Darcy waited for several minutes then, judging it safe to move, emerged from her corner. Something was niggling and ought to be checked out. She glanced anxiously at the exit, in case the bully-boy decided to return, and sifted through her memory. Suddenly, she was back at the priory picking up something from the floor of the chancel; then the scene shifted to the rusty gate at Monk Grange on the night of Miles Standish's murder. And that was it. Swiftly crossing to reception, she inquired about the evening performance of Tristan & Isolde at the Opera House. Whilst the girl was looking up times and seat prices, Darcy dropped a tissue from her bag over the ashtray then picked it up again along with the discarded cigarette. It took all of her will power not to run to the exit. The cigarette in her pocket had the distinctive gold tip of a Sobranie Black Russian.

Expecting at any moment to feel a hand on her shoulder, she hurried away and left the hotel behind with a profound sense of relief. But it was short-lived. A glance behind confirmed her worse suspicions; the heavy black-suited figure was moving through the crowd with surprising speed and agility. Her legs began to tremble and she forced them to work faster. Dodging out of the throng, she made for the Underground. Every minute or so she glanced over her shoulder, terrified of finding herself face to face with her pursuer. However, his swarthy features, occasionally glimpsed, were swallowed up again by the surge of bodies.

Nursing a stitch in her groin, she slowed a little to take stock of her surroundings. The mauve blanket of twilight now draped itself over the City. The changes in light and atmosphere rendered everything strange and confusing. Her breathing was laboured, her legs ached and would not carry her much further. Uncaring of destination, on spotting an Underground access she dived down the steps.

The Underground teemed with individuals of every conceivable shape, colour and culture and each, Darcy thought in despair, seemed to know exactly where they were going and how to get there. Pushing her way through the crowd, she glanced at the entrance. Her heart leapt at sight of her pursuer running down the steps. Half way down, he paused to scan the faces below. In the grip of panic, she could not remember where she had left the car and therefore which tube destination was needed. Rushing aimlessly, and now close to tears, she scanned each terminal then heaved a sigh of relief. Hyde Park Corner, that was the one. In her haste at the ticket machine the coins rolled in all directions along the floor, wasting precious minutes. Glancing over her shoulder, she joined the surge of bodies to the platform. Her stomach heaved with fear; he may have spotted her and be waiting there.

Never at ease on the Underground, Darcy fought off a growing sense of claustrophobia. The lights were yellow and dingy, fresh air a long way off with too many tons of intervening concrete and metal between herself and the sky. For a moment she was transported to the observatory dome and cold sweat beaded her forehead. As she peered around her searching out the Frenchwoman's henchman, the walls appeared to contract, and the roof to lower to crush those who thronged below. As fear reached unbearable levels, a low rumble pierced her panic. Within seconds the tube emerged from its tunnel like a sinister giant earthworm straight from Dunes and swooooooooshed to a shuddering halt. Instinct made Darcy hesitate.

"Does this go to Hyde Park Corner?" she asked a female wearing a grey trouser suit who was boarding. A look of impatience crossed the woman's immaculately made-up face as the crowd pressed at her back, and she almost dropped her document case.

"This is the Northern – you want Metropolitan." She pointed at the sign on the opposite wall before being swallowed by the metallic worm. Darcy, buffeted and elbowed by those wishing to board, stood paralysed by indecision. It was then that she saw him and the cold malice in his face forced her into action. Destination no longer mattered. She watched with a blend of relief and horror as the door sighed shut in his face.

Weariness from strap-hanging and train-hopping followed by disorientation as she became hopelessly lost, induced a sense of unreality. Westminster. At last a familiar name and a point of reference from which to locate the car. Alighting at South Kensington she joined the Metropolitan line and eventually left the Underground. She cast frequent and anxious glances over her shoulder, but saw no sign of her pursuer and assumed he had been left behind at one of the tube stations. Nevertheless, she was dogged by fear and misery. Never had she felt so alone as in that press of people with their stale smells of perfume, tobacco and perspiration. Frank and the paper had defected, her parents were in France, Caro was way up North and there was no-one at all to turn to turn to. And worst of all to handle: there was no Brant. He was an ally of this creature who was hounding her through London intent upon her death, she told herself fiercely, but as she fled the alien streets an ache remained in her breast.

A feeling of discomfort at the nape of her neck made her turn to look. He was there. The dark suit a mockery of respectability, the white shirt bluish and almost fluorescent in the gathering gloom. Fear following on from relief was intensified, and coursed along her nerves like an electric shock. Her footsteps echoed along the pavement as she began to run. The streets were emptying, in the hiatus between the end of the day's activity and the onset of the night-scene.

Rounding one corner, then another she realised with a surge of nausea that she had once again lost her way. Her lungs hurt and terror was sapping the strength from her limbs. From a shadowed doorway a hand stretched out to grab her and she recoiled in terror.
"Buy us a cuppa love, had nowt to eat all day," a drug-dulled voice wheedled. ignoring it she ran on her way, pushing aside the derelict pitiful dregs of humanity that erupted at intervals to block her way. Closing her ears to the muttered recriminations of 'stuck up cow' and 'bitch' and worse, she tightened her grip on her bag and continued to run.

She looked back. The sinister figure was gaining ground. His footsteps pounded the pavement and grew closer by the minute. Waves of malice and evil intent beat against the back of her neck and head. *If he catches me, I am dead.* The realisation spurred her on, kept her going when further effort seemed futile. Fate intervened in her favour as she rounded a corner and almost collided with a uniformed figure.
"Please, can you help me?" she blurted. Never had she been so glad to see a London bobby.

In the end she had not tried to explain her true predicament. It was all too much, too long, and too over-the-top for credibility. Instead, she opted for asking her way and keeping him talking for several minutes. It was enough. Her pursuer was scared off and, as the officer walked away, the street behind her was empty. Never had the steering wheel of her car felt so good beneath her hands, nor the pedals under her feet. Not that there was cause to relax. The respite must be temporary; he could not afford to let her escape and must have followed her to the car park at a distance. Sure enough, within minutes a pair of headlights appeared in her mirror, headlights that kept too even a distance and stayed whatever her manoeuvre. Firstly through the London traffic as the city woke to its night-life, now piercing the anonymous darkness of the motorway where an experiment in lane-switching proves the point. The eyes of the prowling beast remain reflected in the mirror.

Panic knotting her stomach, Darcy wondered where he would strike and how. Perhaps on some lonely stretch of road, or maybe he would bide his time until reaching the North and the isolation of the cottage. Fear threatened her judgment, and the car strayed to the right causing a buzz to her solar plexus. She hauled at the wheel, and it swerved back into lane. There was nothing to be done. She could not bring more danger to Caro, and the police would smirk and blame drink or drugs for what they would take to be paranoid ramblings.

Negative thoughts were sapping her energy and resolve. She was working on being positive and half succeeding when a glance at the petrol gauge turned her cold. It was three quarters empty, which meant a halt at a service station, a thought which filled her with dread. Her eyes constantly moved between mirror and road as she groped for her mobile 'phone. With a rush of mingled frustration and panic, she recalled leaving it in the holdall stashed away in the boot which meant it was not only out of reach, but also uncharged.

North of Birmingham he made his move. Fear gripped her as the eyes of the metal beast drew closer in the darkness. Her foot rammed hard on the throttle. The engine whined and the car body trembled as she demanded first greater then impossible speed. This was the 'lonely stretch' he had been awaiting: no cars in front, only a sporadic few on the opposite carriageway and they inhabited a different world, separated from herself by a metal box, speed and isolation. Darcy's white-knuckle grip on the steering wheel tightened as his vehicle slipped into the middle lane and levelled with her own. A frightened glance showed only a shadow discernible behind the wheel, and anonymity fuelled her fear. Incongruously it brought to mind Spielberg's early film Duel – she had been planning to see the remake – more scary than Dracula, Freddie or Hannibal put together. Because it was real, could happen and was doing now.

Darcy stifled a scream. He was pushing her off-road. She wrestled with the steering wheel, struggling to keep control as the other car nudged her onto the hard shoulder. Her foot pumped the brake: even in the throes of terror she knew that a skid must be avoided. Unless she wanted to do his job for him, she thought grimly, and end up dead behind the wheel. The rattle of tyres on 'stay-awake' road studs jarred her nerves as she hit the throttle, left the hard shoulder and veered back onto the carriageway. Immediately he drew level and swerved towards her; on shock of impact a scream was wrenched from her throat.
"Bastard! Crazy bastard," she mouthed, finding a moment's release in anger. She was vaguely aware of an ape-like head and grin before being forced to look back at the road as he battered her flank again and again. The clash of metal on metal, and the sudden sideways jerk filled her with terror as she veered helplessly to the left. Another mind-jerking rattle, and back onto the hard shoulder, weaving dangerously as she almost lost control. Suddenly the other car cut in front. With a squeal of tyres and a heart-stopping skid, her vehicle screeched to a halt within inches of its rear.

FORTY-SEVEN

Strangely, it was at this time of direst danger that her head cleared and a deadly coolness steadied her nerves. Instinctively her hand moved to depress the door lock. Wait and do nothing she told herself, he has to get out of the car. Resisting the urge to pull off the hard shoulder and attempt a straight race, a strategy that had proved abortive, she bided her time. Her gaze was riveted on the door of the car in front. The coldness inside her head brought a curious sense of detachment and the clarity of ice. He had to be immobilised. The euphemism made what had to be done easier to accept. A car, its driver oblivious to her peril, zipped past causing a moment of distraction then was gone. Her attention focused again on the stationary car in front.

The door swung open and her intending assassin stepped out. *Not yet.* Every muscle tensed in readiness for action. Don't start up the engine yet, give him time to clear his vehicle. Get him out in the open with no chance of cover. Let him think, she thought coldly, that it is you who are immobilised. With a pretence of panic she half-turned the key in the ignition so that it grated a couple of times but failed to start the engine. Momentarily resolve wavered. Could she do it in cold blood? Think of Caro and do it for her, she told herself fiercely. And for Miles Standish – and for what Brant has done to you. To Darcy's shame it was the last in the list that did it. The hurt, disillusionment and sense of betrayal welled up to overpower innate loyalty and justice.

She steeled her mind to the business. Everything about the man standing before her exuded arrogance. His stance was bullish, every movement slow, deliberate and unhurried. He was going to enjoy this, she had made him work at what should have been easy. Now the quarry was in the trap and he would exact every iota of fear, pain and humiliation in payment. His body language conveyed all this to Darcy, making it possible to carry out her plan. She watched his slow advance like a general watching a radar screen, waiting for the optimum moment to activate the killing machine. All thought of Caro, Miles Standish and even Brant had receded into oblivion. This was for self and survival. The faint smell of petrol was in her nostrils. She became aware of the jingle of keys on their ring as they swung from the ignition, and the sporadic flash of headlights from the opposite direction. As she waited, all her senses were heightened.

Now! The ignition key clicked, the gear lever slipped into reverse and her foot pressed the throttle the instant the hand brake was released. The car shot backwards. The hated figure in black, face a white and luminous slash in the headlamps which she had switched to 'beam', threw up a hand to shield his eyes. Momentarily blinded, he halted at the centre of the hard shoulder. Don't think – act! That's right, far enough back to give a run at the target and gather sufficient speed. Her hand rammed the gear lever into first and her foot hit the accelerator.

She tensed herself for impact, deliberately preparing herself for collision with an anonymous barrier, ignoring any suggestion of skin, flesh and bone. The tyres squealed, the car shot forward and for a second she saw the terror in his face as he realised her intent. The bonnet was now within six metres of his body, an instrument of Nemesis ready to strike. She had stopped breathing, was confining her breath along with sentiment in a vice-like grip. She planned to shut her eyes at the last moment, so as not to see his face as he crumpled. At that last moment came divine intervention. An unseen hand turned the cosmic egg-timer horizontal, immobilising the sands of Time and putting the universe on hold.

Beyond the windscreen there was a thickening of the ether, an opalescent milky and shifting quality that breathed and pulsed with life. Particles, suspended in thickening light, danced before her eyes and hung on an atmosphere that was suddenly heavy. In the instant prior to impact, an image flashed through her mind. The scarlet cross glowed livid on white and she hit the brakes instead. She heard the squeal of tyres, and smelled the pungency of burning rubber. The skid flung her sideways, only to be jerked back again by the action of the safety belt. The whiplash must have been painful but she was anaesthetised by fear and shock. She fought to bring the car under control. At the sudden jolt of impact her eyes shut and her heart stopped.

Disorientated, she remained slumped behind the steering wheel. On finally daring to look, she realised that the car had impacted the grass bank and was listing at an angle of some forty-five degrees. At the same instant, and even with the windows shut, she heard the metallic thud of the report. It took a moment to register. She watched as though in a dream: the look of surprise on the man's face, the slowly spreading splotch of red on the white shirt front. Red on white – nothing to do with Anton but a premonition; maybe nothing more than a blip in Time at an instant of crisis. Paralysed, she watched the burly form sink with a dancer's grace to the tarmac, twitch convulsively, then lie still.

There was no time to pause and wonder about his assassin. All that drove her now was the need to get away and save her skin. The engine was still idling. Her hand shook as she tried to engage the lever and the gears crunched. Then it slipped into first, her foot hit the throttle and with a squeal of tyres she pulled away. Would she have gone through with it? The question haunted her progress along the motorway. Initially, a blessed numbness dulled perception, and survival instinct propelled her northwards, to be replaced by gradual realisation and a fit of the shakes that threatened to bring her to a halt. Too terrified to stop, she fought for control and steered the car through dark tunnels strung with hypnotic cats' eyes, and inhabited only by herself and the occasional heavy goods beast on the night-run. As panic and shock subsided, a new pragmatism took its place: given there was no way of knowing the answer it was senseless to ask. She was not about to martyr herself on the cross of speculation.

Which brought her back to that strange experience. Maybe it was nothing more than a psychological phenomenon, she decided, striving to steady her hands on the wheel as the car drifted again. Some coping strategy within her own psyche, to save herself from an act that might have mentally scarred her for life. Resigned to the fact that the answers might always elude her, she still fretted over these questions. Her neck and shoulders ached from the whip-lash and weariness overcame her as she pulled in at the first available services.

Despite constant monitoring of her progress via the mirror and finding no cause for alarm, she had to force herself to leave the car to refuel. Her limbs were shaking as she unhooked the delivery hose, and as the units clocked up on the display she glanced constantly over her shoulder. It was hard to understand why the assassin had not taken a pot shot at her also. She found herself wondering who else had followed her out of London and along the M1. Still no answers, but a decision was made instead. It was time to get out of town while she still could. That decision made, she headed northwards again with a lightening of the spirit.

Upon her arrival at the flat, she paused long enough to swallow a generous dose of cognac, take a shower, throw a few essentials into a flight bag and telephone the airport. 5.40 a.m. and her baggage was checked and she had her ticket. As she made her way to the departure lounge, the voice over the loud speaker system was background noise that blended with the rattle of trolleys, hum of conversation and the plaintive cries of a weary child. But then the shock of hearing her own name jolted her out of complacency.
"Will Darcy West, Miss Darcy West," the female voice repeated, "please go to the enquiries desk at reception." The message was reiterated, the name stressed.

Darcy hesitated. She had not mentioned departure times to her mother, nor Caro – or anyone else for that matter. This could mean only one thing: those fascist bastards knew of her plan. The loud speakers crackled into life again. This time, the voice advised travellers to France that their flight would leave as scheduled at 0.600 hours and that they should make their way to the departure terminal. Striving to look casual and unconcerned, she joined the stream of jostling passengers.

"Miss West? Miss Darcy West?"
The customs officer barred her way. There was nothing to be gained from denying her identity.
"What is it?" she asked sharply.
"I must ask you to accompany me, Miss West." He spoke politely enough, but with dead-pan face devoid of compassion. A female officer stood at his back, ready no doubt to restrain her should she rebel.
"I am about to board," Darcy protested playing for time. She tried not to mind the speculative looks of the other passengers, whilst feeling like a criminal being prevented from leaving the country. What was it to be, a trumped up drugs charge? she wondered in despair. Weariness and trauma robbed her of initiative; better to succumb now than suffer further humiliation. The outfit would obviously stop at nothing to prevent her interference in their plans. The man laid a hand on her arm.
"I'm afraid you have no choice. The police would like to ask you some questions."
"What about?" she snapped, desperately seeking a plan of escape.
"I cannot say, miss."

From the corner of her eye, she saw two men approaching: muscle-bound bodies clad in black suits and white shirt and recognised them as two of Riva Dubois' personal guard. The body of their crony must have been found, perhaps by a patrolling police car, and his I.D. card would lead them straight to Dubois. These two bozos had obviously flown up from London in the expectation of finding her at the flat and

340

had followed her from there to the airport. It was now, or find herself charged with murder. Wrenching her arm free of the officer's grasp, she bolted for the exit.

Shouts rang out, but she carried on running. A groan escaped at sight of the two WPC's on the main exit. Pushing aside a corpulent man and his laden trolley she thought on her feet and formed a daring plan. Pushing her way to the fire alarm, she broke the glass and made a dash for the fire door as pandemonium erupted. Added to the shrilling of the alarm were the cries of panic and shouts of 'it must be a bomb'. The speaker system rose above the cacophony, the voice of authority striving to impose order where chaos reigned. Darcy burst through the fire doors and raced for her car and freedom.

FORTY-EIGHT

Freedom – but for how long? Darcy wondered. A return to the flat would bring a straight choice: being arrested on suspicion of murder or being taken out by Dubois' fascist cronies. There was the cottage, but Brant knew about it and Brant wanted her dead. In this time of greatest need that pain cut all the deeper. But this was not the time to dwell upon personal sorrow. Survival was now the game and the stakes were high.

She drove aimlessly round the City Centre trying to reach a decision. It was a depressing scene: a drunk sprawled on the pavement in a pool of vomit, a down-and-out rummaged through one of a cluster of rubbish bins and a knot of hollow-eyed and old-before-their-time youths shared a joint as they slouched along the deserted street beneath dark and anonymous buildings. There was Jonathon; he would harbour her for old time's sake, she thought, then immediately dismissed the idea as totally unfair. Okay, there was Fran on the Paper. She had loaned her car on the night of Miles Standish's death and would no doubt help again. But primarily, Fran was a reporter and as such could not be trusted to put friendship before a scoop.

That left only Caro. A tide of longing swept over Darcy at the prospect of being crushed against Caro's ample bosom in a protective and welcoming hug. But much as Caro's warm common sense was needed, it would be criminal to involve her further. Wearily, she drove around Albert Square presided over by a pigeon-splattered Queen Victoria, stern and unforgiving in the grey pre-dawn light. Yet if she were caught now, there would be no chance of stopping the fascist movement and the demise of democracy. It was, Darcy decided heading out of the centre, too high a price to pay even for Caro's safety.

Dawn was staining the sky with dusky pink as she arrived outside the stone house in Lancaster. The absence of Brian's car on the driveway brought a surge of relief. Selfish though it may be, she needed Caro to herself right now. She cast several anxious glances over her shoulder whilst waiting for the door to open, but saw no evidence of a stalker.

"Darcy!" Caro stood in the doorway momentarily taken aback, but then reached out and pulled her friend inside. "What has happened?" she demanded, surveying Darcy's weary and anxiety-ridden features.
"It's not good Caro. The police—" Darcy stayed Caro's arm as she was about to close the front door.
"You may not want me here."
"Balls!" Caro said unequivocally, ushering Darcy towards the kitchen. For the first time since leaving the conference, Darcy felt a glow of inner warmth.

After eating at Caro's insistence a couple of eggs from the family hens, several dark plate-like mushrooms from the field behind the house and tomatoes from the greenhouse, Darcy felt a whole lot better.
"So what is the plan?" Caro said after listening intently to Darcy's story to date and commiserating over Brant's betrayal.
"France is out, so I might as well go to Edgeway Hall. Someone has to find out what is planned, then try and make officialdom listen."
"I don't like it, but I guess you are right." Caro looked worried as she refilled their cups with coffee.
"I have something to tell you," she said minutes later as they took their coffee to the conservatory and watched the sun rise over the Pennines. "Whilst you have been tearing around the country," she continued in response to Darcy's look of inquiry, "I've been doing a little research of my own."
"Into?"
"Anton de Beaumont."
"Shoot."

"Well as you discovered, he left his home in the North of England to enlist with the Knights Templar. From records gleaned from the London Repository – 'friends in high places'," she smirked as Darcy's eyebrows went up, "it seems he quickly distinguished himself in battle but also with his scholastic ability. And this is where it gets interesting: he became an influential and radical thinker, and if I read the inferences correctly – an adept at alchemy."

Darcy leaned forward tense with excitement.

"I suspected as much."

"It would have helped," Caro continued, nodding "to ensure his survival following Philip of France's purge of the Order and the charges of heresy. As an adept he would still have commanded respect and not a little fear, despite incurring the displeasure of both the Templar and orthodox Christian hierarchies."

"By falling in love with a Cathar girl," Darcy supplied.

Memories of the nightmare returned, of the French countryside, the cries and screams and the searing flames of the death pit.

"The body found alongside the coffin," she said aloud at last.

Caro nodded agreement. "From surviving fragments of diaries and letters, it became clear that she escaped with him to England. They could not marry, but there can be no doubt they were committed to one another until death."

"And perhaps beyond." Darcy added quietly.

Caro's eyebrows rose. "Pardon?"

"In a way they live on through you telling their story today," Darcy improvised, feeling unequal to the task of relating her more bizarre experiences.

"But Templars were sworn to celibacy," she added changing tack.

"Absolutely. So were Cathars. But it seems they still met, even after Anton was sent to the priory following the order's dissolution. However, whilst monks were tolerant of Templars – they were after all a Church Order albeit a militant one – they

were not so of Cathars. I guess they suspected Anton of
carrying on an illicit affair and—" she paused and shrugged
expressively.
"Had them both put to death," Darcy finished for her, biting
her lip.
"I'm afraid it looks that way." Caro nodded agreement and put
down her empty cup. "I reckon they had a secret trysting place,
that little cove perhaps. We know from his letters that Anton
was allowed to walk the cliffs for exercise. One day they must
have been waiting for them."
"And they believed he took his secrets to the grave," Darcy said
solemnly.
"Absolutely. And that is the reason behind his special
treatment," Caro added.

"It is incredible though," Darcy said frowning,
"that they accepted claims of creating gold, not to mention the
secret of immortality."
"I've looked at that too," Caro said, trying to look modest and
failing so that Darcy had to laugh.
"Okay, let's hear it."
"So, forget the myth of immortality and focus instead on the
gold. It isn't as wacky as it first sounds. Think what we can do
today, the way atoms are split or added and organisms cloned
or their appearance radically altered. What is so different about
taking a base metal, changing its molecular structure and
ending up with gold?"
"Oh come on, Caro," Darcy protested, they didn't have our
technology."
"But they did have the knowledge. Democritus – he was born
about 460 BC – taught that everything consisted of invisible
blocks which were tiny and eternal. He called these blocks
'atoms'! Each atom had its own unique fingerprint. Nothing in
the universe changed, only the patterns of the atoms. Think of it
Darcy! Atomic weights are the building blocks of modern
science. So can we be absolutely sure these latter day chemists
didn't crack the molecular code? But that isn't the issue,

Anton's contemporaries would have no problem with it; they would have believed it, which is the point I'm making."

"I'm mega impressed, Caro." Darcy held up her hands in submission. "But even if they accepted he could make gold, immortality is a different ball game!"

"From your twenty-first century perspective maybe. For 'immortality' try reading 'the ability to cure major diseases'. Remember the stone was also known as the universal panacea. Remember alchemy is about symbols: for 'stone' read 'breakthrough in medicine'. In medieval minds, after plague, and smallpox and God knows what, relative 'freedom from disease - and the increased life span that would bring - might readily translate into 'immortal life'! The alchemists may well have found cures for some of the major diseases which died along with their art. My guess is there was nothing supernatural about it, just a different language and way of expressing things."

Darcy sat back and laid her head against the cushions of the easy chair and thought it through.

"Yes, I can go with that," she said a few minutes later, sitting upright again, "But I don't believe any of it is of significance today nor, although I once did, is the Templar fortune. It's about the generalised mysticism surrounding the Templars. It obsessed Hitler and his Nazi generals, and made them want to emulate them to create a certain aura of fear and importance. Von Schmidt is after employing the same tools to manipulate the masses. Same goes for this Conjunctio thing. It's about dramatic effect."

"I absolutely agree. And I fear they may succeed."

Darcy recalled then an unresolved mystery from their last meeting. "Talking of disease, did you suss the truth behind Dr. Piper?"

Caro nodded. "I reckon Anton's body was deliberately contaminated to keep their guilty secret safe, but also to guard the monks against dark forces!"

"A bit far-fetched," Darcy said with a grimace.

"It is scientific fact that spores can survive the centuries and be activated. But that aside, you're thinking twenty-first century again!" Caro exclaimed. "Anton de Beaumont was known to be an adept in the alchemical arts, and those monks were riddled with superstition. Make no mistake, they would be afraid of what they had done, and use ritual to protect themselves."

"Hold on, something doesn't pan out," Darcy protested, sitting upright again to face Caro, "Why kill him – then preserve his body?"

"Superstition again," Caro said with a shrug of her shoulders. "His body was ritually treated because of Anton's supposed powers. Remember they murdered him, and would be already racked by guilt and terrified of retribution – secular or occult."

Darcy nodded, and twisted a strand of hair around her finger. "I can go with that. But how did Leah," she flushed and covered up quickly: "I mean a female Cathar come to be buried alongside him, and inside a monastery of all places?" If Caro noted the slip she chose to ignore it.

"I figured Anton's respectable burial in the vault was expedient. Don't forget he was sent there by Edward the second. What better way of avoiding an accusation of murder? A fall from his horse could be blamed, or other unfortunate 'accident', which left the Cathar girl".

"An act of compassion?" Darcy suggested. again.

"Something like that, Caro agreed. "His 'sins of the flesh' had to be punished, but he was a sophisticated scholar and traveller; it's my guess those monks secretly liked and revered him still."

"And also a compromise."

"Spot on. They couldn't bring themselves to place her within the coffin, but at least laid her alongside."

"And draped her locks around his chest," Darcy said, struggling with her emotions.

"Or they were buried together to more effectively cover the double murder," Caro suggested with a cynical expression.

"I prefer the compassionate version," Darcy said quietly, standing up ready to depart.

As it turned out, Caro would not hear of her leaving until the following evening, and showed Darcy to the guest room. Despite protesting that she would not sleep, Darcy was oblivious minutes after laying her head on the pillow

The following day was rather more tense as the deadline loomed, but Caro made Darcy help with some mindless task like shelling peas or washing the lettuce, whenever she began to brood. Eventually, it was time for her to leave and they stood together at the door.
"I can't thank you enough," Darcy said emotionally.
"Rubbish. Just let me know you are safe when its over," Caro insisted, her cheerful manner failing to mask the anxiety behind her eyes.
"I will, don't worry." Darcy wished she felt as confident as she strived to sound. A hired car to avoid being traced or stopped, and a telephone call to Clare Cabbala – posing as her protégée – to sanction her presence at the 'rally' meant she had done all she could to ensure success and survival.

FORTY-NINE

As she drove towards Alderley, the roads became
Narrower, and flanking hedges imbued the landscape with an
appropriate air of mystery and secrecy. A fat and buttery moon
bathed the landscape in eerie light and threw the escarpment of
the Edge into sharp relief, then frequently disappeared behind a
tangle of branches, or canopy of cloud, to emerge in an entirely
unexpected position due to the winding of the road. The whole
area, Darcy recalled, was steeped in magic, myth and legend –
shades of Alan Garner and childhood reading – and she felt her
courage begin to wane.

There was a more tangible cause for anxiety. Behind her
headlamps were strung along the darkness like a double row of
crystals. She watched them in the mirror noting how they kept
a steady distance. At least this confirmed the entry in Brant's
diary, now she could be reasonably sure of both timing and
location. On the minus side it was unpleasant to feel trapped,
the lane being too narrow to turn the car, and side roads
apparently being in short supply. The only possible course now
was to carry on and, with luck, bluff her way out at the other
end.

As she drove, Darcy periodically glanced at the sky.
Her research had revealed the Conjunctio, the union of
Jupiter and Saturn in Pisces, was scheduled for three minutes
past midnight, but the compulsion to scan the heavens
remained. Soon there would be no point in looking. Ragged
purple cumuli were shunting in from the west, and the moon-
glow, when visible, had acquired the sulphuric yellow tinge that
foretells a storm.

Edgeway Hall stood at the end of a sweeping drive and
presented a floodlit façade ablaze with crimson Virginia

creeper. It was, Darcy guessed, a country manor of Georgian origins but boasted a huge Victorian conservatory. It housed an ancient vine that snaked around the lamp-lit interior and pressed against the panes as though seeking a means of escape. A situation with which Darcy could identify: to her surprise and consternation some thirty or so vehicles – all swish, and a couple of black stretch limos with sinister smoky glass at the windows – were already standing on the gravelled forecourt and purpose-built parking areas. Frank's warning that this was something big had not prepared her for the reality.

A chauffeur bent to open the rear door of an adjacent limo. Darcy shrank back on her seat as a tall man with fair hair and a matinee-idol dimple in his chin alighted, and was followed by an elegant woman who had the high cheekbones and dark complexion of an eastern European. Darcy remained in her car for a time, watching the scene outside whilst planning her next move. The gathering of people around the house reminded her of exotic moths irresistibly drawn to the source of light. There was something unusual about all these people, nothing overt but an indefinable something that proclaimed them different. The women wore haute couture, triumphs of understatement and cut that whispered elitism and wealth, and sparked coloured fire from discreet gems as they moved beneath the arc lights. The men for the most part were attired in formal evening dress, but some sported flamboyant beards or hairstyles. A man whom Darcy recognised as a principal partner in Conti & Conti the hottest P.R. outfit in Europe, wore a single gold earring. As he paused to laugh and whisper something in the ear of a blonde Amazon, the light caught and sparked the solitaire diamond set at its centre. His male companion carried an ebony cane and paused to languidly sniff the rose in his lapel.

There were the odd eccentrics yes, but about them all even the most conservative, was that elusive aura of difference. Suddenly Darcy knew what it was – power. The power that went with wealth and clique and which generated a sense of being in control, of not being accountable in the way that ordinary citizens were. Each had a careless sort of confidence that stemmed from security, because nothing was too large or too serious to fix. That was the unifying factor between these divergent individuals. Yet she recognised only a few; these were people who worked in the shadows, preferring to keep their wealth, power and activities secret.

Darcy slipped from the car to shelter behind a massive and ancient yew tree to observe the networking operation. Mounting the steps to the portico of the house was the newly-appointed billionaire chairman of the Bank of Federal Europe. Passing beneath a weeping cedar, the head of Medico Pharmaceuticals was deep in conversation with Giovanni Soleni, Italy's premier car manufacturer. Suddenly very afraid, Darcy shrank back into the shadows. These 'names' of commerce and industry may possess wealth and power but nonetheless, if Miles Standish and Frank were to be believed, over the past year or so they had been systematically brainwashed into supporting a fascist manifesto. In the main, she had no doubt, they believed themselves to be here to back a European initiative for federal unity and social improvement, at the same time gaining kudos and spin-offs for their own enterprises. In reality they were being used to endorse a far more sinister project.

Finding courage to leave the shelter of the yew, she mingled with the celebrities who were making their way to the entrance. Fortunately she had opted for a formal black dress and jacket but still felt conspicuous amongst the illustrious guests. As she approached the steps, a man with close-cropped hair, wearing a dark suit, black tie and with a discreet radio receiver in his ear and a microphone attached to his lapel, stepped into her path.
"Are you with someone?" he asked in a conversational tone which detracted nothing from his air of menace. "I mean, are you somebody's guest?" he added, the implication being that she was neither rich nor famous, and unless her presence was vouched for by someone who was both of these, then her

speedy and enforced exit was assured.

Darcy swallowed the upsurge of panic and replied with a touch of haughtiness:
"Clare Cabbala will vouch for me."
The man's features remained impassive. "This is a sanitised area," he said with a politeness that chilled, and as though she had not spoken.
"Official press," Darcy responded with equal sang froid and flashed her card. "Madame Cabbala will vouch for me," she repeated steadily, daring to meet and hold his gaze. Turning his head slightly to the right he clicked his fingers and a second security officer stepped from the shadows beyond the portico. He moved forward effectively barring Darcy's path as the first man moved to one side and spoke very fast and with a low voice into his radio. Darcy held her breath, and concentrated on presenting an attitude of unconcern whilst apparently ignoring the curiosity of the guests. Her tongue passed nervously over her lips as the radio clicked. The muscles of her stomach contracted; the man frowned as he listened and cast a look of suspicion her way. Nausea rose and the urge to flee was almost overwhelming as he stuck out his lower lip, glanced her way again and said something in an undervoice. He nodded, spoke again and, with a jerk of his bullet head, dismissed his underling. He gave Darcy a long hard look then, whilst her heart seemed to do a back-flip, silently nodded at her to pass.

Thank God she had made it right with the Cabbala woman, she thought, walking past on legs that threatened to give way at each step. Having already vouched for her and put her name forward as internal press officer to the Order, Cabbala had demurred at first but then capitulated. Professional pride, and an unwillingness to admit the limit of her authority, had made the woman reckless. My only sin in her eyes, Darcy reassured herself, lay in jumping the gun, which if the need arose could be explained away as a misunderstanding.

Despite airy proportions, the atmosphere of the banquet hall was overwhelming. The air was growing hotter and more sultry by the minute and carried a pall of expensive perfume. All around her Darcy saw faces of men and women with the power and motivation to influence governments and their policies. This operation did not smell good, an impression that was fortified by a glimpse of the ever-so-English looking Ernst Von Schmidt in conversation with a man of military bearing.

The aisle seat in an insignificant position to which she was directed, nonetheless provided an unobstructed view of the lighted rostrum, and the huge piece of sculpture suspended above it. Two silver orbs – presumably Saturn and Jupiter – were diametrically fixed in orbit and linked by a lightning-flash of power. These people were taking this thing seriously, Darcy thought with a sense of incredulity. Something of significance nagged at the back of her mind. Awareness struck, and suddenly she was afraid. The lightning flash motif was the runic symbol for power the Nazi's had worn on their uniform.

On sitting down, she spotted Clare Cabbala seated several rows in front. She was clad in an incongruous puce gown and turquoise pashmina. When the woman turned and gestured to attract her attention, Darcy looked down and pretended to rummage in her handbag. The last thing she needed was for the Cabbala woman to challenge her now, or even engage her in conversation. After turning round several times, the woman's attention was claimed by a tall man with silver hair seated to her right. Which was opportune, but nonetheless the incident set Darcy's nerves on edge. This apart, it was impossible to ignore the atmosphere of suppressed excitement and anticipation; there was a buzz in the air that made the flesh tingle.

There was no time for further speculation. The lights were lowered, a spotlight appeared and Darcy stifled an exclamation as Ernst Von Schmidt walked on stage. Attired in evening suit and black shoulder cape, he presented a distinguished appearance with no sign of the mania that had emerged at their previous meeting. Darcy held her breath as Von Schmidt seemed, for a timeless moment, to stare straight at her in recognition. The knowledge that it was down to her own paranoia did nothing to ease the suspense. She breathed again as he held up his hands for silence and the hum of conversation died. At first, it was the usual conference-type 'speech of welcome' so innocuous – and delivered with a faultless English accent – that Darcy began to think she may even now be mistaken about this being a sinister conspiracy.

Then came a dramatic change of mood, and it was all she could do to prevent herself from rising and quitting the hall in disgust. Subtle at first the speech moved from a broad economic and political forum to the particular topic of ethnic minorities and the 'undermining of Europe's native community, culture and ethics'. From there it was a short step to explaining and ultimately supporting the ideologies and policies of the Right. Persuasive arguments about a 'need for discipline', and protection of interests against 'non-nationals' who sought to monopolise commerce and the economy were thinly-veiled in their anti-Semitism. Darcy looked around her, and saw to her horror that an initial coolness and self-consciousness, perceived in the audience at the outset, had mellowed into acceptance. A head nodded here, and another there, and a muttered 'hear, hear' and other muted sounds of approbation issued from points around the hall.
"We have been too soft on those who infiltrate our respective countries and give nothing in return. It is no longer fashionable or politically correct to show national pride, pride in our roots, pride in our achievements or pride in our aims, but we challenge this assumption!"

Von Schmidt's voice had risen a pitch and two spots of vivid colour showed on his cheeks as he warmed to his theme. Darcy found herself praying he would lose it, would blow his cover and reveal himself for the vile fascist he really was, rather than the champion of infra structure and guardian of culture he now portrayed.
"Now," he continued, thumping one palm with his fist to emphasise the word, "is the time to reclaim our identity from

outsiders who would take all and leave us nothing. And with your help," here he spread his arms to embrace the sea of faces, "we can do it. There is nothing wrong with loving your country and wanting your compatriots to reap the benefits of your labours. Wear your national pride with impunity! Refuse to back governments whose policies cater for the outsider and penalise its own citizens. Join with us in creating a new select society!"

To Darcy's disgust and dismay, this elicited a low rumble of applause which gathered momentum as he held up his gnarled hands to stem it.
"Thank you, thank you, and now ladies and gentlemen," he intoned, "it is my honour and pleasure to welcome our principle guest and speaker."
He bowed – and Darcy almost expected to hear a click of heels as he did so – and disappeared behind blue velvet curtains adorned with the ouroboros symbol worked in silver thread. The symbol of oneness, Brant had called it, and in these surroundings, and within the context of Von Schmidt's inflammatory speech, a euphemism for the Aryan race.

Nothing could have prepared her for what followed. The hall was plunged into total darkness, causing a ripple of surprise and consternation. As though realising with a corporate mind what was required of them, the crowd fell silent. Searchlights clicked on and swooped around ceiling and walls with eerie effect, transforming gilded cherubs into grinning gargoyles. Still in silence, they converged into one brilliant beam that sliced the blackness and pinpointed the vacant rostrum. A brilliant hologram of Saturn and Jupiter within a massive silver ouroboros shimmered overhead. Then came sound. A single chord that boomed and vibrated around the roof-dome. Simultaneously plumes of smoke, highlighted by coloured strobes, wreathed across the stage. She appeared in the flickering web of light as if by magic, silent and motionless, arms outstretched to the mesmerised crowd.

Darcy was no exception. The figure on the rostrum

was disturbingly charismatic with her dark hair and eyes that even from this distance glowed with the fire of the fanatic. The hairs on the nape of Darcy's neck prickled as she stared for the second time at the French Minister for European Foreign Affairs, but this time in a very different role and setting. She stood like that, silent and unmoving, for several minutes, allowing the emotion to rise and beat against her in waves. Then the music started. Spacey new-age strains, evoking infinite energy and the song of the spheres. Far more dangerous than any rallying anthem, Darcy found herself thinking, before the sound took over and rational thought was put to flight. At one moment soaring and plunging, the next triumphant and aggressive, it swept away doubt and scepticism.

The final note died, taking with it resistance as her mind stretched out and away. A thunder of applause broke the silence and snapped her back to reality. A deliberate and staged change of consciousness, she warned herself vehemently, recalling Caro's report of the Nuremberg rallies and the nefarious use of ritual and music. For several minutes the audience was allowed to vent emotion, then the woman on the rostrum raised her arms, commanding silence. The response was immediate and disconcerting. We are being hypnotised into obedience, Darcy told herself in time to throw up a mental barrier. It was a political stunt, and whoever had stage-managed this show would earn the respect and envy of every spin doctor and pop impresario in the country. In that moment she recognised the true threat of this fascist regime.

Riva Dubois began to speak. In order to resist the compelling resonance and timbre, Darcy had to remind herself that this woman was trained for the job.
"Friends, thank you for your wonderful welcome. You have waited for tonight, worked so hard on my behalf."
She shook her head and corrected, "Not for myself – but on behalf of our planet." She bowed her head in apparent humility, waiting for the murmurs of approval to subside. She is far more dangerous than I imagined, Darcy thought, as Dubois raised

her arms and voice: "In my self I am nothing, I am an instrument of your corporate will. We shall open the eyes of the blind, the ears of the deaf and lead those who have lost their way."

Listening, Darcy felt the cold hand of fear clutch her heart. Dubois' words sounded the death-knell of democracy. Here, at best, the good intentions with which the road to hell was proverbially paved; at worst the hapless majority sacrificed to the whims of the privileged few, a minority who were every bit under manipulation as the people they sought to control. She sensed the sonorous voice wrapping itself around the hearts and minds of the listening crowd, dulling their logical and critical faculties, pandering to the sense of moral superiority and reforming zeal that glossed an underlying greed. "The time is right, and the people," she was saying, "will never be more receptive. We have what they secretly want, and can lead them in our direction."

Darcy sighed with despair. How many armies had marched to the beat of that particular drum? As the applause incited by the speech faded, Riva Dubois continued: "People are hungry for spiritual sustenance. Religion has betrayed them, humanism has left them unfulfilled. They are searching for enlightenment and have a need to be led! Methods are justified by results; our right to lead will go unchallenged!" As she went on to extol the need for a 'conjunction' of commerce and politics in federal Europe, and the courage to take crucial decisions 'unfettered by public concern and misguided concepts of political correctness', the atmosphere in the hall thickened. Darcy wiped away the beads of sweat strung along her upper lip and breathed deeply. The air was sultry and hot, the fug of perfume over-powering.

"And now it is almost time," Dubois intoned theatrically, moving forward and to the right of the rostrum. "Time for a momentous astronomical event to launch our new society." Every head turned, and expectant faces were raised as a panel

357

slid silently aside to reveal a giant screen positioned above centre stage. Upon it, between the heads of purple cloud, two bright spheres like giant stars were now visible. "There they are – Jupiter and Saturn live from our satellite." Dubois' voice rang with triumph and rallying zeal, "Tonight is unique; what you are about to witness will not occur again for thousands of years. What better time to pledge our loyalty and monetary support for the new society? This event shall serve to mark the change in our world, the damming of an immigration-tide that threatens to swamp our national identity; the exclusion of those who refuse to accept our laws and culture; an end to sub-cultures, lawlessness and anarchy.

"We have a – template," the slight pause emphasised the play on words, "for power, wealth and – guidance." This second pause was more sinister; for 'guidance' read 'manipulation', Darcy found herself thinking as Dubois continued: "by the enforcement of a moral and spiritual code dating back to the crusades. Only a generation or so ago, our forebears sought to emulate them and their rise to power by inspiring religious fervour and national pride." Here Riva Dubois' previously arrogant tone became subdued and persuasive. "They made mistakes, and because of this are reviled by history, their noble aims forever warped and misunderstood."
Which must be the most trite understatement ever made about Hitler and genocide, thought Darcy with scorn. But this is where she loses or wins them, she realised as Dubois continued.

"Within minutes, my friends, the planets will merge to symbolise a New Age and our rise to power. It will become our inspiration, and combined with the ouroboros, symbol of wholeness," and here Dubois raised an arm to indicate the giant hologram overhead, "shall become our insignia. By this shall we recognise each other – and in turn be recognised."
For 'insignia' read 'swastika', Darcy thought grimly, as she listened with dismay to an explosion of applause. Obviously, this viper of a woman had soothed any qualms and won over her audience. Something, a sort of prickling of awareness along

her spine, caused her to turn her head. Her stomach lurched and contracted. Three rows back, pale and luminous in the semi-darkness, she recognised the face of Brant.

He was staring straight at her, and given the lack of surprise in his expression, had obviously been aware of her presence for some time. In fact, she realised with a buzz of unease, he had probably sat there on purpose in order to keep her under observation. Shocked and sickened by this proof of his guilt, she hesitated over whether to make a dash for the exit then decided against. If Brant intended to expose her he could have done so at any time since entering the hall. Whatever his plan for her, there was nothing she could do at present.

The voice of Riva Dubois took on a deeper and more hypnotic quality drawing her attention back to the stage. "They made mistakes, but we shall learn from them. Where they were over-zealous we shall employ subtlety. Where they relied on military power we shall rule via new legislation. Segregated housing with electronic tagging of non-nationals will ensure compliance. Control of cultural codes and practice will inhibit ethnic identity, whilst a positive programme of learning will promote social conformity."

She might just as well say brainwashing, Darcy thought grimly as the sound of applause filled the hall.
"We must discriminate," Dubois continued, "have the courage to nurture and promote the best, and eliminate from our society undesirable elements. We are being given a wonderful opportunity to build; a New World for a New Age – and there will be no place within it for weakness or anarchy. We shall be the architects of its moral and social infrastructure. But first the people must be educated, be roused by rallies and rhetoric to support us and put us in power. It can be done, ladies and gentlemen. We need to fire the imagination of people and media. Half turning, she raised her arm and pointed, "And he shall be our ambassador."

The hall was plunged dramatically into darkness. Panic gripped Darcy as she wondered what stunt was planned next. Could these people not see the spectre of Hitler looming with his dream of the perfect Aryan race? People shifted on their seats, coughed and whispered. Just as it seemed she was unable to bear the blackout a moment longer, it was lifted. She gasped aloud as a dozen spotlights swooped and arced then coalesced on a figure fixed centre stage. Darcy's hand flew to her mouth. "Anton!"

She fought against a wave of nausea, faintness and shock.

FIFTY

He was propped upright, encased in glass to preserve his medieval flesh from the scourge of twenty first century air. They had clothed him in silk, velvet and burnished armour and the splayed cross of the Templars blazed crimson on his chest. His gauntlet-clad hands rested upon the hilt of a massive sword, and a plumed helmet – visor raised to reveal the ravaged face – adorned his head. The eyes, sunken in their sockets, stared at them in silent condemnation.

Darcy cried out and half rose, then fell silent again as those seated behind vociferously complained. The media will love this, she realised in dismay, and the Far Right would then get access to the forum it craved. A pain stabbed her chest to think of Anton being used for such evil purpose. A single spotlight appeared left of stage and in its beam stood Riva Dubois. She raised her arms to stem the tumult then turned and pointed at Anton de Beaumont:
"He will be our inspiration and icon."

The crowd, Darcy included, rose to its feet as one and stood in silence. Riva Dubois motioned for them to be seated and the wave of bodies subsided. She pointed at the screen, and every face was up-turned at her direction.
"Wait and watch," she instructed. A few seconds later the hush was broken by the striking of a clock. "One, two, three," the crowd intoned, the count getting louder as it progressed, "ten, eleven, twelve!" As midnight struck the crowd roared.

Darcy sat in silence, willing Anton de Beaumont to somehow put a halt to the proceedings. "Stop them, Anton," she whispered, willing with all her strength that he would somehow hear and act. Why had he brought her to this point if powerless to help? Like a laser beam she focused her thoughts upon him. Anton de Beaumont stared impassively back. To her despair there was a complete absence of presence and no hint of a salt-mist breeze teased her senses.

"And now three minutes of silence," Riva Dubois commanded. Obediently the whispers and talking ceased and every face was turned to the on-stage screen. The clouds were shot with light from the thinly-veiled planets. Darcy's fingernails dug into the flesh of her palms. Seconds then a minute ticked by. Until this moment pressing earthly events had claimed her attention, but now she became aware of a strange stillness, that unearthly calm that seems to herald momentous events.

As seconds passed, the sensation intensified and the hairs on her arms and nape of her neck began to rise. The only time she could recall feeling anything similar was whilst watching the total eclipse of the sun. For the two or three minutes preceding Totality, the world had seemed to stand still and be pervaded by an eerie sense of reality suspended. Then, just as now, she became aware of events beyond human manipulation; of the universe and of her own place, however tiny, within it, an experience she had found intensely moving and would never forget. Watching the discs of light on the screen converge, Darcy at last began to understand something of Brant's obsession. The last few seconds ticked by; the clouds parted. A cry rose from the throats of the spectators as the screen blazed with light. So this is the Conjunctio, Darcy marvelled: the union of Saturn and Jupiter in Pisces for only the third time in recorded history. The heavens were ablaze, the atmosphere in the hall electric.

Suddenly all was chaos. With a crack like gunfire the glass in one of the great arched windows crashed and a streak of blue light shot through the aperture. In slow motion, Darcy watched the priceless Pre-Raphaelite window implode. It seemed to hang on the air then collapse, showering the crowd below with a thousand fragments of red, blue, green and gold stained glass. Screams ricocheted off the walls as Riva Dubois held up her arms and pleaded for calm. Seconds later a roll of thunder reverberated around the ceiling and echoed from the walls, the sound intensified by the hall's acoustics to deafening effect as the long-threatened storm finally broke. A second flash streaked across the stage. Darcy, already on her feet, screamed with those around her as it struck the metal structure depicting the planets. The air crackled and stank of sulphur and melting metal as the sculpture, twisted and misshapen, dropped and swung drunkenly from one steel hawser.

"Anton! Anton!" From somewhere far off it seemed Darcy heard her own voice calling his name. Tendrils of smoke seeped through the spangled curtains and minutes later they burst into flames. Fresh screams erupted as the glass case holding Anton de Beaumont shattered in the heat. Awareness of personal danger ceased as, with growing horror, Darcy watched the scene on the stage. Seeking fresh sustenance, the flames licked greedily at Anton's garments. His flesh became scorched, crisped and curled, and the lips drew back in a grimace. Still his eyes seemed to hold her gaze. The crowd it seemed were released from thrall. She was aware of the screams, the crush of bodies in the instinctive rush for the exit, but was unable to join the exodus. Intuitively, she reached out as though to touch Anton de Beaumont.

Gradually, she became aware of the sense of presence that had been absent since her arrival. The air was perfumed with the scent of pines after rain, sensuous sandalwood and the sweetness of a salt-rose breeze.
"Anton," she whispered, her eyes filling with tears. An image of a young and virile Anton, hand raised in salute, formed in her mind.
"Anton," she whispered again as she felt him leave. Screams erupted around the hall as the corpse burst into flames. The air was filled with an obnoxious odour as the flesh crackled and flared like a torch in a sconce. But this is not Anton, Darcy consoled herself. Anton had gone, thus depriving the fascists' of their media bait. Sparks flew, and the air crackled as first the screen then the dais itself went up in flames. People pushed

and shoved and climbed over each other in the panic to reach the doors. Flashes of lightning and cannons of thunder added to the confusion. Darcy, half-mesmerised
by events and the spectacle of the fire, was knocked to the ground in the stampede. She cried out in pain as feet trampled her body and wondered with a strange sort of clarity whether she would die in the flames or be crushed. Smoke caused her eyes to stream and choked her lungs. Losing consciousness, Darcy felt herself being hauled upright. Instinct made her struggle but the grip on her arms tightened. Coughing and protesting she was dragged first, then half-carried, along the aisle to the exit.

Cool air hit her lungs, and gradually the choking sensation eased. So did the pressure on her arms as she was unceremoniously dumped on the dew-spangled lawn. Noise, heat and hysteria abounded as flames spewed and smoke belched from the roof and windows of Edgeway Hall. To compound the chaos, the storm still raged; strobes of lightning frizzled the atmosphere throwing trees and buildings into sharp relief. Each flickering illumination revealed the scene below with a clarity that was surreal. A clap of thunder sounded directly overhead adding to the general cacophony. Darcy ducked as though expecting the sky to fall on her head. Wiping her eyes on the back of one hand, she whipped round in time to see the figure of a man swallowed up by the crowd.

She remained like that for a minute, a dazed expression on her face. The air was filled with screams, the crackle of flames and crashing of roof spars and tiles. Now and then the clamour was sharply punctuated as windows exploded into the night. Then came the rain. Wind-driven and tropical in intensity, it swept the lawn and ravaged façade of the house. The crackle of burning timbers was overlaid by the splutter of dying flames. Plumes of black, acrid smoke belched forth to block out the stars. Sirens ripped through the night, and seconds later a retinue of fire engines and police cars swept up the driveway. Spurred to action by flashing blue lights and wailing sirens, Darcy struggled upright and staggered to her car.

FIFTY-ONE

Several people were injured in the rush to escape but there was no loss of life as a result of the fire. Darcy had to face the unedifying fact of her disappointment on hearing the news. Had Von Schmidt and Riva Dubois perished that night she would have considered it an act of divine justice. Holed up at the flat, she clicked off the television and tossed the remote control unit onto the settee. The fascist order had lost its talisman and therefore its main thrust for the media, but still had its ruthless and charismatic leader. And her bunch of heavies. Maybe Europe had gained some time, but what about Darcy West? she thought grimly. Riva Dubois would be out for revenge.

Deep in thought, she paced the carpet for several minutes. Personal risk apart, somebody had to blow the whistle on this little lot. Frank would back her if he had hard evidence and not everything, she realised, had been destroyed in the fire. Proof lay in the parchment and notes left for her by Miles Standish. But she had given them to Brant. The documents were, she reasoned, too precious for him to carry on his person or leave in the car which left the farmhouse - or more likely, the observatory. Reaching a decision, she moved to the bedroom and packed some clothes in an overnight bag. Pausing only to telephone Caro and let her know she was safe, Darcy snatched up her car keys and emerged from the dubious cover of the flat.

****

To trek the cliffs by night and risk getting lost or by daylight and chance being seen was the crucial decision. After agonising on the journey north, she compromised by opting for twilight. On reaching the cottage, she stuffed waterproofs, chocolate, compass and torch into a rucksack and zipped her skeleton keys into a pocket. It was a sad trip to the car park of the Old Priory and from there on foot to the path that wound over the cliffs. The hills wore the russet of dying bracken, blood-berried rowan and the melancholy mists of Autumn. A short time ago this had been the scene of such happiness between herself and Brant, now it lay in ruins like the priory that had started it all. She trudged on, for the first time in days not pausing to look over her shoulder. The pain of lost love was greater now than fear.

On starting out the amethyst haze had been confined to off-shore, but on climbing higher the air felt moist and chilled her face. The mist was drifting inland off the sea and visibility was worsening by the minute. A familiar tingle at the nape of her neck warned of not being alone, yet there was not a soul to be seen. Jumpy now, and starting at every shadow, Darcy glanced back and stifled a cry of alarm. Heart humping, she cursed herself for a fool when the 'figure' turned out to be a stunted gorse. She paused, and considered the indistinct outline of crags ahead, but decided this was an assignment and as such there could be no turning back, and there was always the compass. She moved forward again, but at steadier pace. The roar of surf over rocks some three hundred feet below warned of the folly of haste.

On reaching the cliff top above the cove, she was engulfed by a wave of panic. The feeling of not being alone deepened with the gathering gloom. So had awareness of her isolation and vulnerability. It had been foolish to come. She stood still, breathing hard and staring into the darkness until her eyes ached. Her hand flew to her mouth as somewhere nearby a twig snapped. Someone was lurking in the mist, a stalker in the shadows. To turn back now would be to run into the arms of her pursuer; her only chance was to keep going. The farmhouse and observatory lay ahead, but even if he was there, Brant was the last person who would come to her aid. It might even be him out there in the shadows. That thought cut like a knife. It was bad enough for a stranger to want her dead, but if it proved to be Brant whom she had loved and trusted, how much harder to bear.

She began to run, and her feet as they strayed from the path stumbled over loose stones, clumps of sea grass and spongy heather. Pitching forward, she lay still for a moment, hearing the sound of her ragged breathing, pounding pulse and stifled sobs. There came the sound of footfalls on the sandy track, followed by the rustle of feet through dying bracken. Frantic with fear, she scrambled upright, ran forward and almost fell. With a stifled cry she drew back from the brink. Both surf and rocks were obscured by the mist, but the muffled roar and echo reminded her of the danger lurking below. Crouching, and feeling her way, she returned to the path and paused to look back. A dark figure was moving inexorably in her direction.

All the demons and monsters of childhood coalesced in that one shadowy form. Darcy stumbled forward, gasping for breath and almost paralysed with fear. A cry was dragged from her as a bat squeaked and skimmed her head.
"Help me, help me," she pleaded aloud to some unknown entity or benevolent force. For a second, it seemed a figure in white appeared in her path, but it was only the shifting of vapour into strange forms. Anton had gone, his spirit released from its vigil. The sounds of pursuit grew louder, the shadow more distinct. She turned; he was almost upon her and he was holding a knife in his hand.

So that was to be the method. She had wondered how they would do it. Standing facing him with her back to the brink of the cliff, she saw it all with a terrible clarity. He intended forcing her off, as they had forced Miles Standish on to the railway lines and her death too would look like an accident. There would be no stab wounds or bullets in her body and a verdict of misadventure would be recorded. The rocks might even prevent her from being identified. So much better for Brant and the hateful regime he had helped to spawn. Prevented by pride from pleading for her life, she crouched like an animal at bay.

"Brant?" she whispered, her voice cracked with fear. She needed to face him, to confront the inevitable rather than fear the unknown. But the mist rendered him faceless, an anonymous creature of nightmare, crab-like with menace as he moved in for the kill. Numbly, she watched the silhouette drawing closer. With each step the blade goaded her backwards to the brink of the precipice. A glance over her shoulder confirmed that another couple of steps would send her hurtling onto the rocks. Her attacker brandished the knife then drew back his arm to lunge.

At last she screamed, the sound torn from her throat but seeming to come from someone else. A sound like the crack of a whip jangled her nerves. She stared at her attacker as he lurched nearer, then felt a tremendous force yank her forward and to one side. As she fell something rushed past, then nothing but blackness and silence. Past caring now, Darcy let herself sink. The scissor-wind snipped at her face: *snip snip snip.* It cut at her flesh, leaving it raw and open to the probing blades. The pain of knowing Brant was about to kill her over-spilled in tears and moisture stung her chilled cheeks.

Overhead, the great drum of the Universe turned, spilling kaleidoscopic patterns of stars with each ponderous revolution. Turning, turning into oblivion, uncaring of her pain and distress, keeping stars and planets turning on their axes those pinpoints of light so cold and remote. This, the power to manipulate worlds and cosmic forces was Brant's real love. Not for him a flesh and blood woman, the entwining of limbs and mingling of heart and spirit. His love cut as deep as the scissor-wind. He preferred the chilly embrace of Venus, the anonymity and promiscuity of a million stars. His heart yearned for knowledge and power for which, if necessary, he would kill. As he was about to kill her now.

FIFTY-TWO

Her head hurt. The light was the cause, the brightness that someone was flashing in her face. Why didn't whoever it was leave her to die in peace? But she did not want to die. In a flash the fog of apathy cleared from her brain. She battled with him then, fought for her life, kicking and lunging out with her fists and shouting obscenities into his face. The palm of a hand made contact with her cheek and the shock made her fall silent.
"That's better."
The voice was familiar. She struggled to rise through the strata of mist that smothered mind and memory. The light came from a flash lamp, it was lowered and she tried to focus but the face above hers remained a blur.
"Can you sit up?"
The cotton wool drifted from her head and her vision began to clear. At first she stared without understanding, then screamed and tried to roll aside and writhe from his grasp.

"I won't hurt you Darcy."
He was shaking her whilst talking but his words were not making sense and the screams kept coming. "I said I won't hurt you. But I may have to slap you again if you won't be quiet."
"Brant?" The threat had got through to her.
"I'm here." His arm went around her and felt like a haven of warmth, but she pulled away in disbelief.
"You tried to kill me," she accused, shrinking back.
"Don't be ridiculous; I would have made a job of it." His voice held the warmth of humour, and she dared believe a little.
"Who then? And – where is he?" she asked hesitantly.
"Jean Perot – a member of Riva Dubois' personal guard." He shifted position and pulled her close to cradle her in his arms, "and he is taking a midnight swim."

Darcy raised her head and leaned back in order to see his face.

"What happened?"

"I shot him."

"I thought you were with the fascists." Somehow she knew he was telling the truth.

"Idiot."

"I have missed being insulted."

"Don't worry, I'll make up for it. Can you stand now?

"I feel sick."

"You fainted. I'll carry you if you like."

"To where?"

"The farmhouse of course."

Doubt and fear assailed her again; he seemed to read her mind. "Darcy, if I wanted to kill you I would have tipped you over there," he explained patiently, directing the beam of the lamp at the edge of the cliff to illustrate his point. "Much less messy than digging graves, and no-one would be any wiser."

"I guess. I think I can walk now," she said with a shudder.

"Then let's go. I would hate to lose you to pneumonia after all this effort and inconvenience."

"You haven't changed."

It was a comforting thought as he led her off the cliffs.

****

It was all too incredible. After weeks of misery and despair, here she was propped up in the huge Victorian bed, sipping a hot toddy and with Brant holding her hand. "I really did think you were one of them," she confessed.

"Nice to know you had faith in me."

"You can't really blame me."

"No? Just you wait and see."

Despite the shock of the night's events, Darcy had to smile at this. The chill that had struck her out there on the cliffs, and was reluctant to leave her body, retreated a little.

"There is something I need to ask," she said hesitantly.

"Fire away."

"Did you also kill the bastard who forced me off the motorway?"

"Sleep now Darcy." Brant rose abruptly from the edge of the bed.

Placing the almost empty glass on the bedside Cabinet, she sat upright.

"Not until I have some answers. For starters, I'd like to know how it is you can go around killing people with apparent impunity," she demanded. "And how did you know I was in London? And what were you doing at Edgeway Hall if you are not a member of that vile order?" The words were fired at him like missiles, discharging pent-up resentment and emotion. "And why did you lock me in and leave me here alone?

He seemed about to depart without answering, but paused at the door. With a frisson of apprehension, Darcy recognised the air of remoteness and authority that she had learnt to fear.

"To answer your last question first," he said in a voice now devoid of indulgence, "For your own good. To avoid scenarios such as the one in London – and what happened out there tonight. As for Edgeway, I saved your life – odd, don't you think - I should be seeking to take it now!" he said with heavy irony. "As to the rest, perhaps I do owe you some sort of explanation, but now is not the time."

"There may not be another one," she said pointedly.

"So be it. Now finish your toddy and get some sleep."

"And you sure as hell do owe me an explanation!"

"Sleep," he repeated remorselessly, opening the door to leave.

"Are you not coming to bed?" she asked tentatively, aware of taking a lot for granted. As he had rescued her and they were on speaking terms again, she had assumed their relationship would be as intimate as before. She willed him to stay, but her eyelids felt unaccountably heavy, her thoughts confused and her limbs leaden.

"I have work to do."

"Don't leave me alone, Brant." Darcy was gripped by panic.

"I won't." For an instant the stern expression relaxed. "At least, not for longer than necessary. I shall return long before you awake."

"Promise!" She was struggling now in the grip of a deadly fatigue.

"Of course."

"Must you go?" she murmured, her tongue thick in her mouth.

"There is a body floating around out there, Darcy – and things to be done."

Darcy muttered some sort of reply. Her eyelids were too heavy to hold open. A wave of relaxation rippled through her body, robbing her of the will to move. Suddenly her eyes flew wide open.

"Brant?" she asked wildly.

"A harmless draught."

"But – why?" The impetus of panic drained away and sleep dragged her mercilessly down. He paused hand on door knob. "I can't have you disappearing whilst I am out of the house. Far too much trouble – now that I have you back."

The door closed, and Darcy pondered the implication of his words. Dimly she was aware of footsteps receding as the waters of sleep closed over her head.

FIFTY-THREE

She awoke to sunlight dappling the quilt and was confused, expecting to find herself in Caro's spare bedroom. Her limbs were leaden and relaxed, her mind lazy and unwilling to tackle reality. Several minutes passed before confusion subsided, and awareness of her present situation dawned. Gradually, facets of the previous night's events arose, then constantly moved and changed like patterns in a kaleidoscope. At last a general picture emerged and solidified and at its centre was Brant. Turning her head swiftly, then grasping the duvet as a wave of giddiness followed this rash action, Darcy discovered she was alone. So where was Brant now? she worried, struggling to sit up against her pillows then slumping back as the effort proved too great. It seemed he had saved her from being murdered, so why this sense of unease? Something niggled, demanding awareness, but threatened to be unpleasant. The languor persisted. It was easier to cease thinking and drift back to sleep. The sound of the door opening, and footsteps across the floor, brought her awake for a second time.

"Good morning."
She turned her head and screwed up her eyes against the light as Brant – carrying a loaded tray – moved to stand with his back to the window. "Feeling better?" he inquired in a conversational manner. The thing bothering her flooded back to consciousness and she struggled into a sitting position.
"You drugged me!"
Brant, however, seemed unperturbed by the accusation.
"I told you – harmless. You needed sleep." He laid the tray before her. "Now you need food. Eat your breakfast," he commanded as though the matter had been dealt with and was no longer up for dispute.

"You had no right!" she exploded, so that milk over-spilled from the jug and formed a pool on the white lace tray cloth.

"I thought you might be hungry," he responded, his eyes brimming with humour.

"You know what I mean," she said irritably. Her gaze moved from his face to the painted wicker chair. "Where are my clothes?" she demanded.

"Drying on the Aga."

"Oh." She deliberated a moment, reluctant to admit to thinking the worst.

"To both drug you and deny you your clothes would seem to be slightly over the top, don't you think?" he said solemnly, apparently having read her mind.

"May I have them please." Darcy had to smile.

"When you have eaten." He pointed to the boiled egg, fingers of toast and pot of tea on the tray. Sensing that he would not be budged, Darcy poured tea into a china cup. Nodding his satisfaction, Brant walked to the door.

"When you are ready, I'll be waiting downstairs."

He disappeared, leaving Darcy feeling oddly deflated. The previous night, she had blamed his aloofness on events, now she could no longer deny that Brant Kennedy was deliberately avoiding intimacy. He had not even kissed her or given her a reassuring hug. Surely their reunion should contain a little more joy? And that parting shot: he was 'waiting to see her', much in the style of Frank Kelly, and the outcome on such occasions was seldom good. It was not that simple, she acknowledged, there were still dirty corners to be cleaned before things could get back to normal. For example the unresolved matter of his involvement in at least two killings. Then there was the comment of the previous night that there were 'things to be done'. Did these things include a massive cover up job, and if so just how much power did he have? Considerable, it seemed. Absently she picked up a finger of toast, then realising that she was hungry, dipped it in the egg yolk and began to eat.

****

374

A little over an hour later, fresh from the shower and wearing the clothes that Brant had brought after critically examining her tray, Darcy entered the sitting room. He rose from his armchair and escorted her to the one opposite. Mab and Brock fawned over her so he banished them to the kitchen. "Are you feeling better?" he inquired, closing the door and returning to his seat. His solicitude was apparent, but so was restraint: he could have been addressing a stranger.

"Much, thank you." A log fire crackled and blazed in the grate and had circumstances been different, Darcy thought wistfully, it would have been a perfect afternoon. The ticking of the clock on the mantel grew louder as the silence between them lengthened. Brant looked away as he caught her watching him and glanced at the clock for the second time since she had entered the room. She tried to break the impasse, sought desperately for something to say but he was unapproachable. He stared deep into the flames before finally speaking and when he did, both voice and expression were grave.

"We have to talk Darcy, but first there is something you should see."

With mounting irritation, Darcy watched him turn on the television.

"Really Brant," she protested, feeling that under the circumstances an afternoon's viewing was less than appropriate. He held up a peremptory hand and she fell silent. The images on the screen settled. Darcy leaned forward.

"That's Riva Dubois!" she exclaimed.

"The French referendum on the Treaty of Brussels Amendment," he explained, nodding.

"That's today. It must be a live broadcast."

"Watch." He raised his hand to stem her words. Frustrated, but instinctively responding to his air of urgency, Darcy turned back to the screen. Riva Dubois, elegant as ever despite a strained countenance and a hand that, given the bandages, had obviously sustained burns in the fire, waved from the balcony to the cheering crowds below. Covertly, Darcy glanced from the screen to observe Brant. Normally scornful of daytime viewing, he had an intense and focused air. There was a tension about him, a strangeness that brought an unpleasant fluttering to her stomach. A frown creased her forehead. Today surely, Riva Dubois was simply functioning as her country's Minister for Foreign Affairs. The referendum was a formality, the outcome a foregone conclusion so the programme scarcely warranted exclusive attention. She glanced again at Brant. Surely they should be discussing their future – if indeed they still had one. And Brant Kennedy should be offering some sort of explanation for his recent behaviour.

As the cameras zoomed into close-up, Darcy was about to demand that he turn off the television to talk. The French minister smiled and waved to the crowd. Suddenly there was a crack, muffled but distinct. Riva Dubois froze in mid wave, a half-smile still on her lips and her eyes expressing surprise as they glazed. Blood slowly welled up from a small hole at the centre of her forehead.
"Oh, my God," Darcy breathed, as the woman crumpled and fell. Security men were instantly at her side. The crowd surged forward and commentators' voices were raised in shock and disbelief. Within minutes the news flash came: Riva Dubois was dead.

Brant switched off the television and stood before her, his expression grave. The silence and tension mounted.
"You knew," Darcy said leadenly. Brant remained silent and watched her with an odd expression. Darcy started to rise, then sat down again as Brant shook his head.
"I told you," he said, "we have to talk." She passed a hand over her forehead in a gesture of bewilderment as he continued: "Or rather I do – and you must listen. But first," he added crossing to the sideboard on which stood a couple of crystal decanters, "you need a drink." He handed her a glass containing brandy. "Knock it back," he commanded, standing over her, "it's medicinal." She coughed as the neat spirit burned her throat. "Again," he said inexorably and she finished it off. Relieving her of the glass, he poured a second smaller measure and one for himself and topped up both drinks from the soda siphon.

"Make this one last," he said with a glimmer of the old humour that brought Darcy close to tears.

"I don't know you," she whispered.

"No." He took a gulp of brandy and soda and looked away. "I aim to do something about that right now."

"Why did you make me watch?" she asked dully.

"So that you would understand why I must send you away."

"Send me away? But we have just found one another again," she said in desperation, sensing the seriousness of his intent.

"In fact," he continued, ignoring her protest, "if you have any sense Darcy, you'll save me that trouble," he said brutally.

"I love you." Voicing it Darcy realised it was true, despite his implication in at least two murders and now the assassination of Riva Dubois.

"By your own admission, you do not know me," he said with a coldness that chilled her heart.

"You don't love me."

"That has nothing to do with it," he snapped, becoming angry.

Darcy made no response. Now all was clear, his aloofness and reluctance to touch or kiss her, his coldness and withdrawal. She repeated her question of the previous night.

"Did you kill the man on the motorway?"

"No." He met her gaze, but then added as her expression lightened with relief: "but had I been on the scene, I would have had no compunction in doing so."

"So you weren't in London after all."

"No."

"Who did kill him then?"

"I am not allowed to say."

"Honour amongst rogues?" she sniped, venting her pain.

"I am bound by the Official Secrets Act," he said stiffly.

She stared at him, then rose and paced the room.

"You're with National Security?" she said at last, turning to face him while striving to keep her voice steady. He made no answer, his silence being confirmation enough. She shook her head and laughed bitterly.

"Ace work, you really set me up."

"It was never like that." He shook his head and seemed distressed. She stared into the fire, her face working in agitation.

"What a gullible fool! How you must have laughed."

"That's enough. Now please sit down and listen."

When she made no effort to move, he gestured impatiently at her seat.

"I said sit down" he repeated. Rising he took her by the arm and pushed her down onto the chair. "For what it is worth," he said seating himself opposite, "I am an astrophysicist, but allied to the Department."

"But hardly sent here to monitor the weather!"

"Hardly," he agreed with a wintry smile. "I am normally involved in Space Programme Security, but given the nature of this crisis, the astronomical and alchemical implications, I was judged best one for the assignment," he explained with evident embarrassment.

She digested this in silence.

"So, did you kill the man on the cliff?"

"I certainly shot him. Whether he was dead on hitting the water is debatable. I hope not." She gave him a quizzical look. "There will be water in his lungs," he explained, "Makes a 'death by misadventure' verdict somewhat easier to reach and sustain."

"Don't tell me," Darcy gave him a scornful look, "The Department can arrange it. Is there nothing it can't fix?"

He made no answer, but bent his head and picking up a log from the basket tossed it onto the fire.

"And Riva Dubois?"

"There was no alternative."

"Okay, so she was an evil bitch, but what about the justice system?"

Brant shook his head and surveyed her much as he might an over-indulged child.

"Had we attempted to bring her and her fascist party to trial, there would have been countless delays, legal loopholes, acquittal on a 'technical point' – not to mention corruption of witnesses or worse. Have you forgotten poor Miles?"

"So the Department opted for legalised murder."

"An emotive term. 'Execution' might be better. She and Von Schmidt seduced the European Parliament with her plan. Had it come to fruition Nazi-style rallies would have corrupted the young and incited anti-Semitic persecution. You heard for yourself at Edgeway Hall. Have you really forgotten Miles already? And believe me," he added when she looked uncomfortable, "there are hundreds like him, innocent people who were murdered or simply disappeared."

"And what of Von Schmidt? Will we hear of another execution, or an 'accident' like the one on the cliff? Your lot are just as bad!" she accused.

"Don't be a hypocrite Darcy. When sickened by atrocities have you never said of say, Saddam Hussein, or Milosovic, or Bin Laden 'someone should take him out?' Plenty say it, then protest when we act." Unable to deny the truth of this, Darcy declined to challenge him further.

"Why the Home Office intervention?" she asked instead, recalling the Manchester News and the blocking of her story.

He stared into the fire as though considering how much to divulge.

"Von Schmidt's obsession was known, as was his Nazi background and recent involvement in neo-Nazi activities," he said at last meeting her gaze, "The Home Office didn't want the culprits drawn away from London into rural hard-to-police areas. Hence the news black-out on St. Gildas Man. There were also break-ins at museums and Templar Repositories across Europe. The word went out internationally, and access to relevant information was blocked, as Miles discovered, in an attempt to contain the situation."

"So, the only connection with Anton and alchemy was Hitler's obsession with secret orders and the occult," Darcy commented, the conflict between relief and disappointment visible in her expression. "And Caro's finding of the body was coincidental, as was the trail that led me to Von Schmidt. A series of events linked only by my imagination."

"Who knows?" Brant shrugged. "I can't answer that one, Darcy." She put down her drink untouched.

"And," she said striving to mask the hurt and humiliation, "your only interest in me was to find out why I was snooping and how much I knew."

"At first, yes," he admitted calmly whilst meeting her gaze, "but even then I was attracted."

"And later?" Darcy bit her lip, hating herself for probing her open wound.

"It was selfish of me, but I couldn't help getting involved."

"And the story you spun me about your wife?" she pressed, steeling herself for the revelation that he was married with two-point-five kids.

"That at least was the truth."

"I'm grateful," she snapped, "I should hate to unwittingly have played 'the other woman' as well as the stooge!"

"Darcy." As he spoke, the distress was evident in his voice and he made as if to rise. She shook her head and rising, walked quickly from the room.

FIFTY-FOUR

She stood on the cliff staring out to sea. The salt spray blended with her tears and blurred the rose-grey line where sky and water met. The scene echoed the desolation in her heart and soul. He doesn't love me. The phrase repeated itself endlessly like a loop recording, as though by repetition her mind would eventually accept what her heart could not. To make things worse, of all the people on the planet, she had chosen to fall in love with a man who had wilfully taken the life of another.

Awareness of her own moral fragility brought any sense of outrage to an abrupt end. Brant had it right when he accused her of being a hypocrite. She had to accept that if the anonymous 'executioner' had not taken both action and responsibility, that thug on the motorway would probably have met his death beneath the wheels of her car. In theory she was just as morally guilty as Brant Kennedy. That apart, her emotions were hardly those of the woman of principle she had previously perceived herself to be. Knowing he was involved in the deaths of at least three people should have cured any grief at his lack of commitment; the fact that it had failed to do so must mean that she was not a very moral person. To complicate things still further, it could be argued that his actions and those of his colleagues were justified. Those lives were not taken irresponsibly, but to prevent bloodshed of innocent people.

It was not the loss of life that gave her trouble, she admitted now, those 'victims' had been thugs, torturers and murderers in the true sense of the word. So far as she was concerned, justice had been done. No, rather her problem lay in that it had occurred outside the legal system and in secret instead of in open court. But given the political power behind Riva Dubois, the chance of success for any moves to bring them to court would have been minimal to say the least. Von

Schmidt and the abortive attempt to charge him with war crimes stood testimony to that. If Brant and the Department had not taken unofficial action, would they have failed their duty of care? She shook her head. Bottom line, she was not qualified to pass judgment. There was a modicum of comfort to be gained from that realisation, a sense of relief from letting it all go.

She sighed, hunched her shoulders and pulled her collar up against the wind and desolation. Besides, none of it mattered now, even if she did come to terms with Brant's profession and its consequences. *Because he doesn't love me.* She had read it all wrong, been taken in by his tenderness and passion when all along they had merely been a means of eliciting information. Memories of their lovemaking, with Brant and Anton at times inextricably joined in her heart, returned to compound her pain and confusion.

Yes, Anton. In that also she had played the fool; Anton de Beaumont had died seven centuries ago, was nothing more than inanimate bone, flesh and sinew preserved against natural decay. The notion that his sense of honour and justice had somehow survived to warn of greed and oppression in the modern world was romantic nonsense birthed by her imagination. Curiously that pain was the hardest to bear. Some sort of faith that was difficult to articulate had been hinging on the belief; faith in something more powerful and enduring than the selfishness and transience of this life. Anton and Leala's story had embodied every tragic love and lover – including herself and Brant, she realised now. The pain at its loss felt like a physical wound in her breast.

The salt-laden wind blew a strand of hair across her face, and she brushed aside a damp curl that had stuck to her cheek. Mist was rolling in off the sea, and rain clouds were sailing in from the west, lost battalions searching for land and a chance to discharge their burden. The thought crossed her mind that even the sky was weeping with her today. Until now, events had forced her to keep an open mind about after-life survival, but the present void made her doubt the whole experience. Something precious had been lost, and in its absence years of emptiness and disillusion stretched ahead. She watched a lone gull glide overhead and into the off-shore mist. Loneliness echoed in its call, muffled but still distinct. A ghostly effect given the bird was now invisible.

Instinctively, she tugged the collar of her jacket still closer as a chill struck the nape of her neck. The mist was swirling around the base of the cliffs, obscuring the foam-flecked rocks. Fascinated, she watched as it rose and fell in soft billows, moulded first this way then that by the sculpting wind into a form that was almost but not quite there. A frown lined her forehead and she sniffed the air experimentally. For a moment it seemed the mizzle carried the familiar scents of cedarwood and frankincense and, she recalled, his particular fragrance was always laced with that of the salt-breeze.

The lines of pain and misery etched on her face relaxed a little. Whatever the logic or otherwise of it, she still believed he had played a part, that something of him still existed. His essence was still out there and striving for recognition. Moving closer to the edge of the cliff, she was filled with an inexplicable yearning. The pull, the desire was beyond resistance. Of their own volition her feet carried her forward to the very brink.
"Darcy!"
The voice came from behind. A shock of electric raced and tingled along her nerves to lodge itself in her stomach. Half in reverie and afraid to look, she whirled round then swayed, temporarily off balance with the movement.
"Brant!"
"Remain still!"

The staccato command cracked the shell of her torpor and obediently she froze. Within seconds he was at her side. Taking hold of her arm he pulled her away from the precipice and led her to safety. He held her by the shoulders until she winced in pain and he relaxed his grip. For a full minute, his eyes searched her face, but he wisely refrained from demanding answers. The dark hair was beaded with moisture, his face pale and drawn with misery.

"I tried to be noble," he said instead, "make it easier for you to leave by letting you think I didn't love you. I couldn't do it. No matter how it hurts you have the right to know: I have loved you from the start."

"I'm not going anywhere Brant."

He searched her face again, his eyes momentarily lighting up then becoming shadowed with pain.

"But my work, I have no right—"

"That's for me to decide."

He held her gaze a moment longer, then apparently finding what he sought, appeared to give up the fight.

"There will be problems."

"No doubt."

"You will have to marry me, the Department doesn't like lose ends," he said solemnly, the ghost of a smile touching his lips.

"Anything to keep the Department happy."

"You'll also have to make up with Frank Kelly."

She smiled then, guessing his 'Department' had cleared her name with Max Dearden. It would be good to see Frank again. He placed an arm around her shoulders.

"Come on, this mist is closing in, I don't want to lose you."

She stopped dead to give him a speculative look, wondering how much he had been aware of back there on the brink.

"What is it?" he asked.

"Nothing." A secretive smile curved her lips. Looking back to the edge of the cliff and the swirling vapour beyond, she offered a silent salute. To Anton de Beaumont, a medieval man with green eyes – and the ultimate story to tell.

Other books in the Pendragon Press Darcy West mystery series

DARK STAR

The first Darcy West novel but all four books in the series are complete in themselves.
Dark Star: a novel of dark and chilling prophecy – the dark star of the North brings retribution, silence and death . . .

Reporter Darcy West, separated from her husband, reluctantly takes in her orphaned nephew Alisdair. Shortly after their arrival at an isolated retreat, he finds a strange meteor on a lonely Lakeland fell. It falls into the hands of a psychotic physicist and disaster strikes. Darcy battles against murder, power-lust and corruption, aided by Mr. Ambrose, a hermit with supernatural powers.

Available from Amazon – Kindle edition (paperback version to follow)

The Third Book in the Darcy West Mystery Series

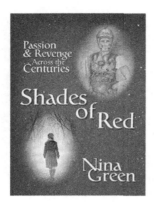

SHADES OF RED

A haunting time-slip novel. The impossible happens…a chink appears in the veil between past and present.

A hardened Roman commander, and a feisty female reporter on a city paper - centuries apart, yet their destinies collide. A grim ruin, spectacular scenery and a legendary lost legion provide the backcloth for a terrifying haunting – but also a love that crosses the barriers of Time.

A compelling story that stays with the reader long after it is read.

Available from Amazon –for both paperback and Kindle editions

The Fourth Book in the Darcy West Mystery Series

WATER RITES
**Exorcism and malicious spirits, medieval murder and
betrayed lovers. A compelling, haunting read.**

A village is shamefully 'drowned' for financial gain but evil
lurks beneath the water. Darcy's task is to expose the corrupt
construction company, but she becomes entangled in a
shocking past. The protection of the ancient church yews is lost,
allowing evil to seep from the ruins of a Medieval convent.

The malevolence that lies beneath the lake's surface rises again.
The troubled spirits of Medieval lovers Miranda Montford and
Sir Tristan Meredith seek justice and release. Nature fights back
with flash storms and torrential rain. If the dam bursts, many
will perish. Darcy is prey to terrifying psychic phenomena, and
she appeals to the charismatic Father John for help. The lovers
must be reunited if the dam is to be saved. As the clock ticks the
horror and tension build to a gripping and unexpected climax.

**For Nina Green's other mystery novels, and her canine
adventures told by the dogs and illustrated with photos of
her own English Setters, visit Nina Green's Amazon Author
pages.**

Printed in Great Britain
by Amazon

43583130R00215